Dark Chapte

Kill For A Copy

Also available from Dark Chapter Press

The Cabinet of Dr Blessing, by Jack Rollins

The Séance: A Gothic Tale of Horror and Misfortune, by Jack Rollins

Kill For A Copy

A Dark Chapter Press Anthology

Edited by Rob McEwan

Dark Chapter Press

Kill For A Copy
Print Edition ISBN: 978-0-9930620-3-2

Published by Dark Chapter Press
20 Royal Oak Gdns, Alnwick, Northumberland, NE66 2DA

First edition: July 2015
This is a work of fiction. Names, characters, places, and incidents either are the product of the author's imagination or are used fictitiously, and any resemblance to actual persons, living or dead, business establishments, events, or locales is entirely coincidental. The publisher does not have any control over and does not assume any responsibility for author or third-party websites or their content.

A CIP catalogue record for this title is available from the British Library.

Kill For The Contents

Welcome
By Rob McEwan

I won't keep you long, I've got Shaun Hutson on the next page and, hell you just want to get to him really and then on to the real reason we're here! That being said, I felt it would be rude not to say a few words to welcome you to this, the first ever anthology by Dark Chapter Press.

When I set up this small press, my mission was to find great new talent in the horror, thriller and dark fantasy spectrum and I'm sure you'll agree by the time you hit the back cover, I made a good start.

What you have in this volume is a great range of stories, from a variety of story-tellers, each with their unique style and vision and their ability to grab you from beginning to end. Some of these writers are going to lock you in a basement, some are going to take you across the globe or in one case, even off the globe and some of them are going to switch off the lights in your own home and let you see the horror that resides there with you. Some of them are going to scare you, some will thrill you, some will even make you laugh, but every one of them is going to entertain you.

These guys are mostly at the early stages of their published writing careers. You may not be familiar with all of their names, but I am certain you are going to read more by them in the future. I want to thank them all for their hard work, determination and talent.

I also want to thank Shaun Hutson for his support of Dark Chapter Press and for kindly agreeing to provide the Foreword.

And you? I didn't forget you. Thanks for picking up this anthology and if you did have to kill for a copy, I hope you didn't kill someone you'll miss.

Over to the big man...

Rob McEwan
Editor and Proprietor
Dark Chapter Press
June 2015

Foreword
By Shaun Hutson

Writing a short story is one of the most difficult disciplines there is.

Writing a short *horror* story is even more difficult. The reason being that most horror stories tend to be concise narratives or sick jokes. The latter is a trap I've fallen into myself. You spend four or five pages describing and setting up characters or story only so you can deliver a "punch line" at the end. "And she held out her hand revealing his freshly torn out heart," that kind of thing.

Writing a short story and a screenplay I've always thought are similar because you've got limited time and space to get character across so it needs to be done economically. With a novel you've got 90-150,000 words to convey the same things so, if you want to, you can take your time. Short stories add restraints that a novelist doesn't encounter. There are no restraints when you're writing a novel. You make up your own rules to a degree. Having said that, the need for brevity and pace has always been something that attracted me as a writer both in short and full length fiction. In a short horror story there's no time for waffle, no space for superfluous material. Short horror stories are bullshit free. Or they should be.

Some of the most memorable pieces of writing I've ever enjoyed have been short stories. "The Graveyard Rats" by Henry Kuttner, "The Outsider" and "Pickman's Model" by H.P. Lovecraft, "The Little Girl Eater" by Septimus Dale, "Children of the Corn" by Stephen King. "The Bats" and "The Fur Brooch" by Dulcie Gray. "The Monkey's Paw" by W.W. Jacobs. There are many more. All those short stories made an indelible mark on me as a reader and also as a writer. They all have that pace, economy of language and lack of bullshit. And they work brilliantly.

A novel can *ease* you in. A short story should *throw*

you in.

Some ideas are just better suited to the short story format. They don't work across 90,000 words. Some ideas have an impact that is only achievable in 10,000 or 20,000 words. One short horror story which appeared in the Pan Books of Horror Stories series, "Tanith" is only about 100 words! What many writers fail to realize is that a story should be told in as many words as it takes. It's as simple as that. If you can tell your story in 10,000 then do it. If it takes 120,000 then you do that. Never add extra detail just for the hell of it. Don't expand characterisations because you think you should. Write from your heart. If it feels right then chances are it is!

The writers of the stories contained within this volume have recognised the restraints the short story puts upon them but they've embraced that. They used brevity, economy of language and have thankfully dispensed with the bullshit. For that they should be congratulated.

There is nothing worse than a story that is stretched beyond its limits. A story that the author hasn't realized has run its course. My own novels have sometimes been criticised for their shortness but any critics who have been dumb enough to do that have missed the point (most critics usually do). When someone reads horror they usually do it to be entertained. They don't want superfluous waffle or self-indulgence. They want to be gripped. They want to be frightened. They want to be taken on a ride they cannot control. One where the only person who knows the destination is the author. And readers will forgive the writer anything if he twists and turns on that journey. They might even forgive him if the ride is a bit bumpy and uncomfortable.

The writers of these stories you're about to read have done the same thing and they've done it brilliantly. If these stories had been any longer they wouldn't have worked. They probably wouldn't have worked as novels.

The art of the short story is one that has been perfected by some authors after years of honing their craft. The stories offered here are the work of authors who are still learning and some who are just starting out. Where they go on their journeys no one knows yet but that is part of the fun. Just like the stories themselves.

Personally, I've written a fair few short horror stories over the years, published in everything from magazines and newspapers to radio and TV. One story I did for Radio was read out as if it was a news story and, within 2 minutes of broadcast, the radio station had CNN on the phone wanting to know where the explosion had occurred and exactly how many fatalities there'd been. That was fun. But, believe me, I'm still learning this discipline. I'm not sure that anyone ever masters it completely but we all carry on writing, hoping we hit the right spots. Some of my stories have been so bad I'd never even consider getting them into print. Writing takes courage as well as skill, you know. Elements of both are displayed in this volume so read on and, if the writers have done their jobs properly, hopefully you'll still be reading deep into the night.

If they've *really* done their jobs you'll be awake long into the night anyway, because they'll have scared you into not sleeping. So enjoy and then sleep tight. Or maybe not.

Shaun Hutson 2015

Home, Sweet Home

By Jack Rollins

"I know it's not our dream house, Keith," Amanda admitted, pressing her firm body against her husband. She kissed the tip of his chin. "But, we can make the place our own and I'm sure we'll be happy here."

"I know, I know. I just loved the old maisonette. I'll get used to it," Keith said, sighing in resignation. The maisonette was sold and he was officially a resident of Tilwick's Golden Acre Park estate.

Peering over Amanda's shoulder, brushing her blonde hair up behind her neck, Keith observed the collection of brown-brick detached and semi-detached homes arranged around the cul-de-sac, washed in the muted orange of sunset. Keith remained silently thankful to have taken up a detached property with a good stretch of tree and shrub-lined garden on all sides, baffling the noise to and from the neighbours. He considered that his battered Ford Focus appeared somewhat out of place among the BMWs and Land Rovers of their neighbours. The patchy lawn of the front garden, the cracked driveway, the *too-small-to-park-a-car-in* garage, the *one-hard-cough-and-down-they-come* fences, all of these things, they made Keith feel as though a huge sign reading *Lowest Earners in the Neighbourhood* should be erected out front.

Keith had voiced his opinion before the move and Amanda reasoned that since the property had been uninhabited for two years, and the landlord had left the running of the place to an estate agent, nobody would be surprised that the place needed some work. Plus, she had added, our friends live here. By *our* friends, of course she meant *her* friends, who had recommended the place to her.

Handing him a glass of a fruity summer red wine, Amanda attempted to free Keith from the mental swamp he kept falling into when he thought about the house and its gardens for too long.

He took a gulp of the wine, recognising Amanda's distraction tactic and hoping that it would work. She slipped a hand to the front of his jeans and fondled him with just the right amount of pressure in the right place to state her intent without hurting him.

"Which room would you like to christen first, Mr Corgan?" she purred.

Keith almost spat his wine across the window, only just managing to swallow his drink in time. In doing so he avoided the destruction of the white vertical blinds he had installed the previous morning. He clasped a hand over his lips and let out a half-laugh, half-cough.

The white baby monitor plugged into the four-gang extension by the TV flickered to life, with two of the three green LEDs blinking, showing that only a low level of noise had been detected. Little Alex's cries usually drove the baby monitor up past the third green light and into the two red LEDs that indicated a loud noise had been detected. A second later, with the LED's still flickering slightly, a snuffling noise was heard through the small speaker. Alex let out a little moan and settled down once more.

"I wasn't expecting him to settle in his new room so well, tonight," Keith commented.

"He's very adaptable," Amanda said. She pinched Keith's bottom, adding, "You could learn from him."

Keith frowned at his wife, something was missing. "Hey, where's your wine?"

Amanda flashed him a grin and rested her head on his shoulder. "I have some news for you... Daddy."

"You're fucking kidding me?" Keith cried, returning his wife's wide grin. "Really? Well, it must be true, or you'd be drinking, nothing as sure as that!" he said, answering his own question.

"You're happy then?"

"Happy? I'm over the bloody moon! How long have you known? The move, Jesus the move... Mandy, are you sure everything's alright?"

Amanda stroked Keith's upper arms. "Everything is fine. I've known for a couple of weeks, but I knew if I told you, you'd probably call off the move."

"Tricky cow."

"Well, it's done now."

"And you won't be lifting a finger 'til he's here," Keith warned.

"*He*? Another little chap, is it? We'll see. And besides, I'm only about six weeks pregnant. I'll be doing plenty right up until I can't move anymore. Alex needs his mummy."

"I know, I know. I just don't want you to get stressed out again. You know how it was when you were carrying Alex."

"Yes, Mr Corgan. But this is different, we're here. We've got a view, and space, and nice neighbours."

"So you say, I haven't met them yet."

"Well, that's the next bit of news. I've invited them over this weekend."

Keith rolled his eyes toward the ceiling. "Oh, brilliant."

After they had chatted excitedly about the baby and how Alex was going to be a brilliant big brother, Keith drained his glass and returned to the kitchen. The wine bottle rattled against the lip of the glass as his hands trembled. The thick red liquid poured across the oak veneer of the work surface, trickling over the edge to splatter and pool on the marbled linoleum floor. Keith cursed under his breath and slammed the wine bottle down before him. He pressed his flat palms onto the work surface and pushed a hissing breath through his clenched teeth.

Closing his eyes he felt the sting of tears and the lurch in his stomach as the reality of the situation – that they would never again leave Tilwick, that the second child would essentially root them to this evil old place – took hold and squeezed all hope from his heart.

Alex squealed with excitement as Keith gathered speed, pushing the toddler faster and faster on his ride-on tractor. The chunky plastic wheels clattered over the stone slabs of the lower portion of the back garden.

Amanda peeked out the kitchen window and smiled as the green tractor trundled past her view. She chuckled as Keith wrestled control of the little black steering wheel to stop Alex steering up the grass embankment leading to the overgrown grass terrace.

"Back down we go, Farmer Corgan," Keith said, guiding the vehicle back to the paved area. "I don't want to lose you in that jungle up there."

Keith had been putting off tackling the terrace, and especially putting of the collection of overgrown shrubs beyond. The truth was, he knew nothing of gardening and the maisonette, with the yard out back, had needed no more than an occasional run over with a broom.

Then again, he thought, *it could be sort of a workout*. The thought of working up a sweat in the garden, of running around with the new tools he had picked up at the local garden centre, suddenly appealed.

"What's this, Daddy?" Alex asked. Keith snapped his attention back to his child, who was off his tractor and stood staring intently at a small item he had picked up from the ground.

"Give it here, son," Keith said, hurrying to Alex's side. He took the curved nail from Alex's hand and noticed a red smear on his son's fingers. "Did you prick yourself with this?" he asked. Keith's mind suddenly raced. *What age do they get their tetanus jab? Amanda's going to fucking kill me for taking my eyes off him. I'll never hear the end of this.*

Wiping Alex's hand with his own fingers, he squeezed gently, trying to promote further bleeding to discharge any dirt driven into the wound. No fresh blood came. Keith realised that the blood had already been on the nail when Alex found it. "Where was this, little man?"

"There," Alex said, pointing at a spot by his feet.

"Everything all right?" Amanda called from the back

door.

"Yeah, it's fine. I just really need to give this garden a good going over." Keith tossed the nail into the bushes. *A cat must have caught a loose nail in the fence or something.* "Come on, Alex, let's get our hands washed and get back into the house, eh?"

Alex made off on his little vehicle, pumping with both legs at once, attempting what he really knew was an impossible escape. He squealed with delight as his father scooped him up, growling and nuzzled the back of his neck. Alex held onto the tractor for a moment before letting go when his dad's tickling became too intense and he scrunched his shoulders up and drew his hands to his face, letting the tractor clatter to the ground.

Keith fastened Alex into his booster seat and Amanda placed an orange plastic *Finding Nemo* plate in front of him. Alex grabbed a wedge of cucumber in one chubby fist and a cube of cheddar cheese with the other.

"Don't forget your sandwiches, Alex," Amanda called.

Alex pretended not to hear, and commenced to eat the cheese and cucumber, picking the ham out from between the slices of bread.

"He really does love that garden," Keith said, smiling as he peered out the window. "I suppose I really should become a gardener."

"Well before you do," Amanda said, her tone becoming a parody of a disapproving mother, "you can get that garage tidied up. You can't see two feet in front of you in there."

"I know, I know, it's *heap-lie-on*, but I needed a place to work from when I was decorating, didn't I?"

"Maybe getting rid of the mountain of empty cardboard boxes from the move would be a good start."

Keith wiggled his lower jaw from side to side. Amanda's tone had changed. She was becoming serious. Her *suggestions*, he realised, were in fact *orders*. "I'll make a start after lunch."

"I thought we were taking Alex to the park after his

nap."

"I can't do it all, Mandy," Keith snapped.

Amanda's eyes immediately turned to Alex, who was still happily munching away on everything but the bread on his plate. "Really, Keith?"

"So what, Mandy? It's the real world. You can't protect him from everything. People get pissed off with each other."

A tiny voice rose from the table, "… pissed off with each other."

Amanda's eyes widened. Keith's closed. He knew he was for it now.

"Daddy said a naughty word," Keith said. "We don't say that."

Amanda hissed, "Don't draw attention to it, he'll just do it all the more."

"Well… whatever… but listen, if you want that garage cleared, I'll do it. But other things will have to wait. And besides, you two will have fun together and I'll get on much faster without the little man checking in on me every two minutes."

"You have a point," Amanda accepted. "Anyway, the sooner you hit the garage and turn your hand to the garden, the better. Want the place looking good for Saturday when the girls come over."

"Marvellous," Keith deadpanned. The girls weren't the problem, he could just leave them all chatting away in the lounge, but it wouldn't just be the girls. He'd have to have awkward, stunted conversations with their husbands and partners about Christ only knew what. Cars and work, probably. And the gym. Keith sucked in the tummy he had gained since Alex was born. *Fuck it,* he thought, *best crack on, I need the exercise.*

Keith flipped the switch and stepped into the garage as the light flickered on. With a deep sigh he took in the scene before him. At the far end of the garage, at the large rolling door, the empty cardboard boxes were stacked, but they had toppled and slid over each other into an unruly mess. *Easy win*, Keith thought, *get them away to the waste depot.*

Moments later he was at the front of the house. He clicked the button on the remote control, activating the automatic garage door. As the entrance opened, flattened boxes slid out onto the driveway and two of them had become caught in the cables on the back of the door, and rose with it, dangling down perilously. Keith playfully smacked the boxes down from the raised door and began to gather the cardboard up. It was then that he noticed the boxes in the storage space just beneath the ceiling.

He frowned, not believing that Amanda would have gone to the trouble of placing anything up there, and knowing that he himself had not. *Probably a load of shit left by the last tenants*, he thought, *may as well get that gone while I go to the depot.*

Keith dropped the back seats of his Ford and stuffed the cardboard in to get it out of the way. This opened up a little room to manoeuvre within the garage as he dragged and scraped some boxes of DVDs and CDs back across the concrete towards the door. Keith closed the garage doors in case any of the neighbours should see him messing about in there, he hadn't any inclination to engage in small-talk. He opened out a red metal step ladder and climbed it until his head was above the level of the storage space.

The space was only large enough for an adult to slide across on their tummy, not even enough room to crawl, but he found three boxes and a battered leather suitcase up there. Without care, he pulled on each item and let it crash to the floor. He didn't really give a shit what was in any of them.

When he was back on the floor, Keith tore away the parcel tape from the first box and pried open the flaps. "Hideous," he muttered to himself, lifting out a garish orange and gold lampshade and a gold painted lamp. He inspected the plug, thinking he might play a trick on

Amanda and set it up in the bedroom. He found that it had the rounded pins of electrical goods of yesteryear.

He delved into the box again and found a neatly folded set of pink pillow cases.

The second box brought no treasures, either. A pink double sheet matched the pillowcases and a few green tinted copper fittings from plumbing jobs before the plastic fittings came along, were all he was offered.

Expecting more rubbish, Keith unzipped the suitcase, purely because it looked more interesting, more personal, than the cardboard boxes. *Probably just some old granny's stinking fucking swimming cozzie*, he thought.

He raised his eyebrows at the mysterious treasure trove within. A dozen small bundles of brown paper greeted him, just begging to be opened. He grasped the first item, a roughly oblong shape, rounded at the edges, about six inches long. Keith cursed as he grasped the item and a point jabbed the centre of his right palm, drawing forth a warm dribble of blood.

“Bastard,” he hissed, unwrapping the item carefully, to find a Stanley knife. The blade looked to be dull, but the triangular tip evidently still had a bite to it. The knife handle had once been chrome, but was now tinged with an orange-brown coating of what first appeared to be rust. Keith soon began to wonder how many people had cut themselves with the blade, and how much blood accounted for the discolouration. For the second time that day Keith wondered about tetanus shots; this time it was not Alex's he worried about, but his own.

He wiped the small puncture wound in his palm against his trouser leg, drawn back to the contents of the suitcase. He found a claw hammer, stained similarly to the blade. There was a tenon saw, complete with dull brass back and well-worn wooden handle. Keith inspected the blade and noted a fine powder between and across the saw's teeth.

He lifted out an almost horse-shoe shaped item and unwrapped it. Keith's fingers opened wide, immediately rejecting the item, letting it fall into the suitcase. He clasped his bleeding hand over his mouth and squeezed his eyes shut for a moment as though expecting the scene to have changed when he reopened them.

But no, the jawbone was still waiting for him.

The door connecting the garage to the kitchen opened and Amanda peered in. "Everything alright?"

Keith kicked the suitcase, flipping the lid over to conceal the bone. "Yeah, it's fine. Just this fucking suitcase. It's fucking stapled together and I cut my hand on it. Dropped it on my head and nearly fell off the steps."

"Mind you don't injure yourself, Mr Corgan."

"I'll be fine, now away with you and get some woman's work done." Keith desperately tried to dismiss his wife so that he could crouch down and gather himself. A wave of nausea swelled within him.

"I'll bloody woman's work you."

Keith's fingers traced across his forehead, gathering up the sheen of perspiration that had gathered there. He affected his best *Cartman from South Park* impersonation and waved his wife away, saying, "Get in that kitchen and make meh some pie!"

Amanda glanced over her shoulder to make sure Alex hadn't followed her from the lounge where he was sat enjoying his beaker of juice and an episode of Peppa Pig. Seeing that the coast was clear, she grinned at her husband and whispered, "Twat." And with that, she closed the door.

Keith heaved a few deep breaths, expanding his lungs fully and letting the air almost shudder out of him. He stared at the case for a long period, not knowing what to do. *Call the police. Let them deal with it*, he thought.

He pried his eyes away from the case lid and looked at the door to the kitchen, imagining he could see his wife through the barrier. His pregnant wife. His pregnant wife who suffered chronic bouts of anxiety and depression during the last pregnancy.

"Fucking hell!" he muttered.

He reached down to the cracked brown leather and flipped the lid back once more. Keith braced himself and grabbed the bone. Something about the delicate shape and size of the bone seemed to suggest to him that this belonged to a female and he guessed the teeth were the right size for an adult, not that he was an expert in these things. He rapped a knuckle against it. *Is it real*, he wondered. *What the fuck would I know, anyway?* It sounded like it could be bone. But then again it could just as easily be hard plastic from some medical model.

That's it, one of those anatomical models, Keith reasoned, turning the jaw over and over in his hands. Then he focussed on the discoloured teeth. And the filling in one of the molars. *Fucking hell! They wouldn't put plaque and a filling onto an anatomical model.*

Keith dropped the bone back into the case and eyed the other wrapped items with narrow, suspicious eyes. He crouched low over the case and steeled his nerves. His fingers found the paper and he began to tear into it like a child on Christmas morning who knew that the gifts were barbed wire and broken glass, but who had no choice but to get it over with as soon as possible.

When he had finished, he inspected the rusted pliers, the dull sawblades, the stained drill-bits and bradawls and he could not shake the feeling that these tools had become rusted and stained, like the Stanley knife, by being left covered in blood. The majority of the tools were wooden-handled, rather than furnished with the comfortable rubber grips of modern equipment. He knew these items were decades old. They might have been hidden away for twenty years or more. Who was to say what happened, when, or who was to blame? Keith knew one thing though, that with the nursing home fire, the dead family at the farm he had heard about, and the Councillor's daughter found dead in an alley, all in the space of a week, Tilwick's police were not going to give a shit about some cold case.

He zipped up the suitcase and hauled it up the ladder, shoving it back to its original hiding place. He stared at the battered case long and hard before descending the ladder once more, wondering *what the fuck am I supposed to do with this?*

Amanda woke to the sound of Keith coughing in the en-suite. After a moment, as she woke up properly and her eyes adjusted to the light which was switched on above Keith, she realised he was actually vomiting into the toilet bowl. She could see his rump as he knelt forward, with his upper body and head out of view.

"Keith, are you okay?" she called.

"Yeah, yeah, I'm fine."

"Not coming down with a stomach bug, are you?" she asked.

"No, babes, I'm okay. Just go back to sleep. I think something just lay heavy on my stomach, that's all."

"Can I get you anything?"

Keith flushed the toilet and stood upright, stepping into full view in the light. "No, honestly, I'm okay." He splashed cold water onto his face, gargled with some mouthwash, patted his face, chest and back with a towel to remove the water and sweat he had accumulated, then switched off the light in the en-suite once more.

Without saying another word, Keith left the bedroom, switched on the landing light and entered Alex's room, leaving the bedroom door open. The landing light illuminated Alex's bed and Keith stood over his son as he slept soundly. Keith's fingers reached out and touched the little boy's face, caressing his cheek, tracing the skin down to the jawline.

This was the third time in the night that he had repeated this action, but it was the first time Amanda had been disturbed. Keith sighed with relief, feeling the firm bone and teeth through his son's flesh. *Still there.*

He walked downstairs, switching lights on as he moved, checking the locks on the front door, back door, the patio door and the kitchen door leading into the garage. He returned to his bed, content that his home was secure and that his family was safe.

Out in the back garden, cloaked in the blackness of the night, hateful eyes watched Keith's every move on the ground floor until he closed the kitchen door and walked back upstairs.

"Disgusting!" Amanda yelled, shocking her husband awake. He hadn't caught the word she'd exclaimed, but when she repeated it, he picked up on it and an instant wave of terror burst against him. All he could think about was *the jaw*.

"What is it?" Keith called, as he sat upright in bed, rubbing his eyes to ease the tight pain that had settled there during his restless sleep.

"You puked in our toilet last night, didn't you?" Amanda asked, frowning in the bedroom doorway.

"Yeah, in there. What does it matter?"

"You didn't use the main bathroom at all?"

"No, what's wrong?"

Amanda rolled her eyes up and thumbed over her shoulder in the direction of the main bathroom. "There's something weird with the plumbing here. I noticed it on the first day, but thought maybe you'd used both toilets. What you flush in one… well, some of it comes back up in the other. Your puke washed through into the main bathroom."

Keith stretched his arms outward and twisted his body gently, extending his muscles a little. He slid to the edge of the bed. "Just be thankful my upset stomach was from the top end and not the bottom end, eh?"

"Too bloody right," Amanda said, turning the corners of her mouth down in disgust as the thought of diarrhoea bubbling through into the main bathroom bowl. She vanished and Keith heard the main other toilet flush as Amanda got rid of the offending material. When she returned to the bedroom she asked, "What was all that about last night? Tossing and turning, sweating, checking on Alex all the time."

"Don't ask me. I'm just getting used to this place, maybe."

"All this news from around town getting you down?"

"The family on the farm is the one that gets me the most, Amanda. Christ, that man butchered his whole family and he's still wandering around here somewhere. If he could do that to his own kids, then he could do it to anyone."

"I know, Keith, I'm worried about it too, but it was a couple of nights ago. I mean, you slept fine the first night in here. It just seems strange you'd be worked up about it now."

Keith thought frantically for an excuse. One came, it was weak, but it was an opportunity to give a sly hint at how tired he was of doing chores. "I was too busy on the first day here to think about anything."

"Oh, poor Mr Corgan has worked too hard."

"Hard work always feels harder in Tilwick," Keith grumbled.

A frozen silence descended as Amanda stared at her outstretched husband. He felt her glare like a laser, seeming to sear his flesh. He propped up on his elbows and asked, "What?"

"This again?"

"What?"

"I know I wanted us to get out of Tilwick once the funeral was sorted, but things changed, okay? Deal with it. I mean, how many times do we have to go over the same thing?"

Keith sat up, puffing out his cheeks. "Listen, it doesn't matter what you say, you dragged me back here and everything you've done since then has been to trap us here."

"Trap?" Amanda cried.

"Just fucking forget it, eh?" he stormed into the bathroom and yanked at the shower cord so hard that the string almost snapped, springing violently against the tiled wall when he released his grip on it and pulled open the shower screen.

"Going to wreck the place now, eh?" Amanda snapped, standing in the en-suite doorway.

"Leave me alone, would you?" Keith moaned, grabbing the shampoo from the shelf and causing the shower gel and conditioner to clatter to the ground. As he reached down to retrieve the fallen bottles, the shower head sputtered and spat as though a large amount of air had become trapped in the system.

He heard the doorbell ring and was aware of Amanda's footsteps heading down the stairs as she went to answer. Relieved to be on his own for a time, Keith righted the bottles and rubbed his thumb over the shower head, trying to remove any build-up that might have caused the interruption in the flow.

The pressure restored once more and a hot jet of liquid splashed against Keith's face and body. He closed his eyes and rubbed his hair and face, savouring the warmth and the peace and hoped that he had avoided another argument. As his palm rubbed over his nose, the pressure incited a dull ache, reminding him of the Stanley knife blade. He inspected the wound to see only a small, triangular scab surrounded by slightly swollen red skin. Nothing life-threatening. Everything would be back to normal in a couple of days.

Amanda answered the front door and found one of the neighbours waiting for her. She recognised the large man from around town, she had seen him at the shops on many occasions and on nights out, too. He was in his mid-forties though and was not from her generation in terms of people she could remember from school; this man fell into the gap between her and her parents.

The man wore his greying blonde hair in a mullet style and in his Black Sabbath t-shirt looked every inch the rocker trapped in the '80s. Despite the fact that his torso comprised of what appeared to be a flabby chest above a swollen paunch, the man's arms were thick and muscular. Clearly, this was a man who carried out a manual job, but whose diet wasn't as healthy as it might have been. Standing at a little under six feet in height, there was just, Amanda thought, *a lot* of this man. He was just *big,* but there was an air of the gentle giant about him, too. His eyes sparkled with friendly energy and his broad face split into a smile as soon as she opened the door to him.

"Hiya," he said. "I'm Sean. Sean Fisher from just over the road." The man turned and pointed to a house only a couple of doors away from where one of her friends lived. "I was in town earlier and there's been an announcement about the *Old Man of Tilwick*."

Amanda found it strange to have someone talking about the town's old master, directly. She had always supposed the resident of Tilwick Castle was not that old – at least, not as old as the local stories suggested – she had rather more expected a descendant of the fortress's original inhabitant. "Oh?" was all she could manage.

"Aye, there was an incident through the night and the master is in hospital."

"Oh dear," Amanda gasped. "It must be very serious."

"From what the Council's released, it's not very good. He's in a bad way. All these murders and fires and all that, it's all connected, they reckon. Now there's been a direct attack on him. The head of the Council, Mr Forster, he was killed last night, too."

It seemed impossible that these powerful, seemingly untouchable figureheads of Tilwick had been brought to such a state. "What do we do?" she asked.

"Well, the Council's just saying brace yourself and prepare for things like power cuts and bad weather. He's not in a position to keep everything flowing at its usual rate. The water might go funny, but they're going to keep testing it in every ward every day until we get through this and they'll let us know if we need to boil it or buy bottled water or whatever. For the moment, they've said just carry on as normal as much as possible."

"Okay, well, thanks for the update."

"My pleasure," Sean said, turning on his heels. "I'll get moving on, I need to catch everyone I can on the estate. Oh, and welcome to the neighbourhood!" he called.

"Thank you. Actually, we're having a barbecue on Saturday if the weather holds up. A few of the folks on the estate are coming over, why don't you come too and meet my husband, Keith?" Amanda offered.

"That sounds great," Sean said. "I'll try to make it. My wife won't come, like, but I'll do my best to drop by. I'll bring a few drinks if I do, is that okay?"

"Perfect. Well, we might see you on Saturday afternoon, then?"

"You might well. Take care," Sean said, giving a short wave as he left the driveway and strode off to the next house.

Amanda closed the front door and hurried upstairs to see Keith. She had forgotten the row they had begun, and instead wanted to tell her husband about Sean and his message. No sooner had she reached the en-suite than she found her hand grasping the doorframe for support as her legs seemed to crumple beneath her. Her scream was caught in her throat as she struggled to catch her breath around her unspoken words. In seconds, her scream did come, and Amanda stared, frozen in shock at the sight of thick, flowing blood coating the shower screen and tiles.

"What's wrong?" Keith cried, seeing his wife crumbling in the doorway. "Mandy, what's *wrong*?"

He hit the button to stop the flow, slid the shower screen open and slipped on the floor as he stepped out, soaking wet, onto the slippery tiles. He managed to catch the wash basin to steady himself, and reached for his wife, who stared at him in horror and disbelief.

"The blood! The blood!" was all she could manage to utter.

"Sweetheart, what blood? What blood?" Keith cried,

wrapping his arms around her to steady her. He eased her back onto the edge of the bed. “Here, sit down. Sit down and have a rest. What blood, darling?”

Her wide eyes brimmed with tears and Keith wrapped his arms around her, struggling to comprehend what was going on as she struggled to free herself from his grip.

Amanda wiped at her hands and arms as though trying to rub dirt away. Keith looked himself over, becoming concerned that he had brought something other than water out of the shower with him and had wiped it on her. Seeing nothing, he looked back at his wife, confused and frightened by her reaction. His hands instinctively moved to her midriff, as though he was checking on the baby who he knew, in reality, was barely a cluster of cells at that point. Certainly not enough to call a baby.

“Mandy, what’s wrong? Tell me,” Keith cried, raising his hands to her shoulders, rocking her gently.

Tears streamed from Amanda’s eyes and her skin took on a waxy sheen, turning white as she went into shock.

“What blood, Mandy? What blood were you talking about?”

“The blood in the fucking shower!” she cried. “You know what blood! It was all over you!” Amanda retched, the spasm causing her head and shoulders to lurch forwards.

Keith brought her head to his chest and spoke in a soothing tone, momentarily terrified by the prospect of his wife having a mental breakdown while carrying the child. “There’s no blood, sweetheart. You’ve imagined it. There’s no blood there.”

Amanda’s reddened eyes seemed to adjust back to reality and she recognised that Keith was simply wet from the shower. She glanced past him at the shower screen and saw that only droplets of water, gathering and tumbling down, gathering the condensing steam, marked the glass. She had imagined the scene, but it was so *vivid*, so *horrific*. Keith had been rubbing litre after litre of thick, dark red blood all over his skin, letting it tumble into his mouth, filling his eyes and slicking his hair.

"I need to get downstairs and have a drink or something," Amanda gasped, peeling herself from the bed.

"Are you sure you're okay on the stairs? Give me a moment and I'll come down with you." Keith grabbed a towel and frantically rubbed as much water from his body as he could in a few seconds before pulling on a pair of grey track suit bottoms. "Come on, I'll get you a cuppa. You get on that couch."

"You shouldn't have called that doctor out, Keith," Amanda insisted. "I was fine."

"Well, look, it's done now, and you just need to keep your feet up and relax." Keith left his wife propped up with pillows on the bed and passed her the TV remote. With a cup of tea in her hand, she seemed a little happier and much calmer than she had all morning. As the TV burst into life, Keith drifted from the master bedroom into Alex's room, where the little boy played with his building blocks in a room made light by two lime green and two pale cream walls, all dotted with transfers of pirates, treasure chests and pirate ships.

"Crash!" Alex cried, making his voice into as savage a roar as his three years would allow.

"What are we building?"

"Not building, smashing!"

"Ahhh, I see," Keith said, taking a position lying on his side with his tummy at Alex's back. "And so, what are we smashing, then?"

"The castle!"

"Oooh! A castle. You must be a giant, then?"

"Not a castle. The castle! Til'k castle!" Alex exclaimed, knocking another pile of blocks over.

Keith smiled, thinking that with the state of the master, according to what Amanda had heard, that it might not be too long before that old castle came down. He pondered that for a moment. What would happen to the rest of the town if the master did die? *Well, what did they do every other time the man they name the master has died? Tell everyone he's taken a new body and introduce the latest member of the Mercer family, I suppose*.

"Are we going to tidy that garden today, little man?" Keith asked, rubbing Alex's hair, ruffling the fine blonde strands up.

"Yeah!"

"Come on then, let's get those welly boots dirty!"

Keith carried Alex down the stairs, nuzzling the boy's neck as he went, causing the child to squeal in delight. Keith enjoyed the closeness of such play. He knew every ticklish site on that boy's body and took every opportunity he could, to send his child into paroxysms of hysterical laughter. "What?" he asked, feigning innocence, "I didn't do anything!" This only caused Alex to laugh out louder as Keith tickled him yet again.

When he opened the door from the kitchen to the garage, Keith let out a gasp and quickly twisted away with Alex, making sure he could not see, right there on the floor, the open suitcase.

"Wait here, little man," Keith muttered, placing Alex on his booster seat at the table. "Stay there while I get your boots."

Keith contemplated the step down into the garage and glanced back at his son. The contents of the suitcase were obscured by the open lid, which had been left flopped against the shaft of the yard broom, leaning against the wall. He knew that Amanda would not have climbed up in the garage to retrieve the case, nor would she have opened it, found a human jawbone and not immediately freaked out about it.

Alex shuffled on his seat. "Want to go in the garden!" he exclaimed, bored of waiting.

Keith knew he had only seconds before the boy would get off his seat and charge into the garage, where who knew what the hell he would discover in the case. He had to just look and get it over and done with. He stepped down into the garage and peered over the lid into the case. Nothing.

No jawbone. No tools. Nothing. The case was completely empty.

Keith felt a sudden wave of nausea, pulling right at the bottom of his guts. Forgetting about the boots, he turned and left the garage, locking it behind him.

"Daddy, where are my boots?" Alex asked.

"You'll just have to wait a minute, son," he replied.

"But I want to go in-"

"Just wait a minute!" Keith snapped, charging out of the kitchen, along the hallway and up the stairs. "Mandy! Mandy have you been in the garage?"

"Why, is it a crime?" Amanda replied, suspicious of Keith's alarmed tone.

"Of course not... just... have you been in there? Has anyone been in there?"

"No, just you."

"Has anyone been around here?"

"No. Just that bloke over the street who told me about this thing with Mammon." Amanda paused, watching her husband's deep breathing and nervous glances. "Something's wrong, Keith. What is it?"

"Nothing. It's all right."

"No it isn't. Has something gone missing?"

"When that bloke was round, you didn't hit the garage door button on your key ring, did you?"

"No. I don't think so."

Keith's eyes widened. "Which is it? No, or you don't think so?"

"Well, no! Keith, what the fuck is this about? You're being really weird and that is the last thing I need today!"

Keith stomped down the stairs, calling over his shoulder, "Just bloody forget it, would you?"

Keith decided that the time had come for the weeds poking through the paving slabs at the rear of the house, to meet their end. He ensured Alex was wearing his little blue gardening gloves, which made his hands look far too big for him. Keith had on his thick rigger gloves and the pair set to tearing out invading broadleaf plantain and dandelions. There was a therapeutic quality to the work, a satisfaction to the job that bypassed tedium and granted him some satisfaction.

"Look, Daddy!" Alex exclaimed gleefully, holding his gloves up for his father to inspect.

"Alex! What have you done?" Keith cried, throwing off his gloves and grasping his child's hands. "Are you hurt?" Alex's gloves were completely soaked through with a sticky red substance that Keith instantly knew to be blood. For the second time that week, he worked over his child's hands to find no evidence of a wound. He peered at the paving stones for clues to where the blood had come from and there, between the slabs, a dark, glistening stream seemed to bring with it more questions than answers.

"Back in the house, Alex."

"But Daddy, I want to help!"

"Get back in, quickly," Keith ordered.

The sharp tone of the order was not lost on the little boy and Alex retreated to the kitchen, occasionally peering over his shoulder to cast hateful looks at his father, who had spoiled all the fun.

Keith replaced his gloves and probed the slick crevice between the stones, displacing the crimson liquid, forcing it to break over the lip of the slabs. Keith grasped another weed and dislodged it, breaking loose a clod of moss as he worked. More blood bubbled to the surface, replacing the dislodged weed. "What the fuck is going on here?" Keith muttered.

Amanda appeared at the kitchen door, "Keith! Why is our son crying hysterically in the lounge?" she cried.

"Not now, Mandy!" Keith called over his shoulder. He braced himself as Amanda's rapid footsteps told of her angry approach.

"Never mind your fucking garden, Keith! Alex is really upset, now what did you say to him?"

Keith stood up, grabbed Amanda's hand and pressed a blood-soaked clump of weeds into her palm. "I chased him into the house because of this. I didn't want you to see it, because you've already freaked out enough, but there is fucking *blood* rising from beneath these paving stones!"

"I'm calling the police," Amanda said, dropping the weeds. "And there's no need to take this out on us, you know!"

Keith watched his wife hurry back indoors. He stared down at the blood spattered ground and felt the tide of curiosity rising within him. Moments later he was jamming the end of a crowbar under the stone, exerting force down on the metal, enough to raise the stone up on one end. One shove with his hand was enough to topple the slab and he could see immediately that the ground beneath the stone was sodden with blood.

Keith drank deeply of the wine offered to him. The bitter tang at the end of the slug sent a shiver up his spine.

"I bet you needed that," Jerry said, smiling at his neighbour.

"You're not kidding," Keith muttered.

"At least Alex is out of the way for a couple of days. And, to be honest, the police have their hands full at the moment. They won't want to disrupt you for long."

"Yeah, a couple of nights with Keith's mum will do him good. It'll do us good, too, but I don't know that we can stay there after this," Amanda said. Immediately, she glanced at her friend Jane for support.

Annette reached out and grasped her shoulder, giving her a gentle squeeze. "I wish we had enough room for you guys to stay here for a few nights."

"I feel awful for recommending the place to you," Jerry said.

"It's not your fault," Amanda assured him. "You did us a favour. I mean, if you hadn't got in touch with that landlord, we would never have been able to live on an estate this nice."

Keith looked around Annette and Jerry's comfortable lounge, glowing soft red in the side-lamp and candle light. The restored furnishings and deep red leather couch gave the place a real homely feel that made Keith decide that his own home was as cold as a grave. Every free piece of wall space was dotted with family photographs and it was clear to both Keith and his wife that the Cooper's home was a happy one.

The open blinds revealed the silhouette of their own home, backlit by the powerful police flood lights as the excavation work continued through the night.

A knock at the door announced the arrival of some more guests. "That'll be Sean and Ellen," Annette said, heading out into the passageway to let them in. "You know what Lynn's like, Mandy, she and Pete are always the last ones to arrive."

Amanda forced a knowing smile, but immediately glanced across at Keith, wondering if they had done the right thing in coming to their neighbours' place. It had been Annette's idea, with the barbecue looking like a total write-off as the police tore up the garden; she had wanted to do something to mark Amanda and Keith's arrival in the neighbourhood.

The doorway filled with Sean Fisher's bulky form, his eyes sparkling and teeth fully displayed in a broad grin. "Ahhh, the new neighbours. Heard about this strange business in your back garden!"

Sean perched himself on a seat near Keith and reached out a hand. "Nice to see you again, Amanda. Keith, is it?"

"Yeah, nice to meet you." Keith shook the hand offered to him by this big, gregarious man. Keith immediately recognised that this was a man who liked to think he was some sort of 'Daddy' of the neighbourhood. As far as he was concerned, the man was nothing more than a gossip and probably just tolerated because he was so forward that he was impossible to escape.

The real surprise came when Sean's wife Ellen

entered the room. In huge contrast to her husband, she was petite, with a thin face surrounded by thick, dark curls. It was clear that she had been very attractive in her younger days, but time had taken its toll on her and she looked simply tired, but well made-up. Her skill with make-up did a good job of covering up most of time's ravages.

The introductions were barely over when the remaining guests, Pete and Lynn, turned up. Keith knew that Lynn and Annette had been friends with Amanda since school, and it seemed that the Fishers were here for no other reason than they were popular on this street.

The Coopers kept the drink flowing, and Keith wondered when Amanda, who was abstaining, would call time on him. He knew, of course, that she would be reluctant to do so too soon, as she had no desire to get home any time soon.

Ellen proved to be a quiet woman, who seemed to have to be tortured for information. Keith wondered if this was because Sean apparently spoke non-stop. His laughter drowned out almost everything else in the room, as though the man constantly strove to keep the focus on him.

The only time he went quiet was when Amanda turned to Ellen and said, "Sean mentioned you didn't like the house we live in. All this business has got me wondering about that. Is there any particular reason?"

Ellen seemed dumbstruck and Keith noticed Pete and Jerry shoot concerned looks at each other.

"No," Ellen said. "Not really. You know when you just have an irrational dislike of a place… the atmosphere, something like that. That's all it is."

Amanda smiled with a sadness clear in her eyes. "Well, perhaps it isn't irrational after all, eh? Depends what gets dug up around the back."

Sean cleared his throat and added his opinion, "You know, Amanda, it could just be a response to what's going on with the Old Man. Strange things happen whenever that old chap gets ill, or wounded, so the stories always say. Well, you know that anyway."

"I'll be honest, Sean, I never really went in for all that. I sort of left that behind when I moved out of my folks' place."

"Which denomination are they?" Sean asked.

Amanda smiled and said the nickname of the *House of Embers*, "They were *mental money burners*."

"Embers. You said *were*?"

"Yes, my parents are both dead now. I mean, they had me pretty late on, my brother is much older than I am."

"Ah, I'm sorry, *hen*. I shouldn't be so nosy."

Keith's eyes narrowed. He knew that this man couldn't survive without nosiness and now he understood why. Ellen was so repressed that it was obvious these two had no life together. That's why the lives of others seemed much more interesting. "Anyway," Keith interjected, "I don't like to talk about religion while I'm drinking."

Sean shot him a look of annoyance. "*You* weren't talking about religion. Amanda and I were."

Keith straightened his spine up, knowing that he was nowhere near as physically capable as Sean, but wanting to look his best anyway. "All the same. I think we should drop it." Amanda frowned at him, upset with his apparent rudeness.

"Sorry, Keith. I mean no harm," Sean said, his face returning to the ruddy-faced, grinning configuration he usually displayed. He knocked back a tall glass of Jack Daniels and coke, then got up to fix himself another. "Anyone else for a drink? Keith, much left in that beer?"

"I'm okay, thanks." Keith knew that his drink was almost finished, but some nagging sensation warned him to slow down, to keep his wits about him.

As an endless supply of coke and bourbon seemed to flow into Sean's mouth, he spoke of his band *Wages of Sin* and their last gig at a local bar *The Silver Bonnets*. This led into many tales of their drunken hijinks over the years, and theories about just why it was his band always seemed to lose their bassists. "I might as well have an advert up permanently looking for one. My brother joined us for a while, but we kept fucking fighting all the time. Hey, the Gallaghers had nowt on us!"

"Does Joe still play, aye?" Pete asked.

"Well, that's a matter of opinion!"

"I've never heard him practising in the house or anything," Pete said.

"What about you, Keith? You ever heard him?"

"I'm not with you," Keith said, frowning in confusion.

"Oh, you won't know. My brother Joe, he's your neighbour. We bought up a few properties on this estate years ago and did them up. Mind, we never spent much time on yours. Dad lived there for a lot of years and we never quite got round to changing as much as we did on the others. I always wanted to sort the plumbing between the en-suite and the bathroom. Had any surprises with that, yet?"

Keith forced a smile across his lips and glanced at Amanda to check if she had picked up on this revelation. *He's the fucking landlord! He has a fucking key!* "Yeah. I seemed to puke in two toilets simultaneously the other day."

Sean chuckled, "Oops! Look, we'll get in there and sort it out for you, okay? We'll let these coppers finish wrecking the patio, then we'll put that right and do the plumbing while our tools are in there. That sound okay?"

Keith took a long look at Jerry, who shuffled uncomfortably, staring at Pete, trying to think of another conversation he could start to move things along.

"So, I mean, I know you said you have the band, but you're what, a builder by trade, then?" Keith asked.

"Yeah, I have my certificates for plumbing, too. I used to do a lot of it, but I set the business up and brought up some apprentices to full plumbers so they could take that over. Too much of a messy job, that."

"I see. Your brother… he's a builder too?"

Sean smiled, his eyes beaming. "No. Not usually,

although he is handy. I taught him everything he knows. No, Joe's a copper. In fact, he's right behind your house now with a shovel and pick in his hand."

Keith stared at Amanda with the intensity of one trying to transmit his thoughts right into her head. *Are you hearing this? Are you getting all of this? This is why I hate Tilwick. It's all stitched up. Someone was killed in that house. He has a key, and now his brother is supposedly looking for a body!*

Amanda continued in enthusiastic conversation with her friends as Keith slowed his drinking, pondering his next move. Sean seemed to be getting increasingly drunk, but did nothing to slacken the pace of his drinking. When Jerry walked through to the kitchen to gather another round of beers, Keith saw his opportunity and followed him.

Keith raised a finger to his lips and spoke rapidly, in a hushed tone. "Listen, Jerry. What's fucking going on with that house? There's something weird, why won't Sean's wife go there?"

Jerry pinched the bridge of his nose and shook his head. "Keith, keep this to yourself, ok? Sean was caught out knocking off his tenant there. We all knew he was up to something with her and it all came out. It was nasty and Ellen really took it badly, poor cow. But, she took him back and Sean ended it with the tenant and she moved away, out of Tilwick, as soon as the shit hit the fan."

"Right, so that's why she hates the place?"

Jerry nodded. "Exactly. That's all it is, mate. Nothing spooky, he just really hurt her and apparently he controls all the money and won't move house."

"Really? That's pretty harsh."

"Yeah," Jerry said, grabbing three beers, "but you've met the man. Is it surprising?"

Keith smiled and tilted his head, a gesture indicating *I suppose not.*

As they entered the lounge once more, Sean's eyes were half-closed and he appeared about to collapse asleep on the chair. Ellen was pulling her coat over her shoulders.

"Oh, Sean's planning on a sleepover," Jerry said, chuckling.

"You're sure you don't mind, Annette?" Ellen asked.

"Not at all. The kids will do a good job of waking him up. I'll put a coffee in him and send him back to you," Annette assured her, wrapping an arm around her shoulder, pulling her close for a hug and a kiss on the cheek.

"Thanks for a lovely evening, it was nice to meet you both," Ellen said, turning to Keith and Amanda.

"Likewise," Amanda replied.

Sean fell asleep fully and began to snore loudly within minutes of Ellen leaving. "Well, I guess that's our cue to hit the road," Keith said, squeezing Amanda's knee. "Thanks for the beers, we'll have to make it up to you sometime."

"Not at all," Jerry said. "I just hope you can get the house sorted and settled soon, then you can enjoy it properly."

"We'll see," Amanda replied uneasily.

Once all the goodbyes and thanks were said, Keith and Amanda took their leave. As they walked over the road towards their home and its spectral illumination, Keith whispered, "Listen to me, Mandy, we are moving out of here tomorrow. I can't put my finger on it, but something very fucking wrong is happening here and that Sean bloke is at the heart of it!"

"Where the hell are we going?" Amanda asked.

"I don't care if we have to camp in mother's back garden, we are not staying in this house! Why the fuck did Jerry not disclose that Sean and his brother are the landlords?"

"Is that a crime?" Amanda asked.

"No, but clearly some sort of a crime *has* taken place there. A murder – the last tenant, probably. She was shagging Sean and he got caught out and she apparently fucked off. He probably murdered her when she didn't want to call things off."

The rain came down heavier with every footstep, until they set foot through their front door and out of a full summer downpour, full of static.

"Listen to me. His brother, this copper, Joe," Keith whispered, "He's going to tell us that nothing has turned up and all the blood and all that, it's going to be passed off as what's happening with Mammon."

"So you're a believer now?"

Keith wiggled his jaw from side to side, letting the tips of his teeth grind together. "Listen, I'm not saying that. But I'm saying *he* is, and everything he has to say on these disturbances is based on that."

A knock at the front door made them both jump in fright.

Keith answered to find a policeman waiting for him. He recognised the broad smile immediately – this had to be Joe Fisher. "Evening, Mr Corgan. I'm Joe, by the way. I just live next door to you."

"So I understand, nice to meet you," Keith said, offering his hand. "And call me Keith." He put on his best neighbour act, thinking, *I'll play the game, you bastards!*

"Great, Keith. Listen, this rain's making a bit of a mess out back. We're going to call off until tomorrow morning and we'll see what the weather does then, ok? I should add, though, there are no signs so far of anything untoward, so I'm tempted to think it may all be to do with the Old Man getting smashed up."

"Could well be. I think we'd all hope that rather than anything else, eh?"

"Too bloody right. Anyway, try to sleep well, and I'll check in with you in the morning, but if anything should happen, if you think you need help just feel free to knock on my door, all right?"

"Thank you so much."

"Stay safe."

Keith closed the door and waited, his hands pressed against the hard white PVC. He turned the handle upwards, engaging the locks, before twisting the front door key, fixing the locks in place. He breathed deeply, trying to force his spiralling mind into a sense of calm, a state in which he could form a cohesive plan.

"Keith!" Amanda cried from the bedroom.

Keith hurried up the stairs to find his wife lying flat on the bed. "What's up?"

"I've got this pain in my left shin. Would you take a look for me, please?"

Keith leaned in close and guided Amanda's left leg, encouraging her to bend her knee. Amanda had not closed the curtains when she had entered the room, but even the light pollution from the floodlights in the garden was not enough for Keith to see clearly. He reached for the bedside lamp and turned it on. "What the hell is this?" he asked, pointing a finger at the pea-sized fleshy bump a third of the way down her shin.

"I don't think it's a bite. It's not itchy, it's just sore."

"Hard to tell what the hell this is…" Keith prodded the lump with his fingertip, eliciting a sharp gasp of pain from his wife.

"Jesus and Mammon, Keith!"

"Tender, eh?"

"What the hell is it?" Keith muttered, nudging the solid little lump aside.

Amanda hissed through gritted teeth.

"Mandy, if it's that sore, maybe I need to get you to A and E."

"What? After all you've had to drink?" Amanda's front teeth pressed down hard against her lower lip.

Keith glanced up at his wife. "Did you do anything over at Annette's? Can you remember bumping anything? You might have driven a splinter in and it got infected."

"It doesn't look infected, though. It's not red."

"No, you're right. It just looks… normal. I want to get a pair of tweezers at it. So tempting just to squeeze it and see if it bursts." Keith wore a playful grin, the mischievous look of one who enjoyed inflicting a little pain under the pretext of helping.

"Fucking dare, Mr Corgan, and I'll take an eye!"

"Just rest it up, that's all you can do. Want some paracetamol?"

"Yes, please."

"Let me get a slash, first."

"Oh, Keith I hate it when you say that. Can't you have a piss like anyone normal?"

Keith chuckled and wandered into the en-suite. "Who says I'm normal? FUCK ME!"

"What is it?"

"Don't come in here!" Keith cried, staring into the toilet bowl.

"What the hell is it?" Amanda cried, inching toward the edge of the bed, teeth gritted against the pain of the mysterious growth in her leg.

"I said fucking stay there! You can't see this! Stay away!"

Amanda ignored her husband and limped to his side. "Christ and Mammon!" she screamed, staring at the tangle of white, shrivelled fingers in the bottom of the toilet bowl.

Amanda staggered backwards and, turning, she fell against the side of the bed, scraping her shin. She howled as the wooden lip around the bedstead caught the small growth, unleashing fresh, searing pain through her body.

"Fucking hell, Mandy!"

Amanda rolled onto her back, clutching her leg. "Keith, it's agony! Have I ripped it open? I can't look!"

Keith grasped his wife's foot and inspected the raw skin, sheared in the fall. Blood leaked from the bump. Keith probed the wound with his fingertip and pinched a tiny thread he found, highlighted by the tiny blobs of blood clinging to the fibre. "Stay still. This may hurt."

Keith teased the fibre away from Amanda's leg, finding that it doubled in length, sliding from the bleeding flesh. "It's a hair. I think it's a hair."

"In my leg?" Amanda gasped.

"It's really dark, though. It isn't your hair."

"Are you kidding, Keith? This isn't the time to take the piss!"

Keith kept drawing the hair from the wound and noticed that it was threaded through Amanda's flesh around the bump. As he continued to draw out the hair, the flesh began to open, like stitches being picked from a garment.

"Keith, it's agony! Stop it! *Keith!*" Amanda screamed, grasping at the bedclothes hanging over the bed above her.

"Just stay still, it's almost open!"

The skin peeled open to expose the interior of the bump, where Keith saw a reddish brown lump. "What the fuck is this?"

"Leave it alone!"

"No way." Keith dug his fingernails into Amanda's flesh, slipping over the tiny item, and he adjusted his grip until he managed to get purchase once more. "Try not to move. I have this."

"Don't, Keith! Please!" Amanda cried.

Keith tugged the little bump free, finding that it led to a longer shaft, about six inches long. Amanda screamed until the entire nail was dislodged from her flesh.

"A nail? How the hell did that get into my leg?" Amanda screamed.

Keith unravelled the black hair, which was wrapped around the nail a dozen times. "How the hell did this hair get in there? And whose hair is it?" He straightened the fibre out and saw that the hair was almost two feet long.

Amanda pressed down on the hole in her leg, trying to stem the bleeding. "Pass me a towel, Keith, would you?"

"Sorry, here." Keith stood up and grabbed a towel from the rail above the small radiator in the en-suite.

Amanda pressed the towel down and glanced up at Keith to see him staring out of the window. "What now?"

The rain looked like a blizzard, cut out sharp in the hard light, each drop a white-hot spark against the blackness of the corners of the garden beyond the burning bulbs.

"There's someone down there."

"What?"

"I'm telling you, there's someone in the garden. She's looking right at me."

Keith raced down the stairs, through the kitchen and slammed the key into the back door lock. In moments stood on the soft earth among small mounds of paving stones, squinting in the floodlit glare. "I saw you! Give it up now!" he shouted.

His night vision ruined by the floodlights, Keith peered into the darkness, shielding his eyes from the raindrops. He strained his ears to hear above the rising wind and staccato impact of the rain all around him.

He grasped the nearest floodlight and wrestled the black plastic handle, twisting lamp around, casting the intense beam around to previously pitch-black areas of the garden. His heart leapt and he found the impossible urge to run away when the pale face and black eyes peered out from behind a bushy honeysuckle.

"Tell me what the hell is going on!" Keith demanded, stepping forwards.

The woman shied away into the shade of the thick bush.

"Get back here! I need answers! I need to know what the fuck is going on *here*!" Keith hopped up onto the terrace above the ruined patio, only a few feet away from this strange woman. He had noted her thick, black hair. It seemed impossible that this was not the same hair as that found in Amanda's leg.

A throaty hiss emerged from the mouth of this mysterious woman. Keith braced himself; the noise seemed somehow primitive, feral even, and he expected an attack any second. Instead of a sudden rush, however, the woman emerged from the cover of the honeysuckle slowly.

Keith closed his eyes when the light caught her

face and her disfigurement became apparent. The whole lower portion of the woman's head was a ravage of tattered flesh and bruise. Her tongue lashed around beneath her upper palette, but the lower lip, gums and jaw were entirely gone.

Despite himself, Keith staggered back as the woman reached for him with both hands, revealing hands devoid of fingers and thumbs, and forearms encrusted with nails driven right through from one side to another. The woman's entrance into the light revealed ever more brutal damage. Holes had been bored into her temples, her kneecaps had been hacked off, and lower than that, Keith noted in utter disbelief that she made no contact with the ground. She was upright, but had no feet and seemed to levitate above the sodden grass.

Terrified, he turned to flee, caught a fleeting glimpse of a broad smile, heard the clang of metal on bone and felt the momentary agonising pressure inside his skull before all went dark.

"He wants you! He wants you! BITCH! Fucking BITCH! I saw how you looked at him! How he looked at you!"

"Ellen, please! Please, Ellen, listen to me. I don't understand."

Keith heard his wife pleading before his vision sharpened. She was terrified. She was in terrible danger. She was in pain.

The light hurt his eyes as he blinked into full consciousness and he registered a heavy, rhythmic knocking sound from somewhere upstairs. The sounds stopped for a moment or two, but Amanda's cries and pleas persisted. The knocking resumed, eliciting a fresh terrified scream from his wife.

Keith made to stand up, desperate to race to his distraught wife, but his arms refused to move and his torso could twist no further. Handcuffs kept him locked to the radiator. He was in the lounge, a matter of metres from his wife, but the distance may as well have been miles.

The hammering stopped and Keith heard a thud against the floor above. He *had* to get up there. He grasped beneath the radiator, tugging it up against the hooks that pinned it to the wall. The radiator seemed to be stuck, but Keith persisted, jerking upwards again and again. Eventually, the dried paint cracked and the radiator shuddered upwards. Keith pulled at the pipe, bringing the right side of the radiator free of the wall, bending the soft alloy hooks at the other side.

He yanked and heaved at the copper pipe, feeling the satisfying *give* of the soft metal as he pulled, but he could only go so far. The solid body of the quick-cuffs prevented him from wrapping a chain around the pipe where he might have been able to bend it and eventually snap it. He fought and fought, but the metal would not give. He felt as though his bones might, though. He braced his forearm and tried to twist into a position where he could snap his wrist.

Amanda stared at the rusty tools in the battered suitcase and the deranged, elfin woman stooped over them. She had seemed so slight, so vulnerable earlier at the Coopers' place. Now she knew otherwise. This woman was pure insanity.

Ellen brandished the short, pointed bradawl, hovering over Amanda's legs. "Ooh, you have a nasty hole there already, I see."

"Please, Ellen. Please, if you put that thing down and just go… just go home… Nobody would know. I wouldn't tell a soul, I swear it."

Amanda writhed against the nails fastening her wrists to the bedstead, wishing she had the courage and strength to force her arms forward and tear the nails out of the wood, or through her flesh.

Ellen used the rusted tool to gentle probe the little wound on Amanda's leg, caused by Keith's earlier extraction of the mysterious nail. "I wonder if I can do this without touching the sides, you know, like that game where it buzzes when you touch the wire. Do you know the game I mean?"

"Please…"

"DO YOU KNOW THE GAME I MEAN?"

"Yes! Yes! I know the game you mean."

Ellen slid the tip of the bradawl into the opening of the wound. "I was never much good at the game, and whenever it would buzz, I used to just hurry all the more, buzzing all the way to the other end. You get what I mean?"

"Yes! I know. Please!" Amanda screamed when the metal point bit into her flesh.

Ellen chuckled and said, "Oh well!" She rammed the bradawl to its hilt, feeling the spike scrape hard shin bone. Amanda kept on screaming as Ellen withdrew the tool a little and jammed it in again, over and over. Eventually she pulled the bloody point clear.

"There, that was a little taster. What shall we do next? I like your legs. I think *he* likes your legs. He liked her legs. She had long legs like yours. Just like yours." Ellen reached into the suitcase and produced the thick, dirty tenon saw. "Long legs just like yours until I shortened them for her."

"Oh Christ! Ellen, please! You have to believe me! There is nothing going on! I've only just met him."

"*She* only just met him. Just met him again and again and even though I begged him, he would not stop shagging her. He promised he would, but I saw him sneaking in here night after night. Making a fool of me. They all knew. They all knew. I should have visited them all. But he never looked at them the way I saw him look at you." Ellen brought the saw blade up to Amanda's right kneecap. "And that slut, she let him come in her again and again. He couldn't get me pregnant, oh but he fucking made sure she was."

"Ellen, you have to listen to me. Ellen! You've got this all confused."

"*Confused*? I am *not* confused. I know *exactly* what

I'm doing. Just like she knew what she was doing, just like you know what you were doing. Did you think I would let you just move in here and let him pick up with you where he left off with her?"

Keith screamed out in frustration and agony as he twisted his wrist to its extent. Sweat mingled with the damp from the rain, all over his body, running down his face in rivulets as he squatted over his crooked hand. "Fuckinghellfuckinghellfuckinghell!"

An impossibly long scream came from upstairs. Keith cried out in response, and forced his knee down, throwing all his weight into the movement. His cry of exertion turned into his own agonised scream as his wrist separated with a sickening, wet crack.

"Wake up. Wake up," came the voice as again the light of the lounge bled into the darkness and Keith's pounding head tried to make sense of the screaming from upstairs and the agony he felt in his left arm.

"There you are. Nice to have you back."

"Sean fucking Fisher…" Keith murmured, his head rolling around on his neck, impossible to control.

"Wrong brother," Joe chuckled. "Not a bad try, though. Sean's wife, she's upstairs, getting to know your wife much better. Inside and out, you could say."

The screams upstairs increased intensity once more and Keith cried, "What are you doing to my wife?!"

"I doubt very much that good-looking wife of yours was actually looking to shag my brother, but by God and Mammon, when Ellen gets something in her head… well, let's put it this way, when the last tenant, Michelle, was running around with Sean, you have never seen a woman laid so low… she just fucking imploded. The only release she had, came after years of knowing my brother could not leave that slag alone. Only after all that humiliation did she finally *explode*. And my God did she. She even used my dad's old tools from up in the garage to do the job. Sean has no idea... Ellen's such a fantastic woman and he just makes a fool out of her. She should have been with me. I would have taken care of her."

"What a... lovely family..." Keith snorted.

Everything had become quiet upstairs. Keith's eyes rolled to the doorway, where he could only see the white spindles on the staircase.

"Don't worry, Keith," Joe said. "She's not dead. Ellen will make this last hours. That gives us a bit of time to talk. It's not like I can just talk about this with anyone. I can't even discuss it with Ellen, for fuck's sake. After tonight, it will be like this never happened. She'll go back to my useless lump of a brother, cook him his bacon and eggs, and carry on terrified that he's sticking his cock into some other woman. He, on the other hand, will believe that another tenant has made a hasty exit from this messed up haunted house, but really, you won't ever leave. I've already made a good start on your new place in the garden." Joe let out a little chuckle, amused at himself.

Keith hung his head low as the impossibility of the situation became clearer. His shoulders juddered with each sob. From the bedroom, a new wave of screams rang out and Keith strained against the radiator, trying to tear his shattered hand free.

Joe sat in his uniform, watching on, amused and casual, as though the tortured screams of an innocent woman did not fill the house around him.

"What the fuck do you get out of all this?" Keith moaned.

"Ellen has her thing, and I have mine. See... Sean wasn't the only Fisher to stick it up Michelle. I was in there too... except I did it after Ellen had finished with her. Your wife is next on my list. She's a bloody good-looking woman, Keith. I reckon she'll be the best-looking bit of dead fanny I've ever had."

Keith's teeth grated against each other until he felt

they would shatter any second. An animal howl escaped his lips and for the first time since seeing this house, he wished he was in a semi-detached property, where the neighbours would have heard him. He remembered something about the sound of Joe playing bass not penetrating his house, and it was implied he didn't play it quietly. With a desperate heave, Keith yanked his left hand out through the cuffs, hearing the snap of his thumb as it crushed beneath the solid metal.

He toppled as the cuffs fell away from the radiator, but he quickly corrected himself. Joe leapt to his feet and caught him with an agonising punch to the jaw. Keith staggered aside, his vision blurring once more as the screams persisted from above. Keith had only one idea in his daze. He had to get to his wife, but Joe was too strong for him. There was only one thing he could try.

He charged at the policeman once more, his fist drawn back. Joe expertly knocked the blow aside, smiling at the ease with which he turned the attack away, but Keith had some momentum built up and the two slammed together hard, knocking the policeman off-balance and onto the couch. Joe grabbed Keith's hair and smacked his left temple with two rapid blows. Keith clung to Joe's uniform but slipped away to the floor.

"Not much of a fighter, eh?" Joe sneered. "I wonder what would happen if I took you up there to see her? Would you have a bit more fight in you then, eh?"

Keith curled into a ball on the floor, desperate to make a dash upstairs to Amanda, but knowing he had no chance to do it with this monster looming over him. Instead he crawled. Inching his way across the floor as the screams echoed down the stairs anew.

"Go on, then!" Joe mocked. "You're a right knight in shining armour, you are! Go up there and fucking save her if you can!" He rose to his feet and kicked Keith's rump, knocking him flat. "Get up you cowardly little bastard."

Keith crawled out to the passage, hearing Amanda's

screams transform into the sound of crunching wet gravel. He heard retching and spitting as his wife vomited between cries. His shattered hand reached the bottom step.

"Nearly there! So close, Keithy! Go up and fucking save your wife. You do it. If only your laddie could see you now, he's be fucking ashamed of you. Crawling on your belly like this... absolutely ashamed of you."

Keith made it halfway up the stairs and stopped. His limbs burned with furnace intensity. His left forearm felt like a water balloon about to burst in an explosion of blood and bone. Amanda's cries came anew and Keith fumbled at his chest.

Joe heard a click and a familiar squawk and beep and a panicked despatch operator was heard to shout, "PC Fisher, respond! Can you hear me? State your location!"

"What the fuck have you got there?" Joe snatched Keith's ankles and dragged him down the stairs until he crashed to a halt at the bottom. He grabbed Keith's shoulders and heaved him over onto his side to find Keith grinning through his cracked, bloody lips. His hands clutched the radio he had stolen from Joe when they collided.

"They've heard the screams, Joe. They'll be here looking for you any minute!"

Joe grabbed the radio and slammed a fist into Keith's nose, breaking it across to his right cheek. "You sneaky little cunt!" The policeman thought for a second. There was no way he could hide the scene. No way could he cover this up before his colleagues arrived.

"Ellen!" he shouted. "Ellen, wrap it up we've got to get out of here!"

Joe knew that his words had gone unheard. Ellen was too busy enjoying herself.

He took a moment to stamp on Keith's chest before turning to run out of the front door.

As soon as the door opened, Keith caught a glimpse of the blue flashing lights out in the cul-de-sac. Through his tear-scorched eyes he could make out no faces, but could see the shapes of his neighbours spilling out of their homes and onto the street, drawn by the sudden police presence. He heard shouts out in the street.

"He tried to kill me!" Joe cried. "That bastard tried to kill me!"

Keith rolled over onto his front once more, leaving the police to hear out their colleague as they tried to ascertain the situation and understand why his radio had been filled with the sound of his threats and a woman's agonised screams. Keith crawled up the stairs one by one and heard the calls of the police who had entered his home.

"Stop where you are!"

He ignored them.

A policewoman's voice rang out below. "Stop where you are, right now!"

He pushed on and his head reached the landing. His back gave out. His limbs had finally taken enough punishment. The adrenaline was all gone and dopamine sapped the last vestiges of strength from his being.

The bedroom door was open and he could see Amanda tied to the bedstead, on the side nearest the door, where she always slept, where she could respond to Alex's cries in the night. Her attacker stood over her, arms working busily, the woman totally unaware of his presence. She hummed as she worked. Amanda's screams had dried out into a hoarse, cracked rumble.

Keith felt hands pulling on him, rough, strong, vengeful. But only for a moment. "Dore, in here!" the male police constable shouted.

Dore, the police woman, stepped over Keith and both constables filled the bedroom doorway.

Ellen finally recognised that she had been caught in the act. Keith caught fleeting glimpses of the gore-stained woman, whose face was caked in drying clots of his wife's blood.

Too drained even to cry, Keith spotted Amanda. Through the blood, it was difficult to ascertain what he was looking at, as the police struggled with the manic woman. Ellen snapped her teeth and struck out with the bradawl, puncturing the palm of the male officer, who cried out in pain. She pushed, driving the tool up to the hilt.

Dore took the opportunity of that moment, when Ellen left the bradawl jammed in the man's hand, to swing her baton, knocking the woman against the cream-coloured wardrobe doors.

Ellen reached for another tool even with her bloody cheek squashed against the wardrobe door. Dore was not having that, however, and stomped on the back of the woman's left knee, sending her down to the floor. Dore cracked the baton across the woman's forearm, smashing her hand away from the toolkit.

Dore knocked Ellen flat to the floor and Keith heard the caution being recited. The policeman groaned as he slowly drew the long, slender bradawl from his palm.

It was then, as the policeman ducked aside to deal with his own injury, that he caught a full look at his wife's face and could finally make sense of the scene. Her left eye was obscured by a brown, rectangular object and blood covered the left side of her face from her hairline to a point above her nose. Keith now knew that this was the tenon saw, embedded in his wife's head, where Ellen had been in the process of sawing through her skull. Her cheeks were a ruined landscape of deep gouges and punctures, her upper set of teeth hovered above a crimson gulf where only a savaged tongue hung, ragged and slick, in an open space where once her perfect mouth had been. Her jaw was missing. It was then, as he tore his eyes away from the sight of her destroyed face, that he noticed her legs poking out from beneath the bed, both with a wrecked half kneecap hanging from tattered flesh.

Keith closed his eyes and felt the swamp of exhaustion consume him once and for all as the stairs filled with the fall of heavy boots as more police officers rushed onto the scene. Screams broke through the darkness once more, but Keith knew that this time, the horrific shrieks did not originate from the lips of his wife. These were the screams of a man. These were his screams.

“That should settle everything for you now. There will be peace in this house.”

“There will be plenty of peace. I’ll never let another person live in it,” Sean said, staring at the small wooden shrine the specialist had just installed in the overgrown garden. The structure itself was somewhat reminiscent of a birdhouse, but with some personal artefacts placed within and holders for incense and candles on the outside.

“I understand, but… well, life goes on. You may feel differently in a while and I just want you to know that if the next occupant honours the dead with that shrine, they should find peace in the house.” The specialist took one last look at Michelle’s hairbrush and necklace, and Amanda’s compact mirror and the picture of the little boy and the father who had left Tilwick a few days before. “I’ve put some of the last tenant’s personal effects in there. I feel awful saying this, but I heard about her injuries and, well… they say her husband has hasn’t made a decision yet about the life support. I’ve done it just in case. She might return here, you know, looking for them.”

“Jack, wasn’t it?” Sean asked, staring blankly at the shrine.

“Yes,” the specialist replied, pulling his leather jacket back on.

Sean offered his hand. “Thank you for setting this up for me.”

“You’re welcome. It was a horrible business all of this… but you can’t blame yourself, Mr Fisher. You weren’t to know.” Jack had read the news at the time and had, of course, heard all the rumours of Mr Fisher’s psychotic wife, who had dismembered a new tenant in this very house. He had heard of the widower who had spent months in Tilwick Psychiatric Hospital, receiving treatment after the whole horrendous experience had caused a complete mental breakdown.

"Do you mind seeing yourself out? I think I'd like to stay here for a little while."

Jack patted the large man on the back and took the narrow path along the side of the house, using the weather-beaten gate to make his exit. As he closed the gate, he caught sight of Sean Fisher kneeling in the grass, shuddering as grief and guilt claimed him once more.

Bon Appetit

By Stuart Keane

The viscous, orbital fluid squirts me in the face. I feel it land on my cheek. A warm, dribbling sensation tickles my visage. It should gross me out, should repulse me. It should stop me from doing what I'm doing.

It doesn't. I simply smile.

I look at the deflated eyeball between my fingers and chuckle. I place it in my mouth and chew, enjoying the squidgy texture. I expect a bubble-gum taste—after all, the shape is reminiscent of a gumball—and, not for the first time, I'm fooled. It reminds me of soggy cabbage. Only more sour. I sip some water, washing it down.

I'm a man of particular taste. Extravagant taste. Unusual tastes.

I look down at the corpse below me.

I have work to do.

I'll start with the kitchen knife. I grab a red pen and draw some dots along the forearm. They stop at the elbow and I angle them upwards across the arm. My task here is to skin the arm from the wrist to the elbow. The cut needs to be lean, lithe. The skin has to be wafer-thin to get the right taste. Crispy flesh is the best flesh.

It's better than bacon.

I make an incision by leaning the razor-sharp, steel blade on the clean, innocent flesh. Blood seeps from the cut with no effort and I dab it away with a towel. Using the tip, I slice along the arm, parting the bronze skin, severing sinew and tendons. After a moment of cutting, surgical in precision, I peel the skin. It sucks away from the slick muscle with a slurping noise. Red mucus, formed from the blood and oxygen between the flesh and muscle, pulls away like mozzarella cheese from a pizza. I watch the mucus snap and the skin is finally free.

I hold it up and I can see through it. It's that thin. One layer of epidermis. Just as I planned. I fold it gently and place it on the white plate beside me. I smile.

My work makes me happy.

I repeat the procedure with the other arm. Again, I pull away a thin sheet of skin and fold it, placing it next to its counterpart.

Next, I take a smaller knife with a serrated edge and I push the blade into the exposed forearm muscle. A small blood spurt hits my shirt but I ignore it and continue to slice. The sound reminds me of cutting through a rare steak. Wet but tender. It also reminds me of fingering a wet, dripping cunt, the squelching noise evidence of my excellent sexual prowess. In my experience, it's soon followed by the cries of orgasm and the throes of death as I strangle the bitch to death. I feel my cock pushing against my jeans.

A slab of muscle falls from the arm. It slaps the metal table with a splat. I place it on a separate white plate. I look at the forearm and see a red, blood-soaked bone with no muscle and shreds of severed tendon. I look closely and I can see scratches on the bone from my cutting.

I love bones. So amazing. Taken for granted too, we all have them.

With that, I'm finished with the arm. For now.

I look at the end of the table and see the decapitated head staring at me. Honey, that's her name. I thought it was a stage name, you know, for a hooker? I checked her driving licence before I burned it and it's her actual name. I wonder where her parents were and what they were thinking, giving their beautiful daughter such a terrible name. I mean, don't they realise people like me—extravagant tastes, remember—are drawn to people like this?

I thought she was a stripper. When I was inside her, her tight, dripping pussy wrapped around me, I envisioned, no, planned this. I knew exactly what I wanted to do to her. How I would use her body to create the best art, the best work I've ever produced. When she screamed for me, the thought of her head severed from her body made me cum inside, hard and fast. She complained, saying I should have pulled out. I didn't. When she made a big deal of it, I punched her in the face. She fell and smacked her head on the table. Then my knee. Seven times.

I can still see the bruises.

I remember eating out her cunt right away. It was still coated in my semen, as I bit into her sex and took several meaty chunks with my teeth. Swallowing them was a pleasure, the semen adding taste to the bloody viscera. You've not lived until you've eaten proper pussy.

A man has needs.

I look at her head and it taunts me. *You're a real man, aren't you? Hitting a woman, taking advantage of her dead, naked body. You're a sick fuck.*

I nod. "I know."

I slap the face. It spins and topples on the table. I unbuckle my jeans, letting them fall to the ground. I pause, considering my actions. Then, I pick up the severed head and slide its stiff mouth onto my throbbing cock. "Shut your mouth, bitch. You're nothing but a useless whore."

Mmghhhghhe she says, choking on my girth. I deep throat her and feel the flesh tear within; it sends a small vibration up my cock, releasing my orgasm. I ejaculate, filling her dead, rotting throat with my seed. I place her back on the table, closing her mouth—swallow, don't spit—and pull my jeans back up.

I'm sorry, that was unexpected.

I'm normally in control of my urges. If you fucked Honey though, you'd know why it was so easy to fuck her again. A truly majestic body, fascinating tits, an arse you could lick all day and *that* pussy. It'll be a shame when she's gone.

You tore my throat. You shit, how am I supposed to eat now?

"You can't, you're dead. Fuck off."

Make me. Cunt.

I pick up the head and punt it across the room; it

spins in the air and its lips open, releasing my semen into the air. The sticky fluid splatters all over the worktop, the walls and the floor. I sigh.

Occupational hazard.

At least it shut the bitch up.

I return to her half mutilated corpse.

Using the bloody knife from earlier—it's so sharp and makes my job much easier—I cut along the abdomen. Blood seeps out onto Honey's flat, toned stomach, pooling in the creases of the skin. Using my fingers, I slide them into the slick gash and pull my fingers outwards. A tearing sound fills the room and the hole widens, exposing her ribcage and organs. The smell of blood, pungent copper and iron, stings my nostrils. I love it, some people wouldn't.

It's a funny old world.

I wiggle my fingers in the air, unsure of what to grab first. I opt for the intestines and grab two handfuls. Now, grabbing intestines is tricky, difficult but I manage with little effort. I've had plenty of practice. I pull a wad of intestine onto the table and proceed to trim them, cutting them into four-inch strips. Blood sluices everywhere. I look at the hose attached to the wall and I intend on washing everything down before I leave today. Once I have a dozen, I place the guts back into the torso. I wash my hands, I'm not an animal.

I'm ready.

I walk into the next room. My kitchen. I close the storage door behind me.

I turn on the gas and place a large frying pan onto it.

I drop a dollop of butter into the pan and it melts quickly. First, I place the intestines into it. The hissing and spitting reminds me of my years at Cookery College, the years I wasted cooking 'food' when the real delicacies were around me each and every day. I once heard that Chinese people do taste of their food. I tried it and I was disappointed. The meat is leaner, yes, but nothing special. However, from that point, I was hooked.

Don't go out trying that, I'm only responsible for my

own fatality rate.

The guts are browning nicely so I roll them over. The smell of cooked meat fills the air, making me smile. Not long now. I move them aside and place the two slabs of meat beside them. Again, the spitting ensues as the meat sears in the pan. I take a smaller frying pan and pop it onto the gas, filling it with oil. I crack two eggs and drop them in. I watch the whites form and the yolks bob on the heat. I move the guts, my makeshift sausages, to a small plate. I then take the sheets of flesh and cut them into strips. I place them in the pan and watch them curl and crisp. It's nearly ready.

A man was put on earth to cook.

And that's what I do.

Am I a cannibal? No. I have extravagant taste. I crave only the best in the world and, despite their appearance, humans are that delicacy. It's been seven years since I ate a cheeseburger. Six since I had a proper steak. I don't ever intend to have sausages again; the human intestine has much more flavour.

Humans or nothing. That's my motto.

Lauren pushes open the door and walks into the room. She pauses for a moment and stares at me. "Oh shit, did you fuck the head again?"

"No," I lied. I continued cooking, my back to my head server.

"You should get your head checked. Anyway, table four is waiting for their mixed grills."

"It'll be one minute."

I toss some mushrooms in the pan and slice a tomato in half, placing it face down. I construct the most popular special from my menu. I check as I go. Three sausages, Steak, three bacon, one egg, tomato, mushrooms and my special ingredient. I spit into the pan and stir it into the sauce of the tomatoes and steak—blood and juice—and pour it on the steak.

Voila.

"Here you go, Lauren. Table four is ready."

Lauren picks up the plates of human body parts and

ambles off. I peek at her arse and smile. I hear the bustle of my restaurant, the hive of activity. I hear two dozen people eating my delicacies, my way of improving the diet of the world. People love humans, my profits confirm this. After all, we all eat food without consequence. We don't know what goes into our food and nor do my customers.

I know what goes into them though.

Love. Passion. I have extravagant tastes, remember?

Lauren comes back in. "I have someone with a complaint. Apparently the steak was too tough."

I sigh. "Send him in."

Seconds later, a burly man who's clearly never seen a gym wobbles through the door. The sheer exertion of walking has brought on a sweat. I smile and grip the knife on the counter. He looks at me, curious.
"My steak was too tough."

"It's supposed to be like that," I reply.

"I get better down at The Swan. Any thoughts on that?"

I did. I think about my profits. How this man will keep me in business for a week. His arse cheeks alone would make for some great hams.

Behind him, Lauren shuts the door and locks it. The look in her eye is one of vehemence and willing. She is willing.

To do my bidding.

I close my eyes and I hear a sickening crack. The fat cunt hits the ground.

Lauren pulls the cleaver out of the man's head and smiles.

"Bon appetit."

I smile and kneel down. I bite the man's neck, taking a bloody chunk out.

Warm blood spills into my mouth.

Yes, this will do nicely.

Out of Sight, Out of Mind

By David Basnett

When I was in my twenties I wasn't scared of much. I still lived in the rural town I grew up in. Drove two miles to work, two miles back and about twice a year took the train into the city to attend book signings and to catch the RSC at the Theatre Royal. I still saw the same friendly faces from school when I went to do the weekly shop or even for a meal. Never felt threatened, never felt... unsafe. The headlines in the local paper always seemed to about things like graffiti or kids playing chicken on the road.

But that was my twenties, and while I was deciding what to do with my life, my forties clocked up faster than I ever thought possible. They brought with them an extra stone and a half of weight, nasal hair and a receding hairline that burnt quickly in the summer sun. My forties also brought me another unexpected surprise.

It didn't seem much when it started. Maybe they had been there a while and I just hadn't noticed. You see, I kept on glimpsing things in my vision, but whenever I tried to look they moved. Damn things drove me near crazy. I went to the local optician, not one of those big chains - I always tried to support local business, be it a coffee shop or a bookshop. The optician asked me to describe them and I thought for a while before responding *tiny black floating spider-webs*. She nodded as if she had heard it a thousand times before and examined my eye with a torch that seemed to be powered by a miniature nuclear power station; I bet if I dropped my pants that light would have shone through my eye and out of my urethra like I'd stuffed magnesium ribbon up there and set it on fire.

I waited a moment with her face uncomfortably close to mine, her breath hot on my cheek. I'm embarrassed to say it was the closest I'd been to a woman in a long, long time and it gave me a not unpleasant tingle of excitement.

"There's no retinal tear," she said and wheeled her chair back to her desk where she started typing up my record.

My heart jumped, I hadn't even considered it could be something that serious and, even though she had dismissed it, my brain raced at the thought of what horrendous conditions it might have been.

"That's good," I said, always the master at stating the obvious.

"If you start seeing white flashes, come back in," she said, her Scottish accent was long on the vowels and made her sound bored. Or maybe that was just my company.

"So how do I get rid of them?"

"You don't," she replied. "It's debris in your eye casting shadows on your retina. In time your brain should learn to ignore them to a degree."

She stood and turned on the light and I emitted a strangled yelp and bit down hard on my tongue. My brain dismissed what I had seen as I trick of the light and I avoided looking at her for the remainder of the assessment in case I proved my brain wrong. Please, please God let my eyes be wrong and my brain right.

As I left I risked another look at her in an attempt to give me a chance of sleeping that night, and to my immense relief she looked normal. She gave me a puzzled smile that I returned, and closed the door after me.

On the walk home my brain started to undermine its earlier, dismissive argument and pondered one thing and one thing only: can a trick of the light make it look like someone has no skin on their face?

Two weeks went by. I'd like to say that I put the visit to the opticians out of my mind, but in reality it had stayed at the forefront of my thoughts for fourteen long days. That morning the floaters were particularly bad in my eyes. I stuffed a pack of cigarettes into my jacket pocket and took a walk down Main Street to get a sandwich from the butchers for my lunch.

I stopped by the window of the local electronics shop. I had a shitty old television in my flat, it weighed a ton and the colour was shot and gave everything a pink tinge. I had a fund for a new one that I kept in an old tea caddy in one of my kitchen cupboards. It was taking a while as I kept on dipping into it to pay unexpected bills and whenever I fancied a Chinese takeaway, but it was starting to mount up and I was on the lookout for what I could afford.

Anyway, I stood outside the shop, looking at all the screens and trying to understand the technical details with all the success as if I were trying to decipher the Voynich manuscript. BBC News 24 was showing and the Prime Minister came on the screen. He wore his normal immaculate dark grey suit with white shirt and royal blue tie. He was speaking into a microphone about the budget and how much better off we were since his party had come back into power. I blinked rapidly as the floaters came back into my eyes and seemed to swirl in my vision as if they were sentient and were trying to communicate with me.

After a moment, the floaters settled and finally drifted out of my vision, but I wished they hadn't. Oh my God, if I could take the time back to that moment I would have closed my eyes, turned and ran until I reached the coast like a poor man's Forrest Gump. What I saw damn near stopped my heart right there in the middle of the street. My teeth bit down hard on my tongue and severed the tip, I assume I swallowed it down like a delicate morsel of tasty pork. My mouth filled with blood, but I hardly noticed it.

As the floaters cleared, my eyes locked onto the television feed from the shop, where the Prime Minister's skinless face stared back at me from forty screens. His jaw moved up and down as he talked but he had no lips with which to form words. Spittle and blood sprayed from his mouth. I sank to my knees in the street, my eyes locked on the screens. I was aware of passers-by muttering and giving me a wide berth. I realise now how crazy I must have seemed to them, but it was of little importance compared to what I was witnessing.

I felt a tap on my shoulder and I turned to see two more of them standing over me. Their faces like medical cadavers stripped of their skin. One of them was Judy Moore. I recognised her by her eyes and the pastel polo shirt she wore. I knew her well, I went to school with her son, Alan.

She talked to me in a kindly voice at first, but the words must have been bounced straight back out of my ears by my overloaded brain because I have no recollection of what she said to me. My pleaded mutterings must have eventually registered with her because for all that she had no face to form expressions, her eyes seemed to take on a hard look and she took a step backwards. I do remember what she said to me at that point, the woman whose house I had visited dozens of times growing up, the woman who always had a spare ice lolly in the freezer or a carton of juice, she leaned in to me and said slowly and quietly: “There’s more of us than you fuckers, now.”

They sectioned me under the Mental Health Act and to be fair, I think I am probably in the best place now. They say that I disfigured myself. That I am a danger to myself. I don’t even get to wear a belt or shoelaces now. Their efforts are pointless, I tell the psychologists at my monthly meetings, but now I just let them do their job if it makes them happy. They don’t realise that I am no longer at risk. That the creatures that walk among us and that once pursued me no longer have an interest in me. For all I know they could all be one of *them*.

But I am at peace. Blissful peace since I picked up that knife. Sometimes the peace evaporates at night when I sleep, as that is when my brain recalls the feeling as I slowly slid the blade into each of my eyeballs, the gentle pop and the damp of the vitreous humour and blood as it wound its way down my face, the tug of the retinas as I pulled and pulled.

I heard a report on the radio that floaters are becoming more and more common.

God help you all.

Blynd Haus

By Robert J. Stava

It seemed like a pretty good summer pick-up job, even if the first one was well, *creepy*.

But the money was good, and as a kid heading into his senior year at Wyvern Falls High with a recession economy still wallowing in the horse latitudes, there was no arguing that money was a good thing.

Ricardo Dimas was a good-looking kid at seventeen, as in *lady-killer* good-looking, with his thick black hair moussed up in a 'fauxhawk', his flashing white smile and cut figure. But he was also a *good* kid, as in that rare combination of charm and charisma with good manners.

The girls adored him.

His household, three generations of Portuguese stone masons, were big on family values, manners and Ricardo, along with his younger brother Luis, had been raised well.

But it was his buddy Billy Vincent – aka *Eugene Visconti* – who landed the roofing gig for both of them that summer, through his uncle Sammy. The first job was at the 'Blynd Haus' Funeral Home.

Billy was also a decent kid at heart but always in and out of some kind of trouble or another, so it was with more than a little surprise (and suspicion) that Ricardo came home one day and told his parents Billy had landed him a three-week gig at the 'Blynd Haus' for the princely sum of twenty dollars an hour.

"Cash?" His father had asked, one suspicious eyebrow raised.

"*Cash,*" Ricardo had assured him.

Victor Dimas hadn't been convinced. Billy Vincent was a slippery customer with a lot of tattoos and a pompadour and into some weird 1950's style music called 'Rockabilly'. And typically any scheme he roped Ricardo into usually involved losing money and was probably borderline illegal as well.

Plus, he spent way too much time working on his hair, in his opinion.

"Who's in charge of the project?" Mister Dimas had asked.

"Jack Curtis," Ricardo had said.

Mister Dimas had grunted. He knew Jack Curtis as a square player around the area who ran odd contracting jobs.

"Fine. Make sure you they pay you every week, cash on the barrel."

"Got it pops."

That's how it began.

The 'Blynd Haus' had been called that ever since anyone could remember, even before it became a funeral home.

Not far from the center of Wyvern Falls, it was an odd, hefty looking Craftsman-style house with diamond-paned upper windows and heavy brick chimneys. It was painted a bright Dutch blue with immaculate white trim and along with its tidy hedges and eerily perfect grass, exuded that aura of austere tidiness that was apparently part of some unspoken zoning requirement for (respectable) funeral homes.

And yet...there was no denying there was something innately creepy – and vaguely menacing – about this particular one, despite its fastidious, no-nonsense façade.

Partly it was the oddness of the various gables, odd recesses, bay windows and rooflines that didn't seem to follow any typical symmetrical house design, partly it was the two main upper front windows that seemed – with their thick crisscrossed window panes – to somehow suggest a pair of square blind eyes.

But it was a job.

A major one, as it were. For starters, it was a complete tear-off: three layers of shingles to be removed and in some locations the roof deck itself would likely have to be replaced if the internal leaks were any indication.

They started on the Monday after July Fourth.

Jack Curtis was already there at seven-thirty a.m. when Billy and Ricardo arrived in Billy's pick-up, after a brief stop at the Dunkin' Donuts on Crichton Avenue. With his cuffed jeans, white t-shirt with rolled sleeves (showing copious amount of tattoos) and black motorcycle-boots Billy looked like a poster boy for Rockabilly roofers. Ricardo had thrown on a sleeveless lifeguard T-shirt that highlighted his cut physique, a pair of veteran 501s and some battered work-boots he'd borrowed from his dad.

There were two other guys there, Jay Ferguson and José Garcia, who were part of Curtis' regular crew. The rest of his regulars were tied up on a major project over on Underhill and apparently the deal was that the Blynd House job had come up on short notice but paid cash, so Curtis had grabbed it. The elderly owner had passed away unexpectedly, leaving his daughter, Melissa Gorman, to deal with handling the funeral home. Miss Gorman was a wealthy widower in her thirties with a house in Briarcliff Manor roughly the size of three Blynd Haus funeral homes. From the start she'd made it clear she had little interest in taking up the family business or its entailing issues. Her stopgap solution had been to appoint a temporary director to keep it running and expediently deal with any outstanding issues, such as leaky roofs.

It was Marcus Kohwalt, the temporary director, who met them out front that morning. Kohwalt was a mousy-haired, diminutive man, with immaculately pressed clothes and a prim, emotionless demeanor.

"I wish to reiterate you agreed to complete the project in four days, yes?"

"Five," Curtis was saying, "The contract was for *five*

days." Curtis was a middle-aged black guy originally from Missouri who had this calm but firm way about him. And though rail-thin, he was tough as nails. Ricardo had only met him in passing but felt an immediate sense of respect for the man.

"I'm sorry Mr. Curtis, but we have a funeral scheduled in five days. It was my understanding…"

"Well *unschedule* it," Curtis cut him off. The look he gave the director made it clear he wasn't one to suffer fools gladly. "You've got a major job here, a complete tear-off to the rafters. And we don't know what we'll find once we get under there."

Kohwalt didn't look happy. One finger kept tapping his schedule book. "Hmpf!" he said finally, "Five days, and no mess. I want everything left as pristine as you found it!" With that he squared his shoulders and with chin up, marched off to the parking lot.

Curtis lit up a cigarette. "Little prick," he muttered to himself. "Probably eats coal and shits diamonds, his Nazi butt-hole's so tight." Then he glared at everyone. "What're you ladies gawking at? Get the lead out of your pants and get to work!"

Billy looked over at Ricardo and grinned, "How much you want to bet we'll find dead bodies stashed in the attic? Rattling their bones and playing strip poker!"

Ricardo crossed himself. Despite a deep roguish streak in him there was still that side that was devoutly Catholic, and surprisingly superstitious.

"Don't say that, man…never make jokes about the dead!"

Billy lifted his shoulders in a classic *whatever* shrug.

As it turned out what they found under the roof was far worse than dead bodies.

It was the following afternoon when they had their first look inside the attic. It was utterly bizarre.

Billy had mentioned in passing to Ricardo that one of the odd things about the Blynd Haus job was that that they had been unable to get access to the attic. Apparently the original staircase up to it had been removed and sealed off during extensive renovations during the 1960s, which was why Curtis had built in an extra day into the contract.

Using tear-off shovels, the guys had most of the three layers of roofing in the dumpster in the rear parking lot below when the full extent of the rot became evident, particularly toward the back of the house. It was there that a couple of towering pines prevented the sun from properly drying things out for decades. Curtis was swearing and cursing as he prodded this area and that with the handle end of his hammer, then next to one of the gables at the back they tore off an entire section of sheathing to see what condition the underlying roof structure was in.

The smell that wafted of the exposed area was indescribable; a mixture of rot, must, rich moldering spice and something else… the feral aroma of animal remains.

The air was strangely cool, as if the breath of underground tombs had been sealed up in there for decades.

Between the rafters it looked like a bunch of antique-looking cages had been stacked in the eave, some which appeared to contain the remains of animals. Curtis made a strange face, then ordered Billy and Ricardo to fetch a tarp from his truck. Five minutes later, the gable was covered over and the five of them were taking a break by one of the back chimneys.

It was a hot and humid afternoon and it was dirty work. Curtis sat atop the peak, forearms on knees, a cigarette dangling in his long fingers, gazing off towards the river. Ferguson was checking his phone messages while nursing a paper cup of coffee – Ricardo swore the guy drank at least a dozen of them a day – and Garcia had parked himself with a water bottle near the top of the ladder. Ricardo didn't know much about him other than he seemed to communicate exclusively with nods and shrugs, worked tirelessly and methodically. Ferguson by contrast was a walking pronouncement of 'too much information'; he talked endlessly to anyone in earshot about his financial woes, his family problems, his health issues, even his stranger sexual escapades with his wife. His entire life, it appeared, was an ongoing train wreck. The only reason Curtis kept him on was that in spite of that, he would work non-stop until he dropped. Probably because going home was a worse option.

Billy and Ricardo were sitting back to back on the ridge near the tarp sharing a smoke when Curtis finally stood up and announced, "Jay, José, you come with me. We're going to need to track down more sheathing to finish this son-of-a-bitch off." He looked over at Ricardo and Billy, "You ladies finish sweeping off and we'll be right back." Then just as he turned to step down towards the ladder he gave them a hard sideways glance and added, "And don't go getting any ideas."

"Yes sir," Billy said, his face a portrait of innocence. He snatched up one of the push brooms and made like he was ready to go at it with gusto.

Billy waited until Curtis's truck had turned the corner then tapped Ricardo's shoulder. "Come on, I've got a couple flashlights in the truck - we have got to check this shit out!"

Ricardo grinned and hitched up his tool-belt. "With you on that, bro."

Pulling back the tarp, Billy dropped down into what appeared to be some sort of partitioned-off storage room. A moment later Ricardo joined him. Flashlight beams teaming with dust motes went this way and that, revealing cobwebbed rafters, stacks of cages and a wainscoted wall with an old wooden door in the center of it.

The cages were what really drew the boys' attention.

The ones that were occupied had creatures that looked like some sort of taxidermist's nightmare.

"What the fuck?" Billy said. In the beam of his flashlight, snarling fangs, maniacal eyes and stained claws sat frozen, coated in a film of dust. One looked like a small monkey caught in mid-screech, but with leathery wings sprouting from its back and a delicate pair of curved horns sweeping back from its skull. Another looked like some sort of massive spidery insect, but with an oddly humanoid head sprouting out between its front mandibles, its dried, leathery skin drawn back in a snarl, revealing tarnished, needle-like fangs. The long cage next to it held a creature that was a hideous sort of miniature mermaid in a tray, its mummified upper torso coiled in a rictus of death, with spidery, webbed fingers and long glossy black hair that looked fine as silk.

There were perhaps a dozen of these strange oddities, decaying in their cages, but what was more troubling were the empty ones, the ones that looked like their occupants had burst out of them. Even more disturbing were the claw marks on the lower part of the door and the large ragged hole in the partition wall near the floor where something, or *things*, had chewed and clawed their way into the next room at some point in the distant past.

Billy looked at Ricardo, brows raised. "This is whacked!" His flashlight played around the floor where the dust had been recently disturbed, but whether by some odd creature or itinerant squirrels wasn't clear.

"Certifiably," Ricardo agreed. His brow was creased in worry. It wasn't just the cages and their contents that had him spooked, there was something in the atmosphere and aromas of the attic that were tapping on his deeper, more primal senses. All it once he just wanted to get out of there, go home and forget the whole thing. Of course with Billy he wasn't going to get off the hook that easy.

"Come on dude, we have to check this out!" Billy said, reaching for the door handle.

"Maybe we shouldn't," Ricardo replied. While he had the wilder streak of the two, there was something in Billy's utter fearlessness that was sometimes unnerving. Of course he hadn't been there when Ricardo and a bunch of other kids faced that hideous witch-thing in the barn on Shadowbrook years back, or the terrible secret they found behind that strange door at the High School. Ricardo had seen already first-hand the terrible things one could occasionally find capering in the darker corners of Wyvern Falls. Billy, whom he had just become friends with over the course of the previous year, did not.

Before he could say anything else however, Billy had opened the door and moved into the gloom of the space beyond. He heard his friend let out a whistle.

"Get in here, bro, you are not going to believe this shit!"

It appeared to be some sort of laboratory, or rather a bizarre cross between a forgotten taxidermy shop, an embalmers studio and a necromancer's chamber. Work-tables, glass cases, bookshelves and trunks, all manner of quasi-scientific looking equipment from another era, festooned with cobwebs and rimed with the dust and decay of decades was revealed in their flashlight beams. Dim light filtered in through the thick, diamond-paned windows and their rotting curtains laced with spider-webs. The only thing marring the image of a derelict Frankenstein's lab was the lack of an operating table with a hoist and a trapdoor in the ceiling. Plus, there was the abundance of magical paraphernalia including the pentagram painted in the middle of the floor.

And then there were the stains, as if visceral matter had spattered across the floor, dripped and drabbled over the equipment and tables....

To Ricardo it was like discovering a lost, Indiana Jones-style tomb in your neighborhood, that was just waiting there behind a trap-door you'd passed a thousand times without glancing at. It was no surprise he was having more than a little difficulty reconciling the immaculate façade of the Funeral Home with the hidden, moldering, nightmarish, chamber hidden within it, like some sort of decaying, sealed-off abscess.

"What do you think this place was used for?" he asked, stepping over to one of the wooden worktables. It had a dusty, globe-style light hanging over it. The table was littered with lab books and odd apparatus that made Ricardo uneasy. He picked up a slim, leather-bound book and blew dust off it. Fanning through it, it appeared to be a journal of sorts.

"Who knows?" Billy answered. He was looking over an alcove in one of the nooks that looked like it had been set up to perform some sort of magic ritual. It was a gruesome tableau of cups, candles and rotting black velvet, surrounding a doll-sized skeletal figure dressed in robes, like the mummy of a shrunken sorcerer.

"And honestly, who cares?" Billy added, picking up a candlestick. "What I can tell you, *hombre* is that this stuff here looks like pure silver and if it is, it's worth a shitload more than we're getting paid on this job!"

"And a shitload of trouble if we're caught stealing it," Ricardo cut in, walking over to him.

Billy gave him one of his 'Gimme-a-break' faces. "Dude, I doubt that rich little Briarcliff bitch has any clue what's up here. We could…"

His voice trailed off as there came a distinct sound of something scurrying along the eave – a heavy clicking like claws on wood. Billy's flash beam shot over just in time to see something dodge behind a stack of crates. It was followed by a muffled *chittering* sound that made the hairs on the back of Ricardo's neck stand up.

It was an unnatural, agitated sound.

Ricardo took the candlestick from Billy and placed it back on the little altar. "We should leave," he said.

Billy shrugged. "Aahh, it's probably a raccoon." Then he stomped his foot. "Hah!" Glass and metal rattled around the attic. And something else.

A faint, almost reptilian-sounding hiss.

Ricardo sensed whatever it was watching them.

Then he heard another sound from across the room – a floorboard creaking as if someone had stepped on it. He fanned his flashlight but there was nothing in the beam… except for the dust motes that momentarily seemed to coalesce… into a hand-like shape.

Any further talk was abbreviated by the distinct sound of Curtis's truck pulling in the drive. It had a perforated muffler that was hard to miss.

"Let's get out of here, bro," Ricardo whispered, suppressing a shudder. He grabbed his friend's arm, "Now!"

Billy looked around distractedly. Ricardo wasn't fooled – he could all but see the wheels turning in his head.

Just as they scooted over to the gable where they had dropped in, Billy paused, then reaching over, twisted the latch on small casement window there.

"Not a word!" he hissed at Ricardo. Then they were clambering up into the bright July sunshine.

It wasn't until he got home that night that Ricardo realized he'd stuck the journal into the deeper pocket of his tool belt., though he would have sworn he'd put it back down on the table.

"*Oi Chata*, are you fucking nuts!?"

"It's only stealing if you get caught," Billy answered as they pulled up across the street from the Dimas house over on Irving Avenue. Ricardo's grandfather Raymundo, whom everyone called 'Rambo', was sitting out front on the low stone wall by the sidewalk in his customary hands-on-knees pose.

Ricardo looked at Billy with a wry, *yeah-right* look but didn't say anything.

Billy took a pull off his cigarette and hung his arm out the window in one of his stock James Dean poses. "What, you going all chicken-shit on me?"

Ricardo turned at him, "Dude, are you really thinking of going back in there stealing that stuff?"

"That's *exactly* what I'm what I'm saying. You heard

what Curtis said, that attic has been sealed for decades. No-one has a clue that stuff is even there, and therefore no one will miss it. I know a guy in Hudson that'll pay top dollar for those cages and all that weird shit – he's got a whole store full of it and *amigo*, you should see what he charges for that junk! We'll make a killing pal. Our ship has just come in..."

Ricardo shook his head. Since he'd hooked up with Billy a year past there had been a few wild adventures. But launching bottle rockets at unsuspecting trick-or-treaters and letting air out of a Police Cruiser's tires was one thing, breaking and entering was a whole other. Even if the occupants of the house in question were dead. But it was more than that. Something up in that attic had given Ricardo a serious case of the creeps, and it wasn't just the weirdness of the stuff that he'd been looking over, there was something disturbing in the atmosphere itself. The sense of unnaturalness, of someone tampering with horrible things...like a violation, or blasphemy. Like those things in the cages.

Along with that came more than a few nagging questions.

Like: *just what in the fuck had someone been doing in that attic?*

"Billy, I think you'd better just let this one slide. Something ain't right with that place bro...there's a reason that attic was sealed off. Just drop it."

Billy let out a soft chuckle. "Really? Okay. You're right. Forget I mentioned it."

Ricardo opened the door and got halfway out. Then he stuck his head back in the cab and waved his finger. "I'm serious. It's bad Mojo. Don't fuck with it."

"Yeah, yeah." Billy answered with a dismissive wave of his hand.

As Billy drove off, Ricardo stood watching the pick-up head down the hill. Billy was lying, of course. It didn't take a rocket scientist to figure that out.

Grandpa Dimas looked up as Ricardo approached, his eyes swimming in the thick lenses of his glasses. His gnarled hands with their long fingers tapped his kneecaps, his cropped white hair sprayed out of his head like a dandelion. To Ricardo he always looked surprised, almost feeble every time he looked up to see the world still in existence around him. Of course that was anything but the truth. Even in his 70s Grandpa Dimas had the strength of an ox. A month previous, Ricardo had watched in awe as he'd methodically split a three-foot wide tree section at their next-door neighbor's, with a sledge hammer and wedge in under six minutes.

"*Alo!*" Ricardo said, taking up a seat next to the old man.

"Hmppf," his grandpa said, along with one of his better shrugs. "You know..." he began, speaking slowly as always and with his thick accent, "everybody always want something else... sheeeze... always need more this, more that! Gimme gimme. Never enough!" He made a couple dismissive waves with his hand. "Ahhhk. Just more headaches. More *stuff*."

"Grandma kick you out of the house again?" Ricardo asked. For a couple that clearly adored each other, they fought constantly. Usually when objects started getting thrown, Grandpa found his way out to his spot on the front wall.

"Yeahhhpa!" Grandpa said, pulling his chin in and frowning.

Ricardo was about to get up, but then he stopped.

"*Vovó*, do you know anything about the funeral home on Oakton Drive – you know, the one everyone calls 'Blynd Haus'?"

"Eh?" Grandpa Dimas said, swiveling around. One gnarled forefinger shook at Ricardo, "*A curiosidade matou o gato!* Stay away from there! No good!"

"Okay, okay!" Ricardo said, patting his grandpa on the shoulder. Then he ruffled the old man's hair affectionately. "I'll go sweet-talk grandmamma until she's begging for you to come back, eh? Grandpa Dimas half-heartedly waved him away. It was an old game with them.

As he walked up the steps to the Dimas' imposing Victorian house he considered what the old man had said; *Curiosity murdered the cat*.

The question was, who was the cat?

Two hours later, Ricardo was up in his bedroom propped up against the headboard and looking through the journal he had found earlier. Amber bars of sunlight slanted in through the bay window as the day drew to a close, bathing the room in golden hues. Compared to his younger brother Luis's neat-as-a-pin room, Ricardo's had the casual flamboyance of a hip high-schooler's hang-out. A soccer ball stood next to a couple of trophies atop the oak dresser; on the wall perpendicular to it was an oversize poster of the model Gisele Bündchen and a Portuguese flag. The only other pictures were a poster of the Foo Fighters, another of Daft Punk and a framed painting of Gaudi's cathedral a cousin had sent from Spain, which hung over a small desk with a laptop.

Ricardo may have had a reputation as a happy-go-lucky Romeo, but he also possessed a keen mind. Next to the usual sports magazines (including one or two mixed martial arts ones) were a bunch of design and architecture glossies that were a burgeoning interest of his.

At the moment however he was engrossed in the disturbing entries and sketches he was finding in the journal. *Seriously fucked-up shit indeed* he thought, looking at a page that detailed several efforts at developing one of the monkey/crab hybrids. Then things took a left turn into major creepy when he found a section on reanimating the dead, accompanied by several small 2x3 black & white photographs.

The first showed a much more orderly version of the attic chamber in its heyday – or at least its peak – when it was being fully utilized for whatever diabolical purposes it had been set up for. The next two Ricardo only glanced at before turning away in disgust – they showed a woman's corpse being dismembered. Nothing worse than any 'Saw' movies perhaps, but somehow more gruesome by virtue of its realness.

The fourth however, was the corker.

It showed two men standing on either side of the altar he and Billy had seen. The elderly man on the left he didn't recognize. Tall and gaunt to the point of being cadaverous, his half-lidded gaze from behind a pair of 1950s Browline glasses suggested a calm, gentle-minded uncle...if one overlooked the blood-spattered apron covering his suit and the gore-flecked saw hanging from his left hand.

The other man however looking startlingly familiar. A handsome kid probably in his late teens with a mischievous face, pale eyes and unruly black hair, he had a self-satisfied smile like the cat who'd just eaten the canary. He had his sleeves rolled up and also sported a blood-spattered apron, standing tilted back with his rubber-gloved hands crossed in front like a man posing after finishing a hard day's work. But Ricardo knew that face. A considerably older version of it lived in the parson's house next door to the funeral home.

Father Rory Dullahan.

That was bad enough. But even worse was the decapitated head of the woman resting on the altar, the same woman whose body could be seen being dismembered in the previous photos. In this shot however it appeared to have been successfully merged with a giant spider or crab, its spindly legs curled up as if it was nesting. And the woman's eyes were open and unquestionably *alive*; they glared out of the photo at him with homicidal malice, the wild-eyed look of someone who had journeyed past the veil of death and returned not quite sane.

Goose-bumps broke out up and down Ricardo's arms.

That was when the face in the photo blinked.

Ricardo screamed.

"*Merda*," Luis said. "What happened!?"

Ricardo's younger brother stood in the doorway. A slimmer, much more serious version of Ricardo, Luis had the studious demeanor of a born lawyer.

"Nothing! It was just a bad dream. I must've dozed off."

Luis looked like he wasn't buying a word of it. He nodded towards the journal on the floor. The photos lay scattered next to it. "What are those? They look like-"

"They're nothing!" Ricardo said a little too quickly, springing out of the bed. He bent over to pick them up but then he hesitated. *What if that head... was alive?*

As if sensing this, Luis glanced at the photos then back at his brother. "Well...you should be careful with that stuff, bro. They look... *off* somehow." He could have sworn himself he saw something move within the images.

Ricardo had a sudden urge to stomp on the photos and grind them with his heel. Instead he rubbed his chin. "On second thought, why don't you run downstairs and get a plastic garbage bag from the pantry. One of the heavy ones."

Half an hour later he was sitting on the front porch trying to call Billy. He'd already texted him twice with no response. Billy's voice came on the line; "Hail, hail, Rock-and-Roll my friend. If you're my masseuse leave a massage..." He was about to hang up when he saw the incoming call flash up on the screen.

It was Billy.

"Hello? Billy?"

A garbled sound came out of the phone in response followed by a sob.

"Billy? Is that you *hombre*?"

There came a strange snipping sound, then what sounded like a weak, pleading version of Billy's voice; "We fucked up man... oh we fucked up bad..."

"What are you talking about?" Ricardo didn't care much for the rising sound of panic creeping into his voice. If this was one of his friend's demented practical jokes, it wasn't coming off as particularly funny.

There was another muffled ruffling noise, then another voice came on the phone; "Hello Ricardo," said an almost jovial, kindly voice. With just a trace of Irish in it. "Such mischievous boys..." There was a faint chuckle, followed by a whimper in the background. "Now, I believe you took something that belongs to me, no? I wasn't aware the Dimas's had switched to raising thieves these days...oh for shame! For shame! Tsk-tsk! Some days I think the whole world is going to hell in a handbasket!"

"Father Dullahan?" Ricardo had a sinking family about all of this.

"So here's how this will work, my fine light-fingered little lad; you're going to come back to the funeral home and return my belongings intact. I'll refrain from turning your good friend here into a choir boy by removing his testicles with a pair of rusty tin snips! Now, how does that sound? Fair enough?"

"Come on Father, he didn't mean anything... look, I'll bring your stuff. I promise. Just don't hurt him!"

"Wouldn't *dream* of it!" the voice chastened; a kindly old man aghast anyone would suggest anything of the sort. In the background came a shrill scream. Then all kindness was whisked out of the voice as the next words came out in an angry hiss, "Now be quick and fleet of foot, little thief, and do not for a second think of telling anyone, or Billy will suffer far worse than a little quick surgery!"

Ricardo found himself listening to a dead line.

He sat tapping his fist into his hand, a look on his face that was a combination of alarm, fear... and anger. What the fuck had Billy gotten them into? And why on earth had he taken the damn journal?

Night had settled in on Irving Avenue. The crickets were in full force; here and there a lightning bug flared its phosphorescent mating signal. Ricardo considered his options for a moment. Should he call that British Detective Easton? He'd helped Luis and his friends out of a few serious jams in the past. But somehow that didn't seem right.

Instead he did a quick Google search on local contractors.

The apartment complex off Crichton Avenue had been thrown up in the 1960s after tearing down the old Wharton Military Academy. One of those typical brick edifices that appeared to have been designed by very unhappy and unimaginative architects, 'Hudson Terrace' afforded – at least for those in the top front apartments – a picturesque view of the upper village and the river beyond.

Ricardo found himself at the door of 214b under the stony-eyed glare of Jack Curtis, looking wiry as ever in a sleeveless t-shirt and jeans. If Curtis had ever had an ounce of body fat on him it had been smoked off of him decades ago, courtesy of the Philip Morris Company. Ricardo wasn't sure if Curtis was seriously PO'd at being bothered this late at night or just at life in general. For all he knew Curtis rolled out of bed every morning PO'd and rolled back into it every night the same way.

Either way he figured the best strategy was to cut straight to the chase: "I'm sorry to bother you Mister Curtis, but I think Billy may have done something bad… and he may be in some serious trouble. Because of Blynd Haus."

To his surprise Curtis pulled him into the apartment and closed the door.

"Sit," Curtis said, after leading him down a short hallway to the main living area where he pointed to the couch. The room itself had a trim, mid-century look to it that was almost Spartan. The one modern concession was a small flat-screen TV. A framed poster of a semi-nude Pam Grier adorned one wall. In another corner was a vintage red Gibson 335 on a stand next to an equally vintage Fender Twin amp.

Ricardo let out a low whistle at both.

"Wow Mister Curtis, I didn't know you-"

"Never mind that," Curtis said, standing with his thumbs hooked in his belt. "Start talking, son."

Ricardo gave him the short version of what they found in the attic and the call he'd received on Billy's phone. Then he showed Curtis the bag with the journal and photos in it. He didn't know if he should warn him or not.

Had the photo really moved?

He was relieved when Curtis looked them over without any apparent effect. Instead, the contractor stood looking at some invisible point out the picture window (which Ricardo saw was a less-than-scenic view of the parking garage at the back), frowning.

Then dropping the bag and its contents on the dinette table he said, "Shit." And shaking his head, disappeared into the bedroom.

He came back a minute later with – Ricardo was shocked to see – an old government issue .45 Automatic. He sat down next to Ricardo and hefted it in his hand like an old, but not necessarily welcome friend.

"Does it have silver bullets?" Ricardo joked.

Curtis snorted and with one deft motion popped the clip, showing Ricardo it was full. Then with one calloused thumb he pushed the top bullet out and held it in front of Ricardo. It smelled of gun oil. The casing was brass but the bullet itself was of a material Ricardo had never seen before, with a curious symbol delicately carved near the point.

"Detroit Steel," Curtis said, "All that's left of my Pa's '66 Chevy Impala." When Ricardo shook his head in bafflement he pushed the bullet back into the clip and after reloading the gun added, "These suckers will blast through anything. Come on, you and I are going to pay someone a little visit."

Ricardo had a million questions he wanted to ask as they drove over to Blynd Haus in Curtis's van, but for the life of him couldn't figure a way to ask them and the contractor's stony demeanor wasn't inviting any small talk. Meanwhile on the car stereo Albert King was stomping his way through 'Born Under a Bad Sign', backed by a melancholy horn section.

Curtis cut the lights and radio as they turned onto Brandreth Avenue, where he parked about a half block down from the funeral home. Minutes ticked by while the two of them sat in silence.

"How do we do this?" Ricardo asked finally.

Curtis sat back, nodding as if contemplating any number of answers. "Well, it looks like you're going to keep your appointment."

"I mean, what are you going to do?"

"Hmpf," Curtis snorted, "Don't you worry about me, I'll be along shortly."

"But what if Father Dullahan hears you? He said he'd..."

"Never mind me, I'll be quiet as a cat." In the dim streetlight coming through the windows, Ricardo could see the white of Curtis's teeth as the contractor grinned. There was nothing friendly in it. Then Curtis leaned over and popping the glove compartment, pulled out a hard rubber flashlight and handed it to him.

"Go get 'em, son."

Ricardo got out.

It was a cool evening with a nearly full moon lurking behind scudding clouds. A moderate breeze suggested a squall might be blowing through in the near future, but for now there was only the sighing of the trees and the occasional twitter of a bat flicking overhead.

The funeral home was completely dark from the front, though even in the night the second story windows looked to Ricardo like the vacant stare of a blind idiot, or perhaps the coiled danger of a mental patient who had only pretended to swallow his meds.

It wasn't until he stepped around back that he saw the ladder propped up at the back of the house and the dim light issuing from the attic window.

Ricardo went up it gingerly as a light-footed monkey, the bag slung under one arm. When he got to the top, the double casement windows in the gable were shut but not locked. Peering in revealed little more than someone had left what looked like a new LED Coleman-style lantern sitting on one of the tables. He couldn't see anyone in there however.

The creak as he opened the right side window and clambered in sounded awkwardly loud - even with the wind - but was unavoidable. He landed as lightly as he could, his heart hammering in his ears. *What if this was some sort of trap? What if Father Dullahan was waiting to step out of the shadows and sink a hatchet in his head, the way it always happened in the horror movies?*

He waved his flashlight around and saw that some items had been stacked up on the table. The strange altar in the nearby gable had been mostly broken down and put into boxes.

That was when he heard a light shuffle followed by the yawning creak of a door being opened nearby. There came a slight movement of air and the trod of a foot.

Ricardo froze.

Then, as if guided by an unseen hand, his saw his flashlight move over to the opposite wall.

He almost screamed.

It looked like a half-mummified baboon's head, jaws open in a terrible snarl, but with six-eyes and two curving, sickle-shaped horns sloping back from the skull. Then Ricardo realized he was looking at an object on a metal tray, which was being carried by two very human hands.

The light beam continued up.

"Jay Ferguson!" Ricardo said.

"Uh, who's that?" Ferguson asked, squinting in the

glare.

He was shouldered aside as another person came in from the other room holding what looked like a stack of lacquered Chinese boxes.

"José?" Ricardo added, sounding even more incredulous. *Who else was here – Santa Claus? The Easter Bunny?*

The voice that called out from the other room was just as much a surprise: "Ricardo!?"

A moment later, hand shielding his eyes, Billy pushed his way into the room.

Ricardo was stumped. "What the…? How the…? I thought you were…"

"Dude, put the flashlight down!" Billy said, placing a set of tarnished silver candelabra on the workbench.

Ricardo was beside himself; he'd been expecting to find his friend horribly mutilated, spindled, or dead, instead here he was same old ho-hum Billy just pulling another stunt.

"Is this your idea of a fucking practical joke!?" Ricardo all but yelled.

"Jesus, keep it down, pal!" Billy said, clapping him on the shoulder, "Look, I can explain… you didn't seem cool with this and I had to move while the job was still on – you know the ladders – and well, Jay and José were up for it…"

"What are you talking about?" Ricardo cut in, lowering his voice. "I got a call on your phone from… *where is your phone*?"

Billy shook his head. "Well, it should be right here…" he began searching his pockets.

That was when the window slammed shut.

Something skittered across the floor, followed by a *snicking* sound.

Then Ferguson screamed.

Ricardo's flashlight swept up to reveal a giant spider-like creature wrapped around Ferguson's head. It looked as large as a king-crab, but with a loathsome humanoid face from which two enormous pincers jutted out of the jaw-line. Insectoid eyes gleamed in the light as it sank its mandibles into the soft flesh of Ferguson's neck; even as they watched, one wicked-looking claw sliced the contractor's ear clean off. It landed with a soft 'plop' on the floor.

"Jesus Christ!" Billy yelled.

Garcia bolted through the door as three creatures dropped down from the ceiling onto him – they looked like foot-and-a-half tall spindly devils with leathery skulls that were all teeth and thorn-like horns. He clutched at one that bit viciously into his hand just as Ferguson went reeling by to crash into one of the bookcases, causing it to topple.

Billy and Ricardo backed up into the rear gable, horrified, when a hiss from behind caused them to stop and slowly turn around.

Poised in the nook by the window was six-legged thing with a skull-like head, pincer teeth and luxuriant red hair that might have been taken out of a shampoo ad. The small, perky breasts were a strange feminine counterpoint that struck Ricardo as perversely erotic. The creature launched itself at Billy just as both boys jumped out of the way, snagging a lock of brylcreemed hair in one of its talons before it tumbled into a table full of instruments, scattering them.

"You bitch!" Billy yelled, clutching at his pompadour even as he ran towards the center of the room. Ricardo snatched up one of candelabra, jumping over the Chinese boxes Garcia had dropped. A myriad of coppery beetles and plated centipedes spewed out of them, scattering every which way.

One of the horned devils disengaged from Garcia and launched itself at Ricardo, its rat-like tail - which ended in a dangerous cluster of needle-like spikes - arching up over its back. For a moment all he saw was hissing teeth and barbed horns. Then Ricardo struck it with the candelabra in an overhead swing, smashing it into a steel tabletop with a sickening crunch.

Nearby, Billy had his hands full with the six-legged

creature which was going at his left foot like an enraged cat. Fortunately the toe was steel-capped under the leather, a fact apparently lost on his attacker despite breaking many of its fangs. Then Billy was able to leverage himself up onto a table enough to raise his boot and stomp it down with all the force he could muster. Once, twice, leaving the thing quivering on the floor, its head a flattened gory mess. Snatching a 3-foot-long metal rod from a pile of lab apparatus, he jumped over to where Ferguson lay, half-buried under dusty books and legs twitching.

Pushing aside the bookcase, Billy saw it was too late – the thing had half-chewed off Ferguson's face, one pincer stuck in his eye socket where it had been broken in the fall. The creature was trying to extricate itself, but several other legs appeared busted as well. Its leathery abdomen quivered as a milky web-like substance leaked out, then with equal parts loathing and anger Billy brought the rod down, imploding the thing's skull.

Ricardo found himself face to face with Garcia - who had dropped to his knees in front of him - struggling with the two critters that had punctured and torn him to ribbons. He hesitated, then dropping the candelabra, snatched up a heavy-looking bottle and smashed it over one creature. Glass shattered and the thing dropped off, its colleague turning around, spitting and hissing at him. For a second, Ricardo wondered if it was blind, then realized it had tiny pinpricks of eyes above the oversized mouth, like gleaming, black BBs. The deadly tail of spike waved gently in the air behind it, as if preparing to strike.

Ricardo feinted a couple of times with the broken bottle, then as the creature jumped at him, caught it on the jagged glass and rammed upwards, his arm like a piston, impaling it on the underside of a rafter.

Garcia rolled his eyes and, gushing blood, toppled over face-first.

Torn up and covered with blood, both boys met by the open door, which led into a smaller room at the front of the attic.

"What the fuck!?" Ricardo panted, fired up with adrenaline and his stomach doing flip-flops. "What the fuck are these things?"

"I… I don't know," Billy answered, "and at this point I don't really fucking care, we got to get out of…"

His words trailed off as a figure materialized out of the gloom of the doorway.

"Mister Kohwalt?" He said, blinking.

Dressed in one of his immaculately pressed suits the Funeral Director looked like he'd just stepped out of a meeting.

Except for the silver-plated .357 Magnum in his right hand.

Before Billy could react, he found his hair snatched by Kohwalt's free hand, the gun barrel pressing his temple.

"*Scheißkerl*!" Kohwalt snarled, "You've ruined everything!"

Ricardo put his hands up. "I-I-It's okay, Mister… we'll put it all back!" he said, wincing at the ludicrousness of his words. At the same time, something else occurred to him; *how did he…?*

"Too late! I had plans to send all of this back to home! Then the water damage! The roof! Now this!" The director was all but foaming at the mouth – bits of spittle flew from his lips.

"No-no, it's never too late!" Ricardo said.

"SILENCE!" Kohwalt screamed.

Then to Ricardo's surprise, he kept screaming. Then he started gagging.

From the front of his suit a cluster of slender black appendages erupted, and with it blood and gore. Backpedaling, Ricardo stumbled and fell on his ass just as the gun went off with a deafening blast. Billy dropped to the floor and Kohwalt staggered forward a step then collapsed, the appendages sliding back out of him with a sickeningly wet, *slipping* sound.

In the director's place stood a nightmare creature. It

took a moment for Ricardo to process what it was.

It sort of resembled a human merged with a giant insect, with the torso split open revealing a cavity from which the appendage cluster had emerged. The human hips and legs were intact as were the head and shoulders above – more or less – though the arms were folded back and hung useless at its sides. The head was tilted back to reveal a torn opening in the neck where a myriad of insectoid eyes peered out, along with a set of quivering feelers or antennae.

Just below that was the giveaway though - the stained clerical collar.

Ricardo had finally met up with Father Dullahan.

The fun wasn't quite over though, as between the Father's legs skittered another creature – a hideously aged version of the thing Ricardo had seen in the photo. Time hadn't been kind to the woman's face however; whatever combination of sorcery, science and taxidermy had been used to create it was now failing. The skin was blackened and wrinkled and the head resembled a half-deflated football with only random patches of hair still connected to it.

Still, the mouth, with its ragged rows of pincer-like fangs, seemed to be in working order as the thing paused before Ricardo's spread-eagled legs and its nostrils flared open and closed as if savoring the fear and horror blazing off him in waves.

"Oh fuck!" was all he could think to say.

Then, like some sped-up Hollywood effect, the appendages out of Father Dullahan's torso shrunk and curled back into the torso cavity, which closed; the opening in the neck sealed itself and the arms came to life. Seconds later, Ricardo was looking at a reasonable facsimile of the priest he'd (thought he'd) known his entire life, if one ignored the splashes of blood and gore across his frock and the not-quite-sane glare of the eyes.

Father Dullahan belched, adjusted his collar and looking down at the Portuguese teen said amicably,

"Well well, glad to see you've made your date with destiny!"

"Glad to see you've made yours," said another voice Ricardo recognized.

Then for the second time, a gun went off in the attic.

Father Dullahan was just in the process of turning his head around when it exploded as three rounds were pumped into it in quick succession. Rounds four and five took the woman/spider thing out of the picture immediately after, sending black ichor and spindly legs flying every which way.

Then, to Ricardo's unbelievable relief, Jack Curtis stepped through the door, smoke curling out of the barrel of the .45 in his hand.

"Any more-" he started to say then dropped into a classic gunslinger's crouch as one last creature rushed out of the shadows; a blur of centipede legs and rats heads. But it was no match for Curtis reflexes nor the Colt with its Detroit bullets.

God he's good, Ricardo marveled as the thing writhed and died. Then he managed to stagger to his feet.

Curtis looked around warily, ear cocked, but if anything else lurked in the attic it was staying out of sight. Finally his eyes rolled around and zeroed in on Ricardo.

"You alright?" he asked.

Ricardo blinked a couple times. Unbelievably, aside from a few bad cuts and scratches, he was.

"Yeah… yeah I think I am…." Then: "Oh God, Billy!"

Even as the words got out of his mouth Curtis stepped over and squatted by Billy's crumpled form, which actually seemed to be *moving.* Curtis looked him over, then to Ricardo's shock half-hauled him to his feet.

"Aw, he's gonna be fine," Curtis said. "Aside from a few singed hairs, that is. Bullet missed him. I think he just plum passed out." Curtis flicked the safety on the .45 and shoved it in his belt.

"Wait, how did you…?" Ricardo said, nodding towards the door.

"Oh, I knew there had to be another way in here, I just had to let the Father here show it to me."

"But he called me on Billy's phone."

Curtis stopped over and nudged the corpse. Billy's iPhone was just visible sticking out of the jacket pocket.

"Always knew there was something funny about that son-of-a-bitch priest," Curtis said. "Now come on, we got a lot of work to do. And hand me that bag with the journal. We gotta hurry, before the law gets here."

Seven minutes later the three of them were back in Curtis's truck. The top of Blynd Haus was already engulfed in flame. Curtis hadn't been happy about destroying his own projects, let alone torching the house, but as he explained briefly to the boys as he broke out his Zippo lighter, there was no way he was going to take any chances about what might or might not be still lurking up there.

Ricardo was amazed how quickly the place went up.

"That's the problem with old houses." Curtis acknowledged as they sat in the cab, watching the first Fire trucks pull up.

Two weeks later found them working construction for a new condo development up on Route 9B, a gainful, if dubious, employment arrangement by Billy's uncle. The Blynd Haus had been a fiasco, not just because Billy's hair-brained scheme had cost Curtis a major job but because it had come a hair's-breadth of landing all of them in jail. Not to mention the Funeral Home had burned to the ground. Once the chemicals stored up there caught, a series of spectacular explosions ensued and it was all the five responding Fire Companies could do but to sit back and make sure it didn't spread to any neighboring houses.

Curtis had gotten them off on a half-lie. He'd told the

police that his four workers had cooked up a scheme to check out some weird stuff they'd found in the attic but got tangled up with a wild raccoon or two that had holed up in there, which Ferguson had dispensed with a handgun. After which Ricardo and Billy had run over to Curtis's apartment to come clean and get their injuries patched up before things went any further. What happened after that was anyone's guess – possibly Father Dullahan and the Funeral Director had heard something and gone over to investigate, maybe Ferguson had lit up a smoke too close to one of the vats of chemicals… hard to tell.

Police Chief Hendricks didn't care much for it, but he'd never had any trouble with Curtis before and wasn't about to start, especially after the report from the Fire Chief and the very strange charred remains of equipment… and *things*… that had been discovered afterwards. The clincher though was that Mrs. Gorman had declined to pursue the matter and wanted it swept out of her life as quickly as possible.

It was Ricardo who had dragged Billy over to Curtis's place afterwards and forced him to apologize and see what they could do to make amends. That's how they wound up washing and cleaning Curtis's truck and tools every Saturday for the rest of the summer.

"I never really noticed that before," Billy said, lighting up a cigarette before handing the matches to Ricardo.

They were sitting on the west side of the new roof they had been shingling, taking a mid-morning break. In the woods between them and the river one could just make out a small mansion of dark grey stone. A 'Juliet' balcony on the second floor was sagging dangerously and on the trim the white paint was peeling in long curled strips. It looked like it had been abandoned for quite some time.

Billy blew smoke up in the air. It was the kind of clear, cool summer morning that would have been perfect for fishing. A couple of sailboats could be seen tacking lazily up the river.

"The foreman told me it's actually on the development property. Been sealed up for at least thirty or forty years he said...." He half turned as a shadow fell on his face, "*What*?"

Ricardo had taken the hammer out of his tool belt and was holding it inches from his friends face.

"Don't even *think* about it."

Be Careful What You Wish For...

By Sharon L. Higa

Jeff's right thumb was beginning to cramp in rhythm with the throbbing of his right shoulder.

The backpack slung to the right side of his body seemed to be growing heavier by the minute, more so within the last fifteen than when he began hitching in this ill-conceived spot two hours earlier. Even setting the pack down didn't help, because it felt like when he picked it back up again, some invisible being had added another brick or three to its weight.

His last ride, an elderly, blue haired woman with the slight spasms of palsy, was hesitant about letting him out here at this location.

She peered anxiously across the seat and through the passenger side window, hands unconsciously gripping the steering wheel to control the minute shakes.

"Are you sure you'll be all right, young man?"

The quaver in her voice was in perfect sync with the persistent nodding of her head. Her blue eyes were glued to the young man's face looking back at her from the open window.

Crouched down alongside the passenger door, Jeff gave her a huge smile of confidence. Patting the windowsill, he said, "Not to worry, Mrs. Samson. I've been travellin' by thumb a while now; I'll be just fine. Thank you again for the ride and you be safe, yourself, hear?"

With an anxious, myopic glance around, the old lady sighed and reached down to release the emergency brake. "All right, then; I guess you know what's best for you."

Jeff stood up and stepped back from the car as she popped the brake and jerked the gear shift into drive. Slowly she pulled out onto the road, gaining speed as she struggled to gain control of the car. Jeff flinched and partially closed his eyes as she angled the vehicle toward the wrong side of the road then over-corrected, heading back toward the emergency lane. She jerkily positioned the car properly between the yellow center and the far right white line, picking up speed and confidence with each rotation of the wheels.

He watched until the car was a tiny speck, finally disappearing altogether behind a scrub-covered hill.

Backpack still set between his feet, Jeff hitched up his jeans and finally took a look around at his current 'rest area'.

It was a crossroads. Stops signs, weathered and pock marked with bullet holes, canted sideways, stood at each corner of the roads leading to the intersection. A white line on the right side cordoned off the emergency lanes, which were simply the edges of the dirt embankments which haphazardly meandered off into the open fields of scrub and stunted trees. The trees, he noted, seemed to march up to the edge of the emergency lane then stopped - as if nature had set up an invisible barrier - forbidding any further encroachment onto the cracked asphalt.

Great, he thought, *A crossroads. Where suicides and criminals were buried in the old days to keep their souls from wandering.* He shook his head but his mind refused to turn the old information machine off. *Also a place noted where a demon could be summoned and a deal made in exchange for a persons' soul.*

Jeff shrugged his shoulders, the action turning into an involuntary shudder of unease.

"Stop it, dammit", he said out loud. "You're givin' yourself the willies, for Christ's sake!"

But God, was it quiet. Not a bird chirp, nor the rustle of any kind of animal. Not even the burring of insects, which, in his experience, could be heard in most every place he'd ever been. But not here; just the wind, the dirt and the lowering sun. Jeff stared upwards, gauging its' position. "*Lookin' to be 4 p.m. or thereabouts,*" he said to himself.

Sighing, he bent down and picked up the backpack, slung it over his shoulder and aimed catty-corner from his current position, toward the road headed in a north-east direction. Moving a few feet down from the stop sign, he turned and faced what he hoped would be oncoming traffic, cheerfully optimistic that a ride would come along real soon.

Two hours later, that cheerful optimism had slowly given way to consternation. In that time, there had only been three cars and one grizzled old farmer on a tractor that had passed his way. The duffer had tipped his ragged straw hat to Jeff as he put-putted on by and down the road.

That had been forty five minutes ago and Jeff was beginning to think that he was either going to have to hoof it, or hang it up for the night and hunker down among a group of three scrawny trees about twenty feet off in the desert.

The wind had kicked up again, this time bringing a chill with it, a hint of what the night temperature was going to be. He slung the pack off his shoulder and flexed his right hand quickly to get the circulation back to normal. Unzipping the front pocket he pulled out his windbreaker and flapped it briskly to get rid of some of the creases and any extra dust from the material.

Dusk was flowing into the darker realm of night as he stuffed his arms into the sleeves and jerked the zipper up, wishing now that he'd taken the old lady's offer to drive him a few more miles.

"Well," he mused out loud, "If wishes were horses, then beggars would ride."

Jeff chuckled at the 'folkism', one of many that his grandfather had taught him throughout the years.

But his thoughts quickly came back to the current reality of his situation. He knew that on a country road like this, trying to walk on until he hit a town could be very dangerous. The roads are unlit, except for moonlight, and who knows who could be cruising. He hadn't thumbed around for the past three years without learning a few things that had kept his hide intact.

He'd pretty much resigned himself to the fact that

he would be camping out with the 'Three ugly sisters' as he had dubbed the trees, when he caught a flash of light from the corner of his eye.

Turning quickly, Jeff saw a pair of headlights in the distance, steadily moving in his direction.

"Oh man, oh please stop! Give me a break!", Jeff muttered under his breath as he thrust his thumb out as far as he could and plastered a friendly, 'I'm a decent guy' grin on his face.

The vehicle - a dusty, beat up old station wagon, hub caps missing - stopped at the crossroads. Jeff couldn't see the driver, but from the angle of the car, it seemed that it was going to pull straight ahead, the way he wanted to go.

The car sat there for a bit, almost like the driver was trying to decide which way to turn.

Jeff kept reciting the same litany in his mind, over and over, the smile plastered on his lips; *Please, don't turn. C'mon man, help a guy out here.* The 'wish litany' seemed to go on forever to him and he didn't realize he'd been holding his breath until the car suddenly surged forward, through the intersection and straight towards him.

Jeff gave a slight nod to the driver of the car and waved his thumb up and down.

The wagon started to pick up speed as it rattled on by him.

Jeff's heart and hope had all but sunk to the pit of his stomach when he heard the squeal of the brakes and saw the red flash of the taillights as the car stopped in the middle of the road.

He stood there stunned for a minute, not quite believing his turn of luck. A sharp blat from the horn got him moving, causing him to snatch up his backpack and break into a shambling run toward the idling car.

He reached the passenger side and leaned forward, finally getting a good look at the driver.

"Hello sir. Thanks a lot for stopping. You're just what I'd been wishin' for; I was beginnin' to think that I was gonna be sleepin' with the coyotes tonight."

"Well, then, you better hop in. I don't plan on havin' you ride on the roof."

The voice was gruff and deep, the face still hidden in shadow.

Jeff pulled open the door, shoved his pack onto the floor and slid in, lifting his left leg up and over the pack. The door closed with a rusty clunk and he reached to the side for the seatbelt. The driver watched this all in silence. With the click of the seatbelt locking in place, he faced forward again and planted his foot on the gas, urging the vehicle forward.

For a few minutes, Jeff just sat there, taking in the car. The seats were faded but clean, the occasional rip patched with an actual patch repair kit, not like the usual duct tape fix. He noted earlier that the car was dented and dusty, the rattle coming primarily from the loose muffler. The body overall was in good shape for a late model car; but the engine, now that was a dream. He'd worked in a few garages in his travels across the country, and he knew a good, strong engine when he heard it. And this engine was top notch. The rumble was smooth and steady, no lurching or hesitation when the man accelerated or decelerated. Jeff was duly impressed.

He turned his attention to the driver.

Rough, gnarled, work hardened hands gripped the steering wheel. The wrists sticking out of the thermal shirt were lean and wiry, as was the arm leading up to the shoulder. Dark overalls, faded but fresh washed from the smell covered the man's body and Jeff assumed that there were 'shit-kicker' work boots on his feet. A farmer or a rancher, Jeff concluded. Someone used to physical labor. A hard, 'salt of the earth' type of guy.

The man's eyes were deep set, eyebrows bushy and thick. The hair matched the wiry eyebrows, its true color, like his eyes, hidden in the night shadows that played within the car. The profile showed chiseled features, the cheekbones jutting sharply out to cut back in and angling down to a smooth plane connecting to the jawbone, accentuating a square chin dappled with stubble. His mouth had a relaxed, contemplative set to it, lips thin and hard, aptly matching the rest of his features.

Many times in the past, Jeff's initial assessment of a driver kept him out of harm's way. He could pick up on whether someone was a 'little off the beam' but harmless, an 'Oh no, not on your life' or what he termed as 'a regular'; someone safe to cadge a lift from. This guy gave him no vibrations of any kind; a 'regular'. Okay, fine.

Jeff turned his full attention to the driver. "My name's Jeff. Thank you for the lift Mr…?"

The question hung in the air between them. When there seemed to be no response forthcoming, Jeff could almost feel his question drop, like a stone, through the empty space between the seats.

Oh great, Jeff thought, unconsciously straightening his shoulders, nervously sliding his hands along the legs of his jeans. *Now what's up?*

Resigning himself to an interminable time of absolute silence, Jeff was startled a few minutes later when the man spoke up.

"Sorry about that, son. I was wool gatherin'. Name's Bowie - J. Bowie. Where ya headed?"

Jeff leaned forward, fiddling with the straps of his pack, giving his mind time to process what was just said.

"I'm headed to a town called Jackson. It's about two hours….."

The man interrupted. "Yep, I know where Jackson is. Matter of fact, I need to be passing through that town; got business about fifteen miles past there." He glanced over at Jeff. "Looks like it's your lucky day; I'll take ya into Jackson, at least to the first exit n' drop ya off."

Jeff sat blinking at the figure who had gone back to focusing on the road. After a second, a grin split his face from ear to ear. "You can? Mr. Bowie that would be terrific!" He slapped his thigh and chuckled. "I guess grandpa was right."

"How's that?" The question was almost a statement coming out of Mr. Bowie's mouth.

Jeff looked at the man and shrugged his shoulders, a little uncomfortable with sharing something that he considered personal with a stranger. But, since Mr. Bowie was giving him a lift to his next destination, he felt he owed the man an explanation.

"Well, my grandpa basically raised me. He was always giving me advice by the way of 'Old Folk Tales', only he called 'em 'Folkisms'. You know - sayings that have good common sense to them."

He looked over to see if Mr. Bowie was following what he was saying. If he sensed any kind of derision from the man, then he would leave his explanation where it was. But Mr. Bowie was nodding his head, a small smile playing across his lips.

He positioned his hands on the steering wheel and addressed the boy. "You mean, like, "A little too late is much too late."

"Yes sir!" Jeff enthusiastically dove in. "And others like, 'A word of praise is equal to ointment on a sore'.

"Or", Mr. Bowie countered, "A chain is only as strong as its weakest link".

Jeff nodded his head, happy to find understanding instead of contempt. "Yes sir, and hundreds of others he taught me throughout my childhood. Just like the one I was thinking of just before you happened along."

The comment quickly warranted a sideways glance from Mr. Bowie. "And which one was that?"

Jeff grinned. "It was, 'If wishes were horses….'"

"Then beggars would ride". For some reason, the last part of the saying sounded creepy coming from Mr. Bowie.

Jeff sat back in his seat and faced forward again. "Yep, that was it."

Jeff pretended to suddenly be preoccupied with the scenery outside his window.

He was grateful to be getting this ride to Jackson and didn't want anything to jinx it so he shut up and they rode on in silence.

Mr. Bowie kept on driving, a calm, serene look on his face.

Soon the rumble of the engine and the smooth swoosh of the tires lulled Jeff to sleep. He angled his head against the window and crossed his arms. Slipping into a deeper sleep, his body pushed down a little in the seat and he began to breathe deep and long, his exhalations accented with gentle, breathy snores.

Mr. Bowie glanced over at Jeff periodically, making sure the boy was truly 'out like a light'. After an hour, the man gently moved his hand down between his seat and the driver's side door. Slowly, so as not to make any noise, he withdrew a hunting knife.

The bowie knife was thirteen inches of cold steel, the tip angled up, smooth at the back. No serrated edges to catch on bone.

The man slowly transferred the knife from his left hand to his right, never dropping the speed of the vehicle or altering its course.

The man looked over at the sleeping boy and picked his spot. With one swift, fully powered motion, he slammed the knife out and up, penetrating between the third and fourth ribs on the left side of the kid's body, punching into the heart and causing instant death. After all, he'd liked the kid and didn't want him to suffer.

Leaving the knife in place to ensure that there would be no blood spurt once he pulled it out, the man drove on, window rolled down to enjoy the cool night breeze.

Twenty minutes later, he started looking about, making sure that they were alone on the road, casting about for the perfect spot. He finally spied a deeper indentation in the shadows alongside the road. The darkness there belied a steeper angle to the ditch that ran alongside the so-called emergency lane.

He casually pulled over to the side of the quiet, deserted road. He looked around, once again making sure that no one or nothing was around to cause him any disruption and listened to the night sounds for any interruption in their normal rhythms. Like a hawk using its whole body to locate its prey, the man sat stock still, using his heightened senses - honed to perfection through many years of practice - to ensure they were alone out here in the dark desert night.

Satisfied, he leaned over the body. With one fluid motion he popped the passenger door handle and with one strong energetic push shoved it open all the way. Only then did he grasp the knife handle and drew it out in one smooth motion as he hit the locking mechanism of the seatbelt. He swiped the bloody blade across the arm of the dead boys' jacket as indifferently as you would wipe a freshly washed dish with a towel. Examining the steel to make sure no excess blood was left he nodded with satisfaction and deftly, silently, reset the knife in the drivers' side door pocket. He turned his attention back to the young man.

The sideways momentum of the body helped him with the final shove. The corpse hit the ground with very little disturbance of the dirt around it. The backpack was tossed out indifferently as well, bouncing off the legs and rolling to a stop a couple of feet away, further down the little ditch.

The man pulled the car forward, the swerve and acceleration back onto the road causing the passenger door to slam closed and lock shut. It was a maneuver he'd perfected a long time ago.

As the engine kicked into a higher gear, smoothing out into a strong, low rumble, the man who called himself 'Mr. Bowie' glanced back in the rearview mirror at the body receding in the distance and chuckling, said out loud, "Here's another saying, son. "Be careful what you wish for…."

Silver Bullets

By Steve Jenner

Blandford Parker, Roland Sami and Thaddeus Field. Three men who started their lives far apart but finally gravitated towards one another, attracted by the violence they enjoyed and the power they craved. Not that the living world wasn't full of such creatures but even at the depths to which some people sank, most could look up and still see daylight. Not these three. The sustaining touch of a cleansing sun had long since failed to reach them through the dense murk in which they travelled. A sinister alliance built on greed and unfortunately for them, mistrust.

When it came to just plain evil, Parker had a head start on his two subordinates as he was descended from a long line of degenerates who had experimented to varying degrees with the dark arts. These ancestors were largely eccentric, invariably selfish and at all times utterly devoted to the most potent forms of magic; a dark sorcery that regularly involved the death of innocents under the most appalling conditions. Blandford Parker was no different. He had blood on his hands and cared little for the victims of his grisly methods.

So then, Thaddeus Field. Nearly seven feet tall with long greasy hair and crooked teeth. An oversized brute built like grizzly bear with the table manners to match. He moved quickly for a big man, usually with a piledriving forward momentum that often swept his foes from their feet before an effective defensive ploy could be devised. He rarely employed subtlety or considered tactics while his choice of weapon was his ham-like fists which he used to good effect, if killing a man noisily and messily was the aim. And to be fair to him, it usually was.

Field moved abruptly from his home in Eastern Europe when his criminal excesses had escalated from the relatively common practice of casual assault to the unacceptable extremes of ruthless murder. As a local mob enforcer, he had enjoyed a certain amount of status in the community but it wasn't long before the outraged citizens claimed on their paid-for protection to protest at his indiscriminate slaughter. The gang bosses agreed as did the infuriated constabulary so Thaddeus Field soon became a fugitive from the law and lawbreakers alike. Only by crossing several international boundaries and the English Channel to London did he find some refuge from determined pursuit.

Due to his size and disposition, Field was conspicuous although not desperately so in a city full of men who relied solely on brute force to stay alive. His background did not betray him as London's underworld was a multicultural society that welcomed criminals of any ethnicity. Employment as muscle for seedy club owners or small-time crooks was easy to come by, however it was not long before he overstepped the mark by murdering two innocent women in the home they shared. The sheer viciousness of the crime coupled with witness reports of a "Frankenstein's monster" fleeing the premises led the police directly to his door.

Once again, Field absconded, this time to the relative safety of rural England and the house of Blandford Parker who promised him protection in return for services rendered. Field did not enquire as to the nature of these services as there was little that offended him and much that attracted him. Money and occasionally women interested him but it was Blandford's more arcane pursuits that really stirred his blood. In Parker's eccentric old mansion, Thaddeus Field witnessed a whole new level of depravity that he had not previously suspected possible. And so the fading daylight vanished altogether from his life as he became one with the darkness.

Roland Sami had known decency once albeit from a distance. In his youth, Sami had run with a street gang that had haunted the suburbs of Melbourne with their painted faces and aboriginal clubs. The Australian authorities had turned a blind eye to their capering and cavorting until a number of burglaries were linked with the membership and arrests were made. Sami was no native Australian, a fact demonstrated by his lack of any personal identification papers or a valid immigration documents. Nevertheless, despite his parents' apparent demise and no traceable point of origin, Sami was still a minor so ultimately the responsibility of the state.

At first, the boy had shown some promise in his studies and the Institution in which he had been placed considered his future bright. Even when items of value went missing he was not immediately placed under suspicion, as his demeanour was that of an innocent immersed in his books and unaware of the world beyond. Short fair hair, smooth skin only brushed by the antipodean sun and the Mark of Cain deeply hidden beneath an air of civility, Roland Sami appeared as other young men who lived modestly. As he reached his eighteenth birthday untroubled by guilt or prosecution, he reached an inevitable conclusion. Life was easy and his only crime was lack of ambition.

The successful mugging of an old woman on a dark street did nothing to change his mind but left him disappointed at the paltry yield. It wasn't long before the limitations of petty theft became apparent and the need to expand his horizons critical. The Institution that had housed him for so long had issued him with an ultimatum upon his achieving adult status. Commit to further education or leave.

Roland considered the proposal and decided promptly. During a final interview with the Governor, he convinced the naive and unworldly custodian to make him a small loan to buy books. When the safe was opened to retrieve the token funds, Sami bludgeoned the old man to death and helped himself to the entire contents.

For the next few years, Sami lived on his wits barely a step or two ahead of the Melbourne constabulary. For the most part, he lived like a vagabond preying on the vulnerable but occasionally he joined up with other miserable wretches to attempt something more elaborate and potentially more profitable. Unsurprisingly, most of these master plans proved to be nothing of the sort and resulted in most of the "master criminals" being incarcerated. Roland Sami somehow managed to remain at large each time but his name was now known and the net was tightening.

In one last desperate venture, Sami and two others tried to relieve a bank of its cash reserves. The robbery attempt was clumsy, ill-conceived and a mess from start to finish. Four people died in a hail of bullets including Sami's accomplices and within minutes the building was surrounded by a division of trigger-happy policemen. By some miracle, Sami managed once more to escape in the confusion but knew as he ran that his time in the city and indeed the country was over. It was not a new thought by any means and the bag he had recently prepared for just such a contingency was now secreted in a station locker near the port. It was the prudent course to pick it up and keep running.

He had the funds standing by for a voyage by ship to England. Luck was with him when he purchased a steerage berth and was at sea within the hour. Sami kept his head down and his nose clean even though the opportunities to purloin any number of valuables presented themselves regularly on board. The passage took weeks but no telegraphed communiqués concerning a fleeing felon reached the ship at any of its stops. Roland Sami arrived at his destination in a cheerful mood, full of dreams about a new life and rich pickings in a decadent land. Unfortunately, that decadence had not spread to the Port Authority who immediately arrested the dismayed traveller for possession of forged documents and illegal entry.

Only his slightly reluctant agreement to enlist in the British Army saved him from being deported straight away. The Great War was less than a year away and few able bodied men were being rejected regardless of their dubious origins. Sami was sent to a camp for basic training and half way through his second night there decided that the cannon fodder life wasn't for him and so made his escape over a wire fence. A search party was sent out for him just after dawn but there was no sign of the deserter. The hunt continued for some days but despite enquiries at local residences, the fugitive was nowhere to be found. As no one had thought to approach the house of Blandford Parker with its protective spells and warning hexes, Sami would remain at liberty to pursue a brutal existence.

Parker, Sami and Field. Together in the rambling old house, away from the noise of war but alert to their own brand of carnage being enacted in the darkened cellars. Parker the adept black magician and his two awestruck but willing subordinates. The sorcery required blood so Field and Sami appended abduction and kidnapping to their list of crimes. Further offences were added during the deviant rites that Blandford practised and it soon became necessary for Parker to instruct his new acolytes in some basic incantations to protect themselves from harm. Not that they were in any particular physical danger but even the most cynical creature can lose its mind amid such degeneracy.

Many months passed as the trio developed their talents. Parker delved deeper and deeper into the black abyss of high magic until his obsession became all-consuming. Sami watched the man's simultaneous descent and climb to unnatural levels but kept his own counsel. He had mastered a few fundamental spells himself but was unable to cope with the stress without the aid of artificial stimulation. Drugs were hardly a new innovation in the world but in rural England their purchase required cunning and caution. Sami found that his trips to the nation's capital were becoming more and more regular as he endeavoured to feed his addiction.

Thaddeus Field put nothing elevating into his mind or body. In one of the rooms of the strange house, he had found some exercise equipment and Indian clubs which he immediately put to good use. His already massive frame became a colossus of hard muscle and tight flesh, the development of which he would not compromise even for Blandford. Not that he was ever asked to do so.

All three men were engaged in their own individual search for stimulation and only convened when some bloodthirsty ritual was scheduled. It was at the conclusion of one such violent episode that Blandford Parker at last told his two house guests what they must do to repay his hospitality.

Sami and Field never really knew the truth. They were given their tasks, provided with items of magical persuasion that would help fool obstructive officials or conceal them from inquisitive eyes and then sent out into the world with words of warning ringing in their ears. No deviation from the plan. No unnecessary flamboyance that might draw attention to their mission and under no circumstances should the objects they had been sent to recover be interfered with, manipulated or lost. For Blandford Parker, results were essential, minions were expendable.

It took a few weeks for Roland Sami to reach his destination. During the journey, he had given considerable thought not only to the item he had been sent to fetch but how he was going to steal it. Blandford had told him that a sack of thirty silver coins was being kept by an obscure order of monks in a monastery high in the Pyrenees. The trek up was not straightforward. Altitude had to be considered. Approach could be magically hidden but security, if any, was an unknown factor. Sami stood at the foot of the peak and plotted his course. The climb, he decided, would be time consuming but not overly taxing.

Sami decided not to rush into action. He took a room at a nearby inn, ate a large meal with gusto and then settled down for evening at the bar. After a tedious hour spent entirely alone he was tempted to visit one of the local establishments for ale and the company of a harlot but instead chose to adjourn to his room for the benefits of his pipe. The mixture that he smoked induced a soothing calm that lasted until he turned in for the night. This drug-fuelled euphoria also brought with it terrifying nightmares of blood-soaked running boys with painted faces.

The next day was bright and cold. Sami did not need too much warm clothing due to his protective charms but did not want to draw attention to himself by strolling off for a mountain walk in light summer wear. The innkeeper provided him with cold chicken, sausages and cheese as well as a bottle of Pyrenees spring water to sustain him on his trek but Sami suspected his supply of stimulants would be the main factor in coping with exhaustion. The sun warmed him as he approached the lower slopes so in unusual good humour, he joined a group of climbers who were clearly hiking for the fresh air and memorable views.

In the end, the ascent was completed without difficulty by following a steep path right up to the monastery gates. He had separated from the cheerful company at a rest station to press on alone up a path signposted for monks and tradesmen only. A cruel wind blew through the higher crags but with his charms to protect him from the elements, Sami progressed easily inside the walls and nearer to his goal.

He had timed his journey to arrive in darkness and to coincide with evening observances which drew the monks conveniently away to worship. Through the torchlit corridors he slid quietly without casting a shadow. No robed figures barred his way, no doors blocked his advance. When he reached the chamber that his compass charm told him contained the sack of ancient coins, Sami allowed himself a smug smile.

His satisfaction was short-lived. When he entered the room, fully expecting to purloin his prize without obstruction or objection, he encountered both in the form of a large dog chained to a wall. The animal immediately reacted to his intrusion by barking wildly and wrenching in frenzied jerks at its restraints. The space was not large, sparsely furnished and contained no room to manoeuvre. Sami assumed correctly that the oak chest currently beneath the beast's great paws held the item he had come for and as his array of charms seemed not to befuddle the canine. A new ploy had to be concocted.

When all was said and done, Roland Sami was not a concocter. A cheat, yes. A liar, certainly. He was even blessed with above average intelligence but if asked to improvise or invent a strategy then he was lost and brute force would often have to do. He thought about killing the snarling dog but using his knife was out of the question and the several necessary shots from his revolver would undoubtedly attract unwanted attention. In the end, he settled upon a tactic that those who knew him would have described as inspirational.

From his rucksack, he retrieved the chicken and sausages that he had not needed during his climb. Inside the skin, he placed a selection of his most potent relaxants hoping all the while that he would not regret the loss later.

The huge hound bounded forward to the limits of its chain and gobbled down the unexpected treat with evident enthusiasm. Sami suspected that the animal was deliberately underfed to increase its effectiveness as a guard dog but on this occasion the gambit had backfired. In a matter of minutes, the dog's growls had turned to whines and finally to great rasping snores.

Roland Sami gratefully stepped in and removed the sack from the chest. He patted the slumbering dog on the head and then made his exit unobserved. The trip down the mountain in darkness held certain dangers but his charms did their job and he reached the bottom unscathed. The lateness of the hour meant that the inn's doors were closed but Sami was not inconvenienced by locks and so made his way silently to his room, once again unnoticed. Early the next morning, he was on his way back to England with his mission successfully accomplished.

Through French vineyards and orchards he swept; the clicking and clacking of the rickety train pleasingly rhythmic and a passable replacement for his sacrificed sedatives. Picturesque villages trundled by and the occasional stops in bustling towns brought at least a hint of urban urgency to an otherwise tranquil day. None of this penetrated Sami's introspection. He was thinking deeply about thirty pieces of silver. Thinking about Blandford's assertion that they dated back two millennia and were associated with death and dishonour. Thinking about why the leather bag was warm to the touch and the objects inside presumably hotter. It was testament to Parker's malign influence that Sami never once peered inside the sack.

If Sami's journey south through sun-drenched Europe had been mainly along the much-travelled tourist routes, Thaddeus Field's return to the east of that continent had been a solitary tour of barely known regions. As a boy, he had known something of the Carpathian Mountains and their myths and legends but had neither wanted nor expected to visit them at any stage of his life. Now Blandford Parker had packed him off to that cold, desolate place to recover a silver dagger from a long-forgotten tomb. Despite his lack of fear in most situations and an unshakable confidence in his physical prowess, the idea of creeping around the vaults of old warriors left him anxious and irresolute.

The landscape through which he drove his motorcycle was a wild and windswept wasteland to one who had dwelt in a city for most of his life. Even Field's unsophisticated upbringing a few hundred miles to the north had included a semblance of urban complexity and at least a few upheld laws.

The further he moved from the larger townships, the bleaker the scenery became until the time came when no signs of civilisation marked the land at all. As he thundered on, cruder, more pagan symbols began to appear etched in the rocks. It was an ancient province steeped in superstition and dread tales that Field remembered as childhood yarns to frighten the unruly. Those stories now filled his head and he couldn't get rid of them.

The higher roads were treacherous with many abrupt drops to the outside of extremely tight bends. His bike negotiated the potholes and rock-strewn stretches as if it were passing through a minefield. He slalomed and skidded for several miles until the path became more even and landslides less abundant. He wondered, as he travelled, how larger vehicles might manage to get through and then quickly arrived at the conclusion that there was no reason for any to attempt it. The region was uninhabited, unsophisticated and ultimately uninviting.

On the lowland paths, fens and marshes veined by ice cold streams prevented any cross country expeditions so Field dipped his head over the handlebars and forged on. When evening introduced a milky moon, Field pulled his bike over into small copse of thin trees and considered the best way to proceed. His compass charm suggested he was heading in the right direction but the distance yet to cover was less than clear.

Field scanned the road ahead but saw no sign of any ancient structures intact or otherwise. Blandford had told him that the tomb was located amidst the ruins of an old fort dating back to the middle ages. Little information was available concerning its most recent inhabitants except for the suggestion that the warrior lord who had ruled there was never defeated in battle. He was, however, hung and dismembered by his own men for atrocities of an abnormal and unnatural nature; the body being interred in the vault with a silver blade plunged through its heart. Ignoble burial it was called, a punishment for devil worship. The resulting struggle for power ended in a conflagration that reduced the fort to rubble never to be rebuilt.

Thaddeus Field did not expect to see crenulated

towers grazing the skyline but some evidence of the stone walls must remain for him to find the crypt. He paced along the line of trees to relieve his cramp and then decided to remount the bike before the clouds he had spotted on the dark horizon either brought rain or intercepted the moonlight. The beam of his headlight would not be enough to pick out the shapes of roadside ruins. He needed the moon. Many times in the past, he had found concealment along the moonlit streets when the shadows had whispered to him to hide in their embrace. Now it was the pale light that he needed to locate his target, recover the damned knife and finally get away from this stark wilderness.

An hour later, he spotted what looked like an old church sitting back from the road between two clumps of trees. Even against the black sky, the jagged outline of broken masonry looked dark and dense with unspecified menace. Field parked his bike out of sight from the road but easily accessible should he need to leave quickly. Why he might need to do so in this silent, deserted place he could not say, yet the atmosphere as he approached the building felt heavy and oppressive.

It soon became clear when he stepped over some shattered stonework and into the heart of the structure that it was no holy place. Faded frescos on grimy walls came alive in his flashlight beam to reveal scenes of bloody battle and merciless execution. Tall statues still in one piece wore thick stone armour and brandished fearsome weapons. Field wondered as he passed whether he might have flourished in such an age when men thrived on strength and aggression alone. With images of breathless conflict dominating his thoughts, he nearly missed his compass charm flickering energetically in his hand.

Field remembered his instructions. If the crystal flashed blue, he was above his target. Red and he was below. Green meant go left, yellow to the right. Now it was alternating between green and blue which indicated that somewhere in the wall to his left, a door leading to a staircase down was hidden. He pointed his torch at the still fully formed wall and was surprised to see a painted mural of several soldiers standing around a door. Much of the colour had faded from the picture and evidence of mould stained the design but most was still clear and easily distinguished.

Even Field, whose wits were not an asset, could not fail to be tempted by the painted door. He guessed correctly that the warrior clan had not been subtle and that the artist not commissioned to be clever. Sure enough, when he ran his fingers around the illustrated frame he found a groove and when the painted door knob was twisted, a wooden portal was revealed and opened. Field smiled grimly at his ingenuity and then directed his torchlight into the space. Dust eddied in illuminated swirls above a grey staircase which disappeared downwards into a dark abyss,

Thaddeus Field had to bend almost double to enter the gap. He crouched and crawled his way down the steps, all the time aware that if his imagined hasty departure ever became a reality, this part of the journey might prove hazardous or even fatal. The thought sobered him as he descended but upon entering the chamber below it became clear that although he would not be able to stand completely upright, he could at least conduct his search without shuffling around on his knees.

That search took less time than he had imagined as the crypt contained only one sarcophagus. He did not waste time admiring its elaborate carvings or the strange language inscribed on its flanks. He cared nothing for the hideous creatures embossed upon its lid or the engraved curses beneath these monsters. What he did pay attention to was the weight of that bulky cover which failed to budge an inch on his first attempt to move it. Maybe it was the ringing in his ears from the effort or perhaps the ghosts of ancient days were gathering to ridicule his endeavours but the vault was alive with strange noises and movements as it accustomed itself to his intrusion.

Field placed his torch on the gravelly floor and returned to the uncooperative lid. He flexed his arms and back before turning his head and neck to try and relieve some tension. From somewhere a breath of air reached him but it did not cool his flesh as the sweat on his forehead ran in rivulets into his eyes. He used his sleeve to wipe his face and then with a growl of frustration, focussed all of his considerable strength into one mighty push.

The stone creaked and ground stubbornly then finally shifted. Encouraged, Field shoved again and was rewarded with still more movement. Eerie tittering squeaks echoed from the dry darkness which Field hoped were the sounds of disgruntled rodents. He narrowed his eyes and peered into corners but only the looming shadows glowered back. Irritated, he wiped his face again then followed that with a titanic heave which sent the great slab of hewn stone crashing to the floor there to break into three pieces. Field grinned. He had not intended to replace the cover so cared little that a man's final resting place had been defiled.

Retrieving his flashlight, Field straightened up and in his haste to complete his task, crunched his head against the crypt's ceiling. The bellow he unleashed had whatever creatures he had disturbed scampering back into their holes. Less tangible observers were probably unimpressed by the explosion but amused by his pain. Field tested his scalp for blood and would have been relieved to find none if he hadn't been so angry. Why Parker had selected him for bumping around in confined spaces he did not know. That shrimp Sami would have been far better suited. Time, he decided, to grab the knife and go home.

Inside the coffin lay the disintegrating bones of an exceptionally large man although what was left of him was largely dust. If he'd bothered to notice, Field might have seen the shreds of a lined black cloak and an untarnished gold medallion still visible next to the spine.

These remnants were ignored mainly because the ornate silver dagger protruding from between the body's ribs was reflecting the torchlight in irregular flashes. Field's grin was equally bright. He grasped the knife by its wound leather handle and tugged it from the skeleton. The bones raised and crackled in protest but soon lay back down, silent and subdued.

Thaddeus studied the gleaming blade for a few moments and then tucked it into his belt. He had seen such weapons before or had at least stolen something similar on occasion. If Blandford wanted it, he could have it. The thing would be a nightmare to sell anyway. Turning away from the remains and dipping his head, he started back towards the stairs. Field had taken only a single step when a bony hand reached out and gripped his wrist. The pain was immediate and electric. In a moment of panic, he almost dropped the torch but recovered quickly enough to twist around again towards the sarcophagus. The thing that had him was slowly sitting up.

More hissing and clicking came from black corners. If whatever lurked in the shadows was closing in then the claw-like clamp on his arm had him trapped. For the first time in his life, Thaddeus Field did not resort to brute force to extricate himself from trouble but took the time to think. Despite the pounding of his heart, he kept a grip on his nerves to face the horror that was slowly rising from centuries of entombment. From his belt, he took the silver blade and held it aloft. The dead bones faltered in their ascent as if they knew what was coming and then Field brought the dagger down in a shining arc to separate the skull from the white-boned neck.

The effect was almost instantaneous. Field's wrist was immediately released as every ancient joint completely lost cohesion and fell back into the coffin in a vaguely human-shaped pile of loose bones. The skull dropped to the floor and gazed sightlessly forward in an accusing stare. A distant scream, like steam being released somewhere, reverberated about the chamber giving Field, if he needed any, a warning to vacate. In a crouching run, he scuttled over to the steps, then up them at a pace he had previously not thought possible and finally out into the hall. He didn't stop there but kept on going until at last he was gunning his motorcycle down the uneven road and back towards civilisation.

In less than a month since they separated, Field, Sami and Blandford Parker were reunited in the old house and drinking Brandy to celebrate their success. Field's unnerving experiences had led to him back to the security of the bottle while Sami was never averse to a glass of quality. Both were interested to hear Parker's plans for the retrieved items and where the third object he had mentioned was to be found. The black magician smiled benignly at his two colleagues. They had performed admirably, he told them, and he was proud of their accomplishments. The last remaining article was indeed a vital part of what was to come but no one needed to go searching for it. The final silver piece had been in the house all along.

"Thaddeus," said Blandford Parker as the three men walked up the creaking stairs of the old house. "You have visited most of the rooms on the upper floors. Did you find anything of interest?"

Thaddeus Field had indeed scoured the entire building in search of something to amuse him. For the first few months of his stay, he had been advised to stay within the grounds and the spells that protected them. He had not understood the warning at first. To him, hexes and jinxes were what the old women of his home town used to scare away scavengers or befuddle their husbands. However, it was not long before he witnessed real magic at work. In the hands of Blandford Parker, sorcery was a captivating thing. When he saw how it was procured, the extraction of blood, the exploitation of fear, he was more than fascinated. He was enraptured.

"Most of the rooms are locked," he said in his gruff voice.

“Indeed they are,” said Parker and then produced a brass key from his pocket. “Now we shall see why.”

Field and Sami exchanged glances but did not comment. Since they had been living in the house, they had found it necessary to not only refrain from upsetting their host but also keep any remarks concerning the dilapidated condition of the old mansion to themselves. Doors had a habit of jamming at inconvenient moments. Taps would not turn off and occasionally the electrics failed to cooperate. Worst of all were the noxious aromas that drifted up through the floorboards from the cellar below although neither man had any trouble imagining the source of those chilling vapours.

On the third floor, Parker used his key to open up a room that neither Field nor Sami had ever seen inside. Warm air flooded out through the doorway and along the passage bringing with it a metallic smell that reminded Field of the lightning strikes that beset his homeland. Parker moved forward and then beckoned the other two to follow. Once again, Field and Sami looked at one another, both sensing that whatever lay inside the room was probably dangerous and beyond their understanding. When the door slammed behind them of its own accord, neither man was surprised.

“Close the curtains, Sami,” Parker ordered.

Sami did so and then rejoined Field who was shuffling about in the awkward way a big man does in cramped surroundings. Sami scowled at the display of nerves. They had never been friends and never would be but they shared enough interests to rub along. Sami’s approach to dabbling in dark magic was a practical one. He saw how its implementation could be a means to an end and had no objections to the methods employed in its generation. Parker’s long term plans were not clear to him but he was shrewd enough to watch and learn as the situation developed. Sami knew that something significant was about to happen and he was determined to benefit from it.

Field, on the other hand, wallowed in the mysticism and occult ceremony of it all. He could not recite the incantations with any accuracy nor could he hope to execute a spell without Parker taking the lead. But that did not matter to him. His ears were not offended by the screams of innocents. His eyes had seen suffering and it did not affect his judgment. All that mattered was that he should be in amongst it, be a part of the show, as he saw it. Whatever Parker had in mind, Field simply wanted to be at its heart and be swept away by the euphoria that high magic produced.

Blandford Parker cared little for the feelings of either man. He did not like them or trust them. Not that he thought for one minute that they might betray him or even attempt to take advantage of their new knowledge. Neither was capable, he was sure. What concerned him was the probability that when asked to play their parts in the forthcoming rite, both would be found wanting in courage and conviction. He had read thoroughly the directions outlined in the formidable grimoire, Veng's Path, and was well aware of what would soon be required. Sami and Field would never know, he thought grimly, and that was how it should be.

In the middle of the otherwise empty room stood a pedestal upon which lay a black box that under normal circumstances might have been used to store shoes. The box had no lid and it seemed that all of the heat and indeed the strange odour was emanating from its depths. Parker indicated that the two men should step forward and take a look. Field immediately moved in and crouched down to examine the box's contents. Sami did the same but did so with more tentative steps. An argent radiance illuminated the faces of all three, igniting a fierce light in their eyes. For Field and Sami, it was merely a gleaming reflection; for Blandford Parker it was the burning lust for power that shone there.

"What is it?" asked Field, who saw only an irregular shaped rock with a pleasing glow.

"Is it radioactive?" was Roland Sami's immediate reaction.

"It is a meteorite, a gift from space," Parker answered slowly. "It crashed into the grounds of this house some years ago. Drawn here, I shouldn't wonder."

The rock flared silver in response to Parker's words, perhaps in agreement to the implied affinity. At least that was what Field thought as he gazed in rapt attention into the box. Something exotic from the far reaches of the solar system finding its way to Blandford Parker could be nothing less than providential; a sign from the heavens that their actions were blessed. Thaddeus Field had never believed in fate or destiny and had no positive views on any popular deities but much had changed since he had come to England. Now he was devout. A convert of the blood.

"That is the third item, the one that makes up the set?" asked Sami.

Parker nodded. "It is. Now you and Field must transport it to the cellar where we will place it with the others. Then the great spell can be cast."

"You haven't told us what the great spell is yet, Blandford. What is it going to do?" said Sami, who after seeing the space rock had begun to wonder where it was all going.

Parker turned slowly to examine Roland Sami. He had supposed that both men would follow him blindly without question or query but he should have known it would be the more insightful Sami who made the inevitable enquiry. How much should he tell him? How much could he handle? It was too late to find a replacement and there was too much at stake to risk a confrontation. Parker smiled at both men and nodded his head.

"Alright gentlemen, listen carefully. Three silver items. One linked with death and dishonour. A second with punishment and revenge. The third alien and ancient. In Veng's Path, the author notes that these are the associations required. The silver is a prime conductor for the magical energies, the blood a catalyst for the conversion. With the correct incantation, these items will be transformed into objects of power."

Field was nodding thoughtfully at every word, convinced that everything Parker was saying was not only the truth but also part of a sacred plan that must be followed. He wanted to voice his complete commitment to the idea but lacked the vocabulary to express himself properly. Sami, by contrast, had not heard anything yet that suggested any great advantage or material benefit that might justify all the effort he had put in. He was worried that the extent of Blandford's immersion into the powerful words in Veng's Path had unhinged him slightly. Sami had opened the pages of the book just once and had felt the nauseating potency of every word sweep through him. They were all on dangerous ground, he thought, but he stayed quiet.

Blandford continued in a passionate voice. "With these objects, the world and the worlds beyond will not only open to us but allow us to rule there. Take what we want, use it how we like. Nothing will hold us back."

Sami wanted to speak his mind but before he could do so, Field had taken up the box and its contents then ushered him to the door and out into the passage. Down three floors they went in single file then through an unlocked portal to the basement.

Once there, Field did what he had been told to and positioned the box alongside the leather sack and the silver blade. Both men waited in silence for Blandford Parker who had stopped to open one of the side rooms in which they had routinely imprisoned drugged women in preparation for their unholy rituals. The thin, barely-conscious girl he had saved for this very night trudged along at his side mercifully oblivious to her surroundings and to her fate.

Parker took hold of the sack and emptied the thirty silver coins at the head of the red-stained surgeon's table that served as their altar. Next he placed the faintly glowing meteorite a few feet away and then the knife at far end. Both Sami and Field were given silver rods like conductor's batons to grip tightly throughout the ceremony and Parker himself held Veng's Path up in the candle light. He took several deep breaths and then instructed Field to lift the girl on to the table where she lay uncomfortably entwined about the three pieces. When all was settled and quiet, Parker began the incantations in a low voice in which Sami could clearly hear the undercurrent of strain caused by the reading.

Each syllable rang like a bell through the gloom, cutting the dense atmosphere with sonorous intonations. Parker read slowly and clearly yet Sami understood nothing of the strange language nor, if truth be known, did he wish to. When Field, at the instruction of the flushed Parker, drew a rush of blood from the girl's neck, wrists and groin, a bright argent glow filled the room touched at its edges with fire-red flashes. Sami felt the ground shudder beneath his feet and a sound like the distant wail of a thousand dying men reverberated around him.

Amidst this tumult, Sami heard Field shouting at him to stand straight and raise his silver wand above his head. As he did so, he felt more vibrations in the air that transferred in full flow to the rod and then down his arm. Eventually, he felt his entire body trembling like a tuning fork as the eerie sounds resonating after each word filled the space in which they stood. Sami watched without emotion as the girl slowly expired, her blood running and engulfing each of the silver items around her. A cold green fire ran swiftly back along the flow and burnt her flesh. In less than a minute, she was an inferno and soon consumed completely.

Parker's voice grew louder as the fumes from the conflagration caught in his throat. He dared not choke in case the incantation was misspoken. The consequences of such an error were too awful to be contemplated. Sami watched the man struggle with the projection. He saw his skin darken like a chameleon, his eyes roll back into his head between words. The reek of decay and smouldering bones rode the waves of smoke as they rose and settled in a layer beneath the ceiling beams. Suddenly, at his side, Field emitted a below of unbearable agony and in his last seconds of conscious thought, Sami knew that his own torment was but a moment away.

The items on the table were now molten globes of incandescent light that heated then super-heated the air around them. Pulses of raw energy radiated in all directions, surrounding and concentrating upon the three men that stood within its sphere. Field again roared in pain and disbelief as the flesh on his body started to shrivel and congeal. Sami's legs had disintegrated beneath him and as he crumbled to the floor, his last sight in this world or any other was that of Blandford Parker with his hands thrust forward in an attempt to repel the light. Within minutes, both Sami and Field were no more than dust.

When the light finally failed, only Parker still remained standing. His physical body was burnt and scorched but otherwise undamaged. His years of immersion in high magic had somehow protected his form against the ravages of energy brought forth by the terrible passages of Veng's Path. He rocked backwards and forwards as if uncertain how to move without falling, the book still in his hand, its pages intact. Blandford shuffled over to the blackened metal table and stared down uncomprehendingly at the three silver objects still glowing but now cold as the void. What he saw hardly registered in his head as the magic shield that had saved his body had not done the same for his mind.

Parker lived through that night but never functioned properly as a human being again. During his remaining years, he completed only three acts of consequence and then disappeared from the sight of man completely. The first of his tasks was to write to his son who was still at boarding school. In his letter he described to him the most recent events of his life in the hope that his heir, his blood, would understand. He also included a copy of his will that left everything to the boy, his mother, not surprisingly, being long dead.

Blandford bequeathed him his collection of esoteric

books with the exception of Veng's Path which he hid carefully but not so discreetly that one of sufficient calibre might not locate it. It was his last malicious act.

Parker's penultimate brush with the world came when his protective spells around the house dissipated due to his weakened state. Officers of the law who had previously been supernaturally persuaded to omit the premises from their enquiries were suddenly inspired to reopen numerous investigations into the disappearance of young people in the surrounding counties. At first, they had been cordial and indeed sympathetic to the clearly enfeebled old man who apparently lived in the house alone but when excavations into the ground beneath the cellars revealed a horrifying collection of corpses, their attitude changed to one of concentrated inquisition.

It was while these deaths were being looked into that Blandford Parker disappeared from custody. One moment they had him, the next he was gone. Summoning his last vestiges of strength as well as a final invocation for magical assistance, Parker managed to perform his ultimate task on Earth. One of contrition? Maybe. Guilt? Unlikely. The collected items that had transformed into such dangerous and powerful objects had taken on the shape of silver bullets. He could not say why but what he did know was that they could not remain together. It is likely that the effort required to hide these objects away from mankind and to mask his trail was enough to drain him of all vitality.

Blandford Parker's body was never found although many magicians looked for it. The ashes of his confederates, Roland Sami and Thaddeus Field were swept away by the breeze that accompanied the first thunder of leather boots that ventured down into what turned out to be a place of nightmares. With their prime suspects absent, the team set up to investigate one of the most ghastly murder scenes in history were obliged to close the case in the most unsatisfactory way.

The house itself lay empty for several years until

one day another younger Parker returned to claim his birthright. He had received his father's letter and although its contents were a mystery, much like his father, he had been intrigued by its melodramatic feel and the implied promise of serious advantage. With his mother also dead and no siblings to wrangle with, the house and all its secrets were his to explore.

The news of Blandford's arrest had surprised him. The breathtaking brutality of his crimes had struck him as absurd and very likely exaggerated although when his father's escape and subsequent disappearance was revealed, he quickly realised that his own course was set. The blood in his veins was already awash with unnatural desire. The images in his head vivid and vicious, undoubtedly the last transmissions from his waning father. He knew what he had to do. What was left to do.

As he surveyed the ruins of his family home, the future was clear if only tinged red at the edges. He must recover Veng's Path and then he must start at the beginning.

Am I Dead?
By Josef DeCory

Dad is gone and I am dead! I think dad is gone. It is a given that I have died because I was there when I died. But how do I know that dad is gone? My death is a fleeting part of my life and it has only been a few minutes since I died. I can see my old self, lying there, on the floor, with no expression of any kind of life. I can only watch as the thick white flakes glide down outside and then blow away with the wind. I can watch as the snow accumulates and then piles into smaller, then larger drifts outside the window of our living room. I wish I knew this was going to happen, but like everyone else, you can only know that you are dead, when you are dead. And death is nothing like what I thought it would be like, at least not for a 16-year-old boy. I never saw anyone in the afterlife that was already dead, except for that one.

This morning I woke up and did not even give life a second thought. Like most teens I think about school and girls and sex, but mostly video games, and sex, which has not happened for me yet, so video games it is. I wake up every morning and go on with whatever the day demands, whether it is a weekday school day, or a weekend sleeping in day. Today, I went downstairs in my jammie bottoms and no shirt and sat at the breakfast bar while my mom got her shit together. My younger brother and older sister were running around trying to get things ready for their busy lives, and my dad, well, my dad left two hours ago for work.

Mary is my older sister and she is in college. She has to be to class in less than an hour and it takes her thirty minutes to drive there from the house. I am a shithead and I hid her backpack and just watched as she ran around screaming at mom to help her find the damn thing. Mary was really upset and near tears when she came to me screaming.

"I know you took it you little son-of-a-bitch."

Mary had a test that day and was going to fail the course without earning a C on this test. She worked hard at succeeding in college and did not need this added stress to her life. She told me that she would kill me if I ever left her in a lurch like this again.

"Where is my backpack you piece of crap" she screamed at me after about twenty more minutes of looking. Then I grabbed it out of the top of the closet and she shoved me backwards and I fell onto the floor. She ran out of the house to her car and I ran after her telling her she was a bitch. Kyle, my 15-year-old brother ran out to get in the middle of us. He was always trying to stop us from fighting and he pissed me off this morning.

Kyle was standing there in his jammie bottoms too, but he was also wearing his t-shirt. The girl across the street, the one who Kyle had a massive crush on, was watching us all fight, and just stood there and let us go at it until Mary pulled out of the driveway with me calling her a bitch as she drove down our cold, newly paved street in Boone. Kyle told me I was a douchebag as he tried to show off for the girl across the street.

When Kyle stopped to talk to the girl he made the mistake of turning away from the big brother who loved to embarrass the kid brother. I grabbed his jammie bottoms and yanked them down around his ankles, along with his boxers. He stood there with his junk hanging out and the girl laughed out loud. She laughed so hard I could hear her as I walked in to the house. It was so funny because he had such a crush on her and now she knows just how cold it is outside. And she laughed.

"You're dead, you mother…" he yelled at me. He ran to the house and was screaming at me about his dick being seen by the girl across the street. I laughed, she laughed, and mom just kept right on making the lunches for us to eat at school.

"Mom, he pulled my pants down outside and the girl over there saw my dick." Kyle was screaming.

"Young man" she pointed at me, "quit being an asshole."

I like being an asshole, sometimes, and was good at it for just about everyone, except my teachers at school and the few friends that I had. I was mostly an asshole to my dad, who was never around anymore because of work, and my siblings, and sometimes my mom, who was usually calm and nice toward me and everyone else around us.

I told my mom that I walked in on Kyle last night when he was beating off and he had no hair down there. He told me to get out and then threw something at me as I shut the door in a hurry. I told her I think he broke part of the door.

"You really are a dick, you know that dude." Kyle said as he headed up the stairs. He pulled his bottoms down and spread his cheeks a part and showed me his butt hole. He was gross that way. Teen guys are gross when they are brothers or really good friends. Kyle and I are both, although we have our moments. We each have a best friend and all four of us are too into the whole homo, no homo part of our lives. Thomas loves to tell us he loves us, which is a little awkward, but then he follows with, "No Homo." It is just the culture of the teen boy, especially two16-year-olds and two 15-year-olds.

We have all been friends for the last five years. We shared everything together, including puberty, and getting hair, and now Kyle, shaving it off. Why? We shared our move into the new house and the freezing terror we feel every time we go into the basement. I cannot tell what it is, but it seems to know us, and is not yet dead. It seems to know that its demise is coming and will not share with us anything else. We can only guess it is someone who either lives here now, or used to live here. Kyle has gone there and made some sarcastic remarks to it and was actually slapped across the face by the wind that came out of nowhere.

Kyle was about six inches taller than me already and Mary was about an inch taller than Kyle. I hated being 16 and the short kid in the house. Shit, even mom was taller than I by a couple of inches. We were, for all intents and purposes, a normal family except for one little thing—that something in the basement that makes it nearly impossible to go down there without being accosted by some piece of shit who apparently lives down there. He got my mom a great price for the house and we were not afraid of whatever lived down there, we were just terrified of the basement and its atmosphere when that thing is there. He just pissed us off sometimes. He seemed like a spiritless spirit. Like I just said, a kind of soul that was not dead yet, but was just waiting for the right person to give him an afterlife. That person was not dead-- YET!. And I do not want to say it out loud, but it almost feels like it is my father.

I went upstairs to apologize to Kyle and he told me to fuck off. I told him I really did not mean to get his boxers when I pantsed him. He just shrugged it off and said he would take care of me later. He was in the early shift of school during our double session days at Wiregrass Ranch High in Boone, North Carolina. I went in later because I was a junior and we got to choose which part of the day we wanted. I liked to sleep in and this was an opportunity of a lifetime for me.

"It's all good," Kyle said. "I'll get you later." And he walked past me and patted me on the head. I knew it was all-cool with him and went to take a shower. I had to go to the basement to get some towels out of the dryer and then run back upstairs to grab my clothes for school. It was my turn for laundry and I already threw in the towels. The person who is down there, that we never see, only feel, never bothers mom, and I am not sure why that is since she is the scaredy cat of the group. She actually thinks the rest of us are nuts about the thing down there and refuses to even allow such nonsensical discussion of ghosts and goblins and shit like that. Either way, *he*, that *thing*, is usually bothering me. He will bother the siblings once in a while, but he always bothers me.

I opened the door to the basement and walked

down the stairs taking each step very slowly. I walked to the dryer and pulled out the towels and then turned slowly toward the stairs. I took very careful, cautious steps, then when I got to the stairs I started to run up them. Out of nowhere he grabbed my ankle and tried to trip me. I made the mistake of running and was now nearly toppling back down the stairs. I can't tell you how many times I was told by my father not to run on the stairs. I dropped the towels, except for one, and then squirmed my way free and finished the slow walk to the door… and freedom.

Shit, I was 16 fucking years old and I was scared to go into the damn basement. I may be an asshole to people, but it is fun, usually. Maybe I pissed this person off and it is going to come after me and scare the shit out of me. Maybe it is trying to teach me something, like a life lesson. Like don't run on the stairs. Hell, I get enough of that from mom and dad.

After school I walked home with my friend Steven and Kyle, who gets out two hours earlier, was riding by with his friend, Thomas. The little bitch mooned me as they drove by Thomas and me as we neared the house. The little bitch through a donkey at me. That is where you pull you penis between your legs and wiggle your butt cheeks like donkey ears. He was disgusting. Thomas said they had to go to his house for a book, then he would come by for his blowjob.

Steve and I went to the house and grabbed some cookies and milk. Don't judge me, I still like my cookies and milk. It is one of the many things that Kyle and I have in common. I heard him and Thomas come in and I left the stuff on the counter. I yelled out to them that milk and cookies were still out and they ran in and finished off the cookies, poured themselves a tall glass of milk each and then joined us in the living room.

Thomas, a super popular 10th grader, punched me in the balls as he stepped over me. I pulled my jeans and underwear down and asked him if he wanted see what a real man looked like. He pulled his shorts down and shoved his shit in my face. It smelled like shampoo.

"Oh my God, you bitch, you shampoo your pubes." I screamed. He pushed his pecker toward my face and told me I wanted to suck it. I gave him a quick upper cut to the balls and he hit the floor. Kyle sat there and laughed with Steven and then we just watched television the rest of the afternoon until Mary got home from college. Washing my hands after touching his junk was not even a thought I had, until the cold breeze from under the basement door wafted into the living room. Thomas felt it and then asked me what it was. It's that thing in the basement that bothers only the three kids in the house, but mostly me. I had a sudden urge to wash my hands before eating anything else. Then I went into the downstairs powder room and washed my hands.

Mary pulled into the driveway and when she walked in she looked right at me and called me dumb shit. She told me I could starve to death for all she cared and then went to the kitchen. She was going to cook dinner because it was her turn. Since dad worked so much, we had to take turns doing things around the house and it was her turn to cook, my turn to do laundry, in the basement, by myself, and Kyle had to either mow the lawn or shovel the drive the next day. Mom had to work until 10 or 11 and then stop by grandpa and grandma's house to check on them. She was busy as shit, but she did everything she could to make sure we were as normal as possible, especially with dad working so much.

The guy in the basement was pretty active today. It was making sounds more than usual and was really bossy. I was a little scared to go down there to finish the laundry.

Mary always made the best suppers and knew how to make a miserable day, caused by this little asshole of a brother that she actually loves very much, and turn it into a great day with food.

"Are the two friends staying for dinner, or is it just the three of us and the ghost in the basement," she screamed as Steve and Thomas got up to leave.

"See ya gorgeous!" Thomas yelled to Mary.

"Grow some hair on your balls, Thomas!" Mary yelled back.

Mary told me I needed to get the laundry started and might as well have a load in while she was getting dinner ready. I hated going down into the basement. Every time I open the door I remember what dad used to say, "If death said hi to you, would you say hi back?" And I thought about that when I had to go into the basement. I just wish it was someone else's turn tonight. I had one run in with him already today.

I told Kyle I would pay him to go do the laundry. I would give him my entire allowance and paycheck and everything he wanted. I meant to tell him my second born, but shit, I wasn't going to go crazy.

"Ten bucks for me, and ten bucks for Mary, cash up front." Kyle said.

And Mary said, "Hell yes!" from the kitchen. They would both do the laundry and they wanted the money now. I thought about it for a second, then took my wallet out, and gave them my last twenty bucks. I really wanted to save up for a new game, but not having to go down there would be worth this shit.

"Oh yea, you also have to shovel the walk and driveway for the next two weeks" Mary told me. I said okay and then watched her put the famous mac and cheese and burger stuff in the oven. She and Kyle went to the basement, and got to the bottom of the stairs. I watched them from the top and then all of a sudden, as I walked away, a warm wind blew the basement door closed. It was as if someone slammed it very quickly.

"What the fuck was that" Kyle screamed. And then I heard Mary running up the steps and then she tried to open the door. "Open the damn door you little shit."

I was trying hard to open the door. I was screaming that I was trying and heard Kyle screaming that something was wrong. He told Mary that he heard it in my voice. I was screaming and pulling and nothing was happening. They were pushing and nothing was going to give.

"I'll run and get the axe from the garage." I screamed.

I started into the living room and the basement being was in the middle of the living room, staring at me.

"Oh shit, you guys!" I whispered, trying to make it louder. I tried to back up and my legs quit working. I looked out the window in the living room and saw that it was snowing outside. Kyle and Mary were both screaming for me to get out of the house. I could not move except for very small steps. The translucent guy moved toward me and then into a light that came from nowhere.

"DAD?" I said. "Oh My God, it was my father down there!" He told me to quit being an asshole to people. I stood frozen, realizing that this had to mean that my dad was now... DEAD! But . .. how... where... when?

He hugged me, told me he loved me, and Mary and Kyle and Mom, and was gone. The breeze, the being, everything, except that light, was gone. He was dead! And then he released the door on the basement without ever telling me why he was doing this.

By the time Mary and Kyle got out of the basement he was gone. I mean he was totally gone out of the house and the basement and everything. It took them 2 seconds, but when they got to me they saw that something horrible had happened.

It was a very calm, cold, quiet in the house as I leaned up against a wall and watched and thought about my death. I watched as Mary and Kyle froze, and then immediately ran to my body, lifted my head up and took my pulse. Then Kyle started to do mouth to mouth and Mary was practically punching me in the chest. Another cool breeze came into the living room and the front door opened up and the white light, the very same light that showed my dad to me, swept across the floor, and I felt a numbness.

I have felt numb before, but this time, it was my death that felt numb. I started to feel my body pulling on me and tugging me to go back in and try again. Beat,

Beat, beat went Mary's arms across my chest. Blow, Blow, blow came Kyle's breath into my lungs. And then I tasted something, it was an Oreo cookie, the cookies that we just ate a little while ago. I tasted them, but felt as if it was not the same thing. Blow, Blow, blow, and the taste grew stronger.

I came from death to unconsciousness and then awoke with Kyle spewing those damnedable cookie crumbs into my mouth.

"Cody," they screamed, "Cody—Cody—Cody!" and I just lay there, bleeding, with fragments of the glass coffee table all over the floor. It hurt, but I am alive again. There was blood all over the floor and the side of the sofa. It was the same sofa that mom loved, it was the one that dad hated, but put up with for the sake of mom.

"Dad" I remember saying a little while ago. He was hugging me, and I freaked out, tripped and fell on the damned coffee table in a whispery disappearance of my father's spirit.

The ambulance came to the house as I sat up and the paramedics barged in with the stretcher as the police officer pulled up to inform us that our father was in a car accident. He was gone. And as they started to take me to the ambulance, as Kyle and Mary stood by my side, we watched as the imprint of humanless footprints appeared in the snow, walking away from the house. "DAD!" Kyle and Mary whispered.

Bovine Rule
By S.L. Dixon

Curtains drawn, light peeking in around the edges. Quiet, maybe, just maybe they had gone.

Quiet, perhaps it had been nothing more than a bad dream.

Quiet, what if theyd survived whatever mess overtook the... *Moo!*

Tears streamed from the girls cheeks, she was just in for a cup of coffee, she and her fiancé on their way to Auroras Landing for the small ceremony theyd (shed) ached over and molded for months straight. Just a coffee, not a standoff, not the world turned upside down.

Moo! Moo! Moooo!

"Try the phone again, what if it's fixed? Please!" she begged, her name was Laila Moore, formally soon to be known as Laila Knowlton, "They'll have it fixed by now."

"Don't be so damn snippy I tried an hour ago when I woke up, nothing," Freddi Downs picked up the phone, fingered some buttons and waited, silence, barely the electric buzz of a world so close but seemingly away at forever's reach. "Happy?" she asked, slamming the phone back into its cradle.

Freddi opened the Cat's Pajama diner more than a decade earlier; it had become something of a boy's club, farmers mostly. Drinking coffee, eating eggs, oatmeal, hash browns and so on, six mornings a week. The money wasn't great, but it worked and it beat the hell out of working for somebody else.

"What do they want?" Laila begged. She'd been in a state of near hysterics for close to twenty-four hours, ever since she saw her fiancé charged, gored and shaken from life by an angry bovine herd.

None of them had seen anything like it, not even on the worst days on a farm did things ever go down like this. It was insanity incarnate. Duke, a local pokey bumpkin, pulled back the curtain and looked out the window; his eyes met a close up shot, steam and nostrils, *Moo!*

"Maybe they's got the rabbids," Duke suggested.

"Could be the diabetes," Duke's brother Luke suggested, pronouncing it *dia-beat-ess*.

"Could have them AIDS even," suggested the third of the trio, Mook.

"Will the three of you just shut the hell up?" asked Maureen Ringer, she'd stopped for an early lunch. She'd been on the road four hours by the time the rest of them were rubbing the crud from their eyes. Outside in the parking lot, where it might as well have been impounded on Saturn, was her rig. She had to ship a trailer full of fireworks that were to meet shelves all over the north. They'd never get there, not at this rate.

"I concur, the three of you have yapped just about long enough for my patience," Robert Mastenn, local farmer. "I don't mean to get on ya, but… I mean, just, shut it a while."

"How about you all shut up? This supposed to be my day off," said Freddi, it had been a long day. She attempted to get through the alley and to her apartment in the building next to the restaurant but met angry eyes, long faces, snorting mad, chewing cud, the typical features of their bovine captors.

Moooo! The animals cried in unison.

A truck rolled into the lot and the shotgun blasts echoed over the asphalt, "Wooo, got'cha!" shouted a boyish voice, excited. Two more shots followed his voice.

"Wooo, boy you did it!" added another boyish voice.

The Frook brothers all looked out the window, slapping their knees, shouting excitedly, making little sense, but appearing genuinely happy about something on the other side of the glass. The rest ran to join them and witness the spectacle.

Moo! Mooooo!

Outside the shots reported and the cows started to fall, one by one. The sea of cows stampeded, forming a revolving circle around the truck and the boys.

"Wooo!" yelled one of the boys.

"That's Jilly's young'uns" said Duke.

"Sure is," said Luke.

"Damn right," said Mook.

Moo! Down another went, it was more than a sea and Robert saw that if Jilly's boys didn't have about a thousand rounds they were doomed to fail.

A lower grumble sounded, it was deep, rising high, it was like a freight train picking up speed, with a howl like a steam whistle blaring as the engine's chaser.

Mooo!

Thump. Crumple. Bang, the truck flipped on its side, Jilly's boys screamed helplessly, showered in shattered glass as the rifle skittered away, lost in a world of shit speckled hooves.

"Oh Rambo, no," Robert whispered, Rambo was his bull, biggest, strongest, meanest bull he'd ever had and he'd had a few.

Rambo stomped the boy who'd carried the rifle first, grinding him into the pavement. The other boy crawled from the truck and tried to run across the lot to the entrance of Cat's Pajama. Two Jerseys charged him from either direction, both catching a leg. His body tore open like a piñata at a birthday party, bearing a shower of crimson and dark purple gore rather than sweet treats.

The show at the window was over before the tally against the cattle herd was much more than a drop in the milk bucket, nobody said a word, stunned at the sight of the devastated boys.

Laila's weeping renewed.

The hours passed, outside the moos became insistent.

"What do they want?" asked Maureen.

"Maybe they're just pissed, don't like being burgers and milk dispensers," suggested Freddi.

It was a joke; nobody truly suspected the cows had anything other than primal, base needs. None of them believed that the herd could have suddenly acquired new cognitive ability. Nobody laughed at the joke, either. Nobody had laughed for more than a day.

"You'd think someone would come save us by now," said Laila.

"Uh-yeah," agreed Mook, his brothers echoed the sentiment.

Morning turned into afternoon and Freddi dropped two baskets of fries. The power flickered when the mobile phones lost initial connection, but the power continued, thankfully, "If we get out of this, you all owe me for food and shelter, don't you forget that."

It was quiet but for the roll and snap of a lighter, nobody asked for permission, but nobody complained. The Frooks all smoked together in the restaurant, a thin blue cloud surrounding them. It wasn't as if someone might ask them to step outside anytime soon.

Robert searched the parking lot for Rambo, he'd gone from sight, but it felt unlikely that he'd leave off; there were a lot of ladies, heifers, in the lot around the diner and he'd fit right in as the herd leader.

Freddi came out of the back with two more large baskets of steaming hot golden fries, Luke looked at her, "What, no burgs?"

It was so stupid and the stress so thick, laughter erupted, even Luke's brothers laughed.

"What's so fuckin' funny?" Luke demanded.

The others laughed harder and gathered around the food, pigs to the trough. Nobody explained Luke's unwitting joke of tempting fate by consuming beef to further anger the herd outside.

At seven, the chorus of moos rang louder than ever, a constant. The power flickered and died, "No good, no good," Laila fretted, "Oh God, we'll starve, they'll starve us."

"Won't starve, all gas. Might die without water though, we ought to fill what we can while there's still water in the heater," suggested Robert. "Got any candles Freddi?"

Freddi nodded.

"Why are they doing this, why?" Laila begged to anybody and nobody.

Outside, the sun glowed orange as it bowed low toward the distant horizon, the day approaching twilight.

"'Hell is they doing?" asked Duke, Luke said he didn't know, but sulked silently, still wanting a cheeseburger and failing to see the humour in this.

The black and white Holsteins dipped their noses into the pools of gore left from the earlier deaths and jogged to the windows. They pressed their noses on the glass, smearing dark blood as they moved. The Frooks watched the display, too enthralled to say anything more. The cows paraded back and forth and back again, puddle to window, a grim, crude grafitti of bodily fluid spreading out before them.

Maureen stepped next to Robert and shook her head. They stood silent, peering through the wall of glass overlooking the parking lot. The diner had once been a Pontiac dealership; that was decades before Freddi overhauled the space to serve coffee and fries.

"Holy Moses," Robert muttered, Laila screamed out.

The mooing had ceased.

Duke frowned and tilted his head slightly. The blood smears on the glass had begun to represent crude lettering. "Su klim?" he muttered. "What the hell does 'Su klim' mean? Is it foreign?"

"Backwards!" Laila announced, leaping to her feet. "Oh God, oh God, they know how to write, oh God," she rambled, "Milk us! They want us to milk them, oh God please, no."

"Like hell, I hope they're miserable, I ain't milking none of them," said Freddi, indignant.

"What if they let us leave… I think…," started Robert, but slowed himself, he didn't think they'd ever let them leave. They were in a pen, living only as far as their masters decided. It had an eerie sentiment, an unenjoyable case of role reversal.

"No way, we have the power if we don't milk them.

They need us," said Maureen.

That settled it, everyone against Robert. They closed the curtains and sat quietly for close to an hour, the Frook brothers staring out the window, the fascination never waning on their dim minds. Duke looked to Mook who looked to Luke (still pissy), "Hell is they doing now?" they asked simultaneously.

Outside the window very near Laila's booth, two plump beef heifers dropped to their bellies and stared at the curtains.

"Look at them go!" shouted Mook, pointing at the animals in the background who hurried into formation, tattooing a beat on the pavement like parading officers, anxious for orders

Moo! Mooooo!

A stream of small calves charged toward the window. They sprang from the backs of the hunched heifers and burst through the glass. Laila screamed and four of the calves took onto her, gumming and sucking. They searched her body for purchase. Without the proper tools to feast as a carnivore, their reflex was to suck relentlessly. Two more calves charged the Frooks and one ran toward Maureen.

The Frooks managed to hold their own, slicing the small animals with their matching jackknives. The calves cried out, the mother heifers pushed their heads through the windows and called back in plaintive wails.

Maureen wrestled the calf that attacked her; she slammed her knees into its head repeatedly, doing more damage to her legs than the thick skull. She could feel her thigh muscles bruising, her legs seizing up from the heavy impacts. Tables toppled and Maureen fell, the calf stood triumphant, poised to latch onto her. It found her breast and sucked through her flannel shirt, she screamed; the heavy mammary bag was sucked with such force that a seam of flesh began to tear away from her chest. She felt around for a steak knife, anything she could use to defend herself.

Robert chased Laila's cries; Freddi ran into the

kitchen and slammed the door behind her.

Mooo! Mooo!

The Frooks ran to Maureen and stabbed their small knives into the immature beast.

Moo!

The calf howled as the Frooks' joint savagery overcame its strength and it soon fell dead. Maureen still had two breasts, but on the left she felt as though the appendage hung by a thread, the skin had separated in a wide gash, bleeding out in a half moon. She fell backwards cradling her chest, the pain indescribable.

Robert heaved and lifted a calf, tossing it aside. The beast landed and chased back to Laila, "Get off her!" Robert demanded. Laila hadn't been so quiet since her fiancé died. Robert turned his attention to another calf as it ran past him, giving space for the first to return. One finally scored pay dirt and shook at Laila's throat, a short-lived red geyser burst from her neck.

The Frook brothers minced the calves into patties, but it was too late, Laila was dead... thankfully. The cows had eaten her nose, lips, one breast and her right hand. It would've been a hard life had she made it through.

The mother heifers at the window cried out in horror at the destruction of their young and the Frooks rushed with their little knives and stabbed for eyes. They cackled happily as the heifers scattered and they pulled the drapes back over the broken window.

Freddi opened the kitchen door, holding a lit candle in each hand. She called, "They dead?"

The Frooks nodded and Robert looked around the mess, "Got a stool?" he asked.

It was civil and orderly the way the dairy cows waited in lines. Robert sat on Freddi's plastic stool. He hadn't hand milked in a good many years, but it's like swimming, once it's there, it's there. The milk splashed onto the parking lot, there was no use for the liquid.

With every happily sapped cow, another stepped

forward. The Frooks watched, they'd never milked cows, goats yes, but never cows. Teets are teets are teets. They each took a stool out into the lot and more lines formed. The cows remained peaceful while the men milked; eyes wary for any aggressive misstep from the beef beasts.

Maureen watched this and considered her options. The cows focussed on the milking, she grabbed a lighter from the serving counter. She glanced down to Freddi who'd hid and latched her lips to a bottle of gin. Coward.

Moo! Moo! Moo! It was an appreciative noise now, lacking the aggression and menace of earlier.

Maureen ran toward her truck.

Moo! This one was unlike the others, deep and rising to an incredible pitch. Maureen reached the back door and fumbled with the handles.

Mooo!

Robert looked around; he knew Rambo's call anywhere.

Maureen glanced over her shoulder and saw the massive beast charging toward her, just a shadow in the night, but she couldn't mistake the shape. The door opened and she hopped up into the trailer. She hadn't worked out a plan, not really, part of her thought she'd never make it to the trailer. She flicked her lighter and saw the fireworks' packaging, a plan formed. On the roof there were two safety hatches, she could crawl topside armed with fireworks and blast those bovine devils to pieces. And maybe, just maybe.

She tore into the packages looking for the deadliest weapons of the arsenal. She opened a hatch and pushed fireworks out by the armload. Robert and the Frooks all yelled, but it barely rose above the mooing.

She caught bits and pieces, *Up, Watch, Sneak, Smarter*, she catalogued it for a later time, perhaps when she led the victory parade. She gathered a seventh armload and piled it topside, she followed it.

Mooo! The call came as she stood up and looked around. *Clop, clop, clop,* the hooves created a hollow metallic sound. Maureen spun and saw the calves charging, “How in the sweet motherfu…?” the first butted her and chased off the side of the trailer. What she hadn’t seen was the bovine pyramid built on the truck’s nose, foreseeing her every move, the cows piled so calves could run topside of the trailer and meet the self-appointed pyrotechnician.

She thumped to the ground and hopped to her feet. Pain shot through her, but she didn’t have time to consider it, not yet.

Mooo! It was Rambo’s heavy steam engine scream and whistle, rising to a crescendo as he reached the full velocity of his charge.

Smack! Wet and full.

Maureen’s body crumbled as her innards tumbled from devastating open wounds. Blood poured from her mouth and she fell to the tarmac, unleashing a rasping, gargling scream until Rambo stomped on her skull.

Robert and the Frook brothers were spared from the view, but they heard it all. Rambo clopped around the side of the truck; blood glistened in the moon shine, his eyes two black blobs of death, his enormous testicles swinging proudly, a testament of his authority.

All night the four men squeezed the teets, spraying milk about the parking lot. Cats and dogs had come to lap, raccoons and groundhogs approached tentative, but unable to deny the bounty of beverage. At first light the line ceased and the milkers returned to the restaurant. Freddi snored gently in one of the booths on the far side of the diner, away from the windows, away from Laila’s corpse.

Robert, Duke and Mook all flopped into booths; Luke hadn’t yet let his annoyance rest. He didn’t like folks laughing at him, especially not his brothers. If he wanted a cheeseburger, he’d have a goddamn cheeseburger.

He cooked in the dark, the patty nice and pink in the middle, dripping blood down his arm, turning the white bun a soggy pink. He ate half of the fat burger before he returned to the dining room.

Moo! Mooo! Moooo!

The calls came from all around the building. A snort and grunt joined it all. Luke stepped to the window and looked out. Rambo scratched his fore-hoof backwards, stating intent, stating a line crossed. Luke glanced around the diner, looked down at his burger.

Rambo snorted, *MOOO!* The bull charged at the gaping window, Luke peered down at his dripping burger again. It clicked, “Oh right, right, beef,” he said. Rambo came through the window. Luke flew like a ragdoll; Rambo continued his pursuit.

Duke and Mook charged at the bull, “Not my brother!” said one, “Not a Frook, you don’t!” said the other.

Freddi jumped up from behind the counter, “I’m try’n sleep!” Drunk as a teenager on prom night.

Rambo trampled the brothers and snorted at Freddi. Freddi remembered herself and fell back behind the counter. Rambo turned his massive head to face Robert. Robert lifted his hands as if being robbed.

Moo, Rambo called quietly and stepped back through the broken wall.

Robert slept until the cows no longer permitted. He got up and dragged Freddi out with him, gave her a crash course in milking and they sat well into the night, the lot a murky pond of animal waste and milk. They returned to their booths after the long day, fell dead asleep in seconds.

Good thing too, they have a lot of milking to do tomorrow.

Redwood
By Angus Fenton

John's feet ached as they pounded the earth again and again. He wanted to stop and rest but he knew he had to keep going. He leaped across rocks and dodged and weaved through the trees, the full moon providing his only light. The exhaustion seemed to gnaw at every part of him but still he pushed on, he had to. His rush up the last hill was too much. Despite the moonlight it was still difficult to find a clear path back to town.

He weaved through yet another clump of trees when the burning in his lungs became too much for him to bear. He desperately needed to rest.

In an instant he got his wish, though not as he would have liked. His toe snagged an exposed tree root causing him to fall forward. If he had the breath, he would have tried to yell but it was too late, he had already begun to tumble down the hill. Everything became a blur as he was flung head first into the earth. Rocks, trees, plants and branches all whipped, grazed and stabbed him. At last he came to a stop in a gully.

After shaking his head trying to regain his senses, he scrambled clumsily behind a large moss-covered boulder and rested his back on it. He tried to slow his heart rate, mask his now erratic breathing. Before long, the irresistible urge to peek behind the rock drilled into his mind, the past half mile had worn him down so badly that he almost forgot to listen and check behind. But now, he heard nothing, nothing but the wind slowly passing between the foliage overhead and the soft rustling of ancient branches. For a second he let himself believe that he had eluded *It*.

He got back to his feet and slowly, bit by bit, kept moving in his original direction, carefully watching his every step. *Nearly there. Nearly home,* John tried his best to reassure himself. He kept his current pace for a few minutes, right until he heard the growl. A shadow moved through the trees in the corner of his eye. That was enough for him; he spun on his heels and began one last desperate sprint for home. It moved effortlessly through the terrain with inhuman agility. *Just one more hill then I'm home. Almost there.* He gave it everything he had left, just one more hill to climb.

The shadow was moving closer, the growling getting louder. John pushed and pushed, he was almost there, just a few more feet then the town lights would be almost on him. Then, he would be safe. His legs were like lead now and every step caused him to wince. Yet still he forced onwards.

Once he finally reached the top of the hill it was no good, he could do nothing but fall to his knees as they gave way. He did indeed see the street lights of Redwood but they were at least another mile away. He didn't realise just how far into the woods he had walked, not that it mattered now.

As the deep growls grew louder, John tried to get back up to his feet but it was no good. In the end he could do nothing but look up at the round, full moon.

"Oi, Scarlet! Another round for us over here!"

Being the owner of The Weeping Willow had its perks but serving alcoholics like Geoffrey Halloran every night certainly wasn't one of them. Scarlet had grown more than tired of explaining to him that patrons were actually supposed to pay for their liquor. Instead, tonight she opted to merely keep ignoring him. He and his buddies weren't far off collapsing anyway, if the eloquence of their attempts at seducing any nearby females was anything to go by.

It wasn't normally Scarlet's problem to deal with Halloran, that honour was usually left with John Clarkes. Scarlet shrugged and went back to cleaning the bar.

Where the hell is he?

It was going to be a long night with only one staff member.

Anthony Clement rose with the sun. He wasn't one for sleeping in but even if he was, a certain sound on the wind had made it even harder to sleep the night before. He wasn't far from another town now, the last sign he had passed made mention of a 'Redwood'.

This part of the country was different to what he was used to, tall trees surrounded him at every turn. He was much more accustomed to the wider open spaces further north. Clement wasn't a claustrophobic man but he did enjoy a clear view of what he was shooting. He packed his small campsite and saddled his horse.

It wasn't long before yet another sign came into view, this one though, bore alterations. "Redwood – 2" had been completely written over with what seemed to be dark red paint. The new sign read 'WELCOME TO BLOODWOOD'. Clement paused but only for a moment to examine the handiwork. He shrugged, *as long as they got cold beer and warm pie.*

Like most of the towns in the area, Redwood consisted almost solely of a single main street. There were several houses branching off but no more than that.

As Clement passed through one last thick arch of trees, the buildings became fully visible. After being on the road for days he actually found the prospect of civilization to be a welcome change of scenery. In the time since his last pass through a town his face had become caked in dirt and he had acquired a stench worse than that of the animals he was forced to hunt for food.

The town seemed different to others almost immediately, Clement dismounted and led his horse in on foot. It was around mid-day, yet the street lacked the 'industrious buzz' that resonated from other settlements at this time of day. The people in the street seemed guarded, as though they were all carefully watching the very steps they took. Even the children walked slowly and close to their parents.

None of this mattered a great deal to Clement though. He had been travelling alone too long to spare much mind to the play habits of children. More importantly, the smell of cooking meat and pastry had already caught his nostrils.

Following the street, and the scent, Clement came to the largest building in the town. For all its height, the structure was a sorry sight. The wooden boards were visibly deformed and a sign that partially read 'Weeping Willow Hotel' now more closely resembled gibberish.

He hesitated briefly before heading for the entrance. But before he could even reach the door, a uniformed body stopped him.

"We don't take kindly to gun-slinging heroes in this town, my friend."

"I'm not your friend." Clement tried to push past, but the officer was unrelenting.

The uniform made a slow reach for his pistol.

"I'm afraid I can't allow armed men in here."

Clement stopped walking and glared directly into the officer's eyes.

"Listen to me Christine. We can't go back to the farm. I know you want to but we just can't. The Willow is our home now."

"But I want to go back to our real home!"

"Please Christine, I'm busy. Just go play in your room."

Scarlet hated having to scold her sister but with John still failing to turn up to work, she was more stressed than usual.

Christine ran back up the stairs with a frown on her little face. Scarlet was about to call her back when she was interrupted by the loud thud of something hitting the boards outside the front door. Before she had time to react there was another thud.

"What on earth?"

Scarlet reached the window just in time to see Officer Peterson sent flying into the mud by an unknown man's uppercut.

The stranger turned and began to walk away from his downed opponent.

He only took three steps before Scarlet saw the policeman reach for his pistol. It did little to even the odds though as the stranger drew his own twice as fast.

"Not wise, *my friend*."

Obviously stunned by the stranger's speed, Peterson took his chance and made a run for it.

The stranger shook his head while holstering his gun. "Shame."

He then turned once again and moved for the hotel door.

Scarlet hurried back to the bar counter, mumbling as she went. "Great! Just what I need."

The Willow's front door flew open and in staggered the stranger, clicking his tongue as he gazed around at the large room.

"I'm not usually an optimistic man, but I really was hoping this place would be just a little better on the inside."

Scarlet didn't know if she was meant to hear the remark but pretended she didn't anyway. She wasn't afraid of the stranger; she had dealt with her fair share of gunslingers. Still, there was a certain look in this one's dark eyes that made her double check the rifle hidden under the bar counter.

The man reached the bar and was about to open his mouth but Scarlet cut him off.

"Was all that really necessary? We've got quite enough trouble around here at the moment!"

"And a pleasure to meet you too. Clement's the name. Anthony Clement."

Scarlet shrugged, unimpressed.

"Well?"

Clement continued feigning ignorance, "Well, what?"

"Nothing. Forget it. What can I do for you?"

Clement smiled smugly and did his best to settle

into the least rotten bar stool.

"Let's see. Maybe a horse? Mine took off when I was unceremoniously assaulted."

This time his efforts to rouse her hit thin air and he was promptly ignored.

"Or maybe not. Well a room would be a nice start anyway. I must say I'm exhausted."

"Yes, I imagine beating innocent strangers senseless must be quite tiring."

Scarlet had stopped drying glasses and now rested one hand on the cold metal barrel of her rifle.

She kept her eyes fixed on Clement's dirty, scarred face. He remained passive but she could tell he knew what she was doing.

"Well more or less. Anyway, like I said, I really could use a rest so may I have a room? Please."

Scarlet hesitated for a moment, still closely watching the gunslinger's eyes. She eventually relented, took her hand away from the weapon and reached for the key rack behind her head.

"Number fourteen. Up the stairs, end of the hall."

She placed the key on the counter and went back to her glasses.

"Thank you," Clement said as he got to his feet, "Oh I don't think I caught your name, either."

"Scarlet."

"Well thank you, Scarlet. But one more thing, I think someone defaced your town sign. You wouldn't happen to know why, would you?"

Scarlet gazed up from the counter, perplexed. She looked into Clement's eyes for a moment before softly answering.

"You really have no idea where you are, do you?"

He made no effort to answer.

The night descended quickly in Redwood. The Weeping Willow's few usual patrons ambled in and resumed their nightly positions. Clement ate at the bar and looked around at the sorry group of individuals. There were at least a dozen of them. Mostly common bar flies and a couple that seemed to have come to eat out.

What each of them had in common, though, was a general look of uneasiness. Rain had just started to fall which only seemed to add to the discomfort. The shaking of one man's hand became so intense that he spilt beer across himself as he drank.

"They always like this?" Clement asked, shovelling more pie into his mouth.

Scarlet also seemed more troubled than before.

"It's fine," she replied, hurrying away to tend to other patrons. She had already gathered that Clement was a perceptive man but, as far she could tell he hadn't picked up on the lie. She stopped in her tracks as the first clap of thunder struck.

No, no. Not now.

The hotel patrons jumped at the sound and one even began to quietly sob. Scarlet quickly strode back to the bar to check her rifle when Christine came running down the stairs.

"Scarlet, Scarlet! The storm, it's another storm!"

Tears rolled down the little girl's face as she ran to embrace her sister.

"I know, I know. It's going to be fine. We're going to be just fine."

Despite her sister's words, Christine continued to cry, gradually becoming more and more worked up.

"But it's coming isn't it?"

"Shh, nothing is coming it's just a storm. We're going to be-"

"No we're not! It's coming! It always comes in the storms!"

"Christine, enough! Please!"

But it was too late. The girl's cries had carried across the whole room.

"What did she just say? W-what was that?" came one voice.

"She's right! It always comes with the storms!"

"Oh God, oh God! We have go! We have to get out

of here!"

The room erupted as the patrons burst into fevered panic. All except for the lone man at the bar, still eating his pie.

"What the hell's the matter with you people?" Clement spat large crumbs as he shouted at the other patrons, "Never seen a damn storm before?"

The others paid no attention. They had gathered at the windows now, staring out with bated breath at each roar of thunder.

Scarlet stood at the bar, clutching her sister.

"Please, *please,*" she whispered.

But her pleading did no good. With another enormous crack of thunder a colossal gust of wind surged through the town and crashed against the hotel. One by one, the lanterns of the town were extinguished and there was nothing but a pitch black mass in their place.

The silence of the hotel patrons turned quickly to panic and shrieks.

"Oh my God! What are we supposed to do now?"

Scarlet simply shook her head and held Christine even tighter.

"No, no! Not again!"

As the panic began to rise, a single voice cut through.

"As much fun as all this seems to be, I think I really am going to have to get some sleep. So if you would all be so kind as to keep your charades down, I would be most grateful."

Totally disregarding the terror of the other hotel patrons, Clement rose from his seat and headed for the stairs. Scarlet snapped out of her daze as he brushed past.

"No, don't go! We need your help!"

Clement shrugged as he began to climb the stairs.

"I think you have quite enough players already, milady. I'm sure you'll be just fine."

"Listen to me, you bastard!"

Clement made no reply except to blow a kiss her

direction before disappearing up to the second floor.

"Damn it! Alright, Christine, I need you to go sit behind the bar, you'll be safe there. Go!"

Scarlet pried her sister from her hip and ran over to the group of still panicking patrons. "I know you're all scared, so am I. But I need you all to listen to me. We will be fine. We will be safe here but I need your help."

The group seemed to settle slightly at Scarlet's words, all of them but one.

"A-and who p-put you, the bar wench, in charge?" came inebriated slur of Geoffrey Halloran.

Scarlet wasted no time and strode right up to the drunk, so close that her nose almost touched his stubbly chin.

"If you wish to continue breathing in my hotel then you can do as I say," she said quietly through clenched teeth, "or perhaps you'd prefer the outdoors?"

"No, no. Here is just fine," Halloran muttered, sitting back down.

"Good. Now all of you, help me get all these tables against the doors and windows."

"A table?" came another voice. "That's not going to make a difference!"

"It will be better than nothing. Now help me!"

Between the whole group, it didn't take long to assemble the furniture barricade. With their work finished, they huddled together in the middle of the room.

The town was still enveloped in total darkness, yet to everyone's surprise and relief the rain had at least lessened to a light pattering drizzle on the earth outside. The panic that had previously held the room had begun to disappear and the patrons breathed normally again. Christine tip-toed over to her sister.

"I-Is it gone, Scarlet?" she whispered.

Her sister hugged her close but said nothing.

Above Redwood, the gloomy clouds parted ever so slightly causing small patches of the wooden hotel floor to glow in the moonlight.

Scarlet was just about to answer her sister when a

splash outside interrupted. She looked around the group but seemed to be the only one to notice.

Not wanting to alarm the others, she walked slowly toward one of the windows. It was still too dark to see anything outside but it didn't stop her from hearing another, quieter splash, closer this time. She was about to return to the group when she heard the boards outside the window creak. Scarlet had heard the creak of drunken footsteps enough times to know it was not the same sound she heard now.

"Alright, I have had quite enough of this," Halloran shoved his way from the group, "I'm leaving. There's no way I'm hiding in here a whole night with you lot! I bet there's nothing even out there".

Scarlet watched in dismay as Halloran began dismantling the barricade at the door.

"Wait, stop! Halloran! Don't!"

She and the others called to him as quietly as they could but he had already vanished into the darkness, leaving the door wide open behind him.

Scarlet ran to the barricade.

"Quick! Someone help me with this!"

"We can't just let him go!"

"He made his choice, now help me!"

The rest of the group slammed the door shut and reassembled the furniture, then resumed their huddle in the middle of the room.

Before long the silence was interrupted by the sound of running footsteps and screams from outside.

"Open the door! For the love of God, open the door!"

The group jumped as Halloran reached the door and began pounding.

"Please! Please, just let me in! I'll-"

He was cut off as the sound of multiple, faster steps reached the door too. Scarlet held Christine tight and covered her ears as she began to cry again.

The sickly sound of tearing, crunching and splattering flooded into the room before all went silent once again.

Scarlet rocked Christine back and forth, whispering to her, “We’re alright, we’re all fine.”

The others similarly tried to console each other, shutting their eyes and attempting to hide their sobbing.

So tightly shut were their eyes that they didn’t notice Halloran’s bloody, thumbless hand press against the window before slowly slipping away.

Clement rose early as usual and withdrew his loaded pistol from underneath his pillow.

To his surprise, he was not met with any warm rays of sunlight as he gazed out the bedroom window. On the horizon, the sun could only just be made out behind the barrier of towering pines surrounding the town.

Redwood appeared deader than the previous day. The puddles in the street had grown to ponds in the night, though the rain had now stopped.

Clement looked back around the room for any more of his belongings, before heading downstairs for the foyer.

He only needed to get halfway down the steps before he could see things were different. He continued to the floor and gazed around the room. Glasses and cutlery were strewn across the boards and all the furniture was piled and stacked by the front door. Only Scarlet remained, hunched over the bar.

“I have to hand to you, Miss, you certainly know how to throw a party.”

Scarlet laid her head in her hands.

“It was no party,” she mumbled.

Clement ignored her and continued,

“If I had have known what fun you were having-”

Scarlet jumped to her feet, marched over to Clement and seized him by the arm. “Alright, come with me. There’s something you need to see.”

She squeezed his arm tightly and led him through the furniture heap and out onto the front veranda.

"Does this look like fun to you?" She pointed Clement to the large and still damp puddle of blood dripping through the wooden boards. Amongst the crimson were several small clumps of what he knew to be flesh. He knelt down for a closer inspection and even noticed three finger nails that had slipped through the boards. Above them, the bloodstains seemed to have faint streaks leading off into the mud.

Clement stood up again and leant against the hotel wall. He knew he was always a heavy sleeper when he finally got a real bed. But as a man who prided himself on his keen senses, the fact he had missed such an attack troubled him.

"Well, you've certainly got a hell of a town here, Miss."

Scarlet crossed her arms and walked up to Clement.

"I asked for your help last night. You could have helped me to avoid this."

"Avoid what exactly? Break-ins happen all the time. Sometimes, people die. Try if you must to blame me, but these things happen."

"A break- a break in?" Scarlet almost laughed, "Is that honestly what you think this is?"

Clement rolled his eyes and stepped off the boards and onto the muddy earth below. "I'm sorry for what you lost and this mess you have to clean up, but I'm leaving."

"You're part of this too now, you know. It knows you're here."

Clement had already turned and began to trudge away.

"It knows you're here!" Scarlet shouted after him.

He stopped and turned back to face her.

She jumped down from the boards and walked up to him. "Please. All I'm asking for is your help. You can handle yourself, I saw the way you scared off Peterson. There's no one left, everyone else in the town is too scared to do anything."

Clement was silent.

"Just help us, please. Help me keep my sister safe. That's all I want."

He finally spoke.

"Just one question. Which one is the road out of here?"

The Redwood stables were in a worse condition than The Weeping Willow. The timber roof was beginning to cave in and the old pines surrounding the structure looked ready to collapse at any minute.

Clement had considered simply stealing one of the horses like he usually did. But every time the thought came to him, he remembered the stunned, speechless face of Scarlet he had seen earlier. Bearing this in mind, he elected to wait until the owner finally showed up.

He had tried to pass the time by napping in the hay but hours had now passed and still nothing. A light misty rain had already begun to blanket the town , bringing with it a fog. Clement liked to think he had the capacity for patience when necessary. Today however, it was not a virtue he possessed.

Picking out a suitable black mare, he began to saddle the animal when a voice came from behind. "Can I help you?"

He froze and prepared to put on his best 'innocent yet reasonable face'. When he turned around he caught sight of an old man he knew could only be the stable owner. Yet to Clement's surprise, he didn't seem to be talking to him, he was facing someone else around the corner of the stable.

A woman's voice came in reply. "No, thank you. I'm browsing."

Scarlet.

Clement considered removing the saddle and feigning innocence. He knew it was too late, though and elected to keep going anyway.

Scarlet walked slowly up to the horse pen fence, clearly unsurprised to see Clement.

“I knew I’d find you here. Oh and stealing your way out, too.”

He stopped and turned to face her.

“Look, like I said earlier, I’m leaving. Why don’t you just go back to your hotel and your sister?”

Scarlet frowned, though still noticeably calmer than before she clearly wasn’t ready to give up. “Why are you so eager to leave? Just tell me that. I’ve seen dozens of gunslingers pass through this town and yet you don’t seem to be the type that scares easily. So if not fear, then what? Where are you going, Anthony Clement?”

He broke her gaze and turned back to the mare, hesitating before he replied. “Nowhere. I’m passing through. I like to travel.”

It then dawned on Scarlet that for the first time in their interactions, she had hit a nerve and gained the upper hand.

“Travelling? Is that so? It doesn’t matter. The only other way out of here without taking a nice day long hike is Mulderson’s road. I don’t know if you saw it or not? It’s the tiny little one to the west. The one that leads straight into the hills. And the forest.”

Clement didn’t reply and mounted the horse, leaving the pair in silence for a moment.

“Look, wherever you’re going, whoever you’re off to rob, can’t it wait? I realise we’ve just met, but we need your help. I need your help.”

“Sorry, I’m just passing through.” And with that, Clement and his stolen mare vanished into the fog.

Clement had been riding at least half an hour, or so he thought. The further he went, the more the fog deepened. If the sun was still up, he didn’t know. He was unable to pick up any great speed, for every time did, he found himself narrowly escaping collisions with trees.

Looking down, even the ground was difficult to see. Everything around him had become a sea of blurs.

Just as he was considering turning back, a snapping sound caught his ears.

"Steady, girl," he whispered, trying to comfort his horse, "It's probably nothing."

Nevertheless, he found himself reaching for his pistol.

Crack.

Closer, this time.

He tried facing the sound and waited a moment.

Silence. Until-

Crack. From behind, now. Clement relaxed slightly.

Great. Bandits. I should have known they'd be out in pairs.

"Alright. You can come out gentlemen. I don't have anything. I spent the last of it on my mare here."

There was no response. His mock surrender failing, Clement withdrew his pistol and pulled back the hammer.

"I tried to play it your way, but very well."

Crunch.

"That's the way, out you come."

Crunch. Snap.

Clement continued pretending he had the upper hand, unaware of the slowly quickening footsteps coming from behind.

"I don't have all day you know."

Crunch. Crunch. Snap.

"What the-"

Out of nowhere, one of the blurs around Clement seemed almost to take flight towards him, knocking him from his horse with a force that left him struggling for air.

He landed on the hard ground with a dull thud that threw his pistol from his hand and left him dazed. As the world around him began to spin, he caught sight of where the gun landed and desperately began to crawl for it. His whole body ached and warm blood trickled down his nose, but he knew retrieving the weapon was his only chance at survival.

Behind him the sound of heavy breathing and steps grew louder.

Clement made one last desperate lunge for pistol.

Finally getting a hold of it, he rolled onto his back in an effort to lay eyes on his attacker and get in just one good shot. He was relieved to finally have a weapon back in his hand, but this quickly failed as he struggled with the hammer, lacking the strength to pull it back.

Little by little, the hulking black blur closed in on him.

"Come on, come on," he mumbled.

The shape was almost on top him when-

Bang!

A thunderous gunshot came from behind, vanquishing the black blur to foggy depths.

Before Clement could process what had happened, he was being dragged away by something.

"Come on, we don't have much time," a voice said, "I'm going to need a hand here; I can't lift you onto the horse myself. Just one push, come on, you can do it!"

Struggling to stay conscious, Clement used what was left of his strength to heave himself up onto the stranger's horse.

"Good, good. There you go, now hold on."

The tight squeeze of the stranger was the last thing Clement remembered before the world went black.

A light pulled Clement's eyes open. His chest still hurt, but someone had propped him against a rock. He appeared to be in the forest but everything was covered by blinding white light.

Suddenly, a voice emanated from within the glow.

"He nears the door, Anthony. The White Eagle has almost reached the door. You know what you must do."

Before Clement could react, everything began to go dark a second time.

"But now you must sleep."

When he finally came to, he found himself staring straight into Scarlet's scowling green eyes. "Well, well. The big tough gunslinger finally wakes up," she chided, draining a bloodied rag into one of several bowls of water.

Clement coughed heavily, but forced himself to sit up on the counter. His torso ached and was now covered with thick bandages. At first the dream had seemed so real, yet Scarlet had clearly brought him back to the Willow and performed some kind of amateur surgery. Hallucinations would have to wait.

"It was you," he coughed. "You scared that thing off! You never needed me at-"

"First of all, it wasn't *scared*, you idiot, it was toying with its food. Don't you think something with speed like that would have killed you where you lay if it wanted to? It wanted sport. And secondly, you're just lucky your stubbornness is matched only by your poor navigation skills. Turns out you didn't stray too far from town. You weren't difficult to find and I already knew following Mulderson's road was certain death for anyone."

"There is nothing wrong with my navigation! I've-"

"Yes?"

He paused, his wounds catching up with him. "I've just never seen fog like that before. It was like blindness."

"Now you know what we're up against. Now, as soon as you're well you can help-"

Clement, seemingly recovering his bravado, cut her off, "I'll help, alright. I'll help right now. I'll enjoy putting down whatever the hell did this to me." He climbed from the counter and gingerly walked over to his clothes to get dressed.

"Good. And I'm coming too. Whether you can muster up the brain power to admit it or not, you need help. Now more than ever."

Scarlet was surprised to find no objections. Clement smiled. "Don't worry milady, I'm not quite as stupid as you may think."

Clement struggled over another fallen tree trunk. He was only just beginning to think heading out so soon may not have been such a good idea.

Scarlet watched from behind as he winced but

quickly tried to regain his stride.

"Are you alright? I need help out here, Clement. Not an invalid to weigh me down."

"You should worry less about me and more about yourself. I'm fine. Besides, we must be getting close now."

The return trip to the woods had been made easier by the parting of the fog. The pair were deep inside now and still had no sign of the shadow.

"Haven't you ever wondered what it is? I mean, it's been attacking the town for how long, a few weeks?"

"Of course I've wondered. Everyday. What it is. And how I can kill it."

The two continued in silence for a few seconds before Scarlet spoke again. "Years."

"I'm sorry?"

"You were wrong. It hasn't been here a few weeks. It's been here years. Five years."

It was late in the night when Clement and Scarlet heard the sound of the steps ahead. Heavy steps, cracking sticks underfoot.

Clement froze at the sound.

"Wait, shh," he whispered. Scarlet stopped behind him.

"What is it?"

"Down there." He gestured to the huge drop in front of them.

The pair gradually edged closer the source of the sound.

Sure enough, in the gully below, Scarlet could see something moving. While it was still too dark to determine what, it was definitely large enough. She couldn't make out what the shadow was doing. It seemed to hug close to the ground as it moved, as though searching for something lost in the foliage.

Clement, though also puzzled, had already begun to move around the edge of the gully.

"Come on, we need to get a better look when it

steps into the moonlight."

"No, let's kill it now and be done with it," Scarlet whispered, lifting her rifle.

"We can't even be sure that this is it. We need a better look."

Scarlet gritted her teeth. "Fine."

She followed Clement as they slowly circled around the ditch until they found a better vantage point atop a boulder.

"Here. And now we wait."

Below them the shadow moved slowly and carefully, its large form pulsating in the darkness.

Scarlet began to grow impatient.

"Clement, look. It's obviously not human. We need to kill it now-"

She was cut off as he put his hand across her mouth. "Look."

Bit by bit, the mass moved from the shadows and out into the moonlight. Scarlet's eyes widened. The shadow wasn't looking for something. It was eating. A pile of red bones and torn clothes lay in a pool of dried blood behind *It*.

"Well, milady, you were right. It's no man."

Within moments, the creature had revealed itself. Its pitch black fur glistened in the moonlight as it dropped a bloodied bone from its mouth.

Scarlet was bewildered. "What- what is it? A cat? I've never seen anything like it. Some kind of giant cat."

"A panther," Clement whispered, drawing his pistol.

"A what? How do you know?"

"I've seen one before," he said, turning to face her, "but it was locked away. A circus attraction when I was a boy."

Scarlet raised her rifle. "And do they all have red eyes?"

"I don't think-" Clement was interrupted by a growl from the gully. In an instant, the panther flicked its tail and made for the other side of the ditch, easily gliding up to the higher ground.

Scarlet got to her feet and began to run.

"Come on!" She shouted.

He got up and staggered after her as quickly as he could.

The pair had a significant head start but the panther was gaining ground, the unnatural glow of its eyes drawing closer and closer.

"Get down!" Scarlet yelled as the panther was almost upon them.

Clement dropped to the ground just as she fired at the animal. The bullet flew past him, grazing the head of its target enough to slow it down.

"I'll lead it this way!"

"What the hell are you doing?"

"Not weighing you down. I'll take it from here!" Clement shouted, cocking his pistol as he headed deeper into the woods. Sure enough, the panther changed course.

"Come on you bastard! Over here!" he yelled, firing round after round.

Three of the six bullets met their marks and the beast reeled in pain, yet still it would not relent. Clement stopped running and hid behind a tree to reload.

"Why won't you just die?"

He managed to get two rounds into the chamber before the panther appeared and effortlessly knocked him to ground. In a single swipe, it clawed at his chest, opening his bandages and the flesh underneath. He tried to fight back but the pain and weight of the animal were too much. He kicked and thrashed only for his face to be slashed with another claw.

Just as the animal prepared to taste Clement's jugular, a shot rang out. Then another, leaving him covered in blood that was not his own. The panther suddenly became still and slumped down on top of him.

"Give me your hand!"

Suddenly, for the second time that day, Clement found himself being dragged to safety by the very same saviour.

Once she had him clear of the panther, Scarlet pulled him to his feet. Quickly redrawing her rifle, she squeezed the wood to try and calm her shaking hands.

"Is- is it dead?"

Clement bent over and picked up his own pistol, breathing deeply to calm his own nerves. "It is. You did it Scarlet. Thank you."

The two looked at each other in silence for what seemed like an age until Scarlet finally relented and lowered her guard.

Still saying nothing, she dropped her rifle, walked right up to Clement and wrapped her arms around him. And he did the same.

The next day, Clement saddled his horse in front of the Weeping Willow as Scarlet watched on from the doorway. For the first time in months, the sun shone brightly on the town as people once again came out into the street.

"Where will you go now? Honestly."

Clement hesitated before answering.

"I'm looking for someone."

"A friend?"

"Not exactly," he replied, mounting the horse. "You could come with me, you know. I could use someone at my back."

Scarlet scoffed at the thought.

"As appealing as that sounds, I have everything I need right here. I need to look after my sister. Besides, there are funerals to hold. Someone has to go and bring those bones home," Scarlet paused and looked at her feet before continuing, "They deserved better than that. Especially John."

Clement wanted to say something to her but couldn't find the words.

"Before you go Clement, one last thing. That "panther", animal or not, I've never seen anything with eyes that glow like that. You can't tell me that was natural. And one day it just shows up. How did something like that even get here?"

He pondered the question a moment but had no answer.

"When I find who I'm after, I'll be sure to ask them."

And with that, Anthony Clement rode for the newly cleared Mulderson's road and out of Redwood.

Bedlam Betty

By Brian Barr

Jason had started to work for Carl Manzetti, the horror comic god, a couple of weeks ago. Since childhood, Jason's dream had been to study art and writing under the great Manzetti. Manzetti's dark, shadowy prints with their fine lines and concentrated attention to minute details had fascinated Jason since the first time he had read Death and Destroy, one of Manzetti's many classics.

Now, living in the filth and scum of a dirty apartment with his girlfriend in a downtown major metropolis, Jason had something to bring sunshine to his desolate life every day. Comics. He was really doing it, taking the metro every morning, and walking into Death Bed Studios, studying with Manzetti, preparing his tools, cleaning the shop. The place was usually a mess, but things had gotten a little more organized since Jason had come into the shop. Manzetti didn't have time to clean anything; the legendary artist was too busy being a genius.

"This is one of my favorite characters I ever created," Manzetti said as he pulled out an old bristol sheet from his desk drawer. On the surface was a semi-realistically drawn portrayal of a woman with a million contradictions that seemed to balance and conflict with one another. She was a beautifully deadly female, yet tragically ugly at the same time, grotesque and appalling. A scary woman, her physique was athletic yet curvy, her eyes raging yet her countenance calm, her head shaven and covered with deadly scars. At the edges of her fingers, where her fingernails should have been, were long, sharp and shiny scalpel blades. "Jason... meet Bedlam Betty. A former prostitute that was murdered on the east side and buried in a garbage bin. She came back to life with a vengeance, and goes on to slaughter johns, pimps... men in general."

"Christ." Jason held the page with honour after Manzetti handed it to him. "This is badass. Mr. Manzetti, I've never seen her in any of your books anywhere."

"That's because I wasn't able to do anything with her." Manzetti shook his head pitifully. "The publishing company I was with at the time said she was too offensive. The murder of a prostitute? Feminists would have been on our ass left and right. The funny thing is... I made her as a symbol *for* feminism."

"A murdered sex worker comes back to showcase her pain and hurt to others." Jason couldn't help but orally analyse Manzetti's statements sometimes. "I get it. But I can see how such a character could end up offending people instead of empowering them. Still... your characters have always offended people."

"That's what I told the company. But they shelved her." Manzetti sighed.

"Well, you have your own studio now. I mean, you worked hard enough to make your own name for yourself. You don't need anyone else. You could release her in a new story."

"I'm thinking about it, kid. Thing is, I signed a stupid contract at the time. The company was going to own any character I created for at least twenty years, whether they were rejected or accepted. The time I created her and introduced Bedlam Betty was only a little over two decades ago. Their ownership of her would have just expired."

"Well, hell, Mr. Manzetti. People are a lot more open minded to fucked up shit like this now. You might as well put her out there. She's your favourite character, right?"

"Right." Manzetti rubbed his beard and looked at the picture longingly. "But with my age.... it's getting harder to just sit at this desk. And all the kids draw digitally now. They turn in their work faster, can do more. What can I do to compete with that, huh? Sure... I got loyal readers. I get paid lots for commission work. But soon, Jason... I'll probably kick the bucket.

"That's why I chose you as an apprentice, kid. I saw the stories you wrote. I liked your artwork. You got a lot of potential, and I could see you were influenced by me. That's why I wanted to tell you about Bedlam Betty. That's why it would be an honour... if you did a story for her."

"Me?"

"It could be a one-shot... a series. Whatever you want."

Bedlam Betty *did* look cool... and what an honour would it be to work on a story for Manzetti. Sure, Jason had a plethora of ideas and characters of his own he had waiting in the wings, creepy crawlies and dead, flesh-burned creatures dripping with blood and pus from every pore. Still, this was a new one, a dark, scary character with some sort of social commentary embedded in its very being. Jason had never thought so deeply about the characters he created, although he had always seen some pretty impressive themes in Manzetti's work. If only that brilliance could rub off on him.

And here, he's giving you a chance, Jason. Just take it.

"I'd be honoured. When should I start?"

"Well, there's no rush, kid. Take a few of these sketches home." Manzetti pulled out a bunch of papers from his draw and handed it to Jason. So many different shots and concepts of the Bedlam Betty character... all so awesome. "Study her. Get to know her. Fall in love with her. Feel her pain and woes. Do a few sketches of your own and make her yours. Then, outline. Come up with a story. Throughout the week, when you feel like you've gotten a solid tale worked out, you can spend your after hours here, in the studio, working on it."

"You'd let me work with your tools here? When you're out?"

"You've done a lot for me in a short time, Jason. Cleaned the place up. Made everything nice and tidy. Get what I need whenever I ask, and take all my advice when I give it. Here. I want to do for you what I wish someone had done for me when I broke out into this business. I had all the talent in the world, but not the smarts, and definitely not the guidance. If I can break you into a dependable and independent business habit, so you can avoid all of the vultures of the field, then I'd say I'm doing my job right, kid."

"Thank you, Mr. Manzetti."

"Good. Now go home. Have an early day. And make Betty shine!"

"I'll make her bloody instead." Jason smirked. "How's that?"

"Even better!"

After waving farewell to Mr. Manzetti, Jason walked towards the door. The smirk hadn't left his face. *Wait till I tell Jocelyn about this.*

"No fucking way." Jocelyn, Jason's girlfriend and fellow horror comic geek, was practically gushing over the pages Mr. Manzetti had given her boyfriend. "He's letting you work on this?"

"Fuck yes." Jason smiled as he pulled out his drawing pad and pulled out a paper. "Never released to the public. A genuine Manzetti character. And he's letting me work on her."

"She looks fucking brutal. I'm jealous." Jocelyn kissed her boyfriend on the face. "If only I could write and draw like you. Character like this would be best portrayed by a female anyway... based on the background info you gave me."

"I swear I'll try to channel my inner ovaries in portraying her," Jason swore as he started to sketch a rough outline of the face. Betty had such a cruel and angular, yet attractive skull-line. "So he wants me to channel her pain... her rage. The whole murdered prostitute thing. Glad I studied Jack the Ripper in high school. That might help."

"Lots of other horrid cases you can study along with that. More modern ones. The way sex workers are treated around the world is fucking horrible."

"You would think law enforcement would do more to protect the women caught in that lifestyle… other than just throwing them in jail." Jason was drawing Betty's body now. Manzetti had her looking like a noir whore, with seductive dress and a boa, but Jason was going more his approach- a punk approach. He was giving her a studded leather jacket, snarling full lips, squinting eyes of hate. Maybe he would add some tattoos...

Jocelyn smirked. "Wow. Are you modelling her after me?"

"She's got your dress sense, that's for sure."

"She's far more athletic than my fat ass, though."

"Babe, you're not fat. You just have a nice ass. Just the way I like it. Anyway. The hands." Jason had waited for this moment. Now, he could draw those scalpel nails, nice and long, shiny and dangerous.

"Yes... fuck yes." Jocelyn looked the picture over. "This is so good. I'd be smart by assuming this project's top secret, huh?"

"Yes, you would."

"Damn... would love to show Dee and everybody what a great character you inherited here."

"Can't have anybody stealing from my future prized achievement," Jason noted. He was drawing the lower body now, very intrigued with the work he was doing. "If only I could do more with this. Trying to think..."

"You don't want to overload it, Jason. It's perfect."

She was right. The design was perfect.

And he was making it his. Entirely his.

"Betty wanted to make something out of herself... to break out of the dark business she had buried herself in. But her mobster boyfriend and pimp wouldn't have it. BLAM! After mercilessly beating her and letting his hired guns have their way with her, he ordered that she was shot in the back of the head. They dumped her down in a garbage bin, found on the side of an abandoned building.

"Little did they know that that building had been used by a bunch of squatter kids playing with magic manuals and rituals. They had opened up doorways that they didn't understand through their dabbling with dark grimoires and ancient spells they found in libraries and discarded books. Such a location made a dead body the prime subject for infestation and possession. Poor Betty's soul didn't have a chance. She was invaded while she was still on her last breath, recoiling for that final gunshot wound that hadn't ended her just yet. The demons read her thoughts, learned her past, saw her desire. They empathized with her, instantly hating her foes. They heard her calling for retribution... and instantly, they saw to her request. They wanted to liberate her, and so, upon her death, they granted her the power..."

"The power that made Bedlam Betty." Manzetti nodded with approval over the punk style interpretations of his character that he was seeing in Jason's submitted work. "Wow, kid. You really put a lot into this."

"I tried." Jason smiled. "Had to make this my own, somehow."

"I never thought of the whole possession and magic, demonic bit. Guess I was just thinking, hey, lady dies, comes back to life. You made it fantastical but logical. How else would she come back?"

"Aw, please, Mr. Manzetti. It's your character."

"No, no. She's yours now. When do you start on the comic art?"

"Since I wrote the first script last night, I'm starting tonight."

"First script." Manzetti smiled.

Jason grinned back. "This will be an ongoing series."

"And I'll help you get it out there. My fans have already liked the prints you've shown on the website. They're already calling you Manzetti Jr. on the forums. Tonight, huh? So fast!"

"It's like a fever, Mr. Manzetti. I have to keep working on her."

"Creativity is like that, ain't it?"

"It's never been like this before. I swear."

Manzetti stared down on another one of Jason's sketches and nodded. "I know that feeling. I felt the same way about Betty when I started planning her out two decades ago. Couldn't stop sketching her. Went into a deep depression when she was rejected... but had to keep going."

"What inspired you, Mr. Manzetti? What made you create Bedlam Betty?"

Manzetti just sat there for a long stretch of seconds. Finally, he replied. "I don't know."

But everything in his eyes said he did.

Every night, for at least a six hour stretch, Jason got to work on the first Bedlam Betty issue. He knocked out 2-3 pages a night, and in less than 2 weeks, he had the Betty origin issue completed. Though he planned on going back and making a few corrections, he was proud of his work, and Manzetti was as well.

"Betty Bedlam #1." Manzetti smirked. "Why not a number 0? Ain't that what you youngsters start with these days? Especially for a origin comic."

"I may have been born a little late, but I'm old school like you, Mr. Manzetti." Jason flipped through some of the pages and smiled as he pointed out a panel. "Have to say this is my favourite part right here."

The panel showcased Betty's official return from the dead. There she was, standing over the motel bed of one of the mobsters that had killed her. His hired prostitutes were horrified on either side of him, and he was in shock as well. Betty sneered with her scalpel fingers dancing in mid-air, ready for the kill.

"I was surprised she killed the prostitutes as well," Manzetti said. Jason couldn't tell from his deadpan tone whether the statement was an approving or denouncing one.

"Betty comes off like a lady that takes no prisoner. I didn't... want her to just come back like some insane saviour of *all* women. No cliché vigilante angle, you know? I just want her to be an avenger of *herself.* Her own needs, her own wants, which were denied during life as she was a slave to her father, her teachers, and finally, her mobster pimp." Jason felt a tinge of fear moving through his body. "I can change it if you didn't like it."

"No. No. Jason, it's brilliant. I'm not here to censor or change you. I gave Betty to you. This is your interpretation."

"So... would you have had Betty become a... no holds barred, go for the kill with everyone type of girl, like I did?"

Manzetti scratched the back of his head. "The sad thing is, as much as I wouldn't want to... I had to. That's exactly how I created Betty to be."

"So you're not disappointed?"

Manzetti chuckled. "I guess I was hoping you would give her some humanist angle that I failed to give her. But Betty has spoken. She remains as cruel and demented as I created her, even in your hands."

Jason laughed. "Surely, my interpretation isn't that similar to yours, Mr. Manzetti. I wouldn't fool myself to being able to do justice to this character as well as you do."

"Jason... despite the new punk attitude, the funky clothes, and the snarl you give this lady... I'm saddened to say that your Betty fits to a T with what I conceptualized."

Was it good? Bad? Neither?

Mr. Manzetti had given Jason mixed signals. He *loved* Betty Bedlam #1, and the pages posted on the website and submitted as ads to horror art magazines had gotten a great response. But at the same time, he was obviously disappointed, even disturbed, that Jason's Betty was as gruesome and dark as the one Manzetti had created. Mr. Manzetti had said that he wished Jason could have given her a more empathetic appeal, a sense of morality or something. But how?

When Jason saw Betty, all he could see was an unbridled monster of sex and violence. Nothing could change that, and to change that would lessen Betty, make her less of what she really was. How could he even dream of doing that?

Another late night, working on Betty Bedlam #2. Jason hadn't wasted any time, and he wanted to get at least 3 issues completed before the first one was released. Now, it was time to lock up the studio and go home. He rose from his chair, checked to make sure the lights were off in each room, and then made his way back to the drafting table-

But there was someone sitting at the drafting table. And it wasn't Manzetti.

Shuffling of pages. Clattering of something sharp on the desk's top. A mixture of rotting flesh and sweet perfume.

That smell. But that's-

Exactly as he had described her on page 16. The scars showed proudly on the back of her head. Her studded leather jacket was mixed with sweat and the smell of garbage. But that perfume... she smelled angelic and demonic at the same time. The ultimate paradox, the greatest household of contradictions, organic and necrotic.

"Not bad," she said with a croaky, smoke and blood-stained voice as she forked her sharp tips through those new pages. "I don't look bad at all."

Jason couldn't be high. He didn't do any drugs, and he rarely drank, especially during his work week. He was sleep deprived, though. Yes, that's it. That's what this mirage had to result from, sleep deprivation. The studio was hot, the room humid. There was no A/C, and with the lights dim and low at the end of the night, Jason was having a hallucination. Surely, and hopefully, it wouldn't be the onset of schizophrenia, but doctors did say that signs of schizophrenia usually showed in the early 20s of a human's development and-

"Carl used to draw me classy," the delusion continued as she spun in her chair, slowly, to face Jason across the room. She surely looked like a real manifestation of the art Jason had portrayed- a dead, rotting, sexy punk vixen with cruel eyes and soft, snarling plump lips. "So dead but stylish in a dress with pretty slippers. Flattering, even cute. But you... you portray me in spiked leather, a collar and bracelets, sharp heeled boots. You make me look deadly and edgy. You show me... my inner nature and outer matching." A tongue flickered across her top lip.

Jason feared he would wet himself and tensed his abdominal muscles, clenching his bladder. This imaginary figure did not fade away. As corporeal as any three dimensional figure occupying real space, she refused to depart from reality. The woman remained and stayed in her seat, still admiring the new pages from issue 2. Carl imagined that some of the ink was still fresh, and even from there, he had noted a few smear marks.

But the pages weren't ruined. Oh no. She wouldn't dare mess them up.

"You revealed a lot in issue 1," Betty stated bluntly. "Too much. Carl nearly had a heart attack right there."

Jason's lips trembled. He could feel her wanting to communicate with him, prying at his mind. *I don't want you to just stand there all night,* her energy seemed to say. *This is a two person conversation. I came to talk to you and you alone.*

He mustered the strength to say something, to respond some awkward way. "You're real."

The woman still flicked through the papers, ignoring the simple statement as if its obvious notation was an insult to her very existence. "Now, you're going even further. Oh, I like this. Here, on page 13, you dared to show a glimpse of the very rituals that made me who I am. And that young man there..." Betty held up the page, showing one of the drawn young vagrants dabbling in magic spells. "Do you think he'll enjoy being outed in such a way? How this must trouble him so."

"You know what made me *me*. And you reimagined

me in a full on, honest way. You didn't hold back in your conceptualization." She tapped her scalpel nails on the arms of her chair. "Maybe *that's* why he's jealous of you. Not talent-wise, no. You haven't surpassed him... yet... though you could.

"Then again... your talents are *natural.* You grew up admiring him. But you never conceived that his greatest artistic attributes came from the same master that granted *me* my second chance."

A part of Jason wanted to run away, either hightail it out the door or risk an inevitable suicide by diving through the building's window-

"Come here, buttercup."

And a part of him wanted to follow and listen to that sickly, alluring voice. The part begging to obey was stronger. He was already, slowly, walking toward her. The dim light was doing her more justice with each creeping motion forward. Her skin was truly a rotting mix of peach and dirt grime black, her smell a horrific mix of sewage debris and royal aromatic scents. Her eyes were all menace, and in that menace was undeniable sex appeal.

"Come to Betty."

Sooner than he had wished, he was there. Standing in front of her as she rose, her gaze never leaving his. An undeniable petrification solidified within him.

Trapped like a delicacy in an arachnid's woven prison. Adhesively held still by some fascinating aura of dark, sensual mesmerisation.

She pressed her palm against Jason's cheek. Her scalpel fingernails teased him, pressed lovingly against his skin, but they did not cut. Oh, they did not dare cut.

Please don't cut me, please don't cut me-

"He gave me to you." Betty's strong, angular face leaned closer, her soft lips so close. Jason could see the worms moving about below the surface of her visage's thin epidermis tissues. Creepy things trailed down her neck as well, over the spiked collar, in and out of her leather jacket, along the borders of her breasts. "He recognized you as the superior, fresher scribe. And now, I am yours."

She leaned in, kissed Jason, and rubbed her hands lovingly against his cheeks. Electricity and sparks of flame rotated through Jason's core. Energies he had never felt, not even in his deepest moments of making love to Jocelyn, were breaking through his fragile spirit.

Betty's tongue danced along his for a while. Her soft lips pressed against his. Then, she pulled away. With only saliva stretching like a temporary ball and chain, she freed him.

"And you are mine."

Her last statement was followed with pain. Jason screamed. Long, sharp blades sliced down his face. The strength to pull away returned, and he tumbled as knife points ripped at the small webbing between his fingers and his hands. Blood dripped. A demoness laughed, so cruel and loving. So evil and enlightening.

Jason stumbled through the door. He refused to look back, refused to look at the woman laughing. Refused to see her demonic face as his bloody hands cradled his own wounded profile. His eyes stared on, as his limbs pumped mechanically, down the stairs and into the night, away, far away.

Home was as far as he could go.

"Oh my god," Jocelyn shouted at the door. "What happened to you?"

"M-ma.. m-m-m-ma...." Jason's mind reached for the first thing that came after such a terrific trauma. "Mugging."

"Oh, baby.. get inside. Hurry! We got to call the police."

"No police, no.... no."

"Did they take your wallet? Did they take your money? Oh, God, Jason!"

Jason's bloody, shaking hands threw his wallet and phone out of his pockets. Maybe that would end interrogations.

Jocelyn stared at the items, relieved, but they didn't offer set answers. "I knew this place was dangerous. I knew we shouldn't be here. I knew. I knew." Jocelyn stared at Jason in pitiful sorrow and disbelief, holding back tears. "My... God, Jason. You're bleeding all over the place. Staining the damn couch. We should-"

"No.... police...."

"I'll get towels.... goddamnit!!" Jocelyn rushed out of the room.

Jason shivered. He could feel the hot cuts, still settling on his face.

Just let me sleep through tonight, Jason thought. *I need to talk to the bastard. Need to talk to him.*

That thing... ain't Betty.

Jason slept beside his loving girlfriend, her arms compassionately around him.

The nightmares didn't end. Pages of pages intermixed. One minute, he saw Manzetti's art, the next, his own. Their stories mixed. The silver, fancy noir dress turned into punk duds. The scalpel fingernails remained razor sharp. Screams and shouts never ended. Mobsters were left memberless, dripping from between the legs. Their prostitutes, mistresses, and girlfriends died with them. Their bodies littered the parks and motels of the rough, rugged city, and the cops couldn't be happier. Slugs that had escaped their jurisdiction were being handled, probably by fellow gangsters- violated brother's codes or something. Either way, bodies of undesirables were filling the dark recesses of the metropolis, and no one cared.

A small-framed, geeky teenager saw it all, every night, and wished it could end. But in the morning, all he could do was get up, start writing, and start drawing, but he could never stop... never.

Jocelyn woke up. *Damn it,* she thought, *I left the fucking faucet on again.*

Slowly rolling to the edge of the bed, Jocelyn looked briefly at her sleeping husband. Then, she stood up, rubbed her arms, and made her way to the door of the bedroom.

Down the hallway she went. Towards the bathroom. No, not there. The sound was coming from the kitchen. Back in the hallway. Through the living room...

She stepped into the kitchen. That's where she saw her- the most horrid and beautiful sight she had ever seen, realized. A gasp escaped her lips simultaneously.

Though Jocelyn wanted to protest as the terrifying thing advanced, she wasn't given the time. Sharp blades descended down against her face, penetrating the skin deep, as Jocelyn's eyes and nose were obliterated. Blood sprayed against the floor from the parted flesh, a torn mouth hanging open helplessly. The blades descended from those devilish hands, one swoop precipitating, and then the next, ripping out hair, ears, and clippings of bone. In the frenzied attack, Jocelyn's shattered, torn head dangled at the neck from only the most slender threads of meat. A swipe later and her head was completely severed.

Working its way down, the monster continued to cut through Jocelyn's body like a mere weed to prune.

The pulpy mess of Jocelyn's cavader lay scattered across the floor. Intestines here, bone there.

Though killing her had been entertaining, Betty only saw her as a momentary detour from the reason she had come to this decrepit apartment. Betty's business was not with *her.* The monster had a more important date with an artist.

Waking up alone, Jason was immediately on high alert.

Where is Jocelyn? he worried mentally. Why was she not beside him? He hoped she would walk into the room soon, back from the bathroom, or holding a midnight snack....

Jocelyn did not come back into the room. *She* did.

Bedlam Betty.

Jason immediately started to shiver. He yelped slightly, but he did not scream. No... her presence robbed him completely of the ability to do so, at least for now.

"You left rudely when I was talking to you, boy!" the woman's croaky, shattered vocal chords grumbled. "Did you think you could run from my love so easily?"

A dripping noise sounded in Jason's ear. Not the sink. No. It sounded like something on the floor.

Betty grinned, homing in on exactly what Jason was hearing. "Oh yes. Let's join your friends."

Jason could already envision it in his mind's eye. He didn't want to go, but she insisted with razor sharp fingertips threatening his throat. She made him rise from bed, go down the hall... and then he couldn't help but scream. Couldn't stop wailing as Jocelyn and Manzetti's blood dripped on the floor, their dead bodies resting on the counters.

"This is how I'm supposed to be." Betty grinned, proud of her work. "Unrestrained. Unapologetic. Untamed."

Jason was weak. He crumbled, falling to his knees.

"Free." Betty raised her scalpel fingers high in the air.

"Wait!" Jason shouted. "What about the comic? What about the comic book?"

"It's served its purpose."

Razor edges tore across Jason's throat, opening deep vents through which he wheezed bloody bubbles.

Jason fell on the floor, convulsing like trout stranded on land as Bedlam Betty walked out of the apartment, ready to start her new life.

"Carl's supposed suicide note was some crazy stuff apparently."

"Yeah?" Marv Matters, president of Marvcore Publishing, leaned in to hear more from his secretary, Dennis. “Like what?”

“Like how he wanted to end it all... and that he knew his apprentice could bring his nightmares to an end by taking over on this Bedlam Betty character of his.”

“Bedlam Betty... ain’t she that horrible idea he shot our way about a decade ago?”

“Two decades, sir. He left to make his own company fifteen years ago. Remember?”

“Years fly by when you’re publishing books and having fun, Dennis.” Marv rolled his eyes as he pulled out a little stress ball and started tossing it up and down. “Anyway... horrible idea. Some bitch with scalpels for hands. What was she, a raped nurse or something?”

“Prostitute, sir. A dead prostitute.”

“Say... remember when the little bastard said she was real?”

Dennis laughed. “He threatened that he would bring her back, sir. That he was the key or something. One of the few things that happened before the nutcase quit.”

“Yeah.”

“Funny thing, sir. This apprentice of his started working on books for this character.”

“Really?”

“Yes, sir. Got a lot of high volume on the website. They probably had high profit margins set.”

“No shit. Carl could draw a pail of water and make it sell good with his fan base. His shit’s still some of our highest selling stuff.”

“This apprentice of his was pretty good too, sir.”

“No shit.... damn. You know, that Bedlam Betty does have some grotesque appeal, don’t she?”

“Indeed she does, sir.”

“Like a mix of blood and sex. People like blood and sex.”

“Only the most American of us, sir.”

“Americans that line our profits. Dennis, assemble our best writers and artists. We’re making a damned Bedlam Betty comic series... under Carl Manzetti’s name, of course.”

"Yes, sir!"

Dennis left the room to fulfil his boss's requests as soon as possible. Marv sat back and thought of what an exciting opportunity this new project would be, fuelled by the fervour of fans after Carl's death.

In another dark zone of the city, an undead whore laughed. Marvcore Publishing wasn't the only entity with plans.

Tactile Living

By Audrey E.L. Coots

Chapter One: Addiction

Brittany was addicted to Tactile Living, a role playing computer game that let the players envision themselves as whatever they wanted to be. It was an extremely addictive game; people could spend hours being the person in virtual reality that they were never allowed to be in the real world. It wasn't a concept specific to the demographic, either. The game was aimed at preteens and teenagers, promising parents that the concept was to encourage their sponge-minded offspring to think about their futures and contemplate possible careers. While this age group did make up a lot of the fan base, a large portion of the game's success came from the disappointed adult population. Grown men and women would leave their corporate offices, loosen their ties and skirts or take off their clothes all together in the comfort of their own homes, and let loose in their Tactile world, where they were rock stars, entrepreneurs, presidents and CEOs, actors, millionaires, doctors and lawyers. Infertile women went to a place where they had a house full of children, and lonely thirty-somethings went to a place where they were never alone.

Brittany found herself closer to the later age group than the former. She wasn't quite thirty, but she was certainly old enough to be remorseful about the career path she'd taken. She was a registered nurse, two years past graduation and too deep into the field to change things now. She chided herself for ever believing that she could actually enjoy the constant, clinical sounds of a hospital, day after relentless day- the beeping, the moaning, the crying and begging. And she didn't even like to think about the job itself- constantly being the *bad guy* who came at people with those hated needles and refusals for more pain medicine. It was an often thankless job, grating on her nerves and wearying her resolve to be a good person who did good things at a good job.

She found that she much preferred the hours between four pm and one am, when she was the stay-at-home wife of a brilliant, handsome engineer. She had a lovely ranch-style home on a green little plot of land, with a large swimming pool fenced off out back. She and her virtual husband had cook-outs on the grill every weekend, lounging poolside with their friends and enjoying life. They spoke often of having children, but for now they were content to live for themselves, vacationing two towns over (there were really only a handful of towns in this virtual world- after all, when it came right down to basics, this was a game, designed by human beings and not all-powerful gods who could create an entire world in 7 days, regardless of their reputations for speedy updates) and fishing at the lake a couple of miles from the house, exercising together in the mornings and having the occasional brief argument. It was not a human-interaction game, but Brittany's computer-generated husband was equipped with three languages, hundreds of words in each one, and appropriate responses were quick at hand. She often forgot that the well-designed man was a fake and lost herself in her perfect world.

Looking around now, she couldn't resist an exaggerated eye roll. Her small, dingy apartment on the uneventful, unattractive Brush Street was a mess; she had no backyard, no pool and certainly no handsome husband. No wonder she preferred her online world. Here, the 40-watt light bulb flickered weakly in the socket above her head, casting dim light across the blank tan walls. The carpet was a faded brown color and the only furniture consisted of an old thrift store couch and a weakened coffee table. She sometimes left the radio on while she played her game, but most of the time she sat in silence and an outsider looking in would almost certainly call this a desolate, isolated existence.

So what, Brittany thought, turning back to her computer. *That's why I prefer the company of a fake husband. Real men judge too much and think too little.*

After a few hours of perfect game play, during which she'd passed two weeks in virtual reality and conversed with her husband more on the prospect of perhaps *next* year starting a family, she glanced up at the clock and realized that it was after two am. She had to be up for work in less than six hours. She sighed, saved her game and padded to her real-life, empty bedroom. She climbed into her real-life, empty bed and closed her eyes, wishing for the entire world to turn virtual. She closed her eyes and pictured her handsome fake-husband, mentally wished him a goodnight, and drifted off to sleep.

Chapter Two: Disbelief

Brittany couldn't believe her eyes. She'd gone to sleep thinking of her virtual world, and now, waking up, she could see it all right in front of her. She blinked several times, rubbed her eyes and squeezed them shut again, trying to clear them.

"Morning, Baby," she heard, and a strong arm slipped itself around her waist. She jumped and fell into the floor.

The perfectly clean, wooden, almost-cartoony-floor.

"Honey? Baby?" She peeped up over the side of the bed- the *nice* bed, no hand-me-down special- and saw the striking features of her husband. He had the chiseled jaw, lightly covered in dark brown stubble, and the heavy lidded green eyes that she'd seen so many times through her computer screen. And he was not quite realistic. He, like everything else, had a slightly cartoony look to him; not quite Saturday Morning, full on animation cartoony but definitely a computer generated look that was somewhat disturbing to look directly at. He was staring at her quizzically, propped up on one elbow. “You okay?”

“Yes!” she said quickly, pulling herself to her feet, which were much daintier than they’d ever been before. *Everything in virtual reality is perfect*, she thought. *Bye-bye, bunions*. “I’m good. I’m great! How’s it going?”

“I’m going to get ready for work now, honey,” her fake-husband said. What was his name again? Brittany furrowed her brow, trying to recall. They normally referred to each other in pet names, adding often gag-worthy sentiment to the unrealistic romance.

“Peter!” she said aloud.

“Yes, honey,” he said, pulling himself out of bed. “I’m going to go get ready for work now.”

“Yes, you said that already,” she said. Was he this repetitive when she’d been on the other side? For that’s where she was, right? On the other side of the computer screen.

She glanced around at the room she’d built from the ground up. She’d painted it, furnished it, decorated it. She knew it well. The bed was a white sleigh bed, the dresser matched and the clothes hamper was a complimenting shade of purple, as were the curtains. There were purple throw pillows that went on the bed every day after she- the stay at home wife, the housewife, the jobless, happy wife!- made it. The closet had a few nice outfits, which she, again, had designed, and the bathroom off of the bedroom was pure perfection. The claw-footed tub, excessive counter space, massive mirror- all of it, her very own design, her very own dream house. She thought she could ignore the odd quality of the visuals around her for this. It seemed like a fair trade. It was like comparing a high quality movie in low definition to a low quality movie in high definition. This was the high quality world, and she was seeing it in low definition, but she still thought this was the better end of the bargain.

She heard the faucet turn on in the bathroom and tip-toed to the door. There he stood in all of his perfectly-perfected perfection. He had a white towel wrapped around his waist, and when it slipped aside, she started to turn her head, wanting to respect his privacy (and so what if he was her husband; she'd never actually *seen* it- he had been fake up until this morning!) but something made her stop and turn back. She was a nurse. The male body was part of her profession, but something was strange here. It took her a moment to figure out that the blob at the apex of his thighs was a pixelated, moving censor. This was how he was viewed when she was playing the game from the other side, so she wasn't exactly surprised that this remained now that she was here, but she was somewhat stumped. Apparently the fact that she was now a part of the game, living and breathing here instead of just playing here, didn't change the rules. When the game was rated PG-13, it stayed that way. There would be no showing of the genitalia here.

A brief glance down her own pants told her that she could see herself just fine, no censor there. *Alright, fine,* she thought. *I can handle that.*

She wouldn't admit to anyone- and especially not to herself- that the beginnings of worry had crept into her mind, like a little nudge that was easy to ignore... For now. She was *inside* of her game! Her greatest wish had come true! She giggled, almost light headed with the thought of it. She had friends here, a husband, a house, *a pool*! And most importantly, she had *no job*. No beeps, no call buttons, no resentful patients, no high-stepping doctors or gossiping nurses. *No responsibilities*. That thought alone was enough to push the worry to the back of her mind.

"Bye, sweetie," her husband said, kissing her on the forehead. "I'll be home at six." He walked out the door, and if Brittany saw his left foot glitch and disappear for just a moment, well, she chose to ignore that. No, she certainly hadn't seen that, and no, she certainly wasn't worried... about *any*thing. She was in her game! What could go wrong?

After she cleaned the house and ate breakfast

(she could choose from three things: pancakes, waffles or pop-tarts, and she'd chosen the latter), she decided she'd go explore her little town. She walked outside and glanced around, and if the neighborhood before her seemed a bit… *thin*, well, that was just fine. She couldn't expect everything to be exactly as it was in the outside world, could she? She felt cold chills prickle her neck when she pressed her hands to the trunk of a tree. It was entirely smooth and somehow empty feeling, like the wooden paneling lining her grandmother's trailer. It looked like real wood, but it was really only a fake, a cheap knock-off of the real thing. She wondered briefly if this world would be exactly like that: a cheap knock off of God's master design. She shook her head, dismissing the thought. This reality was created to be perfect.

The house next to her own came into focus (and *so what* if things more than a few feet in front of her were blurry and had to '*come into focus*,' so what, so *what…*) and then the house after that, and she noticed with mounting suspicion that she seemed to be the only one on the block.

Maybe her husband would like to have lunch with her. She shook the steadily growing worries from her mind and made her way across the small town. She glanced up at the second-story windows of the houses she passed and thought that she occasionally saw people staring down at her, but they disappeared the moment she got a clear view. Her worries intensified.

Find Peter, she thought. *I'll feel better once I'm with him*.

But she didn't feel better. She didn't feel better at all. Because Peter was a fake, and as she stared through the ground-floor window of his office building and watched him, she realized with terror that this was wrong, all wrong. He was in a sitting position, but there was no seat beneath him. He was in a white room, surrounded by empty white space that seemed endless. In the game, the avatars disappeared into their office buildings to discreetly do a hard day's work. What were

8 business-filled hours for them were only a few minutes for the player, so there was no need to ever see the inside of the office buildings, and the creators of the game hadn't bothered to design an area that no one would ever see. What was worse, terrifyingly worse, about the image before her, was that her husband was glitching. Half of his face was sculpted perfectly into an attentive smile, the eye on the right side facing forward. That part of him looked as it should, as if he was patiently listening to someone in front of him talk. The other half of his face, however, was blurry, going in and out of focus, shaking too quickly back and forth, seemingly demon-possessed, and Brittany wasn't sure, but she thought she saw it *crying*.

She suddenly felt very lonely and found herself having trouble catching her breath. She needed to get out of here, now, but a strange thing happened. When she tried to turn to go home, she became disoriented. Which way *was* home? She spun in slow, dizzying circles, her breath coming in heaving gulps that seemed to accomplish little in the way of calming her. She felt a strong hand wrap itself around her wrist and pull, and then there was nothing.

Chapter Three: Discovery

"She's coming to," Brittany heard. The voice sounded as if it were coming from very far away. She squeezed her eyes shut tightly and then opened them slowly, the darkness around her slowly beginning to take form.

Lots of forms... All leaning toward her, watching her.

"Give her some space." It was that voice again, and one she recognized. Her husband?

"Peter?" she said, and she was surprised by the creak in her voice. She sounded as if she'd been sick for a very long time. She felt that it took a great deal of effort to push the word out.

"Sit up, Brittany," he said, gently easing her into a

sitting position. This wasn't quite right... No, this was wrong, all wrong. Peter wasn't supposed to call her by her name. He was supposed to call her "Honey" or "Baby" or "Sweetheart." And why did his voice sound like that? He was always supposed to sound happy; happy to be her husband and happy to see her. Now, he sounded... *Off.* Too quiet and too worried.

"What's going on?" she asked, expecting a computer generated reply, a generic pet name followed by a brief and vague explanation.

"We don't have much time," he said instead, still in that tone. She'd never heard him use it before, and she'd been playing in her Tactile world for a while now.

He squatted in front of her, and she gasped, her stomach rising into her throat. He was grotesquely disfigured. His glitch never stopped. One half of his face was the way it always was, a pleasant, detached expression staring off into the distance. The other half was the half that scared her. A whole head was coming out of the half-face that remained eerily calm. The new head was realistic, like the real world she'd left behind, and his features were twisted into an expression of intense pain. She saw that there were real, wet tears glistening on his cheeks. While the dreamy half face kept perfectly, unrealistically still, the real-world head sticking out of it was moving quickly in semi-circles, jerking back and forth as if it had a nerve twitch of some kind.

"I know, I know. I'm hard to look at. But you have to listen," the real-head said. "We're real. All of us." He gestured to the others standing around her, and Brittany noticed for the first time that none of them were entirely computer generated. Some of them had a realistic leg standing beside a matching cartoony one, some had an arm or just a hand, but all of them had flickering heads coming in and out of focus beside their avatar heads. "This is going to happen to you, too," her husband said. "You have to get us out of here. You're the only one who can."

Brittany's mouth felt like cotton, and she was

vaguely aware of a tingling sensation creeping up her spine. She tried to open her mouth to ask what she could possibly do about any of this, but her jaw muscles didn't seem to be working.

"It's too late," one of the shadowed avatar-people said quietly. "I told you, it's too late."

It's not too late, Brittany tried to say. *I can help! Just tell me what to do!* But none of those words made the transition from her mind to her mouth. She was locked down now, stuck inside of her own body. She watched helplessly as her arm slowly rose in front of her face.

"Excuse me," she heard, and realized that the voice was her own. "I must get home. My husband will be expecting me. Have a nice day." She felt her own legs moving, but she was not the one moving them.

What's happening? She tried to call, but again, nothing came out of her mouth. And was it really her mouth anymore? If she wasn't the one controlling it?

"You're not a player anymore," her husband called after her, and she heard the anguish in his voice, but she thought that this was caused by the rescue that had never happened more than by any feelings he may have had toward her. After all, if he was real, then they barely knew each other at all. She was very well acquainted with the sickeningly perfect avatar that claimed his body, though. "You're being played by... by..."

Brittany glanced up then, using an extreme amount of will power to move her eyes in a direction away from the one she was facing. Above her head, she saw a tag line, much like the one that had hovered above her avatar when she'd been on the other side of things. This one, however, no longer said *BritkinsLyn*. Instead, it said xx*LuCyDaRIINgxx*, and Brittany was suddenly aware of what was happening. She was being played by some outside player, apparently by the name of Lucy, and this Lucy person was in complete control of her own life... Or of what now posed as her life.

She relaxed her muscles and her eyes refocused on the door in front of her. She was going home.

Chapter Four: Life As We Know It

The doorbell rang. Brittany went to answer it, and greeted her neighbors with a smile and a hug.

"Come on in!" her husband called from right behind her. "Weather's fine, water's cool, food's good!" He was balancing a plate of raw hamburgers in one hand and an over-long metal spatula in the other. It was Friday, and they were having another weekend bar-b-q out by their pool.

But the truth was that the weather wasn't fine. It was monotonous. The water wasn't cool, it was luke-warm, and the food wasn't good, it was bland. Brittany had been living here for months now, and she'd grown accustomed to these things. While she could no longer control her own body, she could feel it. Her arms and legs moved without her permission or her consent, but she still felt the muscles working beneath the skin. She didn't get to choose what to eat, but she could still taste the food, and it all tasted the same- sort of like a slightly bitter stick of celery. Every now and then, something would have a slight flavor, a hint of what it was supposed to taste like, but it only lasted for a few seconds, and she thought this might just be her memory, leaving little bursts of taste in desperation. In truth, she was now hyper-aware of these things. It was bizarre sensation.

She could poke her own head out of her avatar now; it had taken her weeks to figure out how to do that, but she'd finally done it, and realized with immense clarity why her husband always seemed to be crying. It hurt. Pulling control of those muscles away from her avatar and using them herself was like separating the muscles from the bone, pulling them out of the body through the skin. It hurt all over, and the first time she'd done it had been so painful that she'd no more than peeked her head out, screamed and returned to the safe, paralyzed haven of her mind. Weeks passed before she dared to try it again, but she had, and now she could manage to keep her head out for several minutes before the pain overcame her.

Peter was much the same, and in the rare moments when she wasn't being played by *xxLuCyDaRlINgxx*, she and Peter tried to talk. They got to know each other in small, painful spurts, and had a growing affection for each other. But always, before anything else, escape reigned in their minds. It was the thought that superseded all others.

Peter had painstakingly explained the situation to her in those weeks when she'd finally been able to keep her head about her, so to speak. He explained that he'd once been a player, and loved the game, and had gone to bed wishing he could be inside of the game, and then it had happened. Someone else had played his body for him, and this had lasted for several months- perhaps even years, he couldn't be sure- and then they just didn't show up anymore. He became an extra in the life of a new player, his wife, who was played by someone named *BritkinsLyn*. He was no longer being controlled by a human being, but neither could he control himself. He was now fully computer-controlled. It was the same for everyone, he told her. One day her *xxLuCyDaRlINgxx* would either grow out of the game and move on, or she'd go to bed wishing she could be inside of the game. Either she'd escape the game, or become a part of it, and then Brittany would be just the same as him: stuck, controlled by a machine, painfully trying to separate her body from an avatar.

"It's like we're covered in wax," he'd said. "We could escape, but we'd have to melt all of the wax off, and it would take all of our skin with it."

Brittany found that to be an appropriate description of the pain she felt when she leaned her head out of her avatar. She burned, from the outside in, and ached from the inside out.

And now she watched, bored, as her neighbors walked through the beautiful house that she'd built and out to the fenced-in back yard. Two men were standing beside the grill, drinking beers with her husband while their wives were lounging in chairs beside the pool, with her. It was like a scene from a Stepford Wives horror movie, eerily without fault or mistake, perfect in every way.

And now she felt herself standing up, heard herself calling for attention.

"Listen, listen, everyone!" she said, and five pairs of eyes turned toward her, their smiling faces politely attentive. "I have an announcement to make," she continued. Brittany wondered mildly what this announcement might be. These weekend bar-b-q's usually went by the exact same script every single time. The same conversations, the same food, the same loosely competitive football game, the same everything, but this was different. "I wanted you all to know before anyone else, because I love you all dearly. You are my closest friends. Peter and I are expecting a baby!"

Peter's avatar ran excitedly toward Brittany's and picked her up, swinging her in a wide circle.

"Careful!" Brittany heard herself say, laughing. Peter put her down and kissed her squarely on the mouth, and their friends congratulated them.

Inside, Brittany was terrified.

She'd had different accounts with Tactile Living, before she'd settled with this story line... First she'd tried being an actress, but she found that lifestyle boring. It was more work than fun. She'd been political, but again, she found this boring and taxing. Her third attempt at a successful Tactile lifestyle had been that of a nurturing mother, a very similar lifestyle to the one she had now. She'd had a handsome husband and three perfect children, but she disliked the constant demands that they'd made on her downtime... Instead of bar-b-q's by the pool, for instance, she spent weekends ferrying them across the town and occasionally to an entirely different town for soccer games and plays and field trips. She decided she wanted to start all over, and wait awhile before becoming a mother, so she'd abandoned that game file and started anew with this one. But she could remember what had happened when her avatar had given birth in that other file, and it was grotesque and awful.

The makers of the game probably intended to scare younger players into taking the idea of pregnancy more seriously. After all, teenage mothers were on the rise and sex education was severely lacking. Having children in the game felt more like a chore than fun- children constantly needed to be fed and demanded new clothes every few weeks. They wanted to spend money every time they went to a store, and their education must be catered to indulgently. If they missed field trips or didn't participate in athletic activities, other parents would give judgmental looks and the child would have an antisocial air about them. They'd start choosing to watch television instead of playing outside, and they'd grow lethargic and dim-witted. Eventually, the in-game version of DHR would show up and whisk the children away, and the parents would be left in a cloud of shame. All of that was bad enough, but the actual event of giving birth was horrifying to behold.

The little pixilated censor boxes held true and nothing technically inappropriate was shown during the birth scenes, but perhaps the creators would have been better off showing the anatomically correct versions of childbirth, or at least a toned down version. Instead, they had the mother physically split apart at the navel. Her bellybutton first popped out, not unlike real-life bellybuttons during those unpleasant, heavy final months of pregnancy. But the bellybutton didn't stop there. It kept slowly expanding, and that's how the player knew that the avatar was in labor and about to give birth. After several hours of the gradually expanding bellybutton, during which the avatar would be breathing heavily and walking around in pain, there would be a grand explosion. The bellybutton would pop, just like a water-filled balloon, and the avatar would be thrown backward onto the floor, covered in green and red and yellow gore. The terrifying scene didn't stop there, however. The opening left by the exploding bellybutton would then begin to throb, and the player would see the first signs of the new baby- a little peep of the baby's hand, waving merrily from inside of the mother's stomach. The baby would reach out through the gaping hole and pull himself through the opening, ripping the mother's stomach as he did so. Finally, after this whole scene played through with repulsive detail, the father would take the child into his arms and a doctor would come and sew the mother's stomach up with a shiny needle. The mother would need several days to recover, but eventually she'd return to her trim waistline and complain no more about it.

Brittany had found this whole process somewhat amusing when she'd been on the other side. As a nurse, and as an adult, she of course knew what really happened during child birth, and she found this macabre display to be disturbing and completely unrealistic, but it was just a game. Back then, *it was just a game*.

Now, however, it would become real.

Chapter Five: Escape

The months went by all too quickly. *Everything* happened all too quickly, here, in this game world. Peter and Brittany talked as often as they could, enduring the pain of sticking their heads out of their bodies so that they could think of what to do, what to *do*. Brittany couldn't have a baby in this game, she told him. She just *couldn't*. She wasn't in control of her body, but she could still feel it, and the thought of feeling herself ripped apart in such an unnatural way while she was unable to do anything to stop it made her panic. A few times, her internal terror actually carried over, and the normally pleasant, starry eyed Brittany avatar would let out a deafening scream. *xxLuCyDaRlINgxx* chalked this up to an in-game glitch and ignored it, or so Brittany believed.

She felt some strange sort of connection to the outside world through this Lucy person, and Peter told her that this was because Lucy was becoming more and more dependent on the game for her kicks. Brittany thought he'd sounded sad when he'd told her that it wouldn't be long now, not long at all, before Lucy fell asleep wishing that she could enter the virtual world.

Brittany was formulating a plan. She wasn't sure if it would work- in fact, she was almost sure that it wouldn't-but she didn't have any other choices. She told Peter of her idea, and his vibrating, rotating head concurred that this was her only option.

"If you do it," he said, his words ricocheting around the currently empty gaming world, "you have to try to help the rest of us. I think you can do it from the outside. I don't know how, but maybe you could come and find us."

She agreed.

"It's going to be hard," he said quietly. "It's going to hurt."

She agreed.

"It probably won't work. It might kill you," he said.

She agreed, and she pulled her head back into her avatar, preserving her strength.

Her bellybutton had started to swell.

Chapter Six: Delivery

The pain was, strangely, durable. Brittany was surprised at how unpleasant the sensation was. She could feel a hot bubbling inside of her abdomen, as if she'd drank too much hot chocolate, but instead of the liquid becoming one with her body temperature, it remained hot inside of her, rolling around, gurgling audibly every time she moved. Unpleasant, but endurable.

The swelling was intensifying. She now had a rather large baby bump and a rather large bump on top of that, roughly the size of a softball, and growing hourly.

In three hours, she estimated it would be the size of a watermelon, and almost as big as her abdomen itself. That's when it would be time.

She took deep breaths, fortifying herself for what lay ahead, as her avatar did the same. Brittany had been stuck inside of this avatar for so long that she actually felt bad for what she was about to do to it, but not bad enough to hesitate. She had to do what she had to do.

Peter paced beside her. His head kept flickering out of the avatar's head, giving her courage. Brittany didn't think *xxLuCyDaRllNgxx* noticed. She was focused on Brittany's avatar and her first virtual baby. She was in for a surprise.

As soon as her engorged bellybutton began to throb, Brittany knew that the time had come. She squeezed her eyes tightly shut and took a deep breath, and with all of the strength she could muster, she pushed.

She pushed her arms out, her legs out, her chest out. Her eyes bulged in her head and her fists clamped tightly closed; her feet and calves cramped and her head felt as if it were about to explode, and still, she pushed. Her teeth ground together, sending white hot flashes of pain through her jaw, and her face felt hot and too-full, *too full* of pressure and heat and blood, and still, she pushed.

All at once, she felt a divine release. All of the pressure subsided, and she found that she was now *outside* of herself. She was staring at her own face, but a cartoony version. She'd escaped her avatar, or what was left of her avatar. The body was covered in a mucous-y liquid, strands of cartoony muck-muck hanging from her hair and shoulders and even her eye lashes. There were deep gashes all over her body, all stemming from that central location where her bellybutton had been. She looked like a gory, bloody depiction of a flash of lightening. Brittany had crawled out of herself, and the avatar was ruined.

The Peter avatar leaned forward and grabbed a

perfect-looking baby off of the floor and cooed over it, while the Brittany avatar lay still, grotesquely smiling through the devastation that was her body. A doctor appeared, walking through the front door of the house with an over sized, cartoony needle in hand.

"Perfection! All is good and well here," he said cheerily. "Let's just get mommy all fixed up." He leaned over the still avatar and began to sew her back together again, but he wasn't programmed to handle all of the damage that Brittany had inflicted. He sewed at her belly for a few moments and then stood, proclaiming her healthy and robust, and left.

The Brittany avatar stood up, and her skin seemed to fall away. The face split into three sections, the left cheek falling sideways and peeling until it came to rest at her shoulder. Her right shoulder ripped until it hung loosely from her elbow in a puddle of skin, and her legs were now just two thick, mucous covered blobs. Most terrifying of all wasn't the gore or the cheerful smile on the face of the decimated avatar- it was the realism that lay beneath. The designers of this game had, for some reason (Brittany supposed for the medicinal purposes of those players who wanted to pretend that they were doctors) designed every realistic layer of the human body. The Brittany avatar had a skull, and her wide eyeballs leered cheerfully from the sockets. Her pulsating, red heart was partially visible where the skin had fallen away.

Brittany stared, horrified. This was more than a glitch. This was evil by design.

Suddenly, she felt very tired. Exhausted, actually. She had fought so hard to get out of there, and she hadn't thought about what she'd do if that actually worked. Before she could contemplate it further, Peter stuck his real-head outside of his avatar. "Run!" he yelled, and so she did.

She didn't make it very far. Just outside of her house, her dream house with the perfect sleigh-bed-bedroom and the perfect claw-foot-tub-bathroom, she collapsed. She couldn't go any further. *It was all for nothing,* she thought as her knees hit the grass. *I tried so hard. It hurt so much. It was all for nothing…*

She passed out thinking of her dinky little apartment on Brush Street: the thrift store couch, the 40 watt light bulb, the faded brown carpet… She passed out wishing she were home.

Chapter Seven: Home

Brittany awoke with a migraine. Her head was pounding, absolutely *pounding* with the beats of her heart, and her ears were stopped up. She was afraid to open her eyes for fear of any light blinding her, making her headache intensify, but she opened them anyway, slowly at first- just a peek, and then wider, in spite of the intensifying pain.

She couldn't believe her eyes. She was home. Home, home, *home!*

She jumped up off of the bed and nearly collapsed from the head rush that resulted, but she laughed giddily. She was home at last! She checked her cell phone and saw with a start that she had several missed calls, several voice mails and several text messages, all from her sister- the only one who would notice if she'd gone off the grid for awhile

Just how long had she been off the grid? She'd experienced at least a year in the game, maybe longer, but how long was that in real time?

She checked the date on her cell phone and groaned. She'd been absent from the world for five days. She mentally went over her body and decided that she was severely dehydrated. Had her real-world body been lying here in this bed, comatose, for *five days*, while she spent a year or so in a virtual reality? It certainly felt that way. She stood slowly, acutely aware that moving too fast would cause her to collapse. She made her way to the bathroom and drank a few steady sips of water. She was thirsty, very much so, but drinking too fast would only cause her to throw it all back up, and she hated throwing up. She had to take care of herself now.

Because she had a job to do.

She had to rescue Peter.

She didn't know how, but she'd promised him that she'd try, and she was going to start by destroying her copy of the game. No, not just her copy- all of the copies she could get her hands on. No one would believe her if she tried to tell them about this whole experience, and she knew that. But she could form her own little army of survivors. She'd get Peter out first, and together, they could rescue the rest.

Because screw being a nurse, she thought, grinning at her pale, real, absolutely *not* cartoony reflection over the bathroom sink. *And screw Tactile Living.*

She grabbed a nearby towel and wiped her face. She stank. She was covered in her own excrement and she was foul with it, but that could be remedied. She knew how to take care of bedsores. She knew how to re-hydrate herself and how to ease her body back into accepting solid food. She would do all of these things, and then, in a week or maybe two, when she was feeling stronger, she would get Peter out. But first, she needed to contact, *xxLuCyDaRIINgxx*. She hoped it wasn't too late. This Lucy person just might believe her crazy story if she had seen anything that had happened during the birth of her first virtual-baby, and if Brittany could trust her instincts and that odd link that she still felt she had with the girl, she thought Lucy had seen it all, and was a little freaked out.

Good, Brittany thought. *Get freaked out. Get worried. Have a nightmare or two. Get out of the zone just long enough for me to find you, and maybe you won't lose yourself in that game.*

She turned on the shower head and peeled her clothes off of her body. That hurt. Everything hurt, but she thought she'd never felt such a good pain. She was going to need some antibiotics, for sure, and some fluids, too, but she could cater to all of that in time. Right now, she had to make a plan, and as she climbed into the hot, steamy shower, she thought she knew what she had to do. She'd start by warning Lucy, for better or for worse. Brittany thought*, and you can lead a horse to water but you can't make it drink and can't say I didn't warn you, Lucy old girl, and don't save, don't save, don't save the game, save yourself!* She was mildly aware that she might be a little irrational; her thoughts didn't seem to be making a whole lot of sense, but she'd feel better once she rehydrated.

After she warned Lucy, she'd look up Peter. If she could find his last name, maybe she could find his address, and if he wasn't a stinking, rotting corpse by now, maybe she could save him.

She slid to the bottom of the tub and wrapped her arms around her legs and let the water pour over her body. As she sat there, she took deep breaths and calmed herself, and when she was no longer giddy about being alive and in the real world again, and when she was no longer thinking in a fast paced ramble about what she'd do next, and when she was no longer covered in her own feces, she laid her head on her knees and cried, her body rocking with sobs.

It was over, it was really over, and somewhere in ether-space, somewhere in the world of tasteless food and windless days and dry water and fake friends with limited vocabulary and pre-programmed social interactions, Peter waited. She wouldn't disappoint him.

I'm coming, Peter, she thought, her eyes picturing his face, his real-world, rotating, shaking face. She closed her eyes and drew his image up more clearly and cried harder, her dehydrated body hating her for it, her eyes and throat aching.

She climbed out of the shower an hour later and wrapped a towel around herself. She was no longer crying. She was no longer thinking in riddles. She was determined now.

She sat down at the computer and searched for a Tactile Living Q&A forum. She suspected Lucy would be there, somewhere, wondering if anyone else had encountered strange, bloody glitches with their games. She knew that she had a lot of work ahead of her, but she was ready. She was determined to never let this happen to anyone, ever again.

I'm coming, Peter, she thought again. *Hang in there. I won't let you down.*

Time It Right

By William G. Chandler Jr.

"It would help if you could bend a little," the wincing man in black complained.

"How much more do you want me to do?" a heavy-set, bald male responded, with his head covered in black soot. Robert Gale, in a grimy, black sweater, khaki pants and black shoes, slid out from a brick chimney. The two men started to force their bodies into the small opening.

"There's not enough space for either of us. It gets tighter as you go up further," Robert declared. "I think it's sealed at the top." He moved away from the chimney and wrapped his right arm across his body, pressing his palm flat against the lowest part of his ribcage, desperate to ease the pain he felt. One side of his sweater carried a wet and sticky Y-shaped gash he seemed to hide from his companion, trying to keep that side away from the other man's view. "We're stuck. Shit!" Robert almost gave up. He knew to hold it together. He had to in order to survive this. The two individuals locked eyes.

The other man, Darin Gale, scrunched his plump body low, waddled to the left, and bounced upright, into the tiny chimney's opening. This shorter male in maroon sweater, brown khakis and shoes forced only his fleshy arm into the chimney. Robert patted Darin's back. "Good effort, bro."

If Robert faltered, Darin would give in. There could be no give. Darin must fight, even if Robert gave up. He looked up to Robert. In the same way, Robert believed in his little brother.

"We have no other options," Darin moaned.

Robert endured for his younger sibling, but knew he had to make him work for praise.

"I said it was sealed," Robert snarled. "You know what? Keep trying."

The plump male moved away from the chimney.

They fervently searched the dusty, cramped, old brick basement. The chimney seemed their clearest option and hope. It proved to be too small. The other possible exit was a slightly raised, grated, portion of the floor, with a rectangular highlight around its edge. They kicked and stomped, disturbing the white layer of dust that lay in wait around dark, sticky stains on the gray cement floor. The grate did not budge. This particular puzzle section had no mystery. The grate simply lets fluids out, not people. Robert continued to pull at the grate.

"What are you doing," Darin inquired.

Robert noted the defeated tone in his brother's voice and yelled, "Come on man! Don't quit now. Feel around, there's gotta be a shovel, a chain, something that we can use to lift this thing! Can you feel anything near you?"

Darin sat in the darkness. His lack of movement said it all. Robert was losing him.

The wounded sibling joined Darin's on the floor. He sighed and muttered his accusation, "You didn't even try."

"I'm working just as hard as you are. The place is clean."

"You're the one that got us down here."

Darin gasped, "That's not fair."

Robert replied, "It might not be fair, but it's true."

Robert quickly rubbed his brother's scalp. "I'm sorry. Come on."

They felt past the brick chimney. The walls of the room had no identifying features. They were just red brickand close enough to inspire claustrophobia. They moved toward a rickety, wooden stairwell, with a glowing doorway, at the apex of the staircase. This, however, was not the preferred means of escape, but something for the brothers to fear. The glow around the door shook the brothers to the core. It was too easy, and obvious an exit.It gradually became clear to Darin that the small basement was a safe place, if only safe temporarily. They were still alive. As long as the captor was on the other side of the door, they were still alive.

Robert, with a focus on the most obvious escape route, blurted, "Why not just rush it?"

Darin pushed his dazed brother back against a brick wall, forcing him down to the floor. This would prevent any ill thought out attack. "Something carried the both of us down here, unconscious," Darin reminded him.

"We don't actually know that."

"You don't," Darin retorted.

"There could be three people upstairs. They could have carried us," Darin said, as he shrugged his shoulders.

"So we take on three possible killers," Robert retorted.

"How did we get here? Remember? We were in a bar with our dates. That fool interrupted our conversation," Darin recalled.

"It was an argument, about Transformers, Generation One, not a conversation," the injured sibling interjected.

Darin recalled the event, "He started talking to the girls. We simply asked him to stop. He threw you on the ground. He beat on me. The bouncers, and bartender, sent us all outside, well, except for the girls. He disappeared. Now, we're here. It was him, alone. I would hate to think two other people are plotting our deaths."

Robert moved closer to the ominous steps.

Darin cried. "I know it was him. He changed. Remember?"

Robert replied, "What? You were drunk."

Darin clenched his fists as he spoke. "His eyes glowed red. His neck got thicker. The thing's muscles peaked. We stepped outside. He disappeared. I turned. I looked, man. We left the bar. We looked for him. He jumped us, with ridiculous speed. Don't you remember that part, at least? Do you remember the fur on his body?"

Robert shook his head.

They heavyset sibling recalled it all. "He took us

by surprise, in more than one way. He's some sort of creature.""Please, that's not possible," Robert said, allowing himself a weak chuckle at the ridiculousness of the suggestion. I'm telling you, there must be three or four guys up there. They jumped us. They have us in their basement. We're going to have to fight for our lives and get the fuck outta here. We've got to escape."

"It's not a joke. It's not three or four guys. It's one. It's one *thing.*You saw it. You don't remember those red pupils," Darin exclaimed.

"This from the man who believes monsters will take over the city of Philadelphia,"Robert chortled.

"Stop," Darin cried.

"What did you tell me about that newspaper story on Pennypack Park" Robert asked. "What was the story you conjured up? Someone let their wolves, or half-wolf dogs loose in the park. They weren't pet owners, but really some sort of cultist?"

Darin smiled. "They might have directed the animals to bite people."

"And turn them into werewolves, right?"

"Possibly. I mean if they're half-breeds they might bite people and turn them into monsters. You never know," the plump sibling snickered. "Robert."

The injured sibling snapped at Darin. "Preposterous. Ridiculous. We're both former college students and understand that facts highlight truths. Werewolves aren't real."

"Humans don't maul the sides of other human beings," Darin said, as he pointed at Robert's damaged side.

The door above the stairwell banged at an impact from the other side. Robert crouched and stepped away from the short set of dusty, wooden steps. They both raised their fists.

Darin dropped his hands to his sides. "I thought I saw something. I just assumed it was the drink messing with me,"

"Oh, now you *did* see something? Punk."

Darin turned away from Robert and focused on the stairs.

Robert froze, a terrifying pain tore through his body, when he realized that his fingertips were actually touching his exposed ribs."I just wanted to believe we were in a normal, honest-to-God fight. But there was nothing normal about it, was there? We can't give up. We shouldn't," Robert said, his fatigue and pain making his emotions bubble to the surface. Tears burned in the corners of his eyes.

Darin hugged his brother, trying not to hurt him, aware of his great pain

Robert wanted to let go. He wanted to tell Darin how terrified he was. His feet were cold. His body shook uncontrollably as the shock and blood loss took their toll. With a feeble effort, he pushed Darin away. "Stop." The wounded sibling wiped the tears from his eyes, and let out a snigger, as he said, "I had the best date."

Darin countered, "I got the bigger dick."

Robert responded, "It doesn't matter if you're dating a woman as ugly as a trout." They smiled at each other, with great effort.

Darin said, "She got a big ass."

"God meant to distract you from the real truth. Is it actually a man, or is she carrying a disease?" Robert cackled.

They laughed. The door above the steps, slammed, then again, twice more, on the other side.

When all was quiet once more, Darin asked, "Why did you hook me up with her? She can cook, I know, but she is a terrible-looking woman!"

"It was a lapse in my judgment, man," Robert acknowledged, quickly. Robert let a tear flow down his cheek.

Darin shook his head. "I wanted a woman that could cook. Her personality was okay. She was real, though," He rephrased his words, "I had a really good woman."

Robert stood up and responded, sharply. He braced the rip at the side of his torso. "Don't say it like that.

We're not through. Whatever it is has to come down here and get us. We gotta fight, man. We've gotta try. Yeah?"The pain took over, though and Robert shook his head and shrugged his shoulders, instinctively, unable to maintain his bravado.

Darin spoke for him, "Mom wanted us to live our lives. She didn't get to see us marry good women. She didn't get to see our great jobs and big families. But she did know how much we value the church, and community. That's something."

Robert tapped Darin's shoulder and mumbled, "She wanted us to live our lives. Didn't we do that?" Darin shrugged his shoulders. He said, "Are you happy with your life, up to this point?"

Robert responded, "I suppose so."

He slipped. Robert felt death on his shoulder and could no longer keep putting a bright spin on things. He only hoped he had inspired Darin to fight, or they were both screwed.

"You suppose so? You had better look back and reflect on what your life is. You better like it. If this is the end, don't you want to think about the good things before you die? Don't you want to use those moments to fight, for everything?" Robert closed his eyes at that. "We're not gonna just lay down and die, but, if this is the end, don't you want to think about those good things too?"

Robert tittered, "Yeah." He opened his eyes, wide. "You better think about that ugly, fat ass."

"Yeah, you're right," Darin chortled.

Robert sniffled. "This ain't right."

"Nothing's happened yet," Darin said.

Robert slipped the floor. "It had a claw," he whispered.

Darin responded, "I'm sorry?"

"We were grabbed from behind, at the pub," Robert mumbled. "It sunk a claw into my side. The pain was bad. So bad I fainted."

Darin stood over Robert.

"I remembered. I just didn't want to admit it," Robert said.

Out on the street a siren screamed, growing closer and closer, two sirens, three. They heard the squawk of police radio scanners and the thump of vehicle doors slamming. Officers pounded the door of the building above them to no avail. Then they heard a heavier thudding. They were ramming their way in!

"Fuck, man! We're saved! Someone must've seen him bring us in here!" Robert cried, jumping to his feet.

They scrambled to the foot of the stiars and Darin shouted, "We're downstairs! Help!"

The door above the stairwell burst open. Robert knew their time was up. He shrugged off death, and its cold touch. He invested in his rage. Together, they would face whatever came down those steps.

Darin said, calmly, "They're not gonna be fast enough."

At the top of the steps, framed in the yellow light of the doorway, a muscular man, their captor, looked down on them. His silhouette loomed tall and dark, with red eyes the only distinct facial feature they could make out. He stumbled down the steps toward them splintering the timber staircase as he fell, and grew.

The captor erupted from his black jumpsuit, his human flesh tore away, snapping as his body expanded until only shreds of skin remained in thick belts over his shoulders, chest and thighs. The monster clawed away the leftover human skin on its body.

Robert and Darin backed into a corner as it grew taller. The creature reared up, stretching its swollen muscle-mass, coated in black, taught fur.

It unleashed an almighty wail, which seemed to intermingle at once, in a snort, a low moan, and a ravenous growl, as the face of a man stretched and contorted, the nose and mouth stretching out into a feral muzzle

Robert, consumed by terror, began to backpedal, but there was nowhere to go. He did not expect this.

He, it, this beast-man, raised its shaggy, meaty arm,

sideways and fell, like a woodsman swinging his ax at full force.

The sharpened hand tore through Robert's exposed ribs, part of his arm and hip, already weakened. Robert could not pinpoint the pain. He just wanted it to stop.

The monster lifted Robert to its mouth and gnashed his neck with its serrated teeth. It pulled the rest of his left arm astray, and off. There was a place just big enough for its large mouth, on the side of Robert's belly. He cried, "No!" and writhed, struggling, clinging to life. The beast bit into Robert again, tearing through flesh and muscle tissue. Chunks of meat hung from the creature's mouth, dripped to the ground and spattered Darin's face and chest. Robert let it happen.

It turned to the cowering Darin and licked his face clean, merely grazing him with its teeth, as it licked him. The beast returned its cruel attention to the still breathing Robert and commenced to tear him in half, like a connected wing and breast in a two-piece chicken meal. Cartilage gave way. Bones cracked, and twisted, slowly. Robert was still alive, through it all. The pain, and agony, seized his spirit. He just wanted to close his eyes. It was time to die, but not before he could be a witness. Darin was still alive. At this point, his only option was to fight.

Darin yelled out in anger at the monster that had dismantled his brother, his bellow became an angry, defiant battle-cry as he rose to his feet, filled with fury and adrenaline.

The beast dropped Robert's body carelessly, discarding his two halves like pieces of paper on a sidewalk.

Darin pounced on the beast, and with no options left, clamped the massive creature's midriff in as stong a bear-hug as he could manage.

He pleaded, "Why like this? Let me live. I'm the last one. Let me live to mourn my brother, please! I just need to bury him. Stop!"

Darin pressed his head in the rooted monster's abdomen and yelped into its fur, "We don't deserve this.

Please! This is not fair."

The monster clutched the back of his head. It pushed a claw through the base of Darin's skull. Darin screeched, with a muffled urgency, "Stop!"

The emotionless beast remained silent to his pleas as his head cracked against its leg. Savage teeth tore into Darin's shoulder; the creature wrenched his head upward, only pulling Darin's head partly off his body. The monster chewed on Darin's shoulder, and savored his hot blood, while working its claws to pry open his chest.

An officer yelled at the top of the stairs, "Focus on the head!"

Handguns roared. The nine-millimeter rounds struck the beast, pounding its muscular form, seeming to have no effect on the monster.

A chunk of Darin's skull rolled around in this creature's maw like a tasty jawbreaker,until two shot gun blasts roared from above.

The monster hit the wall and collapsed on the wreckage of the two brothers. A rookie police officer grimaced and vomited violently on the floor, over the railing of the rickety staircase as two of his more experienced colleagues assessed the bloodbath in the corner.

"Too late again."

"Yeah, but it's one less of those fuckers to worry about."

The Herald of our Times

By Matthew Teah

I am in my bed, cold fear is running through me, mixing with hot dread and a deep sense of foreboding, creating a bitter cocktail of emotions. My body is soaked with cold sweat; it is taking every ounce of my willpower to not physically shake with fear.

I dare not move, I dare not open my eyes. My eyelids are tightly screwed up like a child who believes he cannot be seen so long as he cannot see anyone. Thousands of thoughts are running through my consciousness, flooding too fast to be fully understood; thousands of thoughts, and not one of them rational.

There is something in the quarters.

There is something in my quarters, and I do not know how it got in.

In any circumstance where an intruder is in your home a feeling of fear is as natural as the Earth's orbit around the Sun. But this is different. I can feel my mind unravelling, there should not be anyone here – not for the lack of want for company. It should be impossible. It is impossible. It physically should not and could not be able to occur. But the presence is here. I can feel it as sure as I can feel my heart drumming in my chest.

I can imagine the room around me, the cold and sterile polished steel walls. The functional décor comprising of a cot bed in which I now pretend to slumber, my writing desk, a lamp which sits on my desk and a stool, all of which are fixed to the respective surfaces. The only thing I can't visualise is the intruder.

Somehow, even in the dead silence hanging in the air, along with my eyes tightly closed, I am still aware of it, the way you are aware of someone staring at you from behind, that unexplained sensation of someone's eyes upon you. A vague image begins to form, a simple figure in black, lost in shadow.

I will not open my eyes, for if the interloper has not

attacked me yet, the guise of me sleeping may negate my continued survival until I can pluck up the courage to challenge the intruder.

"I know you do not slumber," Rasped a bitter voice, which barely rose above a whisper. "It amuses me that you think one such as I could be fooled by such a childish ruse, but such amusement cannot last forever."

I feel my pupils fully dilate beneath my eyelids in sheer shock. Something is in here with me. I lie here for a long moment, which seems to stretch out for an eternity. Questions are circling in my head. Is it really here? Am I going insane? Am I dreaming? Whatever is happening I cannot grasp at any form of logic to rationalize any of these thought streams.

"You are not here," I say out loud, dredging up information taught to me in basic training. I say these words even though I do not believe them, how strange the mind works when in situations of extreme stress. "You are a figment of my overstretched imagination brought on by my isolation for such a long period of time."

There is another harsh chuckle, this one longer than the last. "If you truly believed that then you would not have felt the need to vocalize your thoughts would you, Themis?"

At that last word my eyes flash open of their own accord I do not take in my surroundings, my mind is fast falling into a state of shock. It knows my name. Before I can possibly think of how it could know my name, I realise that not only are my eyes now open, but I am sitting up in my cot bed facing the intruder.

I can see it now and how apt my imagination is for the intruder is in black, shrouded in darkness. I cannot be sure but it seems it is just the lack of light in my sleeping quarters, the sole source of illumination being the low wattage bulb in the lamp on my writing desk.

"How do you know my name?" I gasp as hot fear grips me. My head is pounding as the shock of it knowing my name threatens to send me into a catatonic state.

It laughs long and hard. "Your flight suit in what I assume would be the maintenance bay. I had a look around before I came for you. I may know a lot of things but I cannot read minds."

"What are you?" I ask, hoping against hope that I will never find out the answer. Somehow in the pit of my stomach I know it is not like me, it is not human, I can sense that much.

"You are a smart one." It declares. "For you did not ask who, but what. Even in your state of shock you have the wit about you to know I am not one of your kind."

"What. Are. You?" I repeat, this time with a firmness I did not know I possessed. The shock is starting to ebb away, like a patch of ice on a warm winter day.

"The time will come for that, once I have decided if your mind could possibly comprehend one such as I," Replies the voice in the darkness. "Do not take that as an insult, human, not many can comprehend what I am. The mind rejects what it cannot come to terms with, more often than not the effects can be devastating. For now, you may know me as the Herald."

"Why are you here?" I manage, my sudden confidence melting away with every passing second. "What do you want with me?"

"With you, well not a lot." It replies. "What drew my attention was this fine craft you are in. What do you call it?"

"We call it the International Space Station."

"Truly it is amazing to see the human race reaching for the stars. The last time I was here, your saviour was breathing his last breath," Declared the Herald. "Well the scriveners who were deciding the nature of his divinity said he was. How ironic it was that those who killed him would later declare him the saviour of mankind."

I look into the depths of the shadow, the look of confusion must be written upon my features as the Herald laughs its low and amused chuckle once more.

"The one your kind call Jesus." Continued the Herald. "Of course he was not the man the Church proclaims him to be, he was not much of anything to be frank, how the flock are so easily swayed."

"How can you possibly know what the church says about Jesus if you were here well over two millennia ago?" I ask. What I really want to ask is, how is this being that old? What is it? What is it doing here? But I am struggling to think such thoughts let alone articulate them. I am still expecting to wake up and that this will be a bad dream.

"Well, your kind have been emitting electromagnetic radiation at a phenomenal rate ever since you discovered what it could do. We have picked up all of your radio and TV broadcasts since your early 20th century, we have watched the decline of your species.

"You think what you call your modern age has enlightened you. You could not be further from the truth, we watch your evangelical Christian preachers dole out their lies in arenas fit for kings, while the ones in real need are dying in third world countries.

"I think your Jesus would be turning in his grave... oh, he rose from the dead, didn't he?" said the Herald light-heartedly, with what I am sure would be a wry grin on its face, if it has a face, that is.

"A pleasant fiction. Your species is held down by religion, with it you can never truly be free. You are shackled by it.Religion is an interesting topic, but it is not what I am here to discuss, well not for the most part. We have seen your slavery, your World Wars, your persecution, hypocrisy and every possible inequity that has occurred and most horrifically, is still happening to this very day. We have been watching, and we are not happy."

"What are you?" I snap, my fear and unease has been replaced by frustration and anger. I release the harness and free myself from my cot bed and jump to my feet, the manoeuvre looking exaggerated due to the low gravity. My mind is no clearer than a few seconds ago, but my patience has snapped: this thing has intruded and is now speaking in riddles. "You speak of humanity's rise to the modern age as a spectator, you are speaking in tongues about nonsense. You have come aboard this space station unannounced, uninvited and you hide in shadow like a coward!"

A thunderous silence settles on the room, I fear I have gone too far. I fear it is now going to kill me. I draw in what I believe will be my last breath and brace myself. I hope that in my last moments of life I can at least ensure I do not suffer the indignity of soiling myself.

The silence is broken as the Herald steps out of the darkness, upon seeing its true form I lose my tenuous balance, doubling over in mid air, vomiting as cramps tear at my stomach. The pressure inside my skull is suddenly immense as my vision fogs over, I feel my eyes, ears and mouth begin to bleed.

The view now afforded of the room is as if I am looking through crimson cut glass. I continue to vomit as the bitter smell of half-digested food mixed with the iron tang of my blood is making me dry heave even after the contents of my stomach has been emptied into the air.

"I did warn you, Themis," States the Herald. "My physical form in this universe is too much to comprehend, you may not think it now, but you are one of the lucky few. The last being to see me spontaneously combusted, though I believe the high helium, methane composition of the being's genetic structure contributed to it."

Any possible reply is stolen as I continue to dry heave, while I roll up into a foetal position spinning in place trying to stop my limbs from shaking. My eyes are screwed up tight once more, trying to stave off the flashing after images of the Herald's true form which are now plastered to the inside of my eye lids.

"The vomiting shall pass soon enough, however looking upon me will never be an easy task," continues the Herald, I cannot see it but I am sure it is now looking down on me. "You will more than likely experience nightmares for the rest of your days, as your mind tries to expel what you have seen."

"What are you?" I manage through gritted teeth,

as a bitter mix of saliva and vomit taint my tongue as I speak. "Are you a God?"

"No, Themis." The Herald replies in a serious tone, seemingly no longer in the mood for levity. "I am in a position to pass judgement, but I am not a God. There are no Gods."

"Pass judgement?" I ask as the pressure in my skull begins to subside, I am also sure I have stopped bleeding. "On whom?"

"On you, Themis," replied the Herald. "On your entire species, you have evolved into sentient beings and have failed to see what a truly magnificent gift it is. Not only that, you have been squandering this gift for thousands of years. The time has come for judgement, 'you reap what you sow', I believe that is the proper use of the phrase."

"You cannot!" I spit out, the sickly feeling almost subsiding entirely. "You cannot judge an entire species on the same merits. There are billions of people on Earth. There have been countless billions who have died who committed much of what you speak, the ones born today are not responsible for those born yesterday."

"You are wrong Themis. We can, and we will," the Herald's voice rasps again. "I commend you on your analogy. But tell me this Themis, have those born today made amends for those born yesterday?"

"Of course we have," I utter, my stomach cramping as my brain registers I am now hungry due to vomiting up last night's dinner. I stay in my foetal position not because I feel the need to, but because I cannot look at the Herald again. Not yet. "Look at where you are, if you truly were here two millennia ago, you will recognize how far we have come, we are in a modern age. We have advanced technology, we have created health care. We put it to good use helping mankind, we do not live in a perfect society but we are on our way to making it Utopian."

"Themis," rasps the Herald. "Advanced technology does not negate a modern civilization. Yes this technology and health care your species has created does improve your wellbeing.But only if you can afford it.

"The advancements of humanity are used to further improve the standing of the few, while the rest are ignored. The great many of those inhabiting your world suffer lives worse than death. This is needless suffering. The wealth of the few could feed the world twice over. This inequity cannot be allowed to continue, it has to stop now, before the corruption your species carries can be spread away from your wretched cradle. "

"There always has been suffering in the world." I say, trying to make excuses for what I know to be truly deplorable. "It cannot be stopped."

"'The world suffers a lot. Not because of the violence of bad people, but because of the silence of good people,'" said the Herald. "Do you know who said that?"

"Napoleon," I reply. Dredging up knowledge of my high school history lessons.

"Exactly, and that was from the mouth of a despot," said the Herald. "You can say what you like against tyrants but they know a thing or two about suffering. It has not just been said by Napoleon, but by countless other terrible beings in every universe we have encountered. It is the same wherever we travel, not those exact words but the meaning is the same."

I am able to take in what the Herald is telling me, but I cannot believe it, for it is telling me of other civilizations not only in this universe, but in others. Not only am I the first to make contact with another sentient life force. I am also the first to know that there are a great many others. Like before, I cannot articulate any of this; all I can manage is a pitiful question riddled with self-preservation.

"What are you going to do?"

The Herald let out a low guttural laugh as it comes for me. "You already know, Themis."

I am lying face down in mid-air. I am slowly drifting

through a cloud of my vomit and blood. I must have been unconscious for some time, exactly how long I have no idea. I feel groggy. This is more than the feeling of waking up after a long sleep; a deep, cloying fatigue fills me. My vision is fading in and out, accompanied by a low ringing in my ears. I have no idea what happened after the Herald came for me.

The Herald!

I orientate myself vertically faster than any champion surfer could ever hope to accomplish. My heart starts pumping adrenaline through my body as my pupils dilate in panic, I scan my quarters for any sign of the Herald. Seeing none, I do not know if I should feel fear or relief. Was this a nightmare? Was I really visited by a being from another universe?

Just as I try to put the whole episode down to my overactive imagination, I look around at the blood and vomit floating around me. My senses return slowly, I smell the iron tang of my claret red blood and the bitter stench of my vomit. My heart starts to quicken once more as I realize this is potential evidence that the Herald was real, that it was aboard the space station. As my senses begin to sharpen I realize that the ringing in my ears is not a side effect of being unconscious, it is a machine call from the command module.

I try to break into a run, forgetting momentarily that I am in zero gravity. My movements are sluggish and laboured, appearing to be over-choreographed. I half-float, half-bound through the sterile oval corridors of the space station to the command centre. The walls and corridors are covered in aluminium foil.

I enter the command centre, the ringing is far louder as a light on the main console flashes repeatedly, trying to catch my attention. Before I answer the machine call I fire the thrusters of the space station to simulate gravity, for the first time in a week my feet touch the deck and stay there. There is a twinge in my stomach as my body adjusts to the feeling of gravity. I pick up a head set from the centre console and answer the machine call. The console has a small screen built into it which can be used as video conferencing.

"Astronaut, Themis. This is Houston, do you copy?" asks a firm voice edged with distortion. "Themis, do you copy?"

"Houston, this is Themis, I copy." I reply, trying to banish all dread and foreboding from my voice.

Suddenly the screen in the centre console winks into life, it is split into two, one part shows and image of me, the other is the main atrium of Space Command. I can see the man who is speaking to me it is Operations Director Read. His features are craggy and unyielding, just like his temperament

"Damn, Themis, you look like shit!" exclaims Director Read. Behind him are the flight and monitoring teams, all eyes are on their screens which will be relaying the image of me. "What happened to you? Do you realize how long we have been trying to contact you?"
"I have no idea, Sir." I manage, trying to keep my voice level. I glance at the representation of me and see that I do look like shit. "I believe I have been suffering hallucinations brought on by my being up here alone."

"Does that involve opening the external then the internal airlock?" asked Director Read, with his brow furrowing. "Hallucinations be damned, what the hell has been going on up there?"

I freeze for a long moment, the feeling of fear I felt in the presence of the Herald returning. I may not remember what happened after I blacked out, but I know that it would be impossible for me to open the external airlock first without being in the vacuum of space. The Director and the rest of the staff staring at me know this also. It must have been real, the Herald and its message, I feel my face begin to prickle as the pores opened and released a sheen of sweat.

"Well?" asks the Director, who is still waiting for an answer.

"I don't know what I can say that won't cause you to send a shuttle to haul my ass back to Earth," I shrug realizing I am actually going to have to share what the Herald told me.

"Now you listen to me, Themis," said the Director, barely able to reign his temper, his brow is screwed up in frustration. "You do not have a choice in what you can and cannot tell me. I am asking for a report and you better goddamn tell me what happened!"

I let out a pent up breath that I had not realized I had been holding, my shoulders sag and my face is now dripping with sweat as I recount the events from when I woke up and found the Herald in my sleeping quarters.

I tell the Director, and the rest of the staff in Houston, that the Herald described itself as a being from a different universe, and that it had been here in the times of Jesus, and that its kind have been watching and we are to be judged.

I try to describe the Herald's physical appearance. My vision begins to fog and pressure builds in my skull as I attempt to bring up a mental image of the Herald. I am no longer aware of the Director or any other physical thing. I am now looking through crimson cut glass once more, I feel I am close to blacking out.

"Themis!" exclaims the Director. "Look at me, Themis! Focus Themis! Focus!"

At the sound of the Director's voice I snap back into focus. I catch a glimpse of myself in the conference monitor, streams of claret mark my face where blood has been running from my eyes, ears, nose and mouth.

"You are serious about this?" asked the Director in a hushed tone with an incredulous look written across his face.

"Am I serious that I believe it actually happened?" I ask rhetorically while shrugging. "Sir, I don't know. Am I serious that this is all I remember? Yes I am."

This time it was the Director's shoulders that sagged as he let out a long, low whistle. "Right, we have to treat this as First Contact. When you asked what it was going to do, did it answer?"

I shake my head. "I don't know, Sir, I blacked out.

The last thing I know it said was, 'You already know, Themis.'"

A look of unease deepened on the Director's features with each and every passing moment, he asks next what I know is coming, "Before you lost consciousness what did you think it was going to do?"

"I thought of the Apocalypse. Judgement day. The end of the world," I say, realizing one thing that has been in the back of my mind. "Sir you said you registered the external then internal doors opening, did they open again afterwards?"

I look back to the image of the Director, he is looking back at me, but over my shoulder his eyes and nose begin to bleed, he then falls to the ground like a sack of potatoes. I look to the image of me on the conference screen there is a figure in black behind me. Fear bursts in my chest and runs through me in an instant.

The Herald did not leave the station!

There is a harsh hiss of static as the conference screen scrambles with interference. I spin around to confront the Herald, thankfully it is shrouded in darkness once more. It is towering over me, I am physically shaking with fear. It has changed its mind it is going to kill me. I am going to be the first to die on this end of days.

"Thank you, Themis," the Herald rasps. "You played your part extremely well."

"What?" I exclaim with confusion written on my features. "What part did I play?"

"Telling your Flight Director of humanity's impending destruction," Chuckles the Herald. "They will be scrambling over themselves to inform their superiors; you have instilled a far more vintage panic than I could have done alone."

"You planned this!" I spit at the Herald, finding a well of confidence. "I will not be your pawn, I will not dance to your tune!"

The Herald's face lunges out of the shadow, this time I am able to take in its features before the pain hits me, I have but a moment but it is more than enough time. Its raw physical presence seems to bend reality, as if the laws of physics no longer apply. It is in the centre of the module and the surrounding space is somehow warped by it.

Its head and body are massive I have no idea how it fits into the command module. Its huge oval eyes take up much of the upper portion of its head, they are dark as the pits of Hell - to call them black would be an understatement. They are so dark that they seem to draw in all of the limited light in the command module, like twin black holes sucking in both time and matter.

I cannot draw my eyes from them for what seems an age I feel my presence of self diminishing with each passing millisecond. I feel my consciousness being pulled into those void pools of despair. With the last vestiges of my willpower I take in the remainder of its features. Its skin is so pale, bordering on ice white, its hairless head and face criss-crossed with deep scars. They create the effect of if its head having been patched together with odd pieces of flesh.

The most chilling part of its face is its impossibly wide mouth. It runs from one side of its head to the other, its mouth is permanently half open in a leering grin, almost reptilian in nature. It is a grin with too many teeth; hundreds of them, in varying length. They are transparent and look razor sharp, as if they could tear me in two in one bite.

"Now you listen to me," the Herald hisses menacingly, hardly moving its mouth. "Your continued existence in this mortal coil is measured in how long you stay in my good graces. You will dance to my tune. You will do as I say or I will see it done that not only are you the first to be slain. I will make sure it is a most excruciating death, one that will stretch out for eons. Do. You. Understand?"

The extended sight of the Herald has placed overwhelming pressure on my skull. My eyes are closed up tight staving off the burning after-images, all I can do is nod my understanding in what I think is the general direction of the Herald.

I open my eyes once more and find that the Herald has retreated back into shadow. “What happens now?”

“Now we wait,” replies the Herald, from the darkness. “Nothing instils more fear after a threat than inaction. Even in its simplest form, if someone tells you that they are going to hit you, and they don’t immediately, it makes you more paranoid. You know it is going to happen, but not when. We will wait until the leaders of your Earth are saturated with fear and paranoia.”

“How long will we wait?” I ask, the pain and throbbing has all but gone. But I am unable to truly grasp the situation I find myself in. I want to ask what the judgement is, why it is happening and how can this thing judge me? But I find myself only able to carry on with this current conversation.

“We will wait until the machine of lies you call the media mentions a crisis on this space station,” replies the Herald. “We will wait until the word of your message leaks out and hits the people, we will wait for the mass hysteria, the religious riots and mass suicides and the destabilization of your society.”

“How do you know that will happen?” I ask, I am still trying to think independently but the fatigue is still clawing at me.

“I have seen it happen before,” the Herald replies. “On each planet, or system of planetary empires. The paranoia that rules your species will also be its undoing.”

I let out a long, pent-up release of breath and lean against the command console. The idea that this was some strange nightmare has long past. In front of me is a being from another universe, it has traversed time and space to come to the Earth and judge our entire species. I should be climbing the walls in panic, but I somehow feel calm or numb, more likely numb.

Despite my fear, there are thousands of questions swirling around my head, this thing, whatever it is, knows a wealth of information, not only about humanity but of other beings. If I am going to die I will at least try to learn some small measure of truth before I meet my maker, if I even have a maker. Standing before me is the answers humanity has sought for millennia, I wish to be the first to learn them. A kernel of unease forms in the pit of my stomach as I realise I may well be the first and last.

"Can you tell me of others?" I ask, I am growing ever more comfortable in the presence of the Herald. While it is shrouded in shadow, at least. "Can you tell me of others civilizations?"

There is a long pause then the Herald gives off a fiendish chuckle.

"Yes, Themis," rasps the Herald. "I shall tell you of others, it will shed light on why your race needs to be exterminated. You need to understand the significance of light and dark in religion, for example Jesus is the light and Satan is the dark and how these personifications are told in parables and fairy tales?"

"Yes, I understand," I reply. "Like the Ying and Yang, complementary opposites. Life and death."

"Yes excellent, Themis," replied the Herald, a slight chuckle returning to its voice. But not for long, it settles back into a far more serious tone. "I have a perfect story to tell you. In this universe, your universe, there is a system of planets billions of light years from here.

"This system of planets revolves around a gigantic red star a thousand times larger than your own sun. There are fourteen planets, all of which are terrestrial, one of the planets resides in the habitable zone, another resides on the edge of it, well in astronomical terms it does. Surprisingly they both became home to life.

"There is a curious characteristic of which both planets share, neither of them rotate on their axis they are locked in the same position. Both planets have a permanent dark and light side, however they are exact opposites. The planet in the habitable zone has a verdant light side, with luscious pastures and bountiful oceans where life is abundant, of which a sentient race evolved to live in the light and shunned the darkness, fearing it. Darkness became the personification of evil.

"The planet which resided on the edge of the habitable zone, its light side is permanently scorched by the sun and nothing can survive in such intense light. Therefore life managed to evolve in the darkness, eking out an existence from what little sustenance could grow at the border of where light and dark met.

"Religion is a natural process for any newly sentient race, but once they evolve into modern civilisations, they need to shed religion. Sure enough these two races who shared the same solar system created their own Gods in echo of their personal surroundings. Those who lived in the light worshiped it and feared the dark, creating evil personifications. Those who lived in the dark feared the light and created their own religion lambasting the light.

"The sentient races created stellar travel and started fledgling colonies, the only difference between them being the colour of their skin and eyes. Those who lived permanently in the light, their skin was as black as the night they so feared, their eyes varied in colour with perfect vision in the light. Those who lived in the dark, their skin was as pale as ice, as pale as my own, their eyes adapted to see in the dark and were but deep, black pools.

"As inevitable as it was, the two races came into contact with one another. Upon this inevitable meeting, their ambassadors established contact and learned that they lived on polar opposite home worlds. In each other they saw the personification of evil. A 'holy war' broke out as each race's sole vocation became to annihilate the other, to rid the universe of the very thing their religious leaders had warned their followers of.

"They waged war to rid their civilizations of the monsters, the terrors, the very evil in which they had feared for millennia. For centuries after that meeting, apocalyptic battles raged but neither could get the upper hand, it was a struggle that would never end."

There was a long pause, silence hung in the air. I remain silent in case the Herald is going to continue in its parable, seeing that it isn't, I ask, "What happened to them?"

"We killed them," replied the Herald, as blunt and as matter-of-fact as could be. "We murdered every single last one of them. Their civilizations had been so indoctrinated by religion that it permeated their very consciousness. There was no way to change them and as we watched their wars we knew they could not be changed, so we destroyed them. We destroyed them because if their technologies became inter-stellar they would spread their virus of religion and destroy other sentient life forms who had shed their burdens of faith.

"It is not just religion we watch for, Themis. As I told you, we watch for inequities, evils, tyrants and despots. We cannot allow tyranny to spread throughout universe. Your home world contains everything we have watch-words for, your species needs to be eradicated."

My blood runs cold, I do not doubt what the Herald is telling me is the truth, this… this thing, it is going to murder an entire planet.

I am startled by a machine call in the command console, the Herald laughs at my anxiety, I look to the Herald but it begins to disappear into nothingness. "Answer it."

I close my eyes while letting out a long sigh, then answer the call, after a moment of static interference I am once again greeted by the main atrium in space command although the scene that greets me is different from before.

The atrium is practically devoid of staff, I can only see the Deputy Flight Director looking at me but there seems to be no one else. The Deputy Director is a small meek man with massive black-rimmed glasses framing his face, making him look like your classic book worm.

"Deputy Director," I state, not knowing how to proceed. "Where is the Director?"

The Deputy Director shifts uncomfortably on the

spot not speaking, he fidgets with his glasses in a nervous gesture he keeps looking over my shoulder.

"Deputy Director?"

"He is dead, Themis," the Deputy Director tells me, still fidgeting with his glasses.

"What?" I exclaim, my mouth opening and closing like a fish out of water, this must be why the atrium has been emptied. I cannot be sure, but I think I can hear the Herald laugh at the edge of my consciousness.

"He is dead," the Deputy states again. "He saw the Herald and dropped down dead as soon as the screen went to static. We think it was a massive brain haemorrhage or heart attack, he was dead before he even hit the floor.

"The Director isn't the only one, two administrators died the same way. Another five have been hospitalised and are said to be in a critical condition, at least twelve are showing symptoms of severe post-traumatic stress."

The Deputy leans in close to the camera and whispers, "Is it still aboard?"

I nod by way of reply.

"What does it want?" the Deputy asks, but he is obviously not relishing the prospect of what I am about to say.

"The utter annihilation of the human race," I deadpan. "It has not stated any demands, it wants to kill every human life for the religion we have created and the tyranny we have reaped upon the innocent, the Herald describes us as a virus that cannot be allowed to spread. What is happening groundside?"

The Deputy visibly swallows down his fear, trying to contain himself. "The President has been informed but he will stay in Washington. The military is on its way. They will seek to broker terms with the Herald."

Again I can hear the Herald's laughter, before I respond. "Terms?"

The Deputy shifts uncomfortably once more, then shrugs. "I don't know, I am not permitted to know any more, from here on in it is a military matter. They will

be here soon. I was given latitude to communicate this message and nothing more. Good luck, Themis."
The screen is laced with static once more then goes black. I am on my own with the Herald once more.

"Would you negotiate?" I ask the empty room knowing the Herald will be close by.

The Herald laughs again, it is a melodious sound. "Do wolves negotiate with sheep?"

I wait for the Herald to expand on its comment but realise it isn't going to.

"Are you here alone?" I ask, I am able to formulate thoughts while I cannot see the Herald. I wonder if there is an invasion force anchored somewhere in our system. "Did you come to our system alone? Do you have a ship?"

"Yes I came alone and I do have a ship of sorts," the Herald tells me. "Although it is more of a portal, it is a permanent presence in this system that allows me and those of my kin to travel to this verse."

"It has always been here?" I ask incredulously. "How is that possible? It would have been found."

"It was found, that is how I knew to come," said the Herald. "Your people, well the ones who know of its existence, call it the Black Knight satellite."

A wave of adrenaline washes over me, the Black Knight satellite is the stuff of conspiracy legend, it is rumoured to be of alien origin and said to have been in orbit around the Earth for thirteen thousand years. Now the Herald is telling me that not only is the Black Knight real, but it is a portal to other universes.

"I can't believe it," I utter almost to myself. "How could you possibly know to come if you were in another universe?"

"The Black Knight is also designed to pick up electromagnetic waves from the planet of interest," the Herald replies. "As this is always a precursor to stellar flight, my kin place portal crafts in orbit around planets that have the capacity to support life. We monitor the evolution of indigenous species to see if they become sentient and more importantly if they pass the test."

"The test?" I ask, my brow furrows, it has not mentioned a test before.

"Religion and tyranny," barks the Herald, its patience growing thin. "Religion is the first test for true evolution. We need to know if a society that calls itself civilised still believes that there is a man in the sky controlling things, think of it as an IQ test.

"That and we monitor how those in power treat those without it, for if they can treat their own race with such disdain how would they treat beings from another planet, especially one that is less advanced? This is why you and your kind has to be eradicated. You will never learn to live in peace and universal kindness."

I want to shout a denial, I want to refute what this thing is telling me, but I cannot. I know it is true, we call ourselves civilised but we commit atrocities against one another in the name of religion, money and power, we are a wretched species. I feel myself agreeing with the Herald, I think I am starting to suffer from Stockholm syndrome, as I am unconsciously starting to defend the Herald's proposed actions.

There is a machine call again. I have no wish to answer this one as I know military staff will be on the other end of it. I have a sense of unease growing in my stomach. I know that the military staff will treat the Herald as if it is no different from any other invader. I fear the hubris of a military leader who is used to victory will hasten our apocalypse.

Reluctantly I answer the call and as I feared, the atrium is now swarming with military personnel. I recognise those staff nearest to the screen. They are the Secretary of Defence, the Commander of the United States Northern Command and the Commander of the First Air Force. It was obvious that the powers that be were not taking this situation lightly, thankfully the Herald is still invisible I hope it does not show itself.

"Astronaut Themis," states the Secretary of Defence, he is a well-dressed man in his late fifties, and his dark brown eyes are framed by greying brown hair. "It seems that you are in quite a bind up there."

Before I can respond, there is the sound of the Herald's laughter, its brief titter is followed by its crushed gravel voice. "Your Astronaut is in no more of a bind than you are on the ground, human."

The Secretary of Defence's head darts back as though he has been punched in the face, perhaps he had not truly believed the reports."Who said that? Identify yourself."

The Secretary of Defence looks over my shoulder to see if he can catch a glimpse of the Herald. I sincerely hope the Herald will keep out of sight. The loss of the Director and his staff is a tragedy but the loss of the Secretary will be seen as an act of war.

"I am the Herald of your times," replies the Herald with what sounds like relish. "I am the Herald of your impending doom."

The Secretary's face turns rigid, like stone. "I am not here to posture; you have come to our planet and boarded a human held vessel without permission. Not only that, but you have caused the death of three of our people, hospitalised five and scared the bejesus out of the rest.

"You bring a message of judgement and impending destruction, how can you come to such an assumption that not one human being on our entire planet is worth saving? This is our planet, surely we should be the masters of our own destiny."

"There will be no negotiating," replied the Herald with what I am sure is a sneer of disdain. "There will be no talking your way out of this, you and your ilk have the world under your boot, you have this tiny blue planet in your corrupt fist.

"You and your President care nothing for the suffering you reap upon countless billions. Do not even think you can deny it, for I am privy to every single communiqué and radio message that has been sent since its invention on Earth."

The Secretary of Defence is wrong-footed, not knowing how to continue, the Northern Commander seems similarly stunned – or he is merely allowing his superior to take the lead. It seems that the Commander of the First Air Force still has his tongue in his mouth, but I suspect it would be better if he too remained silent.

"Strong words for something that is in orbit with no apparent weapons at its disposal." The Commander of the First Air Force is Lieutenant General Harper, I only know him by reputation, he has the cocksureness of a commander not used to be spoken to with derision. "I wonder if your words would be so strong if we fired a warhead at you. I think you would retreat like a coward."

I close my eyes knowing that the Herald will not tolerate being spoken to with such disrespect. I open my eyes again as I hear the Lieutenant General's sudden cry of panic. I see that the Lieutenant General has been lifted from the ground by some unseen force, he is wriggling in an invisible grasp like a frog before a dissection. The Secretary of Defence and the Northern Commander back away a few steps, caught by surprise at the sight of their levitating subordinate.

At first there is a blood-curdling scream which emanates from the Lieutenant General. It is not immediately apparent why he is screaming, then there is a wet ripping sound and blood starts pouring from the man's feet as his shoes literally explode.

Then his trousers split from his cuffs, tearing upwards towards his fly, the skin and muscle of his legs also gives way with wet sucking sounds. The man is being flayed alive. The flaying extends passed his waist he is literally being torn inside out in front of our eyes. His scream is a terrible sound to behold, it ends abruptly when the flesh tearing reaches his lungs.

For a moment the Lieutenant General's skeleton is suspended in mid-air, dripping with blood as his flesh, skin, muscle and vital organs float in a disgusting cloud of offal above his skull. The Secretary of Defence doubles over and vomits onto the floor, as he does there is a sound of laughter which looks to be coming from the skeleton. The laughter stops abruptly and as it does so the skeleton comes apart one bone at a time, clattering on impact with the blood-soaked floor.

The cloud of suspended offal starts to take the shape of a crude face, only I know that it resembles the visage of the Herald for all others whom have seen it have already perished. I watch in complete disbelief of what I am seeing, it is if I am watching a horror movie.

"Now that I have your attention," the mocking meat visage utters, the sound is not coming from the meat cloud, it is still coming from the station, "take what I have told you to your President, instruct him to prepare your nation for the end of days anyway he sees fit."

The Secretary of Defence looks as though he is about to offer a retort. To ensure he cannot, the offal face grimaces then launches at the Secretary exploding all over him, covering his suit with blood, guts and gore.

The Herald speaks again, but its voice is harsher than I have heard before, I have to cover my ears as a pressure wave hits me, those groundside have to do the same. "You and your entire race are to be exterminated!" the Herald screams. "Do not seek to talk your way out of this, you have limited time as it is."

The Secretary of Defence looks down to his blood stained suit then to the puddle of blood, offal and bone that used to be his subordinate, I can see a well of defiance swell in his chest as his brow furrows in anger.

"You listen to me you… you vile demon!" the Secretary of Defence roars. "We will not run around like whipped dogs, this entire facility is in lockdown, you can slay me and my staff but word will not get out.

"You are on a space station in our orbit. There are over seven billion human souls on this planet and we will fight to save every single last one of them. You are powerless to do anything as we will not convey your message of impending destruction to anyone. The knowledge of your existence will stay on that space station and in this facility. Your continued existence is only down to the fact that one of our own is aboard; that is the value we place on human life!"

There is a thunderous silence aboard the space station and the main atrium groundside, the Secretary of Defence looks around the chamber nervously, as does the Northern Commander.

The silence is broken as the massive monitoring screens which had went dark when the atrium had been evacuated turn themselves back on, the screens no longer show telemetry and live orbital radar feeds. The screens show live television news broadcasts from around the world, the news anchors of each channel stop mid-broadcast as if stunned. I can see what the news anchors are looking at.

They are looking at screens in their studio that are split into two, the screens show the main atrium of Space Command and the view of the command module. The anchors are looking at a perplexed Secretary of Defence and a dumfounded image of me, the Herald must have used satellites in orbit to link feeds. The newscasters have no idea what to make of it.

"Citizens of Earth!" booms the Herald voice, as it does so it reappears behind me. I avert my gaze to not make eye contact through the monitor, instead I look at the news anchors. "Behold the image of your impending destruction!"

At the sight of the Herald, the Secretary of Defence and the Northern Commander double over while clutching their heads and begin to vomit blood profusely. The news anchors on various screens react much the same way as the late Flight Director did, they fall to the ground dead with blood pouring from every visible orifice. Some of the cameras hit the floor and smash, no doubt the cameramen are suffering similar fates.

"Look to me and know that your end of days is it at hand!" the Herald's voice booms, each syllable is crashing against my skull. "Your time of judgement is at hand, it is time to reap what you have sown, not one being on your wretched cradle has led a good life, your world and every inhabitant will be put to the flame. The hell you have feared for millennia will come to your planet and reap the souls of humanity and torture them for eternity!

"Look now to the atrium of space command. Look to the Secretary of Defence of the United States of America, watch him die and know that your deaths will be a thousand times more terrifying!"

The Secretary of Defence had found his feet, the Northern Commander stayed where he lay with a pool of blood forming around his head, which is face down. His legs twitch, but he is stone dead. The Secretary's face is like a rabbit caught in headlights, his death is over in an instant. He is not even afforded the luxury of screaming, his body bursts into a thousand meaty chunks and bone fragments.

The sudden realisation that the images are genuine and the fact that they have witnessed the slaying of the second most powerful man in the United States of America sends those in the studios who still draw breath into utter panic. They flee the studios, they flee for their lives, although I fear it will do them no good.

I feel nothing but despair; the world will tear itself apart, I know that nothing will be able to stop it now, those who believe in end times will blame each other and contradictory religions for this curse. There will be rioting, murder, looting, there will be war and it is all down to the thing that is behind me. Whether it is despair, panic or insanity I find a well of defiance inside my soul, I spin around and with all the force at my disposal I punch the Herald in the jaw while shouting in outrage.

The gesture is pathetic, the Herald does not even flinch. Although if it is able to look startled it does so now. Then with a wicked grin it lets out a terrifying roar, the force of which throws me backwards. I hit the command console with my head.

My world is darkness once more.

I stir from the blackness that enveloped me, my head is pounding and I am rocking back and forth. I assume the sensation comes from disorientation, nausea after being knocked unconscious. I open my eyes and realise that I am lying on the deck, I reach up and touch the crown of my head, sharp stinging pain greets my touch. I look to my hand it is sticky with partially dried blood.

"You are resilient, I will give you that," states the Herald in a humorous tone, the vast creature is in shadow once more.

I push myself up onto my elbows and realise that it isn't nausea causing the rocking sensation, the command module is actually rocking back and forth, no doubt the entire station is following suit.

"What is happening?" I ask, although I fear I will rue asking.

"Look for yourself," replies the Herald. "It is quite beautiful."

I roll over onto my front and with much pain I push myself to my feet, it feels as though I am on a boat in stormy seas, constantly rocking. With some difficulty I ambulate to the nearest Earth side port hole, what I see in the foreground is indeed beautiful, what I see in the background is terrifying.

In the foreground near the space station there are blinding flashes every few moments, the flashes are massive but fleeting, they look like supernovae. I know what they are as soon as I see them, nuclear warheads detonating in zero gravity. The Herald must be blocking the missiles somehow. In the background I see the Earth and the terminator between day and night, on the night side I can see the glow of cities but there are also ruddy orange glows where I am sure cities should be.

"Your government believes it can solve all its problems with nuclear weapons," deadpans the Herald, I know that he is referring to the warheads that are being blocked.

"What is happening groundside?"

"The end of your world," replied the Herald, with a hint of satisfaction. "You have been unconscious for the better part of two days, there is already the total worldwide shutdown of basic infrastructure. Civilisation is tearing itself apart and not to mention the old rivalries rearing their ugly heads, not only are the Americans launching salvoes at us, they are also in a state of nuclear war with the Russians. The orange glow and smudges you can see are the major cities on the Eastern seaboard of the continental United States aflame, the death toll there is already in the millions, although Russia is fairing no better.

"Ironically the Vatican city, Mecca and Jerusalem are under siege, once faithful adherents are seeking revenge for what they call a betrayal. Although the big three are accusing each other for the reason the end of days are nigh. The total population of Earth I can now estimate to be forty one percent."

I cannot believe what the Herald is saying; it is telling me that over three billion lives have been extinguished in less than two days. At this rate the human race may be extinct even before the Herald and its kin get their chance, at that thought another occurs to me which I speak out loud.

"You planned this didn't you?" I ask, there is a long pause as I realise the Herald wishes for me to further explore my commentary. "This is one of the strategies you use, you use the indigenous population's fears against them so that they will tear themselves apart."

"You are correct, Themis," replied the Herald, "my kin are numerous but we are spread across the cosmos in this universe and a multitude of others. To even gather a fraction of us together would take some time and leave some sentient races to their own devices."

I have to ask a question now, it is one that I have felt the need to ask since the Herald came to the station, but it is one I feared learning the truth of.

"Why have you not murdered me?" I ask, but that

isn't the entire question, "Not just that, why have you answered my every question?"

The Herald chuckles. "I thought you would never ask."

"Pardon?" I ask, with a perplexed look written across my features.

"I have plans for you, Themis," replies the Herald, with a serious tone returning to his voice. "I have not been entirely honest, not all of the humans groundside will perish although the great many will. It is not the first time I have done this to the Earth, but not on this scale."

"I don't understand. What are you telling me, you have destroyed the population of Earth before?" I ask.

"Not the entire population," states the Herald. "My kind are not callous or without remorse but we cannot allow an interstellar race who are bigoted, racist or tyrannical to leave its cradle. Therefore we monitor how civilisations evolve in their early stages, if they will become or have already become tyrannical or occult we destroy them.

"This goes for Earth also, the cities of Sodom and Gomorrah, the city of Jericho, the fall of the Roman Empire, the Egyptian empire and other megalith building societies. They all became corrupt and held the great many under the boot of the few so I destroyed them by several different means. Some planets with sentient races eventually learn the error of their ways with the loss of cities or entire civilisations, but not Earth, not humans. No, you have failed to respect one another for hundreds of thousands of years.

"So it comes to this, the last chance for humanity before annihilation is the only option. The scenes groundside will play out unmolested the countries of the world and religions who call themselves pillars of civilisation will be destroyed. There will be billions dead, infrastructure will lay in ruin, military arsenals will be exhausted but there will be survivors. More importantly the survivors will distrust governments and religions they will be resilient against them as they have survived their apocalypse and that is where you come in.

"You will carry a message to them, Themis. You have been seen with me so you will be believed. You will tell them that they have only been allowed to survive, for they have cast down their tormentors and false preachers. You will rally the survivors and form a new order and teach respect, kindness and above all, equality. Through you, humanity will rise from the ashes and prosper.

"Through you, your world will advance enough so that I can withdraw the Black Knight satellite from orbit, safe in the knowledge that you can forge your own destiny. But heed my words, if you do not bring order amongst chaos, humanity will be exterminated and the Earth will be destroyed. The billions of years Earth existed will be for naught and will not be missed, for no one besides me and my kin will ever know that your pitiful blue planet ever existed."

"Why me?" I utter, I cannot believe what it is telling me.

"I could say that it is because you are a woman and that maternal instincts will exude compassion but it is much more than that," the Herald tells me. "I would not say I believe in fate as it smacks of religion, but I do hold stock in strong coincidences. The significance of your name and the fact you were on this station when I came is too much to ignore."

"My name?" I feel stupid that I cannot form more than two words at a time, but I am unable to even think about what the Herald is telling me.

"Your name," Replies the Herald. "Themis to the ancient Greeks was a Titaness and was described as of good counsel. To them she was the personification of divine order, law and custom. Not counting the religious connotations, the providence of your name cannot be ignored. Watch your people come to the brink of destruction, remember it well, for you will teach those who survive the error of their ways. Teach them well, for if you don't, it will be you who dies first."

With that the Herald vanishes and this time for good, I feel his presence leave the station. I stand there at the porthole, watching the ruddy orange glow spread. The fires are devouring the entirety of America, although the eastern seaboard is now in sunlight. As I watch the world tear itself asunder I realise that the Herald has tricked me with wicked irony. It has told me that I am to lead humanity but it has left me stranded on a space station and has brought about the destruction of the very technology that I would need for me to get groundside. I am going to starve to death and die knowing that my death was the last joke of the Herald; I close my eyes as despair rises to claim me.

While my eyes are closed I feel as though a breeze is hitting my face, but I know I will never know the cold touch of wind ever again. I open my eyes and realise the breeze is real I am standing on the blackened lawn of the White House, it seems as though the nukes did not touch the nation's capital. I will not linger here for long. I will not build a new world from the ashes of the old. I am sure that the Herald placed me here as a reminder. I will band humanity together and rebuild the world.

There is a loud bang and I am thrown forward face first into the blackened lawn, I land in the dirt. My world is in darkness again as I am swallowed up by mud and murky water. I try to rise but I cannot move my legs and my arms are sapped of strength. I hear footsteps sloshing towards me; I feel the firm grip of hands on my shoulders as I am hauled over onto my back. I see two men covered in mud and blood who are pointing sawn-off shotguns at me. They have shot me in the back, I know that now. I wait for them to recognise me so that I can begin my ministry. Suddenly I realise they won't, as I am covered in mud.

"I have been sent from the sky!" I scream like a mad woman trying to find the right words. "My name is that of a Greek goddess that is why it sent me, I was sent by the thing in the sky to rebuild humanity!"

One of the men looks to the other while they both

train their shotguns on me, then he looks back down to me. "It's because of God worshippers like you that we are in this mess!"

I try to plead my case, but I realise it is futile. I am sure I can hear the Herald's cackle, but the men don't seem to hear it. The Herald has played me for a fool. I look to the sky behind the men and see that there are fiery shapes falling from the sky, after a moment I can see that they are gargantuan ships. Was this... this Herald... this thing an invading alien sent to soften us up, or was it a guardian against religion like it claimed.

I will never find out, for my world is black once again. The men with the shotguns have opened fire at point blank range, they have shot me in my face. There is an intense feeling of pain that stretches on for what feels like an age but then there is nothing.

I hear the Herald's laughter again.

To See the Well

By Luc Haasbroek

The locals still called it the Well House, although it had been torn down and renovated so often that it looked no different from the other houses nearby. They still whispered about it. All the people in the village agreed that something terrible had happened there, but no one could quite agree on what anymore. It was not something that should have been forgotten.

The locals stayed away from the Well House, but sometimes people from other towns came to it. People who'd heard the stories of the house and its well, and were drawn to it. David was one such man. He was in his twenties, freshly dropped out of university, and ambitious – the kind of combination that causes you to hitchhike from London because of a fairy-tale. He'd heard rumours about the Well, and he had a young man's curiosity. What he didn't have was a girlfriend, or a steady income, or a place to say. Since Elaine had left him and his landlord had thrown him out, he didn't really have a reason to stay in London anymore. He hadn't even sold a sculpture in four months.

After two hours of walking from the main road, David found the Well House. He walked up its garden path. The rain was cold, and he was glad he would be indoors. He found the front door unlocked. The inside of the Well House was cold and dark, but clean. For a moment, David had imagined a witch's cottage or a troll's lair. But this house looked normal, and even had pieces of expensive furniture scattered around it. David didn't believe in stories, he told himself. He was only visiting the old House for a laugh. But then why hadn't he turned back?

He found a large room at the end of the passage. Bulky shapes draped in sheets stood around it – more furniture, perhaps? Wondering if he was at the right place, wondering if he had enough money for a room for the night (not only had his last exhibit not sold well, the reviews were reminiscent of a whipping. In public. Naked), David headed toward the door. One review had stung more than the others: *Although David Emmerson's persistence is commendable, his latest offering is unoriginal and mediocre. He is a hack, and he is the worst kind of hack – because he can't even pretend to be talented.*

"You've come to see the Well."

It wasn't a question. The voice was gruff. David looked round to see its owner. Standing in the doorway was an old man with ratty black hair and a ratty black coat. He was bent and twisted, and his face seemed capable of only two expressions: scowl and grimace.

"Um, yes, I guess I have," said David.

David had first heard the legend of the Well in a pub in Islington a few months before: if you went to the well and asked it for anything, you would receive it. Back then, it had seemed like an amusing fairy-tale. Standing in the dark, cold room with this man, it felt like something else.

"Do you know what you want to ask the Well?"

David thought of the review, of his poverty, of the things Elaine had shouted at him before she vanished into the London darkness forever. Without hesitating, he said, "Talent."

"There's a price," said the old man.

"I don't have money."

A chuckle. "Not that kind of price."

"Then what?"

"You'll know," said the old man. "Come. I'll take you there."

David followed the man down a passage, and finally out into a courtyard. It was beautiful; white flagstones, dotted with rosebushes. At the centre was a simple marble well.

Pulling his jacket tight around himself, perhaps to keep off the chill or the rain or something else David couldn't describe, he walked to the well. Its surface was dark and still. He couldn't see how deep it went down. It could have been a metre. It could have been a thousand.

Taking a deep breath, feeling foolish, feeling scared, feeling a little exhilarated, David asked.

When David walked back inside from the courtyard, the old man was gone. Feeling as if he needed to get out of that place, he hurried out the house and onto the road, where the rain had begun to fall even harder.

David walked to a friend's house in the town, where he just muttered a few words in greeting and fell asleep on the couch. He had turbulent dreams of wells and dark places, but when he awoke he had the idea for his next exhibit. He left for London, wallet full of borrowed money, and began to sketch and sculpt.

The exhibit opened a few months later. It sold well, and the reviewer that had once called David a hack admitted that he was improving. He bought a studio, found a patron, and continued to work. As the weeks turned to months, and the months to years, David felt the pull of the well. For years he ignored it. Told himself he didn't need it. But eventually he went back. Of course he did. And then again two years later. And then again. He asked the well for the same thing, and each time he got it.

Ten years after his first visit to the well, David was a millionaire. Thirteen, and the Tate Modern displayed some of his work. Twenty, and he was hailed as the new Brancusi. But with each year, David's life darkened.

He found himself thinking dark thoughts. They slipped in, uninvited, and took hold. He was angry more and more, and depression followed him like a faithful dog. He was married twice and divorced twice. He was showered in awards. His friends left him. He appeared in Time magazine. His health declined. The White House commissioned him to create an installation. He found himself unable to last more than a few hours without his pills.

At the unveiling of his presidential installation, his hands were spotted and shaking as the president shook them. He looked much older than his forty-nine years. The president didn't remark on it, but thanked him, and praised the sculpture: a simple fountain, with aqueducts that led the water to a white well.

That night, driving home, David thought (as he so often did these days) of the well. It made him bitter. He felt cheated. He wanted revenge or a refund or some sort of recognition that he'd been wronged. He wanted to show the old man that he was David Emmerson, a man of wealth and influence. A man who would not be tricked.

That was why, when he returned to England the following week, David took a taxi (he was too frail to drive) to the town.

He hobbled up the path to the house. It looked the same, but the garden had grown wild and the paint was blistered and flaking away from the door. Again, it was unlocked. Again, he entered. The old man was not there.

"Come out," David yelled into the empty house. "I know you're here! We have some things to talk about."

David searched the house, but found no one. Finally his search brought him to the courtyard. The marble well stood as it always had – unchanged, untouched by time, its water dark.

"You did this to me," David said to the water. "You tricked me."

The water said nothing.

He remembered then the old man's words. *There's a price.*

"No," he whispered.

His reflection stared back at him from the surface of the well. He looked old and sick and bitter, his hair dirty and unkempt, his face twisted. And he understood.

He ran, limping, back into the house, into the large room. He went to one of the shapes under the sheet, the things he'd seen every time he'd come and always thought were furniture. He pulled the sheet off. There was a flutter of dust. The moonlight spilling through the window illuminated the marble.

"Oh my God."

David took two steps away from the sculpture. Not because it was horrifying, which anyone could plainly see it was, or because it looked as if it would topple over, such was the precarious balance of the statue, positioned as it was, on the tips of its toes in the throes of agony. The sculpture's face, twisted in pain, David's trademark, brought the shock of recognition that the craftsmanship was his own. Having disturbed the sculpture with a trembling hand, David scurried back as the piece toppled, struck the floor, and shattered. A marble eye skittered to a halt against his shoe.

David knew then the price. He sat there in the shadows for a long time. After an hour or a day or a hundred years, he couldn't be sure, the door opened. A young man, rainwater dripping off his jacket, came into the room.

Bent with age and twisted with bitterness, David hobbled toward him. Shaking, he said, "You've come to see the Well."

The Coma
By Stefan Lavery

She flung her arms about maniacally to get his undivided attention. He carefully slid the earphones off and gazed up intently at this most beautiful of ethereal specimens, his gorgeous wife, his partner of the last three short, but extremely loving years. She was all of thirty-eight summers old, yet didn't look a day over thirty, he reckoned rather proudly, and Stephen Hawthorne knew full well that he should be thanking his lucky stars for this great fortune in life, and not contemplating killing the poor woman instead. For she'd always been very good to him; she'd never put one single, solitary foot out of place...

But she had to die - and soon.

"Yes, dear?" he asked, a trifle nervously, like a henpecked husband in some domestic tragedy or badly-written soap opera. *Nervousness, or was that guilt, Stevey boy?* He didn't really know, for as yet he was guilty of nothing, surely.

She scoffed teasingly. "Why do you have those infernal mitts on your ears all of the time now? Are my television shows really *that* hard to listen to?!"

He looked over at the cookery programme showing the requisite recipe ingredients being displayed on a list down the side of the screen, and a chef using a blow-torch, of all things, to add the finishing touches to a tempting Baked Alaska.

Now, there was an idea…

"No honey, I just prefer listening to the radio in the same room as you, but I also want you to be able to hear your shows as well. I suppose I *could* go back into the kitchen and listen in there, if it really bothers you any. Certainly would be nice to be liberated of these earmuffs –"

"No!" she exclaimed quite suddenly then chuckled despite herself. "You'll stay in here, you old curmudgeon, where I can see you! It's just that you always have such a strange - I don't know - far away look to your eyes when you're listening with those on. I get worried sometimes. I really do. I never know what the hell you be listening to either half-time, what could possibly be so damn absorbing!"

And she laughed again; a gentle, feminine titter that usually disarmed him.

But not this time...

"Tell her, The Sun Also Rises: *a ten-part audiobook series running on Classics FM,"* the voice in his ears commanded him authoritatively once he had placed them back on again. *"The bitch is getting seriously suspicious here, Stephen, please be aware of that. It will have to be now or never, I'm afraid. Tonight, in other words, just to be on the safe side. Not a moment to lose!"*

He cleared his throat.

"I'm listening to a ten-part audiobook series on Classics FM. *The Sun Also Rises,* it's called. That's why I look so distracted. I'm not just listening to some old hip-hop rubbish, you know, I'm actually trying to concentrate on something *important* here!"

She furrowed her brows curiously then offered him a sly, knowing smile.

"I never knew you were a fan of Hemingway..."

Is that who wrote it? pondered Stephen resignedly, fearing the woman could see right through him and to whatever it was he was secretly planning. He never was the greatest of actors, even at the best of times.

"Turn it up," she continued, baiting him playfully along with that slight grin of hers still evident. "Take those off of you again and turn it up for me. I'd like to hear it as well, this book. It's a really great read. I did it at school."

He began toying with his fancy $400 cell-phone, as if he were adjusting the volume to listen to what she had to say.

"Sorry, what was that, honey? I didn't quite hear you

there."

She sighed, having to repeat herself again. "I said, take those silly things off of you and turn the mobile phone up instead. I'd like to hear this audiobook as well - I did it at school, you see." She turned the television to mute, and waited expectantly, arms crossed attentively.

He shook his head slowly, though tried to appear somewhat nonchalant, at ease with himself, totally innocent of any guile. "It's day seven, so no point, Sarah. You've already missed most of it by now." He attempted a reciprocal grin; utterly half-hearted, he knew for certain, but it was the best he could manage in the circumstances. "Besides, it doesn't actually work without the headphones in. They act as a sort of aerial antenna for the radio, or something... Perhaps you can download it, on that tablet thingy of yours?"

She stopped smiling and turned back to her cookery programme again, turning it up louder this time, then lazing back on the large leather sofa and curling her bare feet up underneath her. Her husband was at the other end of the spacious, well-furnished room, there with his little earmuffs on him and that far-off, distant look to his glazed eyes once more.

"That was close, Stephen. That was far too damn close! I think you already know what you need to do now..."

He sighed inwardly. For the past week or so - ever since he had gotten this damn phone, in fact - he'd been contacted by an eerily husky voice over the radio waves, every single time he had dared to slip these silly little earmuffs on. What began as a simple quest for music and light entertainment had somehow degenerated into a battle royale with himself over whether or not to kill his perfect, oh-so-stunning wife.

She was, the voice said, not real, you see.

A shock, to say the least, Stevey boy...

A shock to the system, indeed.

The voice claimed he was a Dr. Michael Gray, of Cedar Hills Hospital, Boston, Massachusetts. A brain specialist; qualified primarily in the field of abrasions to the cerebral cortex. That Stephen had somehow managed to get himself into a vicious motorcycle accident on his day off work and that he had been, of course, wearing no helmet when he had unfortunately come asunder with the approaching station wagon. And that he now lay comatose in the brain injuries department, a vegetable in all but name until 'she' was ultimately despatched with.

The supposition being, according to this mysterious doctor, was that his whole life here was all a sort of extended 'daydream', that it was a false reality and nothing else. And that the main thing keeping him here was this cutesy, impish dragonlady lolling over there in front of him. *Dispose of her swiftly, Stephen, my good man, and you'll escape this fantasy land now and forever!*

He scoffed at the idea initially, naturally enough. He also knew that these were hardly normal broadcasts by any feasible description, at least not in the traditional sense - the doctor always referred to him on a first name basis, after all - and that he would therefore have to check himself quick-smart into the nearest psych ward in order to discover just what on earth was going wrong with him, and for Sarah's own safety, too.

She'll never let you go! the voice insisted with utmost sincerity. *She'll never let you leave! You wake up now and she doesn't exist anymore - that's the cold, hard fact of the matter. And this she knows... You better believe it, kiddo! She* knows, *and she wants to* exist, *Stephen; make no mistake about* that, *my good man! See, she's already talking of having children, starting a family, something to tie you down with here for all eternity. To keep you emotionally* involved, *in other words. But don't you fall for it!*

Which was true, of course. Of late, she had been getting increasingly broody all of a sudden, dropping atomic-bomb-size hints in his, until now, generally oblivious direction. He thought it was just concern over her body clock, or what have you...

However, he certainly wasn't giving in to these worrying little messages quite so easily - at least, not yet. He still reckoned he was going nuts - "*More* than likely, Stevey, old boy, more than likely" - that is until the voice started predicting stuff that even he, in his warped frame of mind, could not possibly contrive.

He had been lying there half-aslumber one night, listening once again to his favourite spooky radio station...

In twenty seconds, kiddo, go straight to the curtains and pull them open fast. In the darkness you'll see flashing red lights above you from a passing aeroplane, a passenger jet, coming in to land, being at precisely eleven-thousand thousand feet currently. You can then ask your darling wife if she sees it, too.

He did. He had gotten up precisely as instructed, leaping out of their bed with a sudden start, and pulled back those thick, garish, flower-patterned curtains and saw the flashing red lights on each tail fin exactly as described. Then he had asked the freshly awakened Sarah if she saw it, too.

She nodded in the affirmative, yawning irritably, but giving him a deeply concerned appraisal as well, as if her mind was ticking overtime on what this weird act signified. Was she thinking he was going nuts, too? Or was she thinking instead: 'He's catching on to this whole delicate little charade, this make-believe existence, this essentially deceitful set-up, and I had better watch him..." It was hard to tell from her sleepy, somnolent, red-rimmed eyes.

The voice, like all other schizophrenic voices plaguing poor unfortunates throughout the ages, could be conversed with without him having to utter a single solitary word out loud. His mind, therefore, could be read solely from very thought alone. Which confused him somewhat, as the voice itself only communicated speaking through those damned headphones.

"Very neat trick," he had told the good doctor acerbically as he lay back down again, plugging in the earmuffs, "very neat, indeed. I probably heard that plane go over beforehand, however; sort of subconsciously, though."

Oh yeah? came the impatient, thoroughly unsatisfied response. *Well then, explain just how, kiddo, saying you were wearing those thick, heavy-duty earphones all this time?*

But it took more than that to convince one cynical Stephen Hawthorne.

Yes, it took an event of colossal, almost impossible magnitude, a coincidence so great as to get his bullet-proof tower of impenetrable incredulity to waver, then finally topple and make him come round to the utterly fantastic notion of killing his own dearly beloved wife.

It took a TV show.

The following day was Sarah's thirty-eighth birthday, and although he had made plans made for the morrow - a surprise party in *Angelo's,* their favourite restaurant, the voice said he had been tinkering with the latest additions to his hi-tech scanning equipment, particularly the settings of his new 'Neurotransmitter Modulator', and would hopefully invoke a quite different 'surprise' into proceedings, into the advertisements during the breaks of her unmissable weekly serial, *Paradise Beach.*

So there she was, watching the corny, low-budget programme with a low-fat bowl of Neapolitan ice-cream at the ready, and her low-fat legs tucked cosily up underneath her once again, enjoying part one for all it was worth. Stevey boy wasn't sitting tucked up beside her though, however; oh no, he was back in his element, back in his recently commandeered seat set obliquely across from her, earphones at the ready and his vacant, bulging orbs centred squarely on the flat screen as well. For what was about to occur here, he had next to no idea, either.

Then it happened. The advertisements came on. First a commercial for washing-up liquid, then a car, then a candy bar with 'exploding' multi-coloured sprinkles that would 'hold a carnival on your tongue!' And finally, a plump, dowdy-looking woman appeared with two small kids, her holding one of them - presumably the youngest - in her burly, masculine-looking arms. Stephen knew instantly who she was; the previously concealed became subsequently revealed and the scales fell from his glazed, unbelieving eyes with utmost immediacy.

I know this woman!

I know those kids!

They're mine...

He was looking at his real-world wife now, Mrs. Rebecca Jane Hawthorne, and his progeny, Sam and Jennifer, the literal fruit of his loins, squirming delinquently there on camera for his virtual wife and the entire virtual nation to witness.

He took a deep inhalation of breath and let the earphones slide as he listened to Becca wish Sarah a wonderful and enjoyable birthday party tomorrow from her and the kids at the homeless shelter. That without her sterling work in this oft-neglected area, then her and little Sam, and even smaller Jenny, would presumably be out living rough on the streets. For the man of the house had suddenly deserted them.

"You deserve it!" then muttered tiny Sam shyly with a gooey paw in his drooling mouth, like he didn't know why he was there, but had been instructed what to say, nevertheless.

As the commercial came to an abrupt end, Sarah wiped away a tear or two and sniffled softly to herself, then broke into a beautiful, radiant smile that highlighted those large, luminescent, violet-blue eyes.

"Wonderful family," she sighed wistfully. "I'm getting them all set up over there in Hazelbrook Falls, that row of new terraced houses run by the shelter. Makes it all worthwhile to see how the kids are getting along…"

He said nothing, mouth hanging ajar as she turned round to him again, even though the show had resumed.

"You weren't behind any of this, were you?" she beamed knowingly, with a raised brow of inquiry.

He nodded, managing a half-smile in response.

What the hell: the good doctor had obviously arranged it, so he couldn't very well be caught out here. The phone wouldn't ring ten seconds later with a colleague from the homeless shelter asking her how she'd liked it; their little thanks for all that she'd done, etc, etc. No, he could very easily lie here; say that it was well and truly him and him alone, behind the gesture.

He held up his palms in mock submission, in best '*You got me, I confess!*' fashion. "I hoped you'd like it..." he managed again with a faint flicker of a smile translated between two freshly bitten lips.

"Like it?" she laughed. "I absolutely loved it! Thank you, it was tremendously kind of you." And she came over and planted an affectionate kiss on his burning red cheek. The fragrant smell of perfume enveloped the air around him. "It must have cost a bomb, though, to have that on at this time of night!"

He shrugged, like money was of no object where his dearly beloved was concerned.

Later, with his headphones on him again, the voice was back once more, literally chomping at the bit, and eagerly impatient to be believed.

There! it announced somewhat triumphantly. *Do you trust me now, eh? How else could all that have been arranged on such short notice?*

There was a long, almost tortuous silence from Stevey boy as he tried to make sense of his new reality - riffling through every possible permutation of credible explanations - then, ultimately failing, as he knew he would do, he finally agreed that he did trust the disembodied voice. Telepathically agreed, of course; Sarah was still entranced with her hokey show.

"I *can't* believe it - I just can't! - but I also know that it is true. You *are* telling me the truth, whoever you are, whether I like it or not."

Good man, replied the voice, now clearly satisfied and ready to drive home the point with a metaphorical giant sledgehammer, of all things. *Did you ever take a look in the mirror, Stephen, m'boy? A good, long, hard look at yourself? Have you ever wondered why this beautiful lady sitting over there across from you now would ever be interested in a bald, bespectacled, one-hundred-and-thirty-pound weakling such as yourself? A boring, little mild-mannered skunk of a fellow who should be unlikely to charm her otherwise?*

The reality of it all sunk in once again, landing on and hitting Stephen like the proverbial ton of bricks. "I... I just reckoned that I was a successful dental practitioner, that's all, and that she probably valued my pro-active attitude to life. My ambition, my drive... No?"

The voice cackled caustically, laced with bitter sarcasm. *You keep telling yourself that, kiddo. I hate to burst your bubble here, ruin your parade and so forth, but the real world doesn't actually work that way. It is a lot shallower, by far... And what exactly, by the way, do you really know of dentistry, my good man? I mean, outside of the basic, everyday facts such as there are things known as molars and incisors, and that they are thinly coated in enamel. Would you care to share your knowledge on Mesial Occlusal or Distal Occlusal fillings, for instance? Would you care to elaborate on your omniscient expertise concerning these pertinent topics?*

Stephen had to concede that he could not, strange as that may seem to him, share his knowledge on any of it. *Didn't he work as a dentist, for* crying *out loud?! What was going* on *here, for heaven's sake?!*

"I know I am *supposed* to be a dentist, but you're right, I really can't remember any of the specifics at all. I can't remember anything I should reliably know of, and my whole working career seems to be a kind of opaque, distorted blur -"

...with no real substance, added the voice, rather helpfully. *No, I am afraid, kiddo, that in the real world you work in a meat-packing factory, pulling down minimum wage, and that that poor woman on screen during the adverts is your real, living, breathing, worried wife; the genuine article. Think about that, now... You know it makes sense.*

Yes siree, it did make a twisted sort of poetry when you really got down to it, Stevey boy had to admit.

The voice pressed on: *In the real world your comparative lack of financial clout means that your hospital bills are well and truly beyond your modest means. And they are really racking up, Stephen, and your savings have all but gone now, too, leaving poor Rebecca with no choice but to sell the house in order to pay for them. It will be her and the kids who have to suffer in the long run, Stephen - not you - if you don't snap out of this situation of your very own making. For you, too, have a choice here - you can put an end to this sordid little nightmare by murdering that imposter curled up over there in front of you…*

Stephen still had lots of questions for the good doctor, though. He wanted to know, for example, how long he had been lying in the coma? *Two months.* And he had wanted to know when his reality here had actually begun, this utterly bewitching necklace of days that stretched uncertainly back to who-knew-when? The voice indicated that it was impossible to verify that for certain, but that it was obviously less than two complete phases of the revolving moon.

He felt like howling.

"Tell me something else, and tell me no more," he continued inquisitively, prying still further. "How can I be in a coma? I know next to nothing about comas, but I seem to recall from something I've read somewhere that you can't actually dream in one. That your brain has effectively shut down, in other words, like with a crashed computer. So my question to you is this: how can this all be a dream if I'm virtually brain-dead?"

You're right, Stephen, my good man. You are absolutely right. You do know next to nothing about comas. I am the specialist here, and we have been making terrific advances in the past few years in the technology stakes. Advances enough to finally debunk this silly old myth. It is a popular misconception: the brain does actually dream in this perilous state, as it is continuously trying to piece everything back together in painstaking order once more - memories, emotions, etc, as if in a laborious jigsaw puzzle - and the chief side-effect of this slow but necessary process is similar to that of a dream-induced state.

"Well, if this is a dream then how come weird stuff, like trotting donkeymen with snakes for heads, and dogs with suits, top-hats and monocles on aren't prowling about the streets? You know, the batshit-crazy stuff that tends to happen in dreams that you always take for granted, because that is your reality at that particular moment and you're woefully oblivious to the absurdity of it all until you've finally woken up again."

Maybe because the brain itself is aware *that this is a long-term dream, and therefore needs to pace itself accordingly? I don't really know the answer to that one either yet, Stephen. Or perhaps you merely haven't been blessed with that much imagination. It takes an imaginative sort of person to begin with for the neural pathways to fire and conjure such vivid scenarios. Your years of meat-packing may well have dulled your wits senseless, your creative spirit crushed... Or perhaps your brain just doesn't do bullshit, even in dreams. I can't elaborate further on this one, I'm sorry; it would be the purest of speculation. There are still lots we don't know about the mind, after all.*

He was satisfied, however. More than satisfied. He would do it, he reckoned. He would kill her tonight. He would kill her now...

But days later, that vow still hadn't transpired into fruition. The voice was getting impatient once again, and Sarah equally suspicious. Suspicious of his increasingly strange relationship with the radio show every night, that he and he alone, could hear. The radio only worked with the earphones plugged in, wasn't that the reason? Acting as some sort of aerial antenna for his mobile...

So there he sat again tonight, a Thursday, the time approaching eight p.m, meaning his 'show' was scheduled to finish soon, leaving little time for the voice to berate and cajole Stevey boy once more into doing his patriarchal duty.

Do it for the kids, kiddo, if not for yourself, it pleaded desperately. *Think of the kids, for heaven's sake! The kids! Sam and Jennifer… Do you really want them to be sleeping rough? Do you want to see them* starve *to death?!*

Yes, well, when he put it like that…

He slid the earphones off for, hopefully, the final time and made for the open-plan kitchen and there, the knife drawer. No, he couldn't very well do it with sharpened instruments; he was squeamish about blood. Even fake blood, in a fake reality. So he would take a look in his trusty tool cabinet.

"Fix me a coffee, while you're out there," shouted his darling, oblivious wife; the crisp demand reverberating through the hallway between the two rooms.

"Yes, dear," he echoed back, silently cursing this whole insidious affair. Now, *what to use, what to use, what to use?*

He decided on the hammer. A good, solid-metal, wife-dispatching implement that would - if used correctly in the right hands, that is - certainly do the trick. Or wrong hands, according to whose viewpoint you took…

The coffee pot gurgled toward a bubbling, frothing ecstasy and Stephen opportunistically hijacked the growing din to first slide his shoes off, then slip quietly up behind his dearly beloved.

"I'm pregnant..." she announced suddenly, taking him profoundly unawares, making him come to an abrupt and bewildered halt. Had she heard him? Did she know what he was up to? Was she telling him this to emotionally blackmail him still further, to stop him from actually going through with it?

Her head hadn't turned round, however, and besides her unexpected utterance, there was no indication that the woman sitting there with her back to the door actually knew he was there at all.

The coffee pot was coming to the boil now, hissing, foaming...

And then it struck him, as swiftly and surely as the hammer that would ultimately strike her. The revelation of what she had meant came flooding over him like a tidal wave of blessed relief with the subsequent follow-up to that impromptu statement, "... and Ian is the father!"

"I'm pregnant, Bill, and Ian is the father," stated one of the more dippy characters on her second-favourite soap opera, *Port Moresby*, tears streaming down the woman's face at her brave declaration, before her husband, 'Wild Bill' Sullivan, slapped her hard to the ground, knocking off her bonnet in the process.

"Hussy!" he exclaimed, naturally outraged, and stalked angrily away...

The coffee pot clicked off and the din of steaming, bubbling liquid quickly subsided. Stephen held his breath in tortuous anticipation. It had to be now or never.

He hovered over her...

He lifted the hammer high above her perfectly-formed cranium - one endowed with blonde hair so healthy and shining and positively glowing with vitality that it could easily have graced the screens of any shampoo commercial - as silently as he could, then willed himself to do it. *Just do it, just do it, just do it already!* But still he hesitated.

She's not real, *for crying out loud!* he imagined the voice adding, by way of motivational comfort. *So what are you waiting for here? Just do it, for Christ's sake! Just do it! Do you really want her to see your shadow, eh? Or your reflection when the screen turns dark?!*

The voice was right, of course. If she turned round suddenly and looked him square in the eye, he didn't reckon he could then go through with it. No way, Jose. It had to be impersonal to succeed. Utterly impersonal. He had to think of the back of her head as a melon of some kind, a ripe, blonde melon, or that he was a professional golfer at some swish driving range. Her neck the tee, her head the ball... A *Slazinger 1.*

Fore!!!

He took another deep inhalation of breath and then went for it, opting for the melon-squashing approach, the hammer gliding down in hardly aerodynamic fashion, but the power behind it more than making up for this simple shortfall in physics. Work done equals force by distance, or something like that, he had learned once at school... and then her head went slack to one side when the blow successfully landed, unleashing a vicious, fleeting crack, that, although fleeting, seemed to hang in the air an uncomfortable second too long.

He stood there a moment, then the head - only a smidgen of blood seeping out of it, praise the Lord - began to jerk slightly in intermittent paroxysms of fading life. The voice was correct once again. This lady, this non-entity, wanted to *exist!*

He held the hammer to the side of her head this time, in an attempt to finally finish her off, to be somewhat merciful. Then he swung it like a driver at the golf range, slamming thunderously into her inviting temple and nearly knocking her head clean off her shoulders in the process.

It worked. It was *work done*, all right.

He vomited instantly and dropped the offending implement to the ground. He closed his eyes and screamed soundlessly, grimacing as he did so, temporarily losing control of his senses.

However, when he came-to again and gradually re-opened his eyes, it wasn't to the vision of his family in some hi-tech hospital ward, nor into the relieved faces of the medical staff, or the *'I told you so'* crinkles of one obscure Dr. Michael Gray. Oh no, he was still stuck firmly in this reality, glued fast here like nothing had ever happened, nothing whatsoever at all; nothing but a dead woman to show for his conflicted travails.

He thought of heading for the earphones again, spasms of fear now erupting across him, stomach noose tightening, but he wanted a closer look at this so-called 'wife' of his. Wanted to see the damage he'd inflicted. If he'd really done it or not. He inched cautiously around the side of the sofa until he was standing looking down onto her blank, emotionless, depressingly vacant face. Sarah's form was totally devoid of any life or even involuntary movement and he felt like vomiting again. But he didn't, for something far worse was now catching his attention...

Was she trying to speak?!

Was she actually trying to mutter *something?!!*

Sarah was making vague clicking noises like that of the kettle going off, which eventually formed into fully-fledged tutting sounds. She was actually *tutting* at him, he realised to his absolute horror. Her eyes sprung open with a flash and her dead head became a grisly living entity once more.

She shook that dripping, gory head at him like she were profoundly disappointed in him, still tutting as she did so, blood trickling down from her *because I'm worth it* hair and that concave right temple and onto her glowing, rosy cheeks, before spilling further onto those expensive blue designer jeans she was always crowing about. She was grinning malevolently, eyes swivelling upward at her attacker like red-hot coals of the abyss. There was a curiously empty quality to them now; orbs of purest evil.

You blew it, kiddo, she then said softly, but with undoubted, palpable menace and laced threat behind it. *You had your chance and you blew it. You chose poorly...*

Stephen found he was too far gone now to even speak, trembling on the spot, confusion, paranoia and fear making a heady, intoxicating mixture, a most debilitating cocktail as he took in this demon - for want of a better word - lying there resplendent with its feet curled up on the couch and its clothes liberally stained with damning streaks of glistening crimson.

You see, you have led such a particularly uneventful life, my good man, that there was not much to judge you from once you finally began slipping inexorably toward expiration. We had to be sure what type of man you were, therefore - had to be one hundred percent certain, that is - and so this was your first and only test and I'm now pleased to announce that you've failed. The stakes were heaven and hell; and kiddo, there are no prizes for second place...

He meant to scream out loud, protest at the injustice of all of this. That he'd been talked into this - *blackmailed*, more like - by the voice; but he knew full well, to his hideous chagrin, that the voice and her had been no doubt the same entity all along. He had been fooled bigtime, and now he must pay.

You broke the fifth commandment, Stephen - "Thou shalt not kill" - and that's all we needed to know. Would you go through with it? Would you actually go ahead and murder an inoffensive little woman in the coldest of ways? Well congratulations, buddy! You've just passed that *particular exam with flying colours!*

"B-b-but..." he managed to stutter, jaws shuddering involuntarily from the sudden frost that had somehow entered the room. He tried and tried again, to explain that there were obviously extenuating circumstances to be found here somewhere, and that he/she/it surely knew about that, but nothing further came out.

Sarah wiped at her blood-smeared face then got up and walked defiantly toward the open door. Stephen attempted to follow suit and beg for his life, but stood frozen to the spot, his knees trembling beyond control. When she crossed the threshold of the door, the lights of the hallway and kitchen blinked once, then instantly cut out and an impenetrable blackness replaced them. She and everything beyond this very room had somehow disappeared from view.

Another freezing gust of ice-cold wind flailed against him now and the temperature seemed to dip below minus figures. He was sure that he could hear distant laughter from somewhere else as well, from some place far, far beyond, before the *beep, beep, beep, beeeeeeeeeeppppppppppp*........... sound came and the awful realisation that signalled that he had finally and irretrievably flatlined.

Then the floor, ceiling, walls and furniture began to lose their colour, fading away to the deepest of mono-tone greys, then subsequently dissolved before him altogether. Soon there was only his body left which swiftly dissolved, too. There was only a void in place of the previous reality, a hazy, existential consciousness and darkness, all-encompassing, pitch-black darkness, along with its intimidating bride of unadulterated silence, there to accompany him for all of eternity.

Because yes, Stevey boy, he reasoned as the numbing chill set firmly in for good and the pain began to really bite, *the honeymoon period is well and truly over...*

Madness in Death Valley

By M.R. Wallace

I had been camping, alone, as I was wont to do on occasion. Despite the myriad warnings one hears about camping and hiking and otherwise adventuring alone, it centered my mind and allowed me to relax. For several days I would camp by myself, in a little rock nook south of Death Valley. It was out of the worst parts of the place, but still sat securely amidst the sand, rocks and scrub of the desert. A few MREs from a military surplus store, a one man tent, a hatchet, a lighter and my pistol. My entire compliment of equipment consisted of these plus a pack of bottled water. Many of my friends and family thought I was crazy for taking these excursions, but there is no greater feeling than isolation in the wilderness.

At least there wasn't. Now my only solace comes from this morphine drip, meant to combat the pain in my torso. It helps more, instead, to numb the terror that runs rampant in my brain, seizing my faculties and causing me to rip my stitches once more. As I write this, I feel the familiar rigidity of my pistol, tucked under my pillow. It would not be there, but for my insistent coaxing of a friend who I shall not name here. They will feel guilty enough by the end of all this, they need not suffer legal reprimand as well.

That being said, I should probably start from the beginning. The end of my last morphine dose has left my mind a bit disordered, but I need to get this all down before my next dose. Before I succumb to my suffering and press the button again.

It was a week and a half ago, the end of April, when I was seized once again by my desire to get away from it all. Living thirty miles outside of Reno, I had a decent amount of solitude already. But these moods seemed to beckon for total isolation, for the historical Man Versus Nature conflict so sorely missing from much of contemporary society. So I packed my bug out gear, all conveniently stashed in a closet near the front door, and crammed it all into the back of my Grand Cherokee.

I had posted a few farewell-for-a-few-days-and-here's-where-I'll-be-just-in-case type messages with friends and family, cleared out my voice mail and checked my email one last time for any updates. Ah, the life of a homebody content creator. Write a few articles, get paid, rinse and repeat. Add to that a bit of chicken scratch from poems and short stories submitted to assorted publications, and I was living within my means, albeit thinly so at times.

I fired up the little old Jeep and took it south for a few hours, stopping briefly in Tonopah for lunch at the stately old Mizpah hotel. The ancient abode had been around since the gold mining days, along with the requisite ghost stories that seemed to go hand in hand with that time. There were supposed to be two ghosts that haunted the old gal. One, a politician murdered by organized crime and kept on ice until after election. The other, *The Lady In Red*, had been a kept woman who had incurred the wrath of her lover on the fifth floor. There she had met her end. She apparently walked the hallways still, and a mysterious red stain was said to appear frequently in the place where she had died. I had always loved ghost stories, Old West tales in particular.

Finishing my burger, I hit the road once more. I pulled off the road an hour later and put together my pack. It was halfway between a rucksack and a normal backpack, and had plenty of room for my meager survivalist supplies. My pistol, a weathered old Browning Hi-Power, rode on my belt in an equally aged leather holster. My grandfather had given them to me in his will, recounting my visits to him in Arizona in my youth, and my natural skill with that particular gun. His video will had also chided me about my first shot with his twelve-gauge. That was Grandpa Dick, though. Always giving someone a hard time.

I started the two hour hike to my usual spot around one-thirty. It was hot, but not unbearably so. Every once in a while my longings would strike in the middle of summer and I had to double my water ration. Those trips were rough. I reached my camping spot and gazed once more upon the large, rocky outcropping that rose above the desert floor. That formation of weather-beaten sandstone was amongst my favorite places in the world, looking vaguely like an eagle's head rising out of the sand. The beak, as it were, hooked toward the east and provided shade for most of the afternoon. Even from its base I could see the blackened patch of rock where I always lit my campfire.

After a brief scrabble up the less steep northern slope of the formation, I was once again standing atop my usual perch. I gazed out across the Nevada desert, scrub brush and sand stretching far away to the mountains. I set down my pack and unhooked my tent from it. It was a bivouac bag, really, a warm sleeping bag with a miniscule tent over it. I set it up as far back against the wall of the formation as I could, right next to my stash of firewood. I rarely needed to bring firewood out there, perhaps on my next trip out. The temperature started to fall, bit by bit, as the sun crawled behind my roost.

I clambered down to the sand again and set out to gather brush for starting my fire. I found a couple of small tufts of sagebrush and hacked the stems until they came away. Gathering them up, I returned to my site and scaled it back up to the top. I set the brush in a small pile and fetched some of my wood. The sun was well behind the rocks now, and the growing shadow of the eagle head was darkening rapidly. As I groped for the firewood, my hand brushed something slick and wet. Not thinking too much about what I had just stuck my hand in, I flicked it aside. I grabbed the wood and set it up in a teepee-like shape over the brush. Then I extracted the lighter from my pocket and pressed down the button. It was cheating, but I didn't leave my fate to matches anymore.

The tiny blue butane flame hissed, its azure tongue caressing the dry brush. The plant smoldered and started to glow orange. The heat spread, vermilion fingers rising out of it as it blazed to life. As the fire grew and began to consume the larger wood, I saw the wet shimmer of the substance I had blundered into a moment ago. It was a thick, black and blue slime that began to exude fumes as the heat reached it. It smelled awful, indescribable really. It bubbled in its viscous puddle until it was reduced to a sticky residue on the sandstone. A stiff evening breeze picked up, wafting the fetor away from me and my fire.

I kept the fire burning as the sky darkened into the limitless black one can only get in the wilderness. The stars blazed coldly in the void above, providing the only light besides my campfire. A dark patch overhead showed where the new moon hung. The orange circle of light from the campfire flickered in the breeze, shaking back and forth. I stood and looked out over the Nevada desert, the bright sands glowing a muted silver under the starlight. The Milky Way twinkled and I even saw a couple of shooting stars.

The wind smelled of sagebrush, juniper and dust. It was intoxicating. Then I caught a whiff of that stink again, setting the hairs on my neck and arms on end. I shivered, an involuntary spasm that I suspected had little to do with the chilly night air. I climbed into my bivy bag and put a couple of pieces of wood on the little blaze. After the day's activities, sleep fell upon me like a leaden veil. I slipped away from the waking world as though I were drifting out to sea.

A sudden chill swept over me, and my dreams plummeted into the realms of the bizarre. I found myself standing on an island, not unlike the rock formation I lay on at that very moment. All around me surged a sea of fluid, blacker than night and hideously thick. Deep blue streaks of luminescence pulsed in the sludge that lapped disgustingly at the edges of my oasis. The wind stirred up a rattling, shrieking torrent of noise. My flesh prickled at the noisome clamor, causing my jaws to clench tight of their own accord. The waves that slapped against the shore dragged slowly back toward their source.

There was something unsettling about those waves, beyond their color and viscosity. I realized then that the waves were shaped... like creatures. Grotesque, distorted creatures with only the most tenuous connection to anthropoid anatomy. I began to dismiss this weirdness out of hand. I stopped when one finally remained behind, detached from the morass which undulated all around me.

It shuddered violently to hideous life. A head raised out of the muck, shaped like a wedge and dripping slime. Next emerged arms, ending with two wickedly curved claws on one side and a third opposite them, like a thumb. Rather than flesh and bones, they seemed to be composed of the same sludge they had crawled from, twisted and compacted together in black and blue pulsing cords. The thing pulled itself out of the slime into a queerly simian stance. It shuffled toward me and stopped short. Its head tilted back and it let loose a cry, if a cry you could call it. It was a wet, syrupy rattle that ended in a bone-chilling hiss. My mind reeled at the thought of being trapped on this island with such a beast. But neither could I hope to traverse the infinite, seething black mass that surrounded me.

I woke drenched in ice cold sweat, my bag providing little comfort. My fire had gone out and the world was dark. Trying to sit up, I found it impossible to move. I became conscious of a weight on my chest and began to panic. Was I going to die out here, alone, eaten by some wild animal? With the brutal strength born of mortal fear, I thrashed until the weight fell away. I seized the opening of my bivouac and slid myself out. My hips had cleared the bag when I froze. Across from me, behind where my fire had been, came a rattling hiss that sent ice shooting through my veins.

Cold, blue fires burned in a tiny constellation in the

dark. It took me a second to realize they were eyes, and they danced back and forth. The azure lights trembled when came another rattle. They blinked out, and I began to think the abomination had vanished, when a rush of air combined with a solid force knocked me flat again. Its claws raked fire on my chest and shoulders. Hot slime from its slavering maw splashed my face. I seized the thing by its upper arms and wrenched it away again. I kicked away the rest of my bag and lunged to my feet. My foot came down on the remains of the campfire, twisting my ankle and sending me tumbling over the edge.

I struck one of the sandstone slabs, the air exploding from my lungs, supernovae erupting in my vision. I bounced and rolled, finally sprawling on the desert floor. The sand was cold and gritty, shoving its way into my shirt and pants as I writhed in agony. The hideous cry of the nightmare beast reached my ears. I prepared for the end, hearing the creature scrabbling down from my perch. Twisting around, I felt a weight at my hip. My pistol. The sand past my feet crunched as the abomination crawled nearer.

Leather rasped and the night exploded in a series of staccato cracks, each blinding me and making my ears ring. The creature shrieked in pain and fell to the ground, convulsing as its life blood pumped out of its body onto the sand. The stench was overpowering, and I rolled over and retched on the desert floor. The final, ragged breath of the thing was answered by a chorus of wailing hisses from all around me.

I don't remember much after that. I recall stumbling through the desert, my gasping breaths streaming out in rushes of fog. The terrible cries of those nightmarish monstrosities. I remember blindly firing my pistol into the darkness. I ran, headlong into the night. Apparently, I was found several miles into Death Valley, dehydrated and sunburned. My pistol was empty, clutched in my hand so hard that the medics could only pry it out after sedating me. Then I awoke in the hospital, intravenous fluid bag suspended above me. The heart monitor beeped steadily. After a brief moment, a nurse came in. I was informed as to how I was found, the condition I was in, and how long I could plan on staying here.

The first night's stay was peaceful enough. My dreams, if I had dreams, were swallowed by the morphine. The second night, though, I slept fitfully. I woke in the middle of the night and gazed at the window. It was lit by the diffused orange glow of city lights. I was about to close my eyes again. A shadow darted across the rectangular pane. I froze. It returned, spindly arms tipped with wicked claws, and stopped at my window. It scratched, those terrible claws squealing against the glass. I cried madly until a nurse appeared, but the thing was gone.

I was almost certain that I was going insane. But, strangely, it was a dream that convinced me otherwise. My morphine must have worn off for a time, and while I lay there in my hospital bed I could feel the world shift around me. I opened my eyes, in my dream at least, and saw that blasphemous black sludge oozing out of the air vents in the floor. It bubbled into several of the terrible, skeletal beasts that swarmed over my bed and pinned me down. Their breath, hot and rife with the stench of rot and untold years. I thrashed about, struggling desperately to free myself from them. I felt their jaws gnaw at my arms and legs.

I awoke to blood on my sheets and realized that I had been violently tossing about, having ripped my IV out of my arm. My head was pounding. Touching it left blood on my fingertips and I knew that I must have bashed it on the bed railing. My stitches had ripped open, and my broken ribs burned abominably in my chest as a testament to the violence of my episode. I gingerly rubbed my hand against my face. I detected a faint trace of that detestable odor. Rather than believing this to mean I had lost my sanity, it only reinforced the knowledge that I was, in fact, in complete control of my faculties. Though, either way, it isn't a pretty picture.

The next day, I called a friend of mine. It took almost an hour to convince them to bring me back my pistol. God bless them, they even loaded the magazine to the top with my hollow points. All thirteen rounds were stacked snugly in their place, plus one more in the chamber. I thanked them profusely and sent them about their own business. I've spent several days now in a haze of morphine. As much as I appreciate its powers, their capabilities wear thin. I'm probably already addicted to the stuff, not that it matters. Tonight, while that damnable thing scrapes at my window once more, I will thumb the safety off and put an end to the madness. I see no other way, after what I have experienced, to go on and remain sane. If I had anyone else to say goodbye to, I would do so. But my few friends have been here to visit, I don't really have any family, and I can't continue this charade. Staying silent while that abomination scrapes and rattles and hisses at my window is likely to drive me to madness. God, will that thing ever shut up?! I find it morbidly amusing, this irritation I have with an unspeakable horror at my window. I almost feel guilty, leaving such things to live. But, then again, I know nothing about them, other than that they exist. I almost feel guilty, but not guilty enough not to go through with it. Damn them. I'll be glad to rid myself of them.

Found at the bedside of Wilum Crawford.

Hell Awaits

By Feind Gottes

There's nothing quite like the quiet of two in the morning. Everyone is asleep, the television is finally turned off, no pitter patter of feet scampering from one room to another, and it's as quiet as a funeral parlor. No one is moving except me, but no one hears me as I move silently through my dark house, helpless to stop my body from moving. I can't feel the axe in my hand but I know it's there. I watch as my hand pushes open my bedroom door, nothing I can do to stop it. He's taken over now. I am nothing.

The first time I heard the voice, I thought it was just my imagination, it had to be. I was just sitting in my basement man-cave watching the game when it began. It started as a whisper, so faint I blew it off as nothing, just an old house making odd noises like every other old house in the world. Then it kept coming back until I started to question my sanity but I still denied what was happening. There was no way I could ever kill anyone, so it had to be nothing more than my imagination. The voice persisted over weeks and months, while I told no one, not even my wife, whom I had always told everything.

"We're going to kill them all," the voice had told me again and again every time I tried to watch a game or watch some loud obnoxious action movie in my manly sanctuary. When it began, it was so faint I could barely make out the words, though I could almost feel the lips delivering the whispers brushing against my ear. I'd mute my big screen and it would be gone only to return again a moment later. I told myself it was just my imagination or the old house settling or something but then it would return whispering once again. I may not be a saint, but I knew I was no killer.

Now here I was, six months since the voice had begun its whispering, watching my hand push open my bedroom door. My eyes could see my wife asleep on the bed, snug as a bug in a rug, as they say. I was a slave to witness the horror I knew was coming. I could see my hands grip the handle of the axe until my knuckles turned white. He was in control now. All I could do was watch in horrified silence.

I knew what he was going to do, he had told me, but I was helpless to stop him. I was nothing more than an unwilling voyeur now. He was going to kill my family and make me watch. He was going to coat me in their blood. He was going to use my body to satiate his bloodlust, then he was going to leave me as silently as he had entered. It didn't matter how mentally strong I was, there was no way to fight him. I concentrated on preventing my body from moving, but it was like trying to lift a house with my mind, an impossible task. There was no fighting him, not now that he was inside.

He raised my arms over my head in white-knuckled grip, pausing only to taunt me. "Her blood is going to be delicious. Your daughters' will be even better." I could only imagine the maniacal look on my face as he began to laugh, an insane laugh I hadn't known my lips were capable of creating.

My wife's eyes popped open at the sound of my demon driven laughter with a smile, before her eyes registered what they were seeing. Her smile faded while her eyes went wide with fear and she opened her mouth to unleash a scream that never came. The blade of the axe slammed down into her chest, buried to the hilt between her breasts. He stomped my foot into her gut to wrench out the blade; I was helpless to stop it. My wife's lovely hazel eyes filled with fear as she watched the man she had loved, married and shared a bed with for more than fifteen years stood over her, his face contorted in a lunatic's grin, pulling an axe from her chest. I could only watch as those beautiful eyes, the very same ones I had stared into as I said "I do", began to glaze over. I couldn't even shed a tear as the bastard swung the axe down again and again until her chest wasn't recognizable anymore. Her blood was splashed from one wall of our bedroom to the other; her chest looked like it had been mauled by a bear.

"We're not done here, Jack. We'll come back to play later after we play with those lovely little girls of yours. Ever have naughty fantasies about them Jacky? You can admit it now, Daddy. We're going to play all night, Jack." The demon spoke with my voice, though I no longer recognized it.

This can't possibly be real. I'm going to wake up any moment and see this is all just some nightmare. My wife will be beside me in our bed, sleeping peacefully and my little girls will be snug in their beds, all safe and sound. It would help if I could close my eyes. The bastard barely even blinked so I wouldn't miss "the show" as he had referred to it. Why hadn't I believed it was real? Why hadn't I just taken Joanna and the kids and left this place after the first time I heard the voice! But no, I kept telling myself it was nothing, that I wasn't really hearing his voice. I was too afraid of being called crazy, so stupid!

I didn't believe in possession, still didn't want to as he turned away from my wife, heading down my hallway leading to my daughters' rooms. Hollywood definitely knew fuck all about possession. I couldn't feel my body, couldn't feel the axe gripped in my hands or Joanna's blood dripping off my face. I was nothing more than an observation slave as able to control what my body was doing as was any sports fan yelling at the television. I could only watch in horror. I couldn't scream out, "Run!" to my two precious angels. I was conscious and I would never be able to wash these images from my mind.

I imagined I was going to be a blithering, drooling mass once he was done and then what? No one would ever believe that some demon had whispered to me for months then took over my body to kill my family. I wouldn't have believed that before a moment ago. They wouldn't be able to lock me up fast enough if there was anything left of my mind once this bastard was through with me. I pray for a death that won't come, watching through eyes I can't close, covered in my wife's blood. My hand now pushes open the door to eleven year old Amanda's room, my firstborn.

I wanted to cry, seeing my baby girl sleeping so peacefully, knowing what was coming. How many times had I entered just like this to kiss her goodnight on the nights I had to work late. Creeping in, not that much different from how I was entering now; to kiss her forehead whispering "I love you angel".

I screamed, "No!" as the axe smashed down into my baby's sleeping head, popping it like a zit. He forced me to watch while my little girl was turned into a bloody mess, her body not even recognizable as human any more. Luckily I didn't have to watch the light fade and die in her eyes like I had my lovely Joanna, but it was little consolation. Instead I watched as my arms swung the axe over and over, turning my baby girl's head into a picture of scrambled eggs coated in hot sauce. My arms swung down with force, removing hers, then her little legs. He turned her to bloody hamburger with chunks of sausage mixed in. When it was finished, her skinny legs were the only feature distinguishing the bloody mess on the bed as human. I had never felt more powerless, my grip on my sanity reduced to a solitary finger.

The maniacal laughter emanating from my unwilling mouth was the only sound in the house. I only hoped that it would wake my youngest, warning her that something was frightfully wrong. There was nowhere for her to run, I only prayed she might be able to hide. I couldn't bare the thought of my precious little Chelsea seeing her father enter her room dragging a bloody axe looking like something out of a horror movie she was too young to even have seen yet. She was only five years old, apparently that is all she would ever be.

"Two nasty little piggys down only one more to go, Jack. Do you like the way I play, Jacky? Should I make the last one scream, Jack? I need to hear something scream, Jack. Wanna know how I'm gonna make her scream, Jack? Any dark fantasies in this pathetic noggin of yours, Jack? There will be, Jack! I love the screaming, Jack!" My mouth cackled insanely, I only hoped it had woken my last little angel.

I couldn't answer and the beast knew it. He knew I was helpless to stop him from doing as he pleased. The taunting only added to the horror, as if I needed more. I wondered, if he exited my mind right now, would there be any of it left? As bad as this was, I didn't know if I wanted back in my mind now. All I would ever see is the blood, the utter obliteration of my first born and the look on my Joanna's face as she watched me slam an axe into her chest. No more, my God, I just can't take any more! Please, not the baby! Not my little angel! I knew he wasn't laughing at his handiwork, he was laughing at me, mocking me as he hacked my family to bits. He rejoiced at my impotence.

He let my arm go limp as he walked on down the hall, so the axe dragged loudly on the hardwood floor. It scraped and bounced along the boards, sounding like a bowling ball slowly rolling down a lane. He walked ever so slowly, tormenting me with my every step. He paused at the full-length mirror my wife had insisted I hang in the hallway, rearing my head back in laughter so I could see my blood-soaked self in all my current glory. I looked like I had taken a shower in red and black dye. My face was streaked in red with bits of bone, brain and flesh clinging in my hair. I couldn't even tell which was which. Pieces of flesh & bone clung to my blood-soaked shirt like grisly lint. All I wanted to do was scream but only the lunatic's howling erupted from my lips. The image of me would have made my skin crawl if I could only feel it. The beast scanned the full length of the mirror, forcing me to see the axe with strands of my sweet Amanda's once golden hair stuck to it in red wisps like silk. The blade and handle were coated as though the blood had been meticulously painted on. I was transformed inside and out into a bloody grim menagerie of gore. I didn't even recognize myself. I was evil personified and completely helpless to end it. My hand pressed against my last little angel's door, pushing it open, the maniac whispered, "Play time."

Nothing appears quite as sweet and innocent as a sleeping child. I had walked into this room so many times, just to watch as she dreamed the candy coated dreams only the young are capable of dreaming. I would sit and watch, imagining the images of plush bears dancing in lollipop fields, bouncing behind her little lids. So innocent she was, the world not yet having the time to corrupt her precious mind. I couldn't bare to watch my own hands destroy that innocence, but there was no choice. Why did she have to sleep so soundly, so peacefully? I wanted so badly for her to have heard me coming, but here she was, a perfect picture of everything good about my life and this world about to be obliterated by a madman with an axe. A man she called father.

The thing controlling my body just stood there staring at my precious angel, I assumed just to torment me. For the life of me I couldn't see any other reason for him to just stand there staring down at her. Then he increased the nightmare, showing me his intentions. He guided my eyes down the entire length of my sleeping angel's body, then straight down to sheer terror. I couldn't scream, couldn't close my eyes, there was no escape from this vile creature controlling me. I was helpless as he stripped naked staring down at my baby as he did.

Little Chelsea's eyes burst open in fear as he clamped my bloody hand over her mouth. "Scream for daddy." He whispered in her ear.

The screams I heard would echo until I could finally die. Acid could never burn the images of tonight from my eyes. I was completely impotent unable to stop this monster from doing as he pleased. Finished, he stood before the full length mirror in the hallway once more showing me my naked body freshly coated in the blood of my little angel. He had absolutely decimated her body when he was done making her scream.

Those terrified screams that would haunt me until he exited so I could kill myself. Then it struck me, what if he never did? Would it control me forever? Oh God! Oh God! It has to leave, doesn't it? It can't stay in me forever! Oh Fuck! Just kill me you bastard, just fucking kill me! I screamed out, believing it couldn't hear me, then it answered.

"No, Daddy, your suffering has only just begun. Don't worry I'll leave you soon. You've made a terrible mess, Daddy." I was truly laughing at myself now.

"Why me? Why my family? You sick fuck, why!?!" I yelled as the realization hit me that he'd relished in my terror this entire time.

"Why? There always has to be a reason for you peasants up here. Why, you ask? Because you were here, Jack. Just because you were fucking here. Hungry? I'm famished." It couldn't help laugh at my stupidity.

"Who the fuck are you? What are you?" I didn't expect an answer, nor did I get one.

It grabbed a butcher knife from the block in my kitchen, making its way back to my bedroom and the bloody mess that had once been my sweet Joanna. It was still naked with the blood of my family coagulating on my skin. I was thankful I couldn't feel that, but still I had no idea what the thing was planning to do next.

"White or dark meat, Jack? I think that breast meat is a bit ruined. What do you think about a nice fat rump roast?" Once again it laughed loud and hard, delighted by its grisly humor.

It couldn't possibly be serious. He wasn't going to make me eat them too, was he? "Oh fuck! No! No! No! He can't, holy fuck! Please no!" I begged, knowing it was going to get me nowhere, but needing to try anyway.

"Oh yes, Daddy. Playing with your family made me hungry. Very, very hungry." His laughter began again as he carved off a large chunk of my wife's backside.

In the kitchen it began to whistle a happily as it prepared the meat with the skill and care of a five-star chef.

Carefully removing the epidermis and as much excess fat as possible. It seasoned the meat with a bit of garlic, pepper and a sprinkle of rosemary, dropping it into the iron skillet with a sizzle. He seared the piece of my wife on all sides for just a moment. Thankfully, I couldn't smell it. Whistling while it cooked my wife, I couldn't stop screaming.

He plated the rare steak, sprinkled it with a pinch of black pepper, placing it on my dining room table. It sat at my table with a fork in its left hand, a knife in its right as though it was about to address a table full of guests. It just sat there, forcing me to look down at the seared piece of my wife. I didn't know what it could possibly be waiting for.

"Hey Jack, my boy, got any wine? What do you think goes with Filet m'bitch? Red or white?" It couldn't stop laughing at its own morbid humor.

"I can't take this any more, just kill me already, you son of a bitch!" I screamed.

"Oh, we ain't done yet, Jack. I have plans for you, Jacky. Big plans!" I never knew I could sound so menacing; it may have been useful in another time.

I prayed for the nightmare to end as he selected a bottle of Pinot Noir from my wine rack, returning to the table with a piece of our finest crystal. He poured out a glass, then cut into the steak. It was as rare as it could be, squirting bloody juice onto the plate as it cut into the tender meat. All I could do was silently shout, "NO!" as he lifted the forkful of my wife to my mouth. There was no escaping the sound of his chewing, while loudly slurping wine to torment me endlessly. Piece after piece of my wife entered my mouth, driving out any sanity that remained.

He chomped away, guzzling wine until he was finally finished. I longed to burn away the eyes and ears of my stolen body. Unable to be anything but a silent witness to the travesties this monster was committing with my hands. Death couldn't come to me soon enough.

"Man, your bitch was damn tasty, Jack! You can really pick 'em, can't ya? Still with me, Jacky boy? Wanna know what she tasted like, Jacky? I guess they were wrong, not everything tastes like chicken!" Again the maniacal laughter bellowed out as I prayed for death. "Should we have some more, Jack? I hear young meat tastes soooo very sweet. Wanna know how yummy your wife is, Jack? I can let ya. You should really know how fucking delicious she is Jack. I wouldn't want ya to miss it." Again the laughter pounded in my head like a jack-hammer.

I felt nothing until I heard my laughter turn to screams. It took a moment for it to register as my senses flooded back in. I could feel the dried blood of my family pulling my skin tight. Not a sound to hear now that I had stopped screaming which is when it hit me, the taste of meat and wine in my mouth. I was repulsed by the sickly sweet taste and began to wretch. I couldn't throw up fast enough, but before I could it was gone. The beast took back control and I was the powerless witness once more.

"Like how your cunt of a wife tastes, Jacky, my boy? Personally, I fucking loved it. I think we should have some more. Something younger perhaps, something a bit more tender. I tell ya what, Jacky, I'll let you pick. Should we start old or young? I'm thinking save that sweet little thing for last, like dessert, but the choice is yours, Jacky. Whad'ya say?" My ears rang once more with laughter, but I couldn't care anymore. It was going to do as it pleased. It would get no help from me.

I don't know how long it continued. It may have been days or only hours, I had lost all track of time, lost all track of myself. I sat in silent witness while it devoured the family I had loved so much, after butchering them with my axe. It carved off piece after piece, not even bothering to cook it any more. At some point it had gone to the workbench in the basement and used a file to sharpen my teeth to fine points to save itself the bother of slicing. My sweet Joanna, Amanda and Chelsea were reduced, little by little, to nothing more than bones and the few organs the bastard apparently didn't care to eat. He ate them all until my belly was distended, able to fit no more.

His torment was constant. He would ask me which parts he should eat, making quick exits so I could taste what he put in my mouth, though never long enough for me to end my suffering. After his first few exits I ceased bothering to make any attempt at ending this madness, as he would exit for no more than a second or two before entering again. I had no time to kill myself, no time to cry, no time for anything but to taste the sickness in my mouth, gone as quickly as it came. This must have gone on for days, though I can't say for certain.

Throughout it all, his torment of me never ceased. I heard *Jack this* and *Jack that* followed by the laughter, with no escape. I wanted nothing but death, but it never came. I prayed to God to take me, but he wouldn't answer. I offered up my soul to Satan if it would only end, but still absolutely nothing. I was left to witness atrocity after atrocity visited upon my family, helpless to stop it, unable to just lie down and die. It seemed I was doomed to observe until someone, anyone would show up and call the police, but no one did. It had to have been days by now but time had been reduced to a distant a memory.

"Jacky boy, I know you're in there. Seems I've run all out of sweet meat, so we're nearly done. Isn't that happy news, Jack?" It could mock me all it wanted, I wasn't even capable of answering it any more. "I promise, Jack, just a few final touches and you're free to live out the rest of your life in peace. I'll get out of your hair." It couldn't help laugh at its own sick humor. "Oh, out of your hair! I kill me!" It slapped my knee, continuing to laugh hysterically.

I had no idea what to expect from the beast next and I no longer cared. I just wanted it out, so I could kill myself, ending my nightmare. Once again, it took me down to the basement, to my workbench. I watched as it grabbed a hacksaw and my propane torch, having no idea what it was intending to do, not that I even cared any more. Back upstairs in the kitchen, it grabbed the sharpest knife it could find (it tested the sharpness against my thumb, splitting it to the bone) and the shears. He set the tools down on the bathroom counter, looking in the mirror so I could see him smile at me. Dried blood made a mess of my chin and I could see bits of meat stuck in my sharpened teeth. I didn't even recognize me any more. A stranger stared out of the mirror at me, one that I couldn't wait to kill.

"Almost there, Jack, then you're free to go be with your family. I know you plan on killing yourself the moment I leave you, Jacky, but I just can't allow it. No one will believe you if you tell them it was me, but I leave nothing to chance. So you see these things I brought here? These are to ensure you say nothing to anyone ever. Don't worry Jacky, my boy, you're going to live." It smiled in the mirror for me to see, picking up the butcher knife.

It used the knife to carve a pentagram deep into my chest with the number of the beast, 666, carved through the center. "They'll think the devil made you do it now, Jacky!" Another round of laughter burst from blood stained lips.

Using the torch it cauterized the wound that stretched from the top of my ribcage to just below my naval. I would have this scar forever, not that it mattered any longer. There was no way it could stop me from killing myself once it made its exit; if I had to run out into to traffic to do it, I would. Then the thought hit me, what if he waits for someone to show up before releasing me? What if he waited until the handcuffs were on and I'm in the back of some squad car? My mind began to panic at the thought.

"Why are you doing this? Who in the fuck are you, can you at least tell me that?" I screamed out from the confines of my mind.

No response came, other than me smiling at me

in the mirror once again, as it picked up the hacksaw and placed my left hand on the edge of the sink. I was helpless to do anything as it removed my hand as fast as lightning, the flesh smoking as he quickly cauterized the wound. It held it up for me to get a good long look, knowing I couldn't look away no matter how badly I wanted to do so. The only consolation was that I couldn't feel it or smell the flesh char, for now anyway.

"Well, Jacky, it's been an absolute blast but it's almost time to bid you adieu. Just a few last things and I can bid you a long life, parting is such sweet sorrow and all that other shit you idiots say to each other. Now, there is a favor I need you to do for me, Jack and it's very important so listen the fuck up! In fact, it's the only thing that is important. Understand me, Jack?" Its serious tone was a far cry from the hysterical laughter and juvenile morgue humor it had displayed up to this point.

"Fuck you!" I knew it made no real difference what I said to it now.

"Jack, Jack, Jack. I know you're not happy, Jack, but if you want to keep your pathetic little pecker and balls, you'll listen the fuck up right now, because I can always come back, Jack. You can fuckin' count on that, buddy. Now, do I have your fucking attention, or would you like your wife and those two precious little daughters to burn in hell for all eternity? You can save them, Jack, the power is in your hands, well… hand, but to do so you need to do the fucking favor I'm about to ask of you. Are we clear, Jack? You would like to save your family from eternal damnation, wouldn't you, Jack?" I had never believed in heaven or hell but this thing was real, so anything was possible.

"Yes, I understand." I had no real choice anyway.

To my surprise, whatever the beast was, it just smiled in the mirror at me once more, instead of asking whatever favor it wanted. I had no idea what I could possibly do for an entity that could do pretty much anything it pleased. Curiosity was not something I had left in me.

It walked out into the hallway, grabbed the phone

hanging on the wall, returning to the bathroom with a bounce in its step. It made sure I got a good look at my severed hand resting in the sink's basin, setting the phone down in a puddle of my blood.

"When you get to hell, Jack I need you to let Lucifer know what I did here. I know you mortal idiots think he sees all, but he doesn't. You will need not seek him out, he will know who sent you. You tell him Asag has completed his task. Do this and your family will be freed from further suffering. That is your only task. Fail and your family suffers greater than you can ever imagine. Are we clear, Jack?" There was no laughter nor smile now, Asag had said his peace.

"Yes." The single word was all I could muster.

"Good, Jacky!" Asag yelled out, grabbing the phone.

I watched as he punched in the familiar numbers 9-1-1.

"9-1-1 what is your emergency?" Came the operator's voice from the receiver.

"Hello, I seem to have killed and eaten my family. Take your time, we're not going anywhere." The joy in my voice meant they would believe it to be a prank, but Asag knew each call required a dispatch. He added, "This is not a prank, dipshit!" then promptly hung up.

"Now you have your task Jack, don't fuckin' forget. I'll check in on you, just to make sure, but you won't forget me, will ya Jacko?" The laughter returned.

"No, I won't."

"Excellent!" he exclaimed, jamming the shears in my mouth promptly removing my tongue.

He sealed the wound closed with the torch as he had all the others. He then sat back on the toilet, placed the hacksaw between my knees quickly removing my remaining right hand. It fell to the floor with an unceremonious plop, relieving me of any ability to communicate. Asag waved the stump over the torch, burning the wound closed, smiling in the mirror for me one last time.

He could hear the sirens in the distance now, returning to my dining room table to wait. Asag stayed with me as the uniforms entered, finding me naked, covered in blood from head to toe with a smile only the completely insane can muster plastered across my blood-stained mouth. Asag knew I wasn't going anywhere but a padded room now.

I heard his voice in my head as I had in my basement for months, "It's been fun, Jack, but I really must be going. So little time, so many people to kill and all. Be mindful of your task, Jack, your family is counting on you."

My head dropped forward, whacking into the table as Asag left. I couldn't remember my name or where I was. I began to drool. One thought repeating in my head in a non-stop mantra of the damned.

Asag completed his task. Asag completed his task. Asag completed his task...

Author Biographies

Jack Rollins

Jack was born and raised among the twisting cobbled streets and lanes, ruined forts and rolling moors of a medieval market town in Northumberland, England. He claims to have been adopted by Leeds in West Yorkshire, and he spends as much time as possible immersed in the shadowy heart of that city.

Fascinated by all things Victorian, Jack often writes within that era and his period gothic horror works include *The Séance*, *The Cabinet of Dr Blessing* and the forthcoming *Tread Gently Amidst The Barrows* in the J Ellington Ashton Anthology *Under The Bridge*.

Jack's contemporary horror pieces currently published outside this volume are as follows:

Dead Shore, featured in *Undead Legacy*
Anti-Terror, featured in *Carnage: Extreme Horror*

Jack can be found online at:
Twitter: @jackrollins9280
Facebook: www.facebook.com/doctorblessing
Website: jackrollinshorror.wordpress.com

Stuart Keane

Stuart Keane published his first novella, The Customer Is Always... in April 2014. It has slowly garnered critical acclaim and was nominated for a CWA Dagger in the Library Award in 2014. This was followed by Charlotte, which has solidified his reputation as a horror author to watch. His debut novel, All or Nothing, was published by J Ellington Ashton Press in late 2014. His collaborative debut, Carnage: Extreme Horror, was published in December and has received critical acclaim, holding a spot in the Amazon Bestselling Horror Anthologies Top 20 for the first three months of release.

His short story, 'Bon Appetit', was written on the fly during one of his rare free moments. The idea was generated from his experience in several kitchen environments, although the events are purely fictional. As well as taking on editing duties for J Ellington Ashton Press and Dark Chapter Press – and acquiring talent for Kids, DCP's forthcoming anthology – Stuart can be found working on his next three books, Cine, Grin and 89. He is also finalising the line-up for Whispers Vol. 2 and Vol. 3, the sequels to Whispers Vol. 1, which was released in April.

When he isn't writing, he can be found on Facebook or Twitter. Feel free to add him, follow him or Tweet him. Stuart welcomes interaction with the readers, something he will be taking to a new level in July 2015, when he features at the London Film and Comic Con alongside horror author, Matt Shaw. Details can be found at www.stuartkeane.com.

He currently resides in Ipswich, UK with his amazing wife and an unhealthy caffeine addiction.

David Basnett

David was born twelve miles north of Newcastle-upon-Tyne in a small Northumberland town in the UK, and although he enjoys regular forays to the real world, he has lived in the general area ever since. He studied IT and creative writing at university (Not at the same time!) and he says there's no competition to which one he enjoys the most.

He can be found with his nose in any books he can get his hands on, but of course has a particular affinity with horror novels. Strange fact - whilst he enjoys horror movies, he will freely admit that he can't stand slasher/ torture films (with one or two exceptions).

Writing for both the adult and young adult audience, David is quickly establishing himself as a writer to keep tabs on.

https://davidbasnettauthor.wordpress.com
https://twitter.com/dbasnett
https://www.facebook.com/officialdavidbasnett

Robert J. Stava

Robert Stava is a writer who now lives in the lower Hudson Valley just north of NYC, apparently not far from that half-imaginary village he sets so many of his stories in, Wyvern Falls. Originally from Cleveland, Ohio, he grew up in the Finger Lakes region of New York State and after going to college for Fine Arts wound up making his career in advertising at Y&R and J. Walter Thompson in NYC. He went on to become a multimedia Art Director and later as Creative Director ran the 3d Media Group at Arup, an international U.K-based design and engineering company before catapulting into the wild world of writing horror fiction.

His first published short story to be published (Municipal Lot #9) appeared in issue 017 of Sanitarium Magazine. In addition to 'Blynd Haus" another Wyvern Falls short story, "The Anteater" will be featured in an anthology later by Grinning Skull Press - Cranial Leakage: Tales from the Grinning Skull, Vol. 2. His novella "The Devil's Engine" will be published by Muzzleland Press in September of this year as well. The third installment of his "Hudson Horror" novels, "By Summer's Last Twilight", is due out this summer.

He is also author and designer of "Combat Recon: 5th Air Force Images from the SW Pacific 1943-45" (Schiffer Publishing, 2007), a historical account based around his great uncle's service as a combat photographer during WWII.

Visit his author site:
www.robertstava.com

and the official Wyvern Falls feature site at
www.wyvernfalls.com

or follow him on Twitter:
@robertstava

Sharon Higa

Sharon L. Higa was born in Anaheim, CA. but has travelled throughout the U.S.A. and Europe. Writing and telling stories since the age of 6 years old, she finally ettled down to putting her tales on aper in 2008. Having three novels, one novella and several anthologies under her belt, Sharon continues to write in her favorite genres: horror, supernatural thrillers, fantasy/action, mystery drama. She lives in East Tennessee with her husband of 24 years, Mark, one teagle mix pup and nine rescue cats of various breeds and temperments.

My website where you can review all of my
published works is :
www.leapingunicornliterary.com

Steve Jenner

Steve Jenner lives in a rural patch right on the edge of Greater London where the Tube line just about clings on. He has been writing on and off for twenty or so years now, mainly in fantasy but occasionally strays into the horror genre for the odd short story. He has no formal writing qualifications but having been an avid reader for all of his life, he dearly hopes to place one of his own modest efforts in amongst those that he admires so greatly.

In his time, Steve has been a holiday rep, musician and layabout. For many years, however, he worked in the Gaming Industry. Mainly in London casinos but also on board cruise ships. The opportunity to visit many exotic places, meeting colourful and interesting people provided much food for thought. Steve is a firm believer that travel stimulates the imagination and so endeavours to draw upon these experiences to create his fantasy worlds. There is a story waiting on every corner so the more corners you turn...

Steve has a number of favourite authors chief among whom is the much-missed Jack Vance who in his opinion was the master of stylish fantasy. He is also an admirer of the crime novels of John Sandford and the humour of the late Terry Pratchett. When it comes to horror, Clive Barker and Stephen King are the most accomplished and entertaining practitioners. He also enjoys hard rock, hard crosswords and hard cheese. His favourite colour is blue during the daytime and a sort of red-streaked purple at night.

One thing that he considers most important, is to develop a style of writing that differs slightly from the mainstream as the competition there is great and the quality high. Hopefully, some may appreciate this old fashioned approach and enjoy the resulting stories. To this end, Steve has self-published a collection of interconnected tales called The Fragrant Green Hotel which centres around a hotel for the recently deceased. It is a fantasy sequence which currently resides in a far corner of Amazon Books.

Josef DeCory

Josef DeCoryis a six foot nine inch high school English teacher who currently lives in Wesley Chapel, Florida. As a two-year-old, Josef's father took him outside of their home in Elmira, New York and pointed to a hill near the house where he lived. His father told him that Mark Twain is buried up there. Then, at the age of 8, Joseph began reading everything he could get his hands that was written by the famous Author, beginning with The Jumping Frog of Calaveras County. His love for writing began soon after reading the novel Jaws, by Peter Benchley in the early 70's. Josef never had any intention of publishing his work, and figured he would just write and then let it all go into the world of oblivion. Writing comes easy for him, but publishing had no real impression on Josef or his intentions.

Josef likes to teach at both the high school and the university level. His main focus is the high school kids who come in and out of his life every day. He also likes to swim, read and go to the local theme parks like Busch Gardens, Universal Studios, and Disney World. He usually writes at a local bookstore or the coffee shop while listening to his collection of over 300 songs on ITunes.

If you were to ask Josef about writing he would say that it is *easy peasy*, as long as you do not mind taking your brain out, slapping it around a few times, and then putting it back in. Josef has a writing secret that keeps him going when he is not sure what to write next. He writes three or four things at the same time. This allows him the chance to give everything to one story, and then switch to another and start with a fresh brain.

The short story *Am I Dead?* is the first piece that Josef has ever tried to get published. He was very pleased when it was accepted for Dark Chapter Press' Kill for a Copy anthology. Josef is still not sure about publishing anything after this, but the experience and learning has been an extremely valuable exercise.

S.L. Dixon

S.L. Dixon was born and raised in Southern Ontario, Canada. He started into writing the news but found it too a square platform for his creative leanings. From there he failed at selling insurance, stocking shelves, pumping gas, pouring cement, grounds-keeping, general maintenance, ice cream production, dish washing, oil changing, carpentry, scrap hauling, farming and retail sales. Deciding enough he turned back to his college diploma and sidestepped the intended avenue and took a dimly lit alleyway to the world of fiction. Mostly dark and speculative, but occasionally otherwise.

His stories have appeared in magazines and anthologies around North America and in the United Kingdom. Currently, he lives in a British Columbia coastal mountain range with his wife and cat.

www.sldixon.ca
http://www.amazon.com/S.L.-Dixon/e/B00T57ENES/ref=sr_ntt_srch_lnk_3?qid=1426402904&sr=8-3

Angus Fenton

Angus Fenton is currently studying for a Diploma in Professional Writing and Editing, the latest stage in a lifelong passion for the craft. At a young age he remembers being enthralled by J.R R Tolkien's *Lord of The Rings* books and the incredible world they contained. And from here his love of writing began, desperate to create his own fantastical worlds and legends just as Tolkien had done.

Throughout his high school years, Angus was able to pursue writing to a greater degree. Studying the subjects of English and Literature, he received many opportunities to indulge his desire for creative writing. It was around this period that he would generate the early concepts from which he would develop and construct future stories and works.

By time Angus was ready to leave high school, he had many concepts and pre-written stories. As a result, he decided to continue his education of the industry by moving on and studying creative writing at Melbourne University. However, unforeseen circumstances lead to him following a different path for a short time. This was until his admission into the Bendigo Institute of TAFE, where he is currently studying.

Brian Barr

Brian Barr is an American author. He also writes under the pseudonym of Aghori Shaivite. He writes novels, short stories, and comic books. Brian has been published in Autumn Burning, Inanna Rising, and other anthologies. Brian collaborates with another writer, Chuck Amadori, on the comic book series Empress, along with Pencil Blue Studios and colorist Vicki Pittman for the art. His first two novels, Carolina Daemonic and Psychological Revenge, will be published by J. Ellington Ashton Press in 2015.

Audrey E.L. Coots

Audrey E. L. Coots is an award winning author from Lexington, Alabama, USA. She loves to travel, and her favorite place so far is New York City in the wintertime. She has had articles published by USA Today Travel, Shoals Woman Magazine, and Face Magazine, among others, and she continues to pursue her creative writing career in her free time. She has a much loved border collie named Buddy, and she and her husband currently live in South Louisiana.

William G. Chandler Jr.

My name is William G Chandler Jr. I am a native of Philadelphia, Pennsylvania, in the United States of America. I work in the social services industry for an organization, Shared Support, Inc. I help individuals with disabilities achieve their greater goals. I am a graduate of Temple University, in Philadelphia. I studied Film and Media Arts there. I am also a graduate of Philadelphia University where I studied Digital Arts. My writing experience includes my own personal creative writing, and a journalistic period with the Philadelphia Tribune. I have one previous publication before this short story. I wrote a short story, ***Alec's Change***, which is in the anthology **One Real Story**, edited by Kate Cummings. This is on Amazon. I most recently wrote a piece, **Your Life**, for the Leo Spade Production group. The film is on Youtube, under the title **Your Life final**.

Matthew Teah

Matthew Teah is 27 years old and living in Newcastle upon Tyne, with his fiancée Sarah and their cat Narla. Matthew works in a local authority installing care alarms so elderly and vulnerable people can summon assistance if they have a fall or feel unwell. Matthew's influences as a child consisted of watching scary movies, reading horror and science fiction novels and watching too much Bucky O'Hare. Matthew's most favourite pastime is writing science fiction and horror, his piece the Herald of Our Times is his first outing in the horror genre and his first piece of work which has been published.

Luc Haasbroek

Luc Haasbroek is a writer and actor. He has been writing novels and poetry since primary school and has recently work on film scripts. Luc lives in Durban, and is currently studying at the South African School of Motion Picture Medium and Live Performance.

Stefan Lavery

Stefan Lavery is a 32-year-old admin officer who currently lives and works in Belfast, Northern Ireland. He took up short story writing in 2014 and won *Dark Places Magazine's* March competition for that year, with the story, *The Master Equation.*

M.R. Wallace

I was born in 1988 in Pendleton, Oregon. I spent my whole life in eastern Oregon until I joined the army right out of high school. I spent six years in the military as a helicopter mechanic, most of them in upstate New York, where I met my wife Jessica. I deployed to Iraq in 2008, shortly before the birth of my daughter. When I returned, we immediately started preparations for the next deployment. Almost exactly a year later, I deployed to Afghanistan. After that I left the military, had a son added to the family, became a civilian aviation contractor for a while, and now spend most of my free time writing whatever pops into my head. I've always said that my biggest problem with writing was finishing stories. I'm great at starting them. Not so much the finishing bit.

Feind Gottes

Feind Gottes is a horror writer who left the mundane 9-5 world dedicating his life to writing. Feind is the editor for Thy Demons Be Scribblin, his website dedicated to his original work as well as all things related to horror & heavy metal. He has also been a contributing writer for Doommantia and Occult Rock. In July 2013 his story ***Harvester of Sorrow*** was shared by **horror-writers.net** (***Day 1*** & ***Day 2***) and in May 2015 his short story, ***My Shadow***, will be posted as a guest scribe on **The Baked Scribe**, website of author **Chad Clark**.

Twitter https://twitter.com/feindgottes
Tumblr http://feindgottes.tumblr.com/

Final notes from the Editor

Once again, a huge thank you to Shaun Hutson for getting behind this book and for all the help and support offered to Dark Chapter Press this year.

I want to thank my long-suffering partner, Naomi for supporting me through the long nights of editing and typesetting, and thanks to my boys for sleeping all night long. Usually. Thanks to my beautiful, bright and hard-working daughter Caitlin, who has started to see how she can help her old man's business from time to time. Who says child labour is dead? And to my little bro Christopher, who helped me to wade through a stack of submissions last year and even flagged up one or two of the stories that ended up in this volume.

And as ever, thanks for the moral support from Dad, Mam, Mick, Trish, David, Stuart, Kyle, Lisa and Melissa.

Dark Chapter Press took a lot of help from Kickstarter backers to launch this book. Many of the backers this time around originally joined in from the first campaign, for *The Seance* and helped to create Dark Chapter Press with their generosity.

The Honour Roll

Leisyen Keane
Lisa Wood
Patricia Wood
Anne Tweed
Jim Hardison
Douglas Dluzen
Roy Romasanta
Chan Ka Chun Patrick
Andrew Lennon
Robert W. McEwan
Ben Greener
Melissa Bryan
Carl Smith
PJ
Martin Jenner

Hope to see you all again for:
Dark Chapter Press *Kids: Vol.1*
Bloody Heather
&
Under The Knife

Rob McEwan
Editor and Proprietor
Dark Chapter Press

Lightning Source UK Ltd.
Milton Keynes UK
UKOW04f2101080715

254831UK00001B/1/P

9 780993 062032